To HANNAH

SAFE TRAVELS & BEST
ADVENTURES IN THE BIG
APPLE. KEEP IN TOUCH!
~ Isaac

NEW APE IDEA

2019

A NOVEL

by

DAN SOHVAL

The Burlesque Showcase
Georgia

First Burlesque Showcase paperback edition: August 2018

Printed in the United States of America

FIRST EDITION

ISBN 978-0-9997707-0-2

The Burlesque Showcase
An imprint of Incubator Comics Company
www.theburlesqueshowcase.net

Ordering Information:
Quantity sales. Special discounts are available for quantity purchases. For details contact the publisher at isaac@theburlesqueshowcase.net

For individual book orders, merchandise and special discounts on Lazy Eyes visit the book's virtual home at newapeidea.com.

Cover design and illustrations by Isaac Fisher

18 19 20 21   10 9 8 7 6 5 4 3   2 1

For Alkis

NEW APE IDEA

Part I

"This is the key to the problem, how much truth there is in solipsism."
—Ludwig Wittgenstein

"It's not about isolation. It's about time."
—Diarrhea Planet

1.1.0 Hijack

The roar of takeoff doesn't sound as loud as what is coming out of the fat man next to Vreeman. The man sits in the adjacent seat and hogs both armrests for himself, his fleshy belly rising and falling with each snore. His chin tucked to his chest, the man looks to Vreeman like a large toddler. And despite the fact that his body is folded over like a question mark and it sounds like something truly awful is percolating in his sinuses, the man has a peaceful countenance. Like fitful, midday airplane sleep is the best rest he's had in a long while.

On Vreeman's Very Last Flight, takeoff seems to have a sedative effect on most of the plane's passengers. Though they left Newark at a hair past noon, a good amount of the cabin's passengers zonked out the moment the jet engines began rumbling. As the aircraft ascends to max altitude, nobody seems to stir much. There are no screaming babies on this flight, thank Jesus. Every one of Vreeman's practice flights contained at least one insufferable child that would wail and cry and wail and cry, defiant against the ineffective coos from her red-eyed parents.

Perhaps it's because he is flying first class for his Very Last Flight that Vreeman hears only the petulant snores of his neighbor and the whooshing of the plane hurtling through the troposphere. It's his first time too. No more coach and economy class seating like on the practice flights. It is a rare and happy harmony when a personal indulgence and a pragmatic course of action align so perfectly. He initially chose the first class aisle seat for its easy cockpit access. Though the extra legroom and complimentary drinks feel far more sinful than any other aspect of the Flight, which he has painstakingly planned over the past sixteen weeks.

Vreeman casts a glance over each of his shoulders and reaches below the seat in front of him. From his one allowed carry-on bag Vreeman extracts the false carabiner. Even the pads of his fingers seem to sweat, leaving crescents of grease on the fake chrome. He had stowed it in his backpack's front pocket, just like on every other practice flight. Never once did any of the fish-faced TSA agents espy it through their whirring full body scans. Metal detectors were never too problematic: the carabiner is plastic.

The fat man emits a cough and a snort, which elicits a nervous jump from Dennis Vreeman. Dennis wraps his fingers around the carabiner, hiding it in his palm. Based on the large gold belt buckle that digs into the man's corpulence, Vreeman can guess that the man is indigenous to the metro-Dallas area. The man's head falls from his headrest to Vreeman's shoulder. He sputters. A spindle of drool drips down from his maw onto Vreeman's breast. One would think that the airlines would accommodate a slightly greater degree of personal space for their first class customers.

"Shit," Vreeman says, his voice consumed by the plane's in-flight drone. Now he cannot exit his seat and surreptitiously enter the cockpit. Not without waking the Texan, whose breath holds an alcoholic tinge. Vreeman has to wait. Alone with his thoughts, holding the weapon he may not use just yet. He reiterates The Plan in his mind over and over and over until it becomes a spinning ecclesiastical wheel, turning the piceous sky bright with its scorching inevitability.

The Plan

X	Book 1st class tix on midday flight departing from Newark EWR on a Tuesday, Wednesday or Thursday to a destination at least 1500 miles away.
X	If nec. book several practice flights to familiarize self w/ routine.
X	Procure Loder XRG Climbing Carabiner w/ Whittling Knife Attachment (purchasable through "Outdoors" section Executive Traveler magazine).
X	Store Loder XRG Climbing Carabiner w/ Whittling Knife Attachment in carry-on luggage. (If TSA confiscates it, relinquish it and procure a new one.)
X	Board flight from Tues/Weds/Thurs Newark EWR to > 1500 miles away location w/ carry-on luggage.
X	Relax and enjoy flight until maximum altitude is reached.
X	Remove Loder XRG Climbing Carabiner w/ Whittling Knife Attachment from carry-on luggage.
X	Make sure flight attendants are in cabin's rear.
	Enter Cockpit.
	Brandish Whittling Knife Attachment of Loder XRG Climbing Carabiner.
	Assume control of in-flight PA from pilot.
	Announce to passengers and crew intention to commit hijacking.
	Await intervention from Air Marshall.
	Surrender self non-violently.
	Accept arrest by ground forces upon landing.
	Await media.
	Await fan mail, hate mail, and trial.
	Plead guilty, no contest.
	Live rest of life.
	Suicide self if quality of life in jail is < quality of life out of jail AND/OR fan mail, hate mail, general media attention wanes significantly.
	Otherwise die content with identity eternally preserved via Wikipedia/AP databases and Homeland Sec. archives.

The plan is simple. An easy recipe for Vreeman to thrust himself into the mouths of the many-headed hydra that is today's media. An elegant means to have one's face emblazoned across the retinas of every smart-glasses wearing, screen-thumbing, net-surfing plebe of America.

The white-hotness of fame and the slow burn out of it.

The Loder XRG, once cool from the constant breeze of recycled pressurized air is now warm from Vreeman's sticky palms. The air is fresh and alive and electric despite its staleness.

And glory of glories when the long smooth flight of the plane hits a patch of turbulence! The cabin tremors. Pupils flicked upwards from smartphones and lap-top screens and tablets and portable gaming devices to the headrests in front of them. The attendants in their ironed navy business suits remain unfazed, handing out canned spring water and scanning debit cards with their white bloodless fingers. Their mouths are open and their eyeballs are empty; not a hint of emotion of any valence on their faces. The turbulence, though small, through some providence of physics, is enough to roll the fat man from Dallas' head along a 180° arc. His primary chin sloshes from Vreeman's shoulder to the hard plastic shade of the window on the man's other side. He does not seem to wake up.

Vreeman is unburdened. He slides out of his seat and stands in the aisle. His fellow passengers look asleep, their sense-holes plugged with digital stimuli.

The cockpit is open. Small planes like these are usually designed in this manner. It keeps the passengers feeling safe and secure as they may freely keep tabs on their pilots. Not any of that phylum of behavior is going on now, thankfully for Vreeman. If any of the passengers had shown even an iota of paranoia he probably would have marked this another practice flight and rebooked.

He locks eyes with a faraway stewardess in the coach seats. Her eyes say something but Vreeman can only feel his lips twitching and sphincter tightening and does not have the cognitive resources to parse her gaze. He brings his palm to his stomach, obscuring the carabiner. His white cotton business shirt is dotted with perspiration. "Bathroom" he mouths. The flight attendant nods up at a *Fasten Seatbelts* display overhead and purses her lips. Vreeman doubles over, an attempt at beaming the image of painful diarrhea into her skull. The flight attendant shrugs like whatever and hands a seated passenger a 6 oz can of Pepsi.

Takeoff seems to have a sedative effect on the plane, stewardesses included. How else could she have missed Vreeman tiptoeing backwards into the cockpit?

The pilot turns his head as much as his stiff white collar will allow. Everything about the man is thick: jowls, eyebrows, and a salty unironic moustache. What looks like a recent crew cut is already dotted with follicle regrowth. Sausage fingers grip around the half-crescent wheel.

"You can't be in here," is all he says to Vreeman. Another Texan.

In the seat to his right dozes a wiry man. His Adam's apple shows itself with each of his slow turbulent snores.

"Does he usually do that?" Vreeman, somewhere between a murmur and a mumble.

"Christ," the pilot withdraws a hand from the wheel and wipes meaty fingers across a meaty brow. "You do this in plainclothes now?"

The carabiner is slick with sweat. Vreeman slips a thumb under the clip, his nail against the whittling blade.

"Sheeyit. Crane! Wake-up Crane!"

The skinny man rouses with a short quiet moan, as if he is unsure whether or not he was caught in a nightmare. He blinks several confused times as he studies Vreeman, who although rather confused himself, still manages to draw slight offense at the pilot's use of "plainclothes." The navy sport jacket and slacks he wears are about the nicest clothes he owns.

"Wha?"

"Don't what at me." The pilot's pupils dart between the man called Crane and the plane's windshield as he speaks. His moustache obscures a snarling upper lip. "Dee Oh Tee just witnessed you napping on the job."

"_"

"I'm sorry, officer. I don't usually do this." The man speaks at a whisper, his lips varnished with a white film of dehydration.

"_"

"I can vouch for my copilot, he has never acted like this before."

"No sir I haven't."

Vreeman allows himself a breath to stare ahead. His guts are humming with stress; his arteries pump carbonated plasma. His Loder XRG is still hidden in his palm, pressed to his stomach. The flat black brims of the pilots' hats seem to point forward into the ether beyond. The sky is not blue on Vreeman's last flight, but white. Endless, dimensionless white.

"I'm not with the Department of Transportation."

The Adam's apple of the man called Crane bobbed up and down. The pilot just shook his head like, Jesus Christ, Jesus Christ, Jesus Christ.

And here Vreeman is struck by the indelible faultiness of his own planning. How does one announce a hijacking? Do they iterate their intentions to kill the pilots and drive and/or crash the plane? "I am here to commit an act of terrorism," sounds banal, trite. What if a "you motherfuckers!" is thrown in for dramatic effect? Still unsatisfactory. He had rehearsed The Plan countless times, and yet he failed to account for this essential moment.

"I'm not with the Department of Transportation," he says again. A shitty opener, but perhaps a necessary one.

"Goddammit," says the pilot. The co-pilot just keeps audibly swallowing.

Vreeman's skin feels like paper. His whole body swishes with a happy nausea. "I'm here to—"

"We know," says Crane. He sits up in his seat and places his hands on his half-wheel. His skin looks a size too small for his gaunt frame, his bones and veins seem to push out of his body with urgency.

"With all due respect, sir," the pilot now, "this is second visit Homeland Sec has paid us this month."

"What with the U Miami sophomore who tried to sneak kerosene in his Starbucks cup last October. They're now saying it was a protest against the higher ed buyout."

"Heightened security protocol. We understand."

Vreeman turns around and peaks down the aisle. The man from Dallas still snoozes. A flight attendant a few dozen rows down catches his eye. What feels like several seconds pass by. Vreeman shrugs. Crane follows Vreeman's gaze. The co-pilot gives the flight attendant an A-Okay hand gesture. Her eyebrows are thin and plucked and far away but Vreeman can still see they spell anger. She returns her gaze to a screen in front of her. Vreeman swallows and turns.

"May I use the intercom?"

The two pilots share a glance. Crane bites his lower lip and the pilot almost does so himself.

"I don't see why not," says the pilot.

Another gap in **The Plan**. Vreeman has no idea how to use the intercom.

"Hand it to me," he says. "Please."

Crane leans forward and picks the black receiver off of its handle on the underside of the console and holds it out to Vreeman, who quickly pockets the carabiner. The pilots look unfazed. Vreeman takes the intercom in one hand and runs his fingers down the microphone's black spiraling chord. He does not speak.

"Uh, depress the button on the left and talk," says Crane. He speaks with an urgent sweetness. Poor guy will probably get shamed out of his job when Vreeman's testimonial is released to the public.

"Attention ladies and gentlemen." Like most, Vreeman does not like the sound of his voice. The fuzziness of the intercom channel helps though. "My name is Dennis Vreeman and, I, uh."

Crane stares ahead, miming flying the plane.

A clearing of the throat. "Sorry. My name is Dennis Vreeman and this is my Very Last Flight."

Vreeman slouches as he stands. A bad habit he never could kick. At one time he worried that he might acquire scoliosis of the spine later in life. He tucks his chin down toward his chest. It gives a sort of fetal comfort. And how come all these planes have the same blue zigzag-pattern carpeting?

"It is my Very Last Flight because, I, uh. It is my Very Last Flight because we are all going to die. So it's your Very Last Flight too."

Both pilots pout their lips. Their affect is undeniably confused.

"Sorry about this," Vreeman says. He scans the passengers. All seated. Placid. Even sluggish. A few sleepers dot the crowd, though most either stare straight ahead, earbuds in ear canals or fixate themselves toward a laptop screen.

"Is anyone even listening right now?"

Even the flight attendants, blonde hair tied back in neat buns, thumbed the touchscreens of their smartphones. Vreeman removes the carabiner from his pocket.

The Loder XRG Stainless Steel Climbing Carabiner w/ Whittling Knife Attach-ment sets itself apart from all other *Skymall* outdoors paraphernalia due to its unique design. Though made of plastic, the knife attachment is laser-sharpened to cut as finely as a razor. Most Loder whittling knives do not exceed 7 cm in length. They are a perfectly fine size for simple woodcarvings, but unacceptable for attempted acts of ter-ror. The XRG model though, is notable for its employment of what Loder hallmarks as "Cutting-Edge Blade Telescoping Technology". The whittling knife attachment is—in essence—a blade within a blade within a blade. The three fold out of one another and may be locked into place turning the carabiner into a half-size Bowie knife.   "Is there even an Air Marshall on board?"

"Is this a drill?" the man called Crane says, almost frowning.

The blade's unfolding and locking actions take no more than a half-second. He holds the blade up to the pilot's face and drops the intercom the floor.

"This is so not a drill," Vreeman says, his whole physiology awash in the cool minty tingle of self-acknowledged badassery.

"Motherfucker!" The pilot jams a button that glows lime green and hurls himself to his feet, the momentum of which causes him to stumble to his side, his legs falling over one another in a sloppy grapevine. He grabs his copilot, balancing himself on Crane's shoulder and stands erect.

And the copilot Crane shrieks in a full castrato, makes a fist, and punch-es down a round red button on the far right of the console. Vreeman turns to see the blonde-haired stewardess barreling down the aisle screaming "You Bastard! You Bastard! You Bastard!" with a silver fork in each hand. Behind her, one older man manages to look up from his computer screen. His fellow passengers do not. It is only half a second before they are cut off by the thoomp of a thick steel door slamming shut, sealing off the portal to the cockpit.

"Bill you shithead!" the pilot heaves.

"I'm sorry! I'm sorry! Oh my God I'm so sorry!"

Vreeman hears the thumping of the distressed stewardess' fists on 3 inches of solid steel. Her knuckles likely bloodied pretty quickly. He can't quite make out what she's screaming, something animal and atavistic filtered to a low alto mumble through the thick metal. The rodent squealing of steel-fork-on-wall scratching comes through clearly though.

Large globules of sweat collect along Vreeman's hairline and snake downwards to his eyes, nose, and lips. He brings a forearm to mop his face, his blade a silver narwhal's tooth extending from his nose.

The pilot, maybe a linesman in his youth, throws his mass forward toward the hijacker who instinctively blocks his hand with his fists in fear. The pilot's eyeball doesn't make much noise when it pops from his head. Crimson on white starched collar and blue carpet. The optic nerve pulls apart like a glob of putty. The eye itself looks more like a gag gift or up-scale Halloween decoration than a human organ. The iris is turquoise, the milky retina shish-kabobed on the Loder XRG pinkish around the entry and exit holes.

Should one find themselves sans eye, Vreeman thinks, wouldn't logic dictate that they keep their lone remaining eye open as much as possible? Sure, depth perception would be compromised but at least one could have some sense of vision. The pilot though, seems to have let all rational thought evaporate from his mind and squeezes both eyes shut, salmon-colored tears gooping out from his empty socket. He claws at his face and makes infantile shrieks and moans as he stumbles backwards and slumps by the co-pilot's chair.

Crane is still and whitening. He, too, is crying. Vreeman realizes that he can smell fear, and fear smells like urine. Vreeman jukes toward him, knife arm outstretched, the optic nerve of the eyeball dangling off the side. No reaction from Crane; the élan of the whole situation has triggered some infantile behavior primitive in his skull. The copilot continues to cry and blubber and wet himself without ceasing.

"Where do you wanna go?" Crane says. "Just tell me and I'll take you there. Please just don't hurt me."

Vreeman wipes his blade off on the headrest of the pilot's seat. "I don't know," he says.

The floor shifts beneath their feet and Vreeman stumbles forward. He trips over the bloody toddler-like pilot and falls into Crane who embraces him. The whiteness outside the cockpit window has turned to a checkered brown and green and the two roll forward on top of the dashboard, arms still around one another. Crane does not disengage from the hug: limb control becomes difficult when one's spinal cord is nicked by a serrated knife.

The Plan, like an awkward leftover guest at a party, ushers itself out of Vreeman's head. It leaves in its wake a fresh mindfulness. The consuming amniotic hum of the plane in nosedive fills Vreeman's consciousness. That and the liquid warmth of Crane spasming around him.

And what a spectacular end to this, Vreeman's Very Last Flight, to become a bellowing pillar of hellfire on a metro-Memphis freeway along with all those smartphone zombies.

1.2.0 Van

Takashi had several magazine articles on display, primary sources detailing the New York City downtown scene from the 1980's. His gaze saccaded back and forth between the text and a cluster of four music videos playing on mute in his right-hand field of vision. His van's stereo system blasted some decade-old sludgewave as the vehicle wound itself off the parkway and into Teaneck. He blinked twice, closing off two of the music videos and summoned Shackled Uterus' homepage from his peripheral vision. Takashi extended an index finger and swiped at the air in front of his face, logging in to the site's admin area and tabbing down to analytics. No new visitors. There had only been thirteen in the past week.

He focused back in on the texts. Was Patti Smith someone he was expected to know? The whole van's interior shook with the deep bass riffage emanating from the subwoofers. He swiped away the article; a new notification on his media reader blinked in the corner. Tak squinted it open. It was a *Staph Infection* article regarding a management change of a venue space in Hoboken. He winked his left eye, bookmarking the zine piece for later, and opened up a command prompt, though whatever specific scripts he wanted to execute had escaped him.

The van's rumble of locomotion gracefully decrescendoed as the vehicle came to a stop. Takashi tilted his head left then right, cracking his neck and murmured an "Oy vey." The van, perceiving human speech, lowered the music volume in suit.

A handful of children—younger than seven or eight—played ball in the cul-de-sac ahead. They yelled and hooted as they milled about. One shebody snatched a ball, a purple rubbery sphere engineered for no particular sport, and hurled it to the pavement. It bounced off the pavement in a smooth hyperbola and onto the windshield of Tak's van. From there it ricocheted onto the perimeter of a nearby lawn, dislodging some mulch and sending a squirrel zipping up an adjacent oak. The kid took off after the ball while the others, seeming to follow some unsaid rule of the game, swirled in a fleet footed mosh; they screamed as they tagged one another, bearing gap-toothed smiles.

Takashi honked his horn. The van wouldn't move until it registered a child-free road ahead. And yet those little sphincters blocked him from reaching his desired coordinates: the other side of the cul-de-sac. He removed his Lazy Eyes and placed them in the glove compartment. He'd told Doug a year ago he didn't wear them, and it was a lie worth sticking to. Most punks he knew didn't wear them either.

The shebody with the long hair returned, purple ball in hand. She parked herself in front of the van and stuck her tongue out at Tak, who added a second honk, this one longer than the first. This brought the children to a halt. A small pond of stares directed at him. Takashi waved his hands. The shebody flipped her middle finger at him. Her friends squealed and laughed. Takashi returned the flipping-off by an order of two and attempted the meanest, sternest scowl he could. He crossed his eyes, his facial muscles burned with lactic acid from prolonged flexion. All in an effort to transmit the visage of one-who-will-not-be-fucked-with.

They laughed. He too was part of the game now.

Tak, pissed as ever, rolled down a window and leaned out. "Move, fuckers," was all he said. And they did.

The van drove itself through the center of the cul-de-sac to the destination Tak had tabbed in earlier with his bitten in fingernails. Tak ordered it to pull a k-turn, less out of necessity than to just delay the children from further resuming their game. After backing into the driveway, Takashi pinched the collar of his shirt. His white tee shrank two sizes and blackened itself. The Waymo parked itself before he hopped out.

Takashi unlocked the back door of his van and approached the garage. He rapped his knuckles three times against the aluminum door.

"Delivery," he said.

And with that the garage door lifted up and receded into some hidden chasm in its ceiling.

"You're late," said Doug.

Isa, perched atop her amp, fingered the tuning key for her B-string.

"I'll need your help with this, boyo," said Tak as he patted the side of the Waymo.

"Did you pick up the cables?" said Doug.

"Cables?"

"Courtney Christ, Takashi, Isa's old one's burned out. I messaged you about this a week ago. Did you even order them?" Doug pursed his lips and flared his nostrils. "And what'd you do to your hair?"

"Pretty rogue, yeah?" said Takashi. His normal half-Semitic nappiness had been greased and smoothed into a column of liberty spikes. A single devilock, shiny with hair gel, curled along the front of his face, obscuring one eye. "I modded it, should make it harder for facial recognition software to ID me."

Doug's own copper-colored mane was tied up into a tight top-bun, bound with a rubber band. "The fuck Tak. You'll have to go back to Musician's Warehouse and pick them up. Hopefully they won't mind that we didn't preorder them."

"I don't think I will be going back to Musician's Warehouse any time soon," said Takashi.

Doug approached the van. His collar had already begun to darken with perspiration. And it was only March. "I'm coming with you," he said. "If this is a money thing—which I know it isn't—I can find a way to spot you the fifteen K," he said. "But we can't practice without cables."

"Whatever you say boyo." Tak turned to wink at Isa. Her face seemed blank. This usually meant she was immersed in her Lazy Eyes.

"Stop saying 'boyo'," said Doug.

"I like it. I got it from Joe Strummer."

"Who?"

"British indie rocker from the 90's. I can't believe you've never heard of him."

Isa waved her fingers out in front, as if playing an invisible keyboard suspended mid-air. Likely thumbing through endless browser tabs.

Tak rapped his knuckles against the side of his van. "I bet Isa's squeeze in Hoboken would know."

Isa murmured something. Both Tak and Doug paused. She wasn't talking to them.

"You did go to Musician's Warehouse though?" said Doug.

"I did. Last night."

"Today is Monday."

"And yet I'm up before sunrise."

"So yesterday was Sunday."

"That makes sense," said Tak.

"You couldn't have gone to Musician's Warehouse yesterday. Blue laws, everything in the county was closed."

"And yet I did go," said Tak, reaching in through the driver's side window. The synchronized popping of all the locks cut through the suburban air. "Everything's taken care of."

"How'd you get in?" Doug, shirt slowly saturating with sweat, allowed himself a few quick tugs at his collar to circulate cool air along his torso.

"A brick," said Takashi before retreating into his van.

"Excuse me?"

Takashi emerged from the van sporting a Cheshire grin, a slender box of crash cymbals tucked in each armpit. "Help me move these into the garage, Isa."

Isa rose from her seat, stepping carefully over her guitar. Her face, placid and monk-like, remained unchanging as she approached Takashi and took the two cymbal boxes from him.

"Rides are still in the car, let me get 'em," Tak said. "Could you stack those by the drum set, Isa?"

Isa brushed past Doug on her way back into the garage.

"Happy Ramadan, boyo." Takashi emerged from the van, ride cymbals in hand.

"Ramadan isn't until June."

He returned back into the van. "And by the way, I remembered the cables." He popped out again and tossed Doug four different coils of varying lengths supplemented by a second wink before retreating back into the vehicle.

"I don't get this, Tak. Did you steal someone's social security pin again?"

"It's not theft if it's from your relatives, Doug," Tak replied. "And no, I've matured far beyond that."

"Then how—"

"And don't think I've forgotten you, Ms. Spines. I know you're a Gibson acolyte, but wait till you see this Fender I got for you."

From the van Takashi unsheathed it: a powder blue Jazzmaster. Like some Templar of yore brandishing a sword of hyperbolic power, Tak raised the guitar above his head in triumph, the sunlight ricocheting off its finish.

"It's vintage," said Takashi. "From the last millennium."

"I don't know what to say," said Isa.

"You never do," said Tak as he crossed the driveway and handed her the guitar.

"Where is this from?"

"I told you, Musician's Warehouse."

"And how did you get it?"

"As I said, with a brick."

Several southbound geese flew overhead, their biological clocks out of sync with the New Jersey warmth.

"Fuck, Takashi."

"By the way Isa, the Jazzmaster is only part of your gift. I've got a stack in the back. One hundred fifty watts. Pure tube-age."

"You stole this?" Tak could see Doug fight the urge to point at him in condemnation.

"And effects, too." Takashi returned once again to the van. "Let's see. I've got three different fuzz pedals. Distortion, overdrive, analogue delay, digital delay, phaser, wah, auto-wah, sustain, flange, tube distortion, chorus, echo, reverb, another fuzz pedal, and a few I'm not sure about. No labels on 'em."

"How can you be so nonchalant?"

"Oh, and a ring modulator too." Tak could see Doug begin to wilt in the early-spring sunlight. "Hey Spines, come over here," he said as Doug Lamarck-Ganoush retreated into the cool shade of the garage.

Isa approached the van's thorax where Tak gestured toward the bounty of pedals.

"Do you mind if I tweak some of these?"

Isa shook her head.

"I'm thinking of swapping out the capacitors in some of these distortion pedals. We'll get a wider breadth of tones that way."

"--"

Tak could see her pupils bouncing back and forth. She was either inspecting the pedals or swapping between apps on her Lazies.

"Did you see the article in *Staph Infection*? You know that shebody in charge of Rule 30, yeah?"

Isa picked up a half-size red Epiphone and weighed it in her hands.

"I got a bunch of those cheapo starter guitars," Tak called toward Doug. "I saw this Sonic Youth show in Brooklyn. They took all these shitty guitars and tuned 'em to open chords, I guess. They plugged 'em in and laid them against their amps for some extra feedback "I figure we could do something similar."

"How could you? Sonic Youth broke up when you were in your mother's ova-ries." Doug was seated at his throne holding his stomach. A crescent of fat peaked out under his t-shirt and lapped over the waistband of his jeans.

"I didn't say I saw them *live*. I saw a video of them. Y'know, that internet thing?"

Doug closed his eyes and took a deep inhale, which quickly morphed into a brief spasm of coughs. "Listen Tak, I'm not mad. Know that," he said. "I'm just, well, concerned that you seem so confident in this. You don't think anybody could've seen you or caught you on camera or something?"

"I've been scoping the place out for months now. Only two cameras, but they won't recognize me." Tak twirled the devil-lock with his index finger.

"An alarm didn't go off when you broke the window?"

"I'm sure if I broke through the front windows something would've sounded, yeah. But they store all their stuff on the second floor above shipping and receiving. The window I went through was definitely not armed."

"I just can't help but feel you're being reckless."

"Of course I'm being reckless, Ganoush," Takashi ran a confident palm through his thick hair, flattening his spikes and letting them spring up again. "But recklessness does not always equate with thoughtlessness. Besides, I have a plan." Another palm bifurcated his mane.

"Okay."

"So I haven't crunched any numbers yet, but I assume we have somewhere in the neighborhood of two or three million dollars' worth of equipment in my van, right?"

Doug swallowed audibly. "Right."

"I figure I'll take some of this stuff, spend some quality time with my soldering iron and give all the electronics an upgrade."

"This doesn't seem like much of a plan, Tak."

A metal stompbox in each hand, Takashi leapt down to the driveway, landing with more of a pat than a thud. "It's all basic stuff. I can handle it," he said

"That's not what I meant."

"I figure these effects, coupled with our musical expertise, could give us a really interesting noisy-shoegaze kinda sound."

"Still not a plan."

"It's a rogue fucking plan, Lamarck-Ganoush! When did the last good shoegaze album come out? Nineteen-ninety-something? We're breathing life into a dead genre, all the while assembling a new, cutting-edge style. The zines will love it."

"Zines? Who reads zines these days, The Neo-!Kung? Who the fuck even says the word 'zine' anymore?"

"People totally still read zines, and I'm simming pretty soon they'll read about Shackled Uterus." Takashi clicked the overdrive stompbox in his right hand with each word of the band's name.

"I thought we agreed that name was just a placeholder," said Doug.

"We'll see." Tak lobbed each of the pedals onto Doug's lawn. "Courtney Christ, these vintage stompboxes are pretty durable."

A yawn came from Isa, who laid supine on the garage floor. All ten of her fingers were extended and wriggling about as she touch-typed on air.

"You fail to see what I'm simming Doug, I'm—"

"When I said 'plan' Takashi, I meant a thought-out model for how you plan to keep billions of dollars of stolen goods and avoid arrest."

Isa clapped once. A hard reboot of some app.

"Simple. I dye my hair blonde. No one will recognize me, not that any cameras did in the first place."

"What about the van, Tak? Someone could have gotten a look at it."

Takashi screwed up his eyes in contemplation. "We'll give it a paintjob, strip off those bumper stickers and keep it off the streets for a couple months." Takashi paused. From over Doug's shoulder, he could see the screaming children in the street, tagging one another, running this way and that. "Fuck," he said, his voice suddenly flattened.

"What Tak?"

"My van," said Takashi. "I can't just leave a wanted vehicle out on the street."

"You haven't drawn issue with that for the past fifteen minutes."

"Well I didn't realize they might have tagged my license! There were cams in the parking lot."

"This never occured to you?" said Doug, his voice rising in pitch.

"It did. I was going to run my plate numbers through a police scanner I scripted," said Takashi before nodding toward the children playing in the cul-de-sac. "But those little cunts distracted me."

"So take the van home!"

"And drive forty-five minutes to South Orange? Not happening."

"Well you drove it up," said Doug. He looked toward Isa. "A little support here?"

"_"

Takashi swallowed, a look of consternation darkening his face. "Let me store it in your garage. Just for a month."

"Not gonna happen, Tak."

Takashi let a brief look of worry flash across his face. A quick downturn of the lips, no more than a half second. "I'm sorry about this Doug. I'm really sorry."

"Tak, it's not my garage. It's my mother's."

"Barbara doesn't use it. She lets us practice in it, I doubt she'll even notice."

Doug turned toward Takashi, who slumped his shoulders along a calculated trajectory.

"You have one month," said Doug. "By April, I want the van painted, re-liscenced and gone."

A playful scream in the distance. The kid in the overalls beaned another play-mate with the rubber ball.

"Deal." Takashi extended his hand. Doug took it.

"I don't think the van will fit with the equipment," Isa said.

"We'll need a new practice space," said Doug.

Takashi thumbed his nose. "Already simmed that," he said. "Did Isa tell you what happened to the shebody she used to schtupp in school? The one from UZ?"

Figure 1: Takashi Miyagi-Edelstein

"What about her?" replied Doug. He glanced at Isa, who still lay on her back occupied by her Lazy Eyes.

"She's managing a space in Hoboken. You know Rule 30?"

Doug nodded.

"Isa told me the two of them are on good terms. Right, Isa?"

Isa sat up, her greasy hair was matted up on the back of her head.

"You think she'll grant us a favor?" Doug said.

"Honestly," said Takashi, "That depends on Isa, not us."

"Hey Isa!" Doug called into the garage, "When was the last time you F2F'd with this shebody?"

"_"

"You know F2F's aren't exactly her forte, DLG," said Takashi. "But I wouldn't be surprised if they're still sleeping together."

"I always considered it more akin to masturbation," said Isa.

"This does not bode well." Doug removed his glasses and began to massage the bridge of his nose.

"Let's pay her a visit," said Tak. "And what happens, happens."

Isa sighed. Even Tak knew she had little patience for tautologies.

1.3.0 Ward

1.1	Although I am unsure who/what I mean by "they".
1.1.1.	Perhaps a governmental bureau designed to regulate the physical or mental fitness of all medical professionals. Or a similar board of physicians.
1.1.1.1.	I do not know if either group exists.
1.2.	I am also unsure if this doctor is truly paraplegic.
1.2.1.	He could, theoretically, be a man who is fully able-bodied and just happens to use a motorized exoskeleton to move around.
1.2.1.1.	The shell encases him and allows him to walk and manipulate his limbs save his hands and fingers.

1.2.2.	He moves in a way that is almost human.
1.2.2.1.	"Almost" because it does not seem to me that he moves exactly like a human.
1.2.2.1.1.	The differences in movement between the doctor and me show themselves even in how he stands or walks. Although, I cannot quite articulate them.
1.2.2.1.1.1.	I have been told that I am three standard deviations above the average degree of verbal ability for 11-year-old girls.
1.2.2.1.1.1.1.	Whereas I am four standard deviations above the average degree of logical reasoning ability for 11-year-old girls.
1.2.2.1.1.1.2.	I assume verbal ability should correlate with articulateness. Though, I could be wrong.
1.2.2.1.1.2.	Not that I am very athletic or coordinated.
1.2.2.1.1.2.1.	By that I mean the doctor could reasonably believe I move in a manner that is not quite human as well.
1.2.2.1.1.2.2	My second foster mother insisted that I learn to play cello. As I played I would imagine my hands looking like spiders running up and down the neck.
1.2.2.1.1.2.2.1.	My fingers seeming like the angular legs of a spider.
1.2.2.1.1.2.2.2.	Not that I have witnessed any spiders running up and down the neck of my cello before.
1.2.2.1.1.2.2.3.	My original point being that I have witnessed myself moving in a way that was not quite human. Though, I'm not quite sure it makes sense anymore.
1.2.2.1.1.2.3.	When I believe the doctor believes that I move in a manner that is not quite human, the doctor believes nothing.
1.2.2.1.1.2.3.1.	What I mean is that when I think about what the doctor thinks, I am still the one doing the thinking. My beliefs of his beliefs are still my beliefs.
1.2.2.2.	Though isn't any human movement by definition "human-like" regardless of how unnatural it may seem?
1.2.3.	The doctor's name is Wimpfheimer and I have met him once before.
2.	The glasses he wears seem unrelated to his paraplegia.
2.1.	He did not wear them the first time I met him.

2.1.1.	This first time we met in his office rather than an examination room. I wore jeans and a blouse rather than the paper gown I'm wearing now.
2.1.1.1.	I believe it was his office because the walls were covered with diplomas that said "Bruce Wimpfheimer" on them. Though, the doctor has yet to formally introduce himself to me.
2.1.1.2.	He only smiled twice: when the wardens left and entered the room.
2.1.1.2.1.	Not that he seemed necessarily like an unhappy man. Though smiling is often an indication of happiness.
2.1.1.2.1.1.	I mean to say when I see Dr. Wimpfheimer smile I think to myself, "Dr. Wimpfheimer smiles because he is happy."
2.1.1.2.1.1.1.	Or better yet, when I see Dr. Wimpfheimer smile, I think to myself, "I believe Dr. Wimpfheimer smiles because he is happy."
2.1.1.2.1.1.1.1.	Though when I believe the doctor is happy, the doctor believes nothing.
2.1.1.2.1.1.1.1.1.	(Ibid 1.2.2.1.1.2.3.1)
2.1.1.2.2.	The doctor has yet to smile currently at this appointment.
2.1.2.	He does not wear the glasses now. Instead he consults a large clear tablet which seems to display all the information he needs to access.
2.2.	It is obvious, of course, why glasses would not necessarily be related to paraplegia.
2.2.1.	Though he may not necessarily be paraplegic as well.
2.2.1.1.	(Ibid 1.2)
2.3.	I'm not sure if they are prescription lenses. They are boxy and seem to have a small USB port on the side of the right frame.
2.4.	He touches the rims with his thumb and index finger, projecting a chart that is mine.
2.4.1.	"Mine" because it says "Isabel Spines" across the top.
2.4.2.	Not that the chart belongs to me.
2.4.2.1.	Really, I do not see the chart, rather I see a projection of a chart.
2.4.2.2.	It is actually just a picture of a chart with my name on it. Not "my" chart.
2.4.3.	The picture incorrectly lists my "Past Foster Units" as 4.
2.4.3.1	Actual value: 5.
2.5.	"Pretty soon I won't even need these frames. They're coming out

with smart contact lenses."

2.5.1	I don't reply.
2.5.2.	But now I see a smile.
3.	"You don't like to speak much, do you?"
3.1.	I don't reply.
3.2.	"Quiet type?"
3.3.	I don't reply.
3.3.1.	Dr. Wimpfheimer does not like silence.
3.3.1.1.	In that now, when he reads the projection, he frowns and mumbles to himself.
3.3.1.1.1.	I do not know if it is still a projection, because he currently has it on 'private browsing' mode.
3.3.1.1.1.1.	I heard the term 'private browsing mode' from my third foster brother, who had similar glasses.
3.3.1.2.	Though his frowning/mumbling could have nothing to do with his like or dislike of silence.
3.3.1.2.1.	A frown is typically a picture of dislike.
3.3.1.2.2.	Of course, it is not much use to think about Dr. Wimpfheimer's thoughts.
3.3.1.2.2.1.	(Ibid 1.2.2.1.1.2.3.1)
3.3.1.2.2.2.	I could imagine someone frowning when happy and smiling when sad too.
3.3.1.2.2.2.1.	Meaning that what happens on the outside doesn't necessarily relate to what's on the inside.
3.3.1.2.2.2.1.1.	I get anxious when thinking about myself on the outside.
3.3.1.2.2.2.1.2.	I get anxious when thinking about other people on the inside, too.
4.	The syringe is long and thick, the needle wider than any other I have seen before.
4.1.	Of course this makes me nervous.
4.1.1.	"This will pinch a bit."
4.1.1.1.	He is wiping iodine along my shoulder.
4.1.1.2.	I should say "no!" or "stop!" or "please don't."
4.1.1.2.1.	I do not.
4.1.1.3.	Will the pinching happen to me or him? He does not specify.
4.1.1.3.1.	How does he know what my pinching will feel like?

4.1.1.3.2.	And what is the "This" that will pinch? The silver needle that is as thick as a drinking straw? Or his puncturing my skin with it?
4.1.1.3.2.1.	Likely both.
4.1.2.	It does not pinch. It does not pinch. It does not pinch. It does not pinch. It does not pinch.
4.1.2.1.	Instead, I feel a sharp, cutting pain. The needle feels both hot and ice cold. He depresses the syringe.
4.1.2.1.1.	Could it be possible that this pain is what Dr. Wimpfheimer meant by "pinch"?
4.1.2.1.2.	This is why I do not like speaking. Nobody says what they mean. It's not that they are liars, it's just that our language makes telling the truth impossible.
4.1.2.1.2.1	I prefer silence.
4.2.	I suppose it is impossible to give an injection without a little bit of blood seeping back into the syringe.
4.2.1.	That is, the liquid injected into my shoulder was purple and almost shimmery as if it had small flecks of quartz or confetti in it. Now it is crimson.
4.2.1.1.	Though the liquid inside the syringe could turn blood-colored after injection.
4.2.2.	It is not necessarily my blood currently inside the syringe. Thinking about my blood makes me anxious.
4.2.3.	Anxiety is a bodily response to stress. I feel fluttery and energetic but also tired and nauseous.
4.2.3.1.	I get anxious when I think about my blood, my guts, or any other part of my insides.
4.2.3.2.	I also don't like to think about my outsides either, for different reasons.
4.2.3.2.1.1.	(Ibid 3.3.1.2.2.2.1.1)
4.2.3.2.1.2.	I get anxious thinking about the insides of other people because all they can show is their outsides. I get anxious thinking about my insides and I get anxious thinking about my outsides.
4.2.3.2.1.2.1.	I am therefore anxious all the time. I suppose it is also impossible to give an injection without feeling pain as well.

4.2.4.	Pain is interesting because it involves both my insides and my outsides.
4.2.4.1	Insides: The hurting feeling of the needle ripping through my skin and nerves and muscles and poking a hole in my vein and squirting cold shiny purple fluid into it.
4.2.4.1.1.	Outsides: Me gritting my teeth or crying or tearing up or even saying "ouch!"
4.2.4.1.2.	I don't want to think about this anymore.
4.2.4.1.2.1.	"We'll now have to wait forty-five minutes."
5.	Dr. Wimpfheimer initially turns off the lights when he exits the room.
5.1.	Sometime later he comes back and turns them on before leaving again.
5.2.	"Okay Isabel, let's see if this worked."
6.	He depresses the rims of his glasses and a projection of a young girl with translucent skin shows itself in front of us.
6.1.1.	"Translucent" is not the right word, as the whole projection has a cyan tint.
6.1.2.	You can see her organs and her lungs breathing and there are little dots running along her blood vessels all over the place. Beside her are numbers and graphs and charts always changing, but I don't know what those pictures represent.
6.1.2.1	He points to a series of numbers.
6.1.2.1.1	"Blood pressure. There's your heart rate, systole and diastole."
6.1.2.2.	Another figure. This one a line graph with a several jagged lines extending forward.
6.1.2.2.1.	"That's the concentration of various hormones in your blood."
6.1.2.2.1.1.	My blood?
6.1.2.2.2.	"Estrogen, Testosterone, Cortisol. All completely healthy."
6.1.2.2.3.	Only now does he smile.
6.1.2.3.	A similar chart, up by the picture's head.
6.1.2.3.1.	"And that is your brain activity. The brain is made up of millions of little nerve cells called neurons. They send tiny electrical jolts to each other. That tells your heart to beat, your lungs to breathe. I can see what regions are active and which ones are not. That's a

picture of you thinking."

6.1.2.3.1.1.   I don't like this. I don't feel good. I don't like thinking about my insides or my outsides.

6.1.2.3.1.2.   And now I've learned I especially don't like looking at pictures of my insides.

6.2.   "The shot I gave you had millions of little tiny robots. They check in on you and let me know how healthy you are. Think of them like a million little foster mommies and daddies."

6.2.1.   Why do I have to have this injection?

6.2.1.1.   Was it because a jet engine fell from the sky onto their car when my non-foster mommy and daddy were driving home from Memphis?

6.2.2.   What is to prevent them from clogging up my blood vessels?

6.2.3.   What is to prevent them from getting lodged in my brain?

6.2.4.   What is to prevent them from dissolving in my stomach acid?

6.2.4.1.   All of these questions make me anxious.

6.2.4.2.   Of course, I do not ask any of them.

6.3.   "If you experience nausea or have trouble sleeping or have diarrhea that's okay. This can sometimes cause that for the first week."

6.3.1.   "Do you feel sick at all right now?"

6.3.1.1.   I do not reply.

6.3.2.   "Good, because my readings don't show any abnormalities."

6.3.2.1.   He presses the rim of his glasses again.

6.3.2.1.1.   Now a keyboard is projected in front of him. He types on it.

6.3.2.1.2.   Under the picture of the girl (me?) are several lines of words I do not understand, despite having a verbal acumen three standard deviations above the average.

6.3.2.1.2.1.   As he types another word is added to the list.

6.3.2.1.2.1.1.   I do not know what this word means either.

6.3.2.1.2.1.1.1.   A funny thing about words: very many of them I do not understand. The ones that I do understand, I do not like to use. They are imprecise and I never can say what I want to say.

6.3.2.1.2.1.1.1.1.   And by "funny" I mean strange or uncomfortable. Not something that makes me laugh.

6.3.1.2.1.2.1.1.2.   "Funny" is a good example of a word that I know the meaning of but still do not like to use.

7.   "Okay, you may get dressed now, Isabel."

7.1.   Dr. Wimpfheimer leaves the room.

7.2.   The paper gown is loose, and the air in the room is cold.

7.3.   I do not know where they took my clothes.

1.4.0 Banana

Doug leaned forward as he drove, his nose only a few inches from the windshield. The afternoon's cerulean sky and sunshine had given way to heavy rain. Doug had the wipers on full blast as he hydroplaned down the highway. Automobile travel in New Jersey was historically a dangerous endeavor; the stuff of heroic Springsteen anthems from two-thirds-of-a-century ago. To manually drive southbound along the New Jersey Turnpike could be considered suicidal behavior by some, what with all the Waymos zipping along at triple-digit mph's. The overcast skies and rainfall didn't make the driving any easier.

The driverless cars had impeccable reflexes. They could safely and smoothly jettison around bodies moving much slower than Doug's sputtering hipster sedan, their passengers napping or chatting or playing the simple onboard games luxury vehicles came equipped with. A Waymo would never hit Doug. If an accident were to occur, it would be purely Lamarck-Ganoush's fault. The result of errant drifting or a poorly-executed lane change. Knuckles white on the steering wheel, seat belt strap cradling a fleshy breast, Doug simmed a dozen different crashes, wrecks and explosions he might cause as he drove toward Hoboken.

It didn't help that Takashi sat shotgun. Upon putting the sedan in gear, Lamarck-Ganoush put on an old Miles Davis CD. Bebop was his preferred narcotic for highway death anxiety. Tak spoke louder than the music, comparing jazz to complex systems theory. He used phrases like "time-output series" and "nonlinear dynamics" when describing various riffs. The beauty of jazz, the hebody maintained, centered on the network of feedback loops present between the musicians. Isa sat in the back, cocooned in the endless paradiddles of rainfall and the motherly hush of Waymos Dopplering past. She emitted projections the size of pizza boxes from her Lazy Eyes.

"You know DLG, if you sketched out a graph of that last verse," said Tak as they merged onto the left lane toward Hoboken, "It'd look awfully like a Koch Snow-flake."

Doug released a wet cough. From the rear view mirror he could see Isa blink into view a cascade of jagged fractals.

"See? Isa gets it," said Tak. He twisted the volume knob, Coltrane's roaring sax crescendoed in. Tak slung a wiry arm around his headrest and turned back toward Isa.

"Let me in," said Tak.

Isa waved two fingers in front of her face. Tak licked the pad of his thumb and traced over the stills of the fractals in time with the music. He drew up and down with the raising and lowering of the pitches of the jaunty sax solo, leaving a translucent maroon line in his thumb's wake.

"See boyo, it's a near perfect fit."

"I need to keep my eyes on the road, Tak." Doug leaned an inch farther forward. "I can't have any distractions." He lifted a sweaty hand from the wheel and dialed down the volume. "Isa, could you please turn those off?"

Isa blinked into private browsing. She turned toward the window, away from Tak, and began to draw small squiggles in her window's condensation.

Tak faced forwards and cranked the music up. The head of "Straight No Chaser" blasted in. The bass, overdriving the car's worn stereo, caused the seats to vibrate. Doug let out a gasp as an eighteen-wheeler swerved around them and rocketed past at twice their cruising speed, the sound of which was swallowed up by Monk's drunkard's walk of a riff. The truck splashed the left side of the car with a wave of rainwater.

"This is some rogue shit Lamarck-Ganoush," Tak yelled over the music. He twirled an over-gelled spike around his index finger. "We should try to incorporate such computational complexity into the structures of our music."

Doug lowered the volume a few decibels. "Like you could handle that on bass, Tak. Everything you write is pretty, shall we say, straight-forward."

"Straight-forward doesn't exist in this universe, DLG. TANSTAALF."

"What?" said Doug.

"There Ain't No Such Thing As A Linear Function."

Doug wanted to treat himself to a long blink but couldn't, lest he take his eyes off the road. "You're so full of it, Miyagi-Edelstein."

"If there is anything having a Jewish dad and a Japanese mom has taught me, it's an unflinching and undying respect for the numerical."

"Do you want us to get into an accident?"

Tak reclined his seat and put his feet up on the dash. The laces of his combat boots were untied. "If we took my van we'd be totally safe."

Lamarck-Ganoush decelerated as he ramped off the highway. Urban driving was always easier; the density of people made even the Waymos move at a crawl.

"Well you eliminated our ability to do such," Doug said. "Courtney Christ, Takashi, you've stirred up some real shit."

"And it's not an isolated incident I'm afraid," Tak replied.

Doug clicked off the windshield wipers. The rain had begun to subside. "What do you mean?" he said. "Straight No Chaser" had ended. The stereo played a static whisper of emptiness. "What else did you do?"

"Nothing I know of," said Tak, clicking his steel toes together. "Haven't you ever heard of Poisson Distributions? Random events do not occur equally spaced in time. They cluster. Shit— stochastically speaking—tends to storm."

"I believe the building should be 300 meters on the left," said Isa, still staring out her window.

"So you've been here before?" said Tak.

Isa blinked on a projection of a navigation applet.

"Thanks Isa," said Doug. He straightened his spine and took a hand off of the steering wheel.

"_"

"Thar she blows," said Tak.

Doug slowed to a stop in front of an empty shopfront. Across the street stood a giant black and white sign, slicked with rain. It displayed a grid with some chaotic arrangement of triangles within triangles within triangles, geometrically spiraling endlessly into itself. **RULE 30** was spray painted in hot pink across it. He shifted into park and unbuckled his seatbelt. Neither Tak nor Isa were wearing theirs.

"So it's named after the infamous Wolfram automata," said Tak, withdrawing his feet from the dashboard. "Thought so."

Doug could feel a mild sinus headache blooming between his eyes. "What?"

"See the sign." Tak pointed at it with his elbow. His seat was still fully re-clined. "Imagine a grid of squares, all white, save one which is filled in black."

"_"

"_"

"Now let's say I write a set of rules. The color of a square—whether it's black or white—is determined by the colors of the three squares above it. Even seven or eight of these simple rules is enough to generate a totally chaotic shape. The one on the venue's sign is the most famous example of such."

Doug opened his door. "I barely follow you, Tak."

"Determinism begets chaos." A thin pinkness of gums circumscribed Takashi's smile. "It's the cardinal rule of complex systems: great complexity comes from great simplicity."

"How very Tao of you, Takashi."

"Well I am half Japanese."

"The Tao came from ancient China."

Takashi opened his door. "I do math, not history."

Hoboken Venue under New Management, Less Bullshit Ensues read the *Staph Infection* printout tacked to the wall by the entrance. It sparkled under the veneer of packing tape. The only bit of luster in the otherwise dank dungeon of rock. Like a septum piercing on the pope, the sheet stuck out against the dingy walls of Rule 30. The printout was crisp, white and neat. It overlaid a whirling sea of the most repulsive lexemes the angsty basement-dwelling youth of the east coast could stitch together: *Phantom Enema, Dennis Vreeman Sodomizes Gandhi in Purgatory, Rita Rectal & the Rug Munchers.* A few PG-rated band names too. It was the crusters, the thrashers, the bearded guitar wizards who affixed -core to the end of every other word, though, who seemed to sign the walls in the vilest ways.

Doug was the only one who bothered to read the laminated printout. The other two gave it a passing glance as they descended the stairs into the space's atrium. The article was a review of a spazzcore group from Weehawken finishing off a state-wide tour. Mickey Mallorey, the zine's theebody editor-in-chief, described the smell of Rule 30 as "if gym sox could fart". This was not an insult. Apparently in past years Rule 30 had been in even worse condition, Mallorey had mentioned in a footnote. The show was sweaty, bloody and brutally good. Though the *Staph Infection* article was dated from over two weeks ago, the venue still somehow smelled faintly of mildew and warm Mediterranean cheese.

As he descended the staircase, Takashi stopped every now and then to read a tag of some obscure punk band. Isa seemed lost in thought and couldn't be bothered with them. Neither acknowledged the heavy thumping of Doug's mass plodding down the stairs behind her.

"Oy," said Takashi as he emerged from the mouth of the stairs. "There must be a few hundred of these." He gestured toward many more signatures, stickers, and curses flashing across the walls. His nose not six inches from the plexiglass, he began to scan each bit of graffiti slowly and diligently like a Turing machine clicking through some ticker tape. Isa followed, the crown of her head parallel to her toes: the stance of a mind frozen by a kind of logically-induced ice cream headache. Doug was the last out of the staircase, and the only one to lock eyes with the old hebody lying on the couch dragging a thumbnail-sized joint.

"Sorry, didn't mean to intrude," said Doug. His mouth felt dry.

The hebody lay supine on a cushionless brown loveseat. A stringless acoustic guitar laid by his feet. He wore a thin *Rancid* t-shirt, which arced gently over his domed belly. A pale, hairy donut of fat peaked out the bottom, spilling over the waistband of his torn blue jeans. His cheeks, thick and low hanging, were clean-shaven, unlike his bald head circumscribed by a torus of salt and pepper stubble. All this above one major-league schnozz that sloped down toward a pair of lips cracked with dehy-dration. The joint was perched between them. His hands behind his head, he managed to hit the joint without touching it in an impressive feat of stoned laziness. The joint's crimson tip arched up with each inhale and descended limply beneath two columns of smoke from each nostril. He only stared at Doug, puff after puff after puff.

"Oh shit! Did you guys know The Ghost Boners played here?" said Takashi, oblivious.

The man's eyes slid between Doug and Isa. She chewed at a hangnail as if, should the nail become detached from her skin, some grand metaphysical truth would seat itself in the crevices of her brain. The man's gaze settled upon her and shifted from a horizontal vector to a vertical one. His pupils rose and fell as he toked and stared at her in the leery way balding men sometimes do.

"Wait, no, not The Ghost Boners...The Goat Boners." Takashi stepped back from the wall and turned. "Hey Isa, have you heard of The Goat Boners?"

"Mmm, couple'a ska kids from the Oranges," said the old hebody, eyes on Isa.

Tak was silent.

"Sorry, I didn't see you."

"--"

"Is, uh, Ruth here?" Doug asked. He could hear the gunky buildup in the man's sinuses with each wheezy breath he took.

The man lifted a soda can that had been occluded by the broken guitar on the floor, and stubbed out the smoldering non-synth joint.

"Ruthie McRogers?" Doug again.

"Coming!" a smooth alto chimed from the other room.

From a doorless frame across the room the shebody emerged. Tall and thick though not ungainly, she wore a purple sundress that swelled under the cheerful round of her stomach and thighs. The sleeveless dress exposed two muscular arms with a small spray of red hair sprouting from her armpits. Her left shoulder displayed a stick-and-poke tattoo of a colorless banana mid-peel. Hazel eyes sat upon a round face that seemed almost doll-like against her frame. Below them, her nose, the same high-caliber schnozz as the man on the couch, fell in perfect line with her hair: a billowing mohawk of fiery curls rising above a crown of peach fuzz. She held a monkey wrench in her right hand, which she bounced against her hip rhythmically as she spoke. "All apologies. I've grown a bit deconditioned to that name."

Isa ceased gnawing at her index finger and looked up.

"Good to see you, Isa Spines."

Isa pulled back the corners of her mouth into a close-lipped smile. The white of her face turned beetish.

"Ruthie McRogers, you are a sight for sore eyes," said Tak. "I meant to say hi to you last week—I was in here for the garage band from New Haven."

"New Haven? We haven't had a band from out of state in years." The shebody looked toward the man on the couch. He nodded in agreement. "I don't even have enough sway with the Neo-!Kung to import a band into New Jersey." She scratched the back of her head with the wrench. "And, please, don't call me Ruthie. Not in here at least."

Tak inserted a thumb into each of his front pockets. "Must've misheard."

"What do you go by now?" said Lamarck-Ganoush.

"When in here, I like to go by **Futurabold**. Last name stays the same."

"Like the font?" said Takashi, his voice rising in pitch with either incredulity or admiration.

"Yup, like the font."

"I thought that was a typo," said Doug.

"What was?"

"The article." Doug began to perspire in sheets. "The one above the stairs."

"Ah so you're the literate one here I guess. Name?"

"Uh, I'm Douglas Lamarck-Ganoush. Doug. Whatever. Traditional name, not a typeface."

"Right, right." **Futurabold** crossed to him and extended a hand. "Pleasure."

Doug wiped his hand on the flank of his shorts before grasping hers. "Thanks. We actually went to University together. We were in the same philosophy lecture I'm pretty sure."

"Yeah? Which one?"

"Uh, Modern European. Some Hegel and Nietzsche all the way to Heideggar and Wittgenstein."

"Uh huh, Uh huh. Funny how Zappos threw in a few humanities into the course load. Y'know, make us feel like we were doing something with our education other than preparing for a life of corporate dronedom. Did you like it?"

"I did actually. I found Nietzsche really inspiring."

Futurabold screwed her mouth into a smirk. "You white suburban hebodies and your Nietzsche."

Doug choked on something between a laugh and a scoff.

Figure 2: Rule 30

"I don't understand," Isa interrupted. "Why change your name?"

"A few years ago I assisted my thesis advisor on an ethnography he was writing on the Neo-!Kung up in Rockland. It was initially just a short research project, for the summer, but long story short, ended up joining for a year."

"And you survived?" said Doug.

"They're perfectly friendly people," said **Futurabold**. "A mix of folk, united in their disdain for the modern technocracy. Cryptocurrency burnounts, gun lovers, tree-huggers, nudists, vegans and the like too. It's a lifestyle change, sure. No Lazy Eyes, no tablets. If you wanna eat you gotta learn how to hunt. Or at least pick what local vegetation isn't poisonous."

"Any actual members of the !Kung?" said Tak, "These people sound whiter than Doug's philosophy reader."

"To a degree. And of course they're largely not the type to admit that they're name is appropriative," said **Futurabold**. "It's not like I would pick fights though. As I do now, I don't hold myself in a manner too condescending to my hosts."

In one swift, liquid movement the man on the couch brought a joint to his lips, lit it, and took a hit. The hacking wetness of the following cough ricocheted across the room.

"The research was with professor Ezra Stickles if any of you guys took a class with him back in the day."

"_"

"Anthro department?"

"Well my degree's in Evolutionary Ludology."

A shared blankness extended across the faces of the three.

"It's amazing the baroque names modern academia will create to justify their bullshit," said **Futurabold**. "Zappos was interested in the Neo-!Kung, initially because they were fucking up any delivery drones or truck caravans that passed by their encampments. Stickles though proposed that the Neo-!Kung might serve as a cheap but effective security force, hence all the research into them. Really though I just chose the major so I could get a degree without having to study all that tech shit."

"Security force?" Tak, again.

"Here," **Futurabold** laid a hand on Isa's thin shoulder. "Let's go to my office shall we?" She pivoted on the balls of her feet—compact, pretty, shoeless things— and sauntered toward the doorway, her zaftig tush like a Lorenz Attractor, coordinates swaying side to side as she walked.

The walls of her office were white stucco, bare, save for the several dozen sheets of notebook paper tacked up on them. They were all covered in sloppy and prolix arrays of scribbles. In the corners lay milk crates filled with various cables, condenser microphones and power strips. The whole place reeked of air freshener and a scattered intellect. A swivel chair sat behind a cheap wooden desk cluttered with

Chinese take-out boxes and an old, boxy monitor. An enormous PC tower sat on the ground to the side. The monitor displayed a screensaver of randomly generated tropical fish swimming about; it looked about a half-century old to Doug.

Futurabold pulled three empty milk crates from the corner and flipped them upside-down in front of her desk.

"Have a seat," she said.

She looped around her desk, plopped herself down in her chair and clicked the screen to life. Instantly the fish disappeared, replaced by the toothy smiling face of a black-furred bonobo dotted with icons for a breadth of folders, documents and programs.

"Essentially, the Neo-!Kung attempt to live as close to a Paleolithic lifestyle as possible. They sleep in yurts, hunt game and pick berries. You get the idea."

"Is that where you got this piece of shit?" said Takashi.

"What, the computer? I inherited it when I took over the place. It works just fine."

Tak sucked air between his teeth.

"I'm pretty technologically illiterate for a UZ grad," added **Futurabold**. "The panels in the main space I had to have installed. Maybe that's why I liked the Neo-!Kung. The only real piece of technology we used were guns."

Takashi laughed a bit. "Guns? How'd that happen?"

Futurabold leaned back in her chair. "Our lifestyle habits attracted a fair amount of pretty radical libertarians. They saw the Neo-!Kung as their entryway into an anarcho-capitalist paradise. I don't blame 'em. Everything was voluntary and law enforcement were too afraid of us to bother. But when you have libertarians, you have guns. Lots of goddamn guns. I will admit, they made the hunting much easier."

Doug crossed his legs, uncrossed them, and then crossed them again, rocking back and forth as he did so. "So you came here," he said. "Dropped the Paleolithic life and took over this place to try to get a foothold in the music industry."

"Sorta." **Futurabold** leaned back in her chair. "I mean, I certainly don't view myself as a primitivist any longer. Not by any Neo-!Kung standards at least."

"So why did you leave?" Doug, again.

"Because you can't really learn all that much about your human origins sniping ducks on the side of Route 4," **Futurabold** replied. "I honestly believe watching these punks mosh around you can learn a lot more about early homos. The genus I mean."

"Is that why you got the antique PC?" said Tak. "It's what the australopithecines used?"

"Ignore him," said Doug. "The hebody speaks more than he thinks."

"Basically I figure here, with Rule 30, I could conduct my own little primatology research while generating some income—which is not easy for a young shebody to

do these days. Not to mention I'd help out my uncle. Give him some company."

"That hebody's your uncle?" Takashi this time.

"Yeah, my Uncle Dee. He operated the venue before me. But he was losing a lot of money on the place so I took it over from him, did some renovations, blah blah blah. He's something of a bouncer or security now I guess."

"Real animated character."

"Yeah well, lithium will do that to you."

"_"

"_"

"He's pretty benign though. Usually stoned quiet during the off hours. When we're having a gig he'll stand by the door. Look all intimidating. It really does keep the crowd capped at a manageable level of chaos. I really wouldn't be able to handle this operation without him. With him here I can join the crowd, talk to people, you know, conduct research. Been here for a couple months and I still can't figure out whether it's the dullest or most supremely interesting culture on the planet today."

"One middle-aged man?"

"The twenty-something east-coast suburbanite. I mean, look at this place!" **Futurabold** flung out her arms forming a W with her mohawk as the central vertex. "This is as lame and shitty as lame and shitty venues go. Still, I'm constantly getting an obscene amount of booking requests: emails, texts, fucking handwritten letters sent in the *mail*. It feels like every group of four twenty-somethings in the state who can gun out an old Titus Andronicus cover wants to play here. You wanna know why?"

Doug palmed at some wetness on his forehead, waiting for Tak to say something. For once, the hebody was silent. "Why?"

"Because, in the twenties this venue had some significance. Back when Uncle Dee ran the place. He and his equally-manic friends put on a few good shows, McJagger and the Nuggets played here before they broke big. Underground acts too: Judith Butthurt, Moshed Pitatoes. This place got a half a paragraph on a few punk wikis, a couple nods in various music history tomes, and now it's become this bastion for every band who wished they were alive to play at Maxwell's."

"So your uncle is *that* Dee McRogers?" said Tak, leaning forward.

"Oh, don't pretend like you've heard of him," **Futurabold** spoke with an amelodic frankness. "I hear that from poseurs like you every day."

Doug stifled a laugh.

"See, it all boils down to the disease with these kids. You know, they're all more or less talented musically, and, being products of the digital age and whatnot has made them top-shelf networkers. They've largely grown up with all the middle-class comforts their parents could afford, honed their musical acumen in their basements. Then, pow!" She brought her hands down to the desk with a resounding thud. "They hit a wall, proverbially speaking. Can't get a job out of University of Zappos. No income, paternal approval, whatever. So, of course, they form a band with a few of their friends from home. Friends chosen more out of geographic proximity than any sort of shared kindredness or mutual love or respect or whatever emotional mortar modern friendships are adhered by. Friends whose noses are similarly proverbially flattened from hitting similar proverbial walls. And they practice a lot and write a lot and blog a lot. And, nine times outta ten, they sound fantastic. They're amazing at booking shows and promoting and they usually draw huge flat-nosed crowds."

"So what's the disease?"

"Because everyone at these shows are more concerned with archiving the concert rather than experiencing it. There's always invariably the group that stands by the perimeter, arms folded, recording songs on their Lazies. When a more aggressive act plays, few will mosh, but almost all will post about how they lost their shoes or bloodied their nose in the pit.

"The bands themselves aren't much better. I mean, for all their musicianship, the lyrics these groups spew just royally suck. Everyone has a hand-coded RSS of their favorite music media these days, but nobody knows how to craft a coherent sentence. It's a good thing they scream most of the time or their mics malfunction. If the crowd could understand half the shit they belt out they'd probably punch the singer in the face. Or not. I don't know. Musicians our age bewilder me. No offense."

"_--_"

"_--_"

"None taken."

Futurabold leaned forward and exhaled. Her breath smelled of burnt coffee and herbal toothpaste. "Which brings me to the name change. When I was with the Neo-!Kung I couldn't go by Ruthie. Not paleo enough, go figure. Instead, I was Mai. One meaningless syllable, but it sounded somewhat primitive. And with a name like that, the results were astounding. The Neo-!Kung were so much more open.

"So I figure I'd do the same here. Name myself after a font; let them think I'm some sort of post-postmodern cyberpunk, so indulgent in her own pretensions that they should feel guiltless in indulging theirs." She leaned forward, her elbows on her desk, her breasts cradled by her forearms. "I'll tell you, it *works*."

From the corners of their eyes, Doug and Tak shared a look: one of the rare moments of nervous synchrony that reminded them why they were still friends.

"But that's me. I'm sure you didn't come here to listen to me wax ethnographic. So what's the deal, you three wanna book a show?"

Tak spoke first. "In a sense."

"Uh-huh." **Futurabold** pulled the keyboard toward herself and pressed a few keys. She typed slowly and attentively, the way a self-proclaimed cyberpunk would not. "According to my calendar, I have bookings every Tuesday, Thursday, Friday, Saturday, and Sunday for the next eight weeks. I suppose you could open for any of them if you want." Another set of keystrokes, clunky and audible. She bit her lower lip as she typed. "Yeah, if you want to headline anything you're going to have to wait until June at the earliest. Remind me though, what do you guys go by?"

"Shackled Uterus," Tak said.

"Tak's idea, not mine," Doug added. He glanced at Isa. She sat on her crate mouth slightly agape, Lazies set to private browsing. "Ours."

"Uh-huh."

"Yeah, we're developing this old school Riot Grrrl vibe." Tak crossed his legs. His jeans looked impossibly tight. "I've always considered myself a strong fifth-wave feminist. Even considered identifying as a theebody for it."

"There's a fifth wave now?"

"Something like that," Tak wore a hesitant grin.

"Why? Because you have a queer shebody on bass?"

"Isa plays guitar actually." Takashi swallowed his smile. "Doug has been pushing for a name change, though."

"Right, right. I remember listening to a couple of demos you put online."

"Yeah? You like?"

The shebody flared her nostrils and clicked her tongue. "Not bad," she said.

"You do have two competent musicians in your ranks from what I could hear." At this Doug smirked.

"I'm sorta new to bass guitar. I have a good ear though. I'm practicing—"

"—Which is what we came here to talk about," Doug interrupted. "What Takashi here is neglecting to tell you is that we aren't so much in need of a place to perform as much as we are in need of just a general place."

"A practice space?"

"Exactly." Doug drummed his fingers on his kneecap in neat little triplets as he spoke.

"You don't have one? A basement? A garage? A laundry room?"

"Well, we did, but Tak made that space impossible to use."

"I needed a place to hide my van. I'm sorta on the lam currently."

"I'm sorry," she said. "I'd love to help you, really, but I'm not sure I can do that for you here."

"We have a shit ton of equipment." Tak pulled his torso forward, his fingers clamped around the edge of the disk. Exasperation bristled out of him like spines on a sea urchin. "And I couldn't help but notice you don't have too much for yourself. You let us practice here, mi gear es tu gear. For whoever you want. Touring bands, whatever."

"I've done perfectly fine having bands bring their own stuff."

"This's top shelf though. Primo shit."

Doug could see Tak's offers bouncing off **Futurabold** like moths against a porch light: pathologically insistent but ultimately ineffective at breaking through.

"I'm sure it is. I appreciate the offer. It's generous in a weird way, but—"

"—I'm talkin' a drum kit, P.A., bass *and* guitar stacks—"

A muffled report of hacking coughs from the tarred gullet of **Futurabold**'s Uncle Dee sounded across the room.

"Is he alright?" Doug asked, ever sympathetic to respiratory malfunction.

"He's fine. Everything is fine. You three will be fine too I'm sure. I just can't let you use my venue for your own personal needs." Her pupils saccaded from Isa to Doug to Tak and back to Isa. "If you give three unemployed college grads a space, they'll want spare keys, squatters rights, creative control—"

"—I'll have you know that I am currently employed." Tak wrapped his thumbs around the edges of the desk. "Or at least I have a steady income flow."

They locked eyes as Tak released his grip on the desk. His hands dangled by the sides of the blue milk crate he sat on.

"C'mon. Say something Isa."

"A banana."

Futurabold turned her attention away from Tak. "This?" The shebody grazed her fingers over the tattoo on her shoulder. "I got it a few months ago. A throwback to my year with the Neo-!Kung."

Isa blinked off her Lazies. Somehow **Futurabold** had at least briefly popped the shebody's digital bubble.

"It sounds cliché but so were all the evolutionary descendants of apes. The Neo-!Kung take the notion too far, but it's otherwise forgotten in this modern age. We're all primates, it's the newest old idea out there. That's my philosophy at least."

"I don't see what the writings of Darwin have to do with philosophy at all," said Isa.

Futurabold let Isa's statement hang in the air a bit before responding. "It has everything to do with philosophy," she said. "Our whole evolutionary history. Our past lives as primates. They inform every aspect of our existence. Our thoughts, our languages, our cultures. Once you start thinking evolutionarily about your identity, how you are irrevocably a primate borne out of the successes and failures of millions of generations of great apes past, your whole sense of self disintegrates and reassembles anew. Everything you see here in Rule 30 is still chimpanzee tribalism."

"That is reductive," said Isa. "And not in the good way."

"Just cause you can't break something down into p's and q's and, like, little pyramids of dots in between doesn't make it false."

"It is speculation about the distant past. That is empirically unknowable."

"Really, Isa?" **Futurabold** tapped her foot on the tile floor. "When you turn on your Lazy Eyes there is such an emphasis on the now. It's a constant feed of news updates, pictures, social ephemera. When was the last time you asked yourself how we got here or why? Even at University of Zappos nobody would. Not unless you were content poring over the skull measurements of Pithecanthropus Erectus jawbones for hours on end."

"So 'how' and 'why'. Those are your questions?" Isa spoke without making eye contact.

"Yeah, well, that's what I said."

"I see." She traced a visitat on her wrist. It morphed into a leafless brown tree, its branches sprawling out in all directions. "Those are poor questions. You wish to articulate what cannot be spoken of."

"Courtney Christ, Isa," Takashi lurched forward, his head in his hands, "Do you have to do this now?"

"_"

"_"

"You know, as much as I've enjoyed the F2F, I have to set up some promotional info for a show next week," said **Futurabold**. "I'm going to need some space. Thanks for stopping by, and good luck finding a space."

Isa blinked back on her Lazy Eyes.

"Wait." Tak shot up, his back erected. "I think we can help you."

"As I said, I don't need any equipment. Thank you."

"How often do you bring bands in here?"

"I have three or four shows a week.

"No, in here."

"My office?"

Tak whirled his hands over his head. A tornadic affirmation.

"Usually whenever I book someone."

"You're undermining yourself."

"Okay, time for you to leave." **Futurabold** tapped at an imaginary watch on her wrist.

"Seriously. Hear me out. How many of those tags on the wall are real?"

"The graffiti? In the main room?"

"Yup."

"I never really intended them to withstand much scrutiny."

"Hey, I'm not tryin' to call you a poseur or anything. I get it. Yr an anthropologist trying construct a certain atmosphere. An ambience."

"Sure."

"Well every time you bring a band in here, into this room, you risk completely destroying it. You probably have already and don't even realize it."

"Excuse me?"

Tak rose to his feet. His tall and winter-thin frame loomed over the desk.

"What kinda self-proclaimed 'cyberpunk'," he flexed his middle and index fingers around the word, "uses a piece a shit desktop like you've got?"

"As I said, it's my uncle's. He gave it to me."

"What OS are you using? Mac?"

"I'm not sure what that means. It's a PC I think. Microsoft."

Tak gagged before whirling around her desk. He placed the tips of his fingers to the keyboard and deftly typed. "Windows Vista? Seriously? Shit's from, like, 2005."

"Well it serves me just fine."

From **Futurabold**'s side Tak typed a few commands, grunting and moaning in frustration as he did so. "It's dragging ass. I bet you're not the only one it serves." He leaned over her shoulders in a manner that might have been flirtatious if it was not saturated with Takashi's signature vibe of aggression and histrionics. His arms enclosed her body; her mohawk bristled against his neck. He typed and clicked, typed and clicked, his fingers displaying the adroitness of a Baroque pianist.

"Yr uncle's a big fan of internet porn."

"What?"

"And he's not even that good at it; downloading the stuff I mean."

"How can you tell?"

The monitor was black and littered with clusters of numbers and small, almost unreadable fragments of words.

"Well, your PC is loaded with every Trojan, worm and piece of malware the internet could cook up. Seriously, this thing is more virus than it is software. I hope you don't have anything too personal on it."

"Can you get rid of them?"

"Some, sure." Takashi backed off and began to circle the room, his hands held behind his back, both smarmy and clerical. "But half of them have probably sent yr name, address, credit card number and university transcripts to Bulgaria or wherever. Even I would have trouble wresting some of the more masterfully programmed bugs out of yr hard drive." He stopped, his back to the rest of *Shackled Uterus.* "We've been three sheets into the digital age for a near century now. You're not with the Neo-!Kung anymore."

"So what are you saying?"

"You let us practice here for the summer, and I'll build you one hell of a computer. Better than anything money can buy. Any visitors with half a brain for technology will be impressed when they see it. Plus, it'll keep the vast majority of yr uncle's pornobots at bay." Tak let his offer sit. All was quiet as he retook his seat on the overturned milk crate. "The way I see it, you'll have a much more efficient tool for Rule 30, and it'll look sleek as fuck. Yr chances of getting outed as the monkey-brained technophobe you are will decrease greatly, and yr charming Uncle Dee will be able to jerk it with minimal risk of damage."

Doug flashed some teeth toward **Futurabold**. Behind her, he could see a rectangle of loose-leaf paper thumb-tacked to the wall. A to-do list from several months ago, scrawled in pink marker.

His smile was returned, this one with closed lips.

"This is just an exchange of favors?"

"Of course. You scratch our back, we give yours a thorough clawing."

"Okay, I suppose I'm fine with this. For now."

"A wise choice Miss McRogers. We'll be forever indebted."

"Just don't fuck things up."

"Fuck-upage will be kept to a contained minimum," said Tak.

"Thank you so much," Doug added.

"By the way," Tak added. "Any idea where I could snatch some hair dye?"

*   *   *

While Tak was in the Rite Aid Isa and Doug waited in the car. The sedan sat double-parked outside the store. Doug tapped out polyrhythms on his thighs. Four beats per measure on his right hand, three on his left. A simple drummer's exercise made simpler by repeating the phrase to oneself while polyrhytmizing. Isa, in the backseat, was several leagues deep in techno-solipsism.

Eat-Your-Goddamn-Spinach. Eat-Your-Goddamn-Spinach.

The handle of the door clicked and Tak entered the vehicle. The waistband of skinny jeans bulged with various vegan protein bars, breath fresheners and individually-wrapped artisanal carob squares. He likely plucked them all from the tall and labyrinthine shelves inside. He gripped a thin plastic bag, which he plopped into his lap when he sat down. It contained three differently colored bottles of blonde hair treatment: one for Strawberry Blonde, another Vanilla Crème, and the third dubiously labeled "Extra Light Neutral." Given the bag, he must have paid for them in full.

"Change my appearance. You know, just in case," he said.

"You're using all of them?"

"I figure I'll dump them all in a bin and comb whatever emulsion I make into my hair. Watch some pre-millennial music videos while I wait for it to dry."

"_"

"_"

Tak clicked his seatbelt in. "I guess we'll have to take a couple'a trips back and forth. To get all our shit over."

"That makes sense."

"_"

"_"

"Are we going?" Takashi asked. Doug had yet to turn on the ignition.

"Yes. Sorry."

And they drove. The road was slick and pocketed with dark puddles, the sky above, gray and cloudy.

"So will we need to stop by an electronics warehouse?"

"Why?"

"For **Futurabold**. Ruthie. Parts for her computer."

"Eh, I can get'm online. Easier that way. More time for you two to repay me."

"We're repaying you?"

"Yeah. Only, like, twenty thousand bucks apiece. I have to check pricing and shit first."

The car rumbled and sputtered over the cracked bumpy road

"Twenty thousand? Tak, you never said we had to pay anything. I thought you had it covered."

"C'mon boyo, it was implicit in my offer."

"I have probably two K to my name," Doug replied. "The ATM won't even let me withdraw money I'm so broke."

"I could always snag another array of credit card numbers."

"Do that, Tak,"

Miyagi-Edelstein snorted. "You threw such a shit-fit two hours ago about stealing band equipment. And here I thought you had a moral compass. Must be that Nietzsche you read in college."

Doug stared forward. He had fallen for Takashi's oldest of tricks. Tak always dropped bombs while safely buckled into a car in motion, when driver and shotgun passenger had their respective gazes set forward, saccading between the endless Morse code of yellow dashes on the pavement, punny license plates, and flashing LED billboards that hung above them like missionary messages from on high. With the conversants facing forward and thus relieved of the burdens of eye contact, facial de-coding, and synchronizations, inconvenient truths could roll off Tak's tongue like they were written in air. Doug should have seen this coming since the door lock went click.

"__"

"__"

"Just try and pay me within the next couple weeks." Tak wrapped an elbow around the headrest behind him, his solar plexus opened to the dashboard. "You too, Isa."

"__"

"Y'know, a 'thank you' might be nice. I totally got us access to the space, meaning A) we'll get to F2F with tons of bands and B) play shows all the time."

"__"

"__"

"We need to practice first," said Doug. "A lot. And I'm all for taking things more seriously which is why I refuse to play under the name *Shackled Uterus* anymore."

"I thought you liked it!"

"You liked it and you projected your own liking it on to me. My true feelings on the matter vacillate between eye-rolling and a strong degree of dislike."

"Well, what does Isa think?"

But Isa never really looked like she cared much, as long as there was music and the slight sting of nickel-plated string under fingertips.

Takashi faced forward. "Got it," he said. "New Ape Idea."

"What does that mean?" replied Lamarck-Ganoush. He winced as a self-driving eighteen-wheeler bolted by in the adjacent lane.

"Like with **Futurabold**'s banana tattoo. She's onto something." Tak looked at Isa in the rearview mirror. "It has a ring to it, no?"

The highway seemed largely cleared out. Doug put on a blinker and merged over into the left lane.

"Whatever you say, Takashi," he said.

Tak snapped his fingers, pleased with himself. "Darwinism is the new thrash."

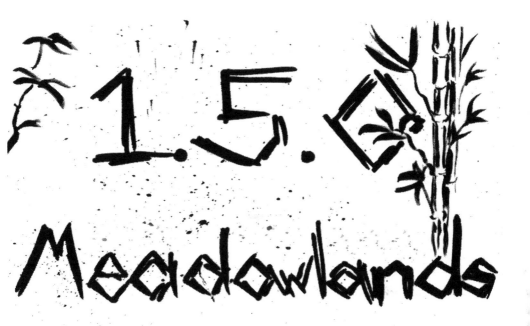

1.5.0
Meadowlands

That damn light above Halisdol's cubicle will not stop flickering. Piece of shit is probably incandescent. Melodica spent trillions on greening up the building above ground and now corporate is too cheap to even order fluorescents for the technicians' office in the basement. And how is Halisdol supposed to get anything productive done with his desk shuttering in and out of darkness, the light clicking indecisively? On a Friday no less, when a failure to meet deadline means weekend overtime. Sure the light might stay on just fine for an hour; let Halisdol at least get a few messages out to his consult at Big Data or maybe finish a lab prelim. Not that any requests to Mercado or even Buildings & Grounds will even get processed. This is infuriating.

In front of him plays a video of two toddlers, both males born with congenital blindness. Their milky white retinas sapped them of any endearing qualities, big baby eyes being a primary cuteness vector. To Halisdol they seem more spectral than human. All the better. The studies come easier when there are no ethical palpitations throbbing between his ears.

The two wear thick black harnesses around their meaty little bodies. They have on diapers and shirts; in a previous iteration, the straps had broken the skin on one subject's belly causing it to cry and wail and bleat. It had to be replaced by another. The cotton shirts protect the skin from irritation.

The harnesses hang down from a large wheel on the room's ceiling. Thus, both subjects are confined to crawl in a circle. This video is of a control case. This week, Halisdol has managed to chart three of the experimental cases. It is a record for him, and yet he is still under quota.

Alongside the video runs a real-time tracker of rates of change in arm extension, crawling speed and leg movement. A grid of force plates had been installed beneath the carpeting they crawled on, and vectors for their movement are measured as well. Halisdol scans the data printout, kneading his toes in anticipation of some juicy eigenvalues. Should the phase space level out into a Markov equilibrium, he might even get promoted to an above-ground workstation. Mapped together, the variables should look something chaotic but patterned, ideally a nice set of eigenvectors varying in magnitude and displacement but not direction. Or so Halisdol hopes, lest his work should lose Melodica some precious government funds. Information scrolls by too fast for Halisdol to read. Hopefully the funky little map reduce suite those interns made could munge through these myriad values. Halisdol really just needs to make sure no huge irregularities pop out. Or if they do, he hopes they could at least be explained in the context of every other irregularity that comes about. Dynamical systems are always less about order than framing the chaos as something tangible or anticipatable.

A *click* and shadows engulf the cubicle. The glow of the computer screen gives Halisdol's face a zombified pallor. This can't be good for his vision. Halisdol blinks twice and adjusted the brightness meter on his Eyes. Comfortable enough.

One of the subjects stops crawling. It rolls backwards onto his heels in a caveman squat. The vector printout goes wild. Negs where there shouldn't be, thousands of off-kilter measurements in need of flooring. Halisdol swipes through a few menues and switches to another experimental group. Another two toddlers. Same harness and carpeted floors. Now though, a looping recording of a woman speaks to them. She coos to them, her voice slow, rhythm and pitch maternally exaggerated. Already they begin to crawl faster and more efficiently. Their little arms extended fully, sausage-like fingers digging into the shaggy carpet with each upward inflection of the recording. Halisdol can smell the eigenvectors.

He depresses a trigger at his station: a small tab on the side of the console. The speakers in the crawl room begin to rotate with the harness mobile. The intended effect is to give the subjects the illusion that they are constantly crawling toward the sound's source. They coo and babble along with it, sliding knees they would never see below their bulbous diapered rears. Already the incoming data —measurements of the entire experimental élan including force, acceleration and jerk of each limb's movement, subject vocalizations per second, all in relation to the inflection of maternal speech—seem incommensurably cleaner than before. An easy write-up for Halisdol. Perhaps he'll even get a bonus this month if he can finish it in time.

Click.

The strong yellow overhead lamp, combined with the lens backlighting nearly blind Halisdol. He throws his head back, giving himself some mild whiplash as he brings his hands to his eyes. Even with lids shut his Lazy Eyes remain backlit: an unfortunate design flaw. He tilts his head forward and removes the lenses. Halisdol prefers to work without them generally, but the built in statistics applets proved to be a great boon to his research. He blinks. Nothing in his visual field changes. Halisdol presses his fingertips against a few buttons on his computer screen. A line graph extends before him. A crude reading of the data would have suggested a slow logarithmic assent; but no, it zigzagged up and down indiscernibly. There is a good chaos: a complexity that may seem daunting yet is easily described with some fun nonlinear equations. And then there's randomness. This seems to be the latter. Motherfucker.

Halisdol has an ace up his sleeve for these situations, when analysis gets too frustrating. A simple script designed to automate data retrieval, programmed to launch with only a few motions. Halisdol swipes it in and before he can say "analysis of covariance" to himself, NO SIGNIFICANT RESULTS presents itself across his screen. Halisdol predicts another sleepless night, ordering Korean fried chicken delivery to the lab at twilight. He takes a slow nasal inhale—simming whether or not Popeye's may taste better this time—when the light flickers back off. The mark of a truly awful job: when a lab tech may not even commiserate with himself.

He opens his desk and removes a dropper of saline solution and lubricates his Lazy Eyes. Although the room is dark, the glow of the computer casts enough light for him to do so. With one hand he peels back his eyelids and inserts the contact over his iris. He repeats with the other eye.

Perhaps the only perk to this otherwise crap job he has at Melodica is the top of the line smart lenses. Halisdol is not necessarily a fan of them himself, but once he was assigned them he became enamored by their convenience; their simplicity. He only has to look back and forth and wink a few times and a projection of an email from Mercado appears before him.

Evander,
I request your company in my office at my earliest convenience.
Thank you kindly,
Maximillian

What a tickle in the sphincter Maximilian Mauritius Mercado is. And what an unhappy joy it is when the will to procrastinate is achieved through a trip to one's supervisor.

The eggshell walls and dowdy navy carpets of Halisdol's laboratory seem like a design anomaly compared to the rest of Melodica's Manhattan complex. The skyscraper houses one hundred and twenty one stories of lush green living walls and ceilings. The bamboo floor has a comforting give to it when Halisdol treads upon it, cool and not too slick. Although the floors require a constant low-grade irrigation system to stay healthy, they never feel moist. It seems all the flooring save the basement and the technicians' offices have the veneer of freshly mopped and buffed hardwood. Stalks and leaves and flowering buds thatched together in snowflaking arrays make up the walls and ceilings of most rooms; they were engineered to grow around a hyper-compressed carbonite frame.

Before the buyout by Palantir, the Melodica tower housed a design akin to Halisdol's office. The whole building was drab and painfully white-collar. So it goes, Palantir had some marketing trouble in the early thirties. Advised by several of the city's top consulting firms, all the corporation's buildings were made green. It was purportedly a big initial hit, in Melodica's Bridgeport, CT HQ. And so one morning 18 months prior, Halisdol came to work to find construction workers bent over the walls with watering cans, while others installed giant reverse-tinted windows that gave the city the appearance of being cleaner and less polluted than it actually was.

Though renovations began a year and a half ago, R&D was behind to behold such architectural changes. Mercado is a shrewd businessman and a seasoned financier, though he never had much interest in research and development. And yet he is the regional Head of Product for a cornerstone of the modern technosphere. It had to be out of ignorance, Halisdol sims, that Mercado left the technicians literally in the dark. The man came to Melodica, New York after a long stint as a financier at Amazon. Halisdol had been here for three years without promotion. And yet Mercado gets to enjoy the view from his 30th story office while Halisdol waddles around the base of this unending corporate ziggurat.

Something about the clean fresh indoor air gives Halisdol the feeling that he needed to wash his face. That and Halisdol realizes the 32 ounces of instant coffee he drank two hours prior needs excreting. He pivots to the right and enters one of the many restrooms along the main corridor.

The men's room sells pleasingly sulfurous. It too had yet to be remodeled. In the mirror he gives himself a once-over. His jaw looks stubbly, eyes racoonish. To cover greasy unwashed hair he wore his lucky straw Panama hat, despite working indoors. The ceiling and floor resound with the soft tinny babbles of urine hitting linoleum and water. Halisdol takes a stand at a urinal; giving at least one empty urinal breadth on each side to prevent any possible infringement of the tacit mensroom code, and waits for a stream. Nothing. He closes his eyes. Still, nothing. The acrid stink of unflushed urine works its way up his nostrils.

When micturational difficulties arise, Halisdol likes to double numbers. 2^1 through 2^{10} are easy as breathing, memorized after years of urinary anxiety. Once past 2048 though, computation becomes problematic and Halisdol has to start some serious crunching, usually diverting his focus from matters below the belt and freeing up a nice stream. This particular time it takes him until 2^{15} to free up. He stops doubling numbers when he can hear the sound of his trickle harmonizing with the soft whir of the fluorescent lights. Thirty seconds pass. He zips himself up, washes his hands again, gives a polite nod to a man who is inspecting his hairline in the mirror and exits the men's room.

Mercado's office takes up the whole 30th floor. It contains dozens of empty workstations. At one point they were populated by staff engineers, though their work had become largely automatable fifteen years prior. Now, Mercado gets to either enjoy a sense of privacy, or mourn the loss of his ability to deprive his underlings of that same feeling. The elevator doors open and Halisdol faces the bamboo door to his supervisor's office. MMM is etched in at about eye level. The bamboo slides open before Halisdol can even knock.

Maximilian Mauritius Mercado sits with his feet up on his desk. He gnaws at the orange tip of a carrot. From his Eyes he projects a GIF of a gaggle of Brazilian women in full Carnivale lack of attire. They undulate midair in a never-ending loop.

"Have a seat," says Mercado. He gestures toward the space in front of his desk. There is no surface to sit on, so far as Halisdol can see.

A beat. And another. Mercado's hand was still outstretched. Halisdol planted himself on the floor in front of him, his legs crossed. The dancers still swung their hips, nipple tassels swinging annularly. Mercado does not turn off the projection or even privatize it upon Halisdol's entrance.

"And take off your shoes," says Mercado. He is obliged, and yet the silence continues until Halisdol clears his throat and removes his Panama hat. He sits it next to him on the ground.

Mercado blinks off the GIF. His office smells of tobacco, though smoking was banned in all Melodica's green buildings. The ceiling is not high, though the enormous tinted windows give the office the illusion of opulence.

"You are aware there is a seat over there," he says.

Halisdol cranes his neck around. A phalanx of fashionable bamboo chairs sit against the back corner of the room. Halisdol stands up, wheels one over in front of the desk, and takes a seat.

"Mistakes are in the making with regards to the toddler studies." Mercado holds the carrot like a cigar between his index and middle fingers.

Halisdol swallows. He hopes it isn't audible. "The results leave something to be desired, I suppose."

"No supposition is required." Mercado's business shirt waxes full with an inhale. "The whole thing is, if I may be so vulgar, fucked. If it was up to me I would have the whole project scrapped, shredded and rolled in a leaf of tobacco from whence it may be smoked."

Boats sail by on the over-dyed Hudson outside. Their sails little pinprick polygons from Halisdol's POV.

"Just on an ideological level. I'm not a mathematician, though I fail to see why management is so invested in your, what is it, measuring how fast these babies crawl."

Mercado does not break eye contact with Halisdol. He has the penchant for real intimidating F2Fs. He chomps on the carrot, masticates, and swallows.

"You use such obtuse jargon. Phase states. Attractor basins. Markov equilib-riums. I read these memos from your lab and I feel as if you are trying to insult me, beguile me. I hope this is not the truth Evander."

"No sir," Halisdol replies, fighting the urge to rock back and forth autistical-ly.

"Alas Evander, I am merely a rook here at Melodica, forever below the King and Queen. And you, Evander. You are a pawn. Or maybe a knight, though in the middle of the game when it is not worth so much." Another bite of the carrot.

"It's just Evan."

"_"

"Not Evander."

"_"

"_"

"You understand what I say?" says Mercado. "I make choices here. I have moving power, material presence. I have made several keen decisions that have advanced this conglomerate immensely. Yet the burdens of our continuing business efforts do not rest solely upon my back."

"Like your canned noodles?" Halisdol, unable to contain himself.

Mercado flares his nostrils.

"That was over fifteen years ago," the Argentinian says. "And we had never intended to sell them in cans."

"Was it your idea to make the bots edible?"

"We had to find a way subjects could become easily inoculated, yes. Though I of course did not design the robots myself. That was a team of organic engineers. We were the first to create automatons that could enter the bloodstream through intestinal pilli."

Halisdol can sim pushing Mercado further. All he has to do is keep mention-ing his boss's failures with the last incarnation of his microbots. By the time Mercado had inherited the project, prototypes of the bots already existed: carbon microbots designed to monitor the cardiovascular stats, blood-hormone levels and even neural activity of their subjects. Mercado's brilliant plan in the late twenties was to market them in an edible form. He had them sprinkled over a can of high-glucose wheat noodles shaped like dinosaurs with a low-casein Alfredo sauce. Each serving contained about 8.5 x 10^{12} microbots which, after entering the bloodstream, monitored the multiplicity of bodily functions in the prepubescent ingestor.

Mercado had imagined that after sending a text message of the coupon code —retrievable on the inner lining of the pastabots' tin—to an API endpoint, customers could have downloaded an applet to their tablet or smart glasses. The applet, in bright pastel colors, would have presented the wakefulness, activity, latitude, longitude, and bodily functions of the ingestor. The target demographic of such a product chiefly being parents of young children who wish to track the bodily states of their offspring whilst geographically separate. The dish was to be marketed as an edible babysitter of sorts.

"Don't get me wrong," Halisdol says, "It was a solid concept."

This much is true. The product could have made a killing. Though the younger Maximilian Mauritius Mercado did not possess a strong degree of lexical facility in English. The product's failure laid in the terrible name he coined for it: *Chaperoni and Cheese.* Of course Palantir dropped the whole venture.

Strong and aggressive F2Fing is rare these days, Halisdol supposes. Rare enough that what should have been a failure resulting in complete corporate exile instead turns to a promotion at a totally different company. This, Halisdol often sims, is why Mercado got a sub-penthouse office made of bamboo while Halisdol himself has asbestos insulation and malfunctioning incandescent lights. Strong computational ability was a default among developers. Interpersonal ability less so.

"I do hope you are serious," Mercado says. "It would not be wise to speak with sarcasm to your superior."

"No sarcasm at all," says Halisdol.

"I have heard it said that sarcasm is the lowest pedigree of humor," says Mer-cado. He sets his carrot on his desk. "Verily I did not summon you here for comedic relief. Had I wanted humor I assure you, Evander, you would be among my last options." Mercado chortles a good three or five seconds after his own wisecrack.

Maintaining eye contact is sometimes difficult for Halisdol. He finds it easier to just stare at the portion of the bridge of the nose between the eyes of his inter-locutor. Others, he sims, often can't tell the difference. Mercado and Halisdol smile together, though likely from different emotional vectors.

Looking up at the Head of Product from the floor, Halisdol cannot help but feel that his outstretched neck is naked, his Adam's apple in full view, and that his jugular feels a bit overexposed. He shifts his weight from one ass cheek to the other, then back again, his palms pressing into the arms of his chair. The bamboo cools away any accumulating perspiration.

"Tell me sir, why am I here?"

The Argentinean purses his lips together almost flirtatiously before speaking. "Evander, you know I have very little respect for your work."

"I've picked up on that, sir." Halisdol replies, scratching at his neck.

"Although this lack of affection is not entirely your fault. As stated, I have little tolerance for your discipline."

Mercado opens a desk drawer and removes a cardboard box of designer cigaril-los and a zippo lighter. Without offering one to Halisdol, he plucks one out, lights it, and takes a drag.

"I consider myself a learned man, Evander. One cannot successfully navigate the turbulent rivers of the marketplace without knowledge of economics, psychology, philosophy, sociology, and mathematics. And as a revolutionary figure in the nascency of microtechnology, I have had to teach myself chemistries of both organic and inorganic varieties, particle physics, human physiology, robotics, and information science, not to mention the intricacies of the human palette."

Twin tendrils of Arabic script pour from each of Mercado's nostrils. He glances outside his oversized windows; Halisdol falls into synchrony. New York City has begun to grow dusky. None of the city's metropolitan din can be heard inside the office, only the whispered silky hum of the building's nanotubules filtering away outside pollutants and poofing in cool, scented air. Mercado nods his head then shakes it, brightening the room's fluorescents.

"I am a man of the academy, I am fluent in seven languages. I am an intellectual. And I do not say this as hubristic exaggeration; I say this with a level of objective access to truth that comes with being a polymath. But yet, I do not understand what it is you complexity technicians do, Evander. The math that is not math. Your tangle of strange attractors and phase spaces. It is meant to make the learned feel bewildered and the bewildered feel learned."

Halisdol finds himself with better posture than normal, as if Mercado's disdain for him has calcified his bones and energized his musculature.

"Alas, I have superiors who, although less learned than I, are more powerful. And they, they, see use for you." Mercado removes his feet from his desk and straightens his spine. "It is my displeasure to offer you a promotion, Evander Halisdol. The director of Research & Development at our Meadowlands complex has fallen ill. The higher ups, for reasons unbeknownst to me, have asked me to offer you his position."

A sick sweetness percolates in Halisdol's gut. His heart rate gleefully trounces toward tachycardia. A strange non-sexual tingling sparkles in his gonads.

"How are your management skills, Evander? Hiring? Firing? Team building?"

"I've never had to hire or fire anyone," says Halisdol, unsure of why only now he stops referring to Mercado as "sir".

"As expected. I took the liberty to hire your lab manager. A recent graduate from Zappos, an exceptional talent by all measures."

Mercado winks and an animation shows itself in front of them. Her name appears in bright bold letters. "I suggest you turn on your Eyes," he says.

Halisdol blinks twice instinctively before thumbing the pockets of his jacket. Dammit, he'd left the contacts in the lab.

"Are you without them?"

Mercado ashes the cigarillo and smoothes over his moustache with index and middle fingers.

"I sing praises to the Gods that your lack of responsibility will soon no longer burden me," he says as he retrieves a spare pair from his disk and slides the two wet disks toward Halisdol.

Halisdol arises from the chair, his legs prickly and head heavy with vassal vaso-vagal syncope, tilts his head back, and places each of the Lazies on his eyeballs. There is a stinging moment while his corneas remoisturize, followed by Mercado giving him one of those flippant "sit down" waves of his hand.

The projection comes alive once Halisdol and Mercado are synched in the same visual channel. "Julia Sets" floats in midair between them. Halisdol shakes his head back and forth a bit. The image shifts with his POV. Shit, enactive interfaces were the stuff of tech expos, something Halisdol read about on the commute to work but had until now never experienced firsthand.

"Julia," says Halisdol. "That's her name?"

"Why don't you try zooming in," Mercado replies.

"Okay." And Halisdol squints, commanding his Eyes to telescope in on the projection. This gave the name the illusion of accelerating toward him. Just as Halisdol feels as if "Sets" is about to smash into the tip of his nose, the name—like a spider egg sac pulsing with jittery young— explodes, leaving smaller lexical fragments hanging in the midair. He pinches a cursive "Curriculum Vitae" to his upper right and expands it. Its letters disassemble and reorder themselves spelling out:

University of Zappos: Class of 2041
BS — Enactive Interfaces, Applied Bayesian Systems,
Evolutionary Robotics
Summa cum Laude

"Triple major," says Halisdol. "Impressive."

"She architected and implemented the resume herself," replies Mercado. "Verily, she should have your job."

Experience, Skills and Recent Publications bob around Mercado's head. Without bothering to read further, Halisdol stands, retrieves his Panama hat from the ground and replaces it on his head. He dusts his slacks off as he steps into his shoes.

"Is the offer to your pleasure?" says Mercado.

"Absolutely," says Halisdol, a bit lightheaded.

"You will begin Monday," says Mercado. He outstretches his hand for a shake. Halisdol takes it. "Melodica will provide transportation."

"Transportation?" Mercado's palm feels paradoxically both leathery and greasy.

"You will be stationed at our Meadowlands center in Moonachie, New Jersey. Your office view of the mighty Hudson River shall be supplanted with one of the humble Hackensack. We have kindly provided security for your crossing of the state border."

As Mercado removes his hand Sets' resume evaporates. It is replaced with a feed of what Halisdol recognizes as the curb outside his apartment. There is parked a large tan van. A manual, not a Waymo. Leaning against it are what look like five half-nude twenty-somethings. Their faces are slathered with tribal paint. They do not seem to be speaking. Submachine guns are slung across each of their breasts.

1.6.0
shebody

Not much noise came from Isa. That much hadn't changed over the past years. The shebody's legs felt so thin, **Futurabold** could sim snapping them in half by accident. She planted a few light kisses along Isa's taught hamstrings before lifting her head up to see Spines' face.

"Courtney Christ, will you take them out?"

"They aren't on," Isa replied.

"I don't care. I can still see you're wearing them."

"--"

"It's rude you know, like keeping your socks on. Maybe worse."

"I never sensed this was a problem in the past."

Futurabold sat up and folded her arms. "You should try to have an analog fuck. Just once."

Isa rolled over and brought a pair of fingers to her eyeballs. She tilted her head forward, removed her Lazy Eyes and placed them on the nightstand next to **Futurabold**'s cot before laying down again.

Isa's breath rate remained constant as **Futurabold** worked her over. Even after several minutes of cunnilingus, when the shebody should have been in the throes of vertebrae-liquefying pleasure, Isa's small, high breasts continued to rise and fall in a measured placidity.

Only Isa's steely silences, her constant inward turn could make **Futurabold** McRogers doubt her fucksmanship. **Futurabold**'s aptitude for romance—to use an antiquated term—usually drew tremendous accolades from those shebodies graced enough to enter her naked confidence. One on-again-off-again Neo-!Kung fling told **Futurabold** she "knew her way around a clit like most men here know a Beretta" on an on-again week. Shakespeare that shebody was not. But perhaps Isa's unyielding solipsism across all vectors, sexual or otherwise, was what so attracted **Futurabold** to her.

Futurabold grabbed Isa by her bony hips and pulled herself away from her. Isa's tattoo writhed in post-coital excitement: whirling around her arms, slithering from her ribs to her pelvis and edging up against her pert breasts and stomach. It was the only sign that Isa was experiencing any pleasure at all. **Futurabold**'s own stick-and-poke on her deltoid seemed primitive compared to Isa's dynamic visitat full sleeves. They sometimes showed themselves as marine creatures, other times naked autumnal trees. Now they were neon fireworks, high-chroma and stimulating.

Isa sat up. "I think I should take a shower," she said.

"Okay. I wasn't expecting a snuggle anyway."

Isa did not look back as she walked naked to the bathroom, the dimple on her lower back winking at **Futurabold** as she left.

An aged ceiling fan spun overhead. The slow currents it generated cooled the sweat off of **Futurabold**. Her room, she realized, smelled peaty and warm, the aroma lit up her hippocampus with memories of her Neo-!Kung yurt up in Rockland county. The smoky discharge of rapidly-firing machinegun paradiddles were noticeably absent from Rule 30 though. The bed springs, old and worn, groaned as **Futurabold** laid back and the mattress curved parabolically under her.

The amniotic whoosh of the shower is followed by the sound of Isa softly stepping inside the tub. The babble of conversation from the outside room is muted by the concrete walls. It was likely roadies for the evening's show, kvetching while hauling equipment as roadies often do. Didn't they get the memo that they could use the venue's gear? **Futurabold** took her tablet from her nightstand, scaled it down to three-quarters size and swiped her index finger across the screen three times. Her door lets out an audible snap as it locks itself. The murmuring outside grew louder and more aggressive. Someone probably forgot to pack a cable or a stompbox **Fu-**

turabold simmed. That would have to be dealt with later.

A cryptic Phrygian melody snaked its way in from the bathroom. **Futurabold** felt a palpitation in her chest. Isa Spines was singing. It was a totally novel sound, even to McRogers. Isa would barely speak when spoken to, usually. The noise of the shower obscured whatever lyrics Isa vocalized, but her melody came through clearly, the shower curtains and bathroom door serving as a makeshift high-pass filter. It was the most beautiful species of singing in **Futurabold**'s opinion: the kind produced by a trained musician but an untrained singer. The vocals were not too pitchy and were still sung with a sense of musicality, but without the polish that comes with years of instruction. It was artistic yet earnest. Aesthetic yet unaffected.

Isa's company—if it could even be called that— was perhaps the only perk that came with New Ape Idea staying at Rule 30. **Futurabold** never had too much of a problem getting laid, though with Isa the lack of intimacy felt intimate in its own way. Some shebodies are just in it for the chase. That, and the new PC. Miyagi-Edelstein was right, her old setup was a piece of shit, especially compared to what he built for her. A string of paranoia around Tak's burglary of Musician's Warehouse still sometimes vibrated in her chest. Tak had engineered a police scanner on her desktop. She scanned the feed multiple times a day, and yet nothing regarding the theft had come up. She'd checked all the equipment for RIFD chips, and Tak had disassembled most of the stompboxes to the point where he insisted they couldn't be tracked. Still, the sense of impending doom was not want to leave her.

The singing decrescendoed into silence. The shebody must have simmed that **Futurabold** could hear her. Now there was only the sound of water. **Futurabold** exited the bed and opened the bathroom door. Though the mirror was fogged, she could still see her mohawk was matted down to one side. She closed the door behind her, pulled back the shower curtains and stepped inside with Isa.

"You've got quite a set of pipes I," said **Futurabold**.

"I hate singing."

"Only when you know others are listening."

A full head shorter than her, Isa reminded **Futurabold** of a sparrow. Her chestnut hair, clipped short, looked somehow darker when wet. The shebody stood with her back to **Futurabold**, making no sound or gesture when she entered the shower. She continued lathering a yellow bar of soap between her palms wordlessly.

"I'll never take a hot shower for granted anymore," said **Futurabold**. "Not after leaving the Neo-!Kung."

"--"

"Or soap for that matter. Amazing though. After six months of not washing my hands, all my allergies disappeared completely. My immune system to date is much more potent."

Isa scrubbed under each of her armpits. A purple wave, likely a facsimile of a Hokusai print, formed along Isa's shoulders and triceps. It grew then collapsed into itself, leaving Isa's skin a bit more jaundiced than its natural tone.

"Really no modern conveniences whatsoever. Except armaments. I don't think we'd be able to eat without them."

"I sim you did not enjoy this lifestyle," said Isa. "That's why you left."

Futurabold placed her hands on Isa's shoulders and kneaded, the knots in her muscles crackling under her fingers. Isa did not move much, she seemed neither to accept nor rebuke the massage.

"I enjoyed it quite a lot for a while. Maybe too much. The naked F2F, with no digital filters or distractions is powerfully sobering. The human face alone is an incredibly high-bandwidth information channel. Not to mention your tone of voice, language, body gestures. It's a lot to process. It can be stimulating to the point of pro-voking anxiety yet numbingly simple, F2Fing."

Despite being in the shower, **Futurabold** felt dry and thirsty. She could taste swampiness on her own breath.

"The modern world is a drug we're addicted to by pubescence. With the Neo-!Kung you can feel the withdrawal effects. Phantom vibrations of tablet messages never sent. Your eyeballs begin to hurt from the lack of backlighting. It's nauseating. I think in the end I didn't have the nervous system to handle it all."

"It's a fallacy," said Isa. Her back was still to **Futurabold**.

"What is?"

"That you're interacting with anyone but yourself. Whatever sobering agents you talk about were placebos."

Isa had turned up the water temperature. **Futurabold** could barely see anything in front of her through the thick steam.

Futurabold ran a finger along the ridge of Isa's ear.

"Suppose I attempt to enter your mind," began Isa. "I do not have access to your thoughts, your emotions. I run a simulation. I put myself in your shoes as the idiom goes. I create an assemblage of impressions, deductions, and inferences about your mental state."

Futurabold picked the soap bar from Isa's hands and began to message suds out of it. She washed her face and neck while listening wordlessly.

"You are a virtual machine I run on my own hardware. Not a separate com-puter."

"So there is nothing to me independent of you? I'm just a piece of your own little world."

"It's not little, my world."

Futurabold replaced the soap on its shelf and reached over Isa, lowering the water temperature. "I take that back. It's not little, it's huge. Vast. Consuming." A note of energy worked its way into her voice. "Why else would you choose to be stuck there?"

"I don't choose anything. Everything I see, feel, smell, it's all tainted by me. I can't know anything without putting my I in it." Isa swallowed. "Accept that and the whole universe falls into place. It becomes understandable, or rather you understand how little is understandable. How attempting to even speak creates meaninglessness. I sim you may call it sad or lonely, but it's not. It's honesty."

A shiver began to germinate within **Futurabold**'s vertebrae. It was as if her veins began pumping antifreeze instead of plasma and hemoglobin. "Can you turn up the water temperature?"

"Are you familiar with the Jewish parable of the four sons?"

"Isa, I'm cold."

Isa turned the knob to the right. "It regards the ethics of teaching children about the holiday of Passover. There are four archetypical sons. The first is a genius. He is inquisitive and eager to acquire knowledge. The parent should engage the child's intellect and help him learn. The second is bitter and ironic. One must be stern and reprimanding with him. The third is the simple son who requires patience from the parent. The last is the dumb child, unable to speak or ask questions."

"_-"

"I sim most of my parents pinned me for this child, suffering from some disability or retardation. The parent is instructed to teach the child without receiving any feedback from it."

Futurabold leaned forward and let some of the hot water run over the back of her neck.

"What I do not understand is why silence is equivalent to a lack of intelligence. Why is he labeled disabled and not lauded as brilliant? He is the only one who understands the uselessness of trying to articulate questions."

"I have to say Isa," said **Futurabold**. "For someone so philosophically opposed to speaking, I don't think I've ever heard you talk so much."

Isa turned and faced **Futurabold**, who offered her a flirtatious smile. Isa's stomach looked nearly concave, and she slumped slightly when standing, emphasizing her hip slenderness. **Futurabold** once found her almost waifish ectomorphism attractive. Now though, she seemed more hollow than full.

"You underestimate yourself I," said **Futurabold**. "You think that you're an island. That you can't know others. It's wrong."

"And how are you so certain?"

"Because you're a fucking human being," said **Futurabold**.

Isa blinked twice. **Futurabold** recognized it instantly. It was a defense mechanism of sorts. As if, by closing one's eyelids and reopening them she could push a refresh button on the world.

"Move," Isa said and hurried out the shower.

Futurabold turned off the water and stepped onto the bathroom floor. Isa had left behind wet footprints along the linoleum. She didn't towel off before entering the bedroom. **Futurabold** dried herself quickly but deliberately before following after her.

Isa left small elliptical indents in the carpeting as she moved about, picking up stray socks and shoes strewn across the floor. Her arms and back were the color of autumnal leaves. Ferocious, jagged patterns spun across her limbs.

"What the fuck Isa?" said **Futurabold**. She stepped into a pair of pants, pulled them up and set them to black denim. Braless, she slipped on a white analog cotton tank overhead. It clung to her half-dried body.

"I don't know where they are!" said Isa, scanning the floor. "I don't know where they are!"

"What?" said **Futurabold**. She removed a wet curl of hair from her face.

Isa's vertebrae enunciated themselves under her bare skin as she kneeled down, looking under the bed. "My Eyes. I can't find my Eyes."

Futurabold sat down on the mattress. "You put them on the nightstand."

Isa sat back, her buttocks to her heels then stood. Though she had just bathed, **Futurabold** could see that the shebody was perspiring. In strides that seemed impossibly long for her stature Isa bolted toward the nightstand. She tossed **Futurabold**'s tablet to the mattress and ran her fingertips all along the wooden face.

"They're not here," she said before checking the drawers. "I don't see them."

"I'm sure they'll turn up I," **Futurabold** replied.

"Get up," said Isa.

"What?"

"Get up," she said again, this time more deliberately.

Futurabold stood up, after which Isa grabbed the bed sheets and gave them three strong shakes, the sheets ballooning up with each one. She bunched the mattress and tossed it to the floor before crawling on to the bed. On all fours, she groped the surface of the naked mattress.

From outside **Futurabold** could hear the roadies, still arguing. Fights at Rule 30 tended not to stay verbal for very long; how long until the two or three hebodies outside escalated into violence?

"They're in here somewhere," said **Futurabold**. "Just relax. And put some clothes on. I need to step out."

"Don't leave me," said Isa. Drops of water pooled and dripped off her body.

"And now she wants company," said **Futurabold**. She crossed the room and slid her feet into a pair of shoes.

"Help me look for them. Please?"

"Put some clothes on," said **Futurabold**. She heard two shouts and a thud from outside. "I'll be right back."

Two shirtless and bearded hebodies wrestled on the floor of Rule 30's atrium. Both were bald and had hip stick-and-pokes of old band insignias on their neck and forearms. Their hairy ass cracks peeked out above their over-tight jeans.

"What band are you with?" **Futurabold** folded her hands across her chest.

And like two children hearing the consternated voice of their mother, the two hebodies stopped what they were doing, their hands receded from each others' throats.

"Cunt$," said the bigger one, still pinned to the ground by his partner. "With a dollar sign."

"Thanks for clarifying," said **Futurabold**. "We're scheduled to have Cuntzz with two Z's in next week."

"Halitosis forgot the cymbal stands," said the hebody on top. "We don't have the gas money to get back to Little Egg to pick it up."

"No problem, you can use our equipment."

"I told you it was no problem," said the bottom hebody.

From **Futurabold**'s bedroom Isa let out a piercing simian howl.

"Shit on a cracker," said **Futurabold**. "You two don't happen to have any smart lenses to spare right? Preferably Lazy Eyes?"

"Halitosis wears smart lenses," said one of the roadies. "But they're off brand."

"Of course they are," said **Futurabold**, shaking her head.

"And not for fucking sale," said Halitosis.

"What kind of self-respecting punk even wears Lazy Eyes?" said the roadie, standing to his feet.

"Apparently the kind that respect the Self a little too much," replied **Futurabold**, heading back toward her bedroom. "I'll be back in fifteen. There's a pizza place across the street, but you'll have to put on your shirts."

Futurabold reentered her bedroom to find Isa absent. The bathroom door was locked, the shower running. She knocked on the door.

"Did you find them?"

"_-"

Futurabold laid her head against the door and exhaled. "You have 10 minutes Isa. Then I'm turning off the hot water."

"_-"

It was another thirty before Isa emerged, passing over the room in silence.

1.7.0 PUS

As advanced as most medical technologies had grown in the past two centuries, those the dermatologist employs seem to have remained unchanged since the Civil War. The paper gown Lamarck-Ganoush wears does not drape far below his pubescent paunch. His genitals lay exposed on the doctor's vinyl chair, shrunken against his body for warmth. He had removed his glasses at the dermatologist's request, who placed them on the metal trundle with the rest of his skincare tools.

Since turning seventeen, Doug Lamarck-Ganoush had previously gone to see Dr. Baek six times. A colleague of a colleague of his mother, Dr. Baek gave the boy treatment at a heavily reduced price. He probably forwent the insurance paperwork with each visit. Skincare was his passion, he would say to Doug and his mother. And that there was no reason the kid should have to live with severe cystic acne in this modern day and age. Not with such advanced treatment options available.

Such advanced treatment options seemed to largely include various metal lances, which Dr. Baek would use to puncture and drain the pustules dotting Doug's forehead and chest.

Like a figure in an impressionist painting viewed too closely, the dermatologist stands a blurry mass above Doug, who lays supine on a chair. A shifting flesh and eggshell blob cracking lame puns and jokes as he snaps latex gloves around his hands.

"Your mother says the isotrennin I prescribed has been affecting your mood."

"--"

"I could give you steroid injections, though that may cause some weight gain. But, hey, maybe that'll work for you. You play football?"

"--"

"Well Douglas, I think I'll take you off the isotrennin. I'll give you some topical agents instead. I will say, though, your skin is starting to clear up."

"Is it?"

"Such optimism. And who says you're depressed?"

Doug can hear the quick clip of a nurse walking down the hall, followed by the creak and click of the dermatologist closing the door to the office.

"Do you like Quentin Tarantino movies Douglas?" The blur sat adjacent to his patient.

"Who?"

"Eh," the blur responds, "Before your time I guess."

With gloved fingers, the dermatologist squeezes a few nodules on Doug's chest.

"You've been popping," he said. "I told you not too."

"Isn't that what you're going to do?"

Dr. Baek laughed a bit too vigorously to sound genuine. "I went to eight years of medical school to learn how to pop zits. You just don't have the same qualifications."

The dermatologist removes a thin lance from his tray. Somehow, the needle-sharp tip is acutely visible to Doug. Dr. Baek pokes at a cyst on Doug's chest, squeezes out the blood and pus, then wipes at it with a square of gauze. He repeats the procedure twenty times: Doug counts them all despite his trying not to. The pain of the drainage procedure is manageable for zits along Doug's chest and forehead: he can bear them with a grimace. The lancing of one large pustule on his neck evokes a whimper from him though. The squeezing and draining that follows is more painful than the lancing.

"Trust me, that hurt me a lot more than it hurt you," Dr. Baek says with a chuckle.

Doug reaches over to the tray and puts on his glasses. He cannot simulate whether the ordeal would have been easier if he was able to F2F with the dermatologist throughout. He sees the doctor leave two small tubes by the sink in his office.

"Wash up, disinfect, and moisturize," he says. "When you're done changing, you can pick up the script from the receptionist."

Barbara, his mother, had been thumbing through a dated housekeeping magazine on one of the waiting room's tablets. Dr. Baek chats at his receptionist, a zaftig silver-haired shebody who either scans insurance docs or surfs the web on her smart lenses; it's impossible to tell. When Doug approaches the desk, the dermatologist produces a white tube of prescription ointment and holds it out to his side.

"Twice a day after washing," says Dr. Baek. "Your skin may become slightly inflamed the first week. Don't worry, it will look worse before it starts to look better."

Doug takes the cream and pockets it in his thrift-shop cargo shorts.

"Oh honey," Barbara says, sliding the tablet off and lifting herself up from her seat. Doug should have known better than to wear a white shirt to a dermatology appointment. His cotton tee is dotted with pinkish blooms of greasy blood. She approaches the desk and squeezes her son's shoulders.

"And after Labor Day too," says Dr. Baek, elbows on the receptionist's desk, twirling an expensive-looking gold stylus in his fingers.

"Have a seat," Barbara says to Doug.

Doug plops his adolescent mass down by the tablet rack. Each one contains a series of brochure applets for patients to peruse while awaiting treatment. Doug's thumbed through them a half-dozen times before. *Eczema and You* proved to hold more rereading value than *Living with Psoriasis* or *Melanoma Do's & Don'ts*. Thumbtacked to an otherwise empty bulletin board above the rack was a lone paper flyer, the only print media in Dr. Baek's clinic.

Learn Theremin: North Jersey Only

Doug cannot remember the last time he saw a real paper advertisement. Thirty years ago they must have been everywhere. Whoever put this up, Doug sims, must be desperate for customers. Or else the hebody has a strange attraction to the old times, a sort of retro faddism Doug Lamarck-Ganoush holds as well. Few whom Doug has met seem to find endearing beauty in the innocent blockiness of a non-smart cell phone, or the refreshing awkwardness of an unadulterated F2F.

A series of rippable phone numbers make up the ventral side of the flyer. None had been taken. Doug rips and pockets two, then untacks the flyer. He folds it in half crisply and slides it into his pocket. He pretends to be skimming over *Surprise! You Have Cystic Acne* when his mom returns. As if anyone is obtuse to the fact they have horrid, uncomfortable cystic nodules all over their body before seeing the dermatologist.

"I could be a bad skin model," he says to her, zooming in on a picture of an anonymous acne patient.

"Come on," she replies. "Want some Dairy Queen?"

"What am I, five?"

"Milk products won't help anything," Dr. Baek calls out behind them.

That evening, his lips glazed with hot dog grease, Doug learns he is lactose intolerant. Ice cream had never been problematic for him in the past, though perhaps puberty had brought with it the digestive changes.

It is the true sign that one is no longer a baby, Doug thinks, hunched on the toilet, when one's body won't accept milk anymore. His stool is loose, foamy and comes out painfully and sporadically.

From the kitchen he can hear Barbara washing dishes. While working around the house, she often would sing. Usually vestiges of lullabies she sang to Doug while he was an infant. Now though, she is silent, as if attuned to the gurgling, frothing discomfort in her son's abdomen. It's a mother's sixth sense, thinks Doug, the unceasing visceral awareness of any illness her offspring faces. A vestige from when their two selves weren't so anatomically separate.

Between painful squirts Doug tries to meditate. Or at least find something non-corporeal to himself that isn't shackled completely to his malfunctioning body. It had become ritual by now, the meditating. A familiar practice reserved for when his mood became big-D Depressing, which was often. Overweight with astigmatisms in both eyes, his skin cystic, spine lordotic and now bowels distressed, Doug's greatest asset is his mind. The early acceptance to University of Zappos pinned to the fridge with a magnet is just one piece of evidence. Without a high degree of sapience, the homo knows the invisible hand of selection would snatch him up before senescence. That was the case with his father: the Lamarck half to his surname. He had lost his life a decade ago to prostate cancer. An early death was wrapped around Doug's histones, iterating throughout all the cells in his body.

Not that Lamarck-Ganoush doesn't try to take proactive measures. Yes, nearly all 16 year-olds masturbate; however Doug does so with scheduled conviction. He does it twice a day, upon waking up in the morning and while lying in bed at night. For his prostate health. For his own longevity.

His reproductive organs seem to be the only area of his anatomy that functions relatively well. Perhaps they too will atrophy. Doug thinks he may need to take a night off, as he reaches behind him for a baby wipe. He is dehydrated enough already.

"There are bananas on the bowl on the counter," Barbara Ganoush says to her son as the hebody exits the bathroom. "And I can boil up some white rice if you want."

"I'm okay, thanks," Doug replies, before doubling back into the bathroom, lighting a match and then re-entering the kitchen.

He picks up a few fruits until he finds a peel spotted to his liking. He removes the browning coat from the banana and takes a bite. The fructose covers up the faint acidic taste indigestion had left on his breath.

"So tell me," his mom says, elbowing off the water faucet, "What's a theremin?"

Doug chews and swallows. "Why?"

Barbara nods and the unfolded flyer flattened on the kitchen counter.

"It's an instrument, invented by a Russian physicist. You know *Good Vibrations*?"

He gets a side-eye from his mother. "Do you?"

"Sure. The Beach Boys. I found a few albums with Dad's stuff in the closet."

"--"

"You can hear on the titular track. It's the sorta retro science-fiction sound."

"That?"

"The instrument is essentially two heat-sensitive glass tubes. They sense the warmth of your hands. You can modulate pitch with one hand and volume with the other."

Doug's right cheek bulges with masticated banana as he speaks. The flaccid peel lies on the kitchen table.

"Are you that bored of drums?"

"No, of course not," says Doug. "You hear me every day in the garage." He swallows. "This is my chance to expand my musical expertise, train up the neural nets in my skull."

Barbara crosses from the sink and picks up the flyer.

"Where would you buy one?" she says.

"I wouldn't," says Doug. "I think I'd build one."

"--"

"Courtney Christ Mom, I'm going to be surrounded by techies and engineers next year. My tinkering muscles have totally atrophied. You want me to fail outta college?"

"There will be several Rutgers kids getting grandfathered into the new school. I doubt they are all engineers."

"Well that's only upperclassmen. My class will consist of all first-generation acceptees."

"Zappos wouldn't have accepted you, let alone give you a scholarship if they didn't think you were qualified."

Doug thumbs at one of his nostrils, dislodging a bit of crust left over by a rhinovirus he'd suffered through a few days ago.

"Why are you so against this? I can comp for the lessons myself. The guy couldn't even afford board space for any digital advertising so far as I could see. I doubt he'll charge much."

"--"

"And even if he does, I'll take a few lessons and teach myself from there."

Barbara smooths the theremin ad and replaces it in front of the hebody.

"Douglas, honestly, I don't think you need another reason to stay inside the house.

"_"

"Sure, I'm proud of how musically talented you are. You take after your father."

"And he would drum for hours every day. Use and disuse Mom."

"But I never see you outside. What will you do at university, stay inside your dorm room?"

"I'm honing my talents."

"Dr. Baek said you need to be getting vitamin D for your skin."

"I'll get a UV lamp."

Barbara picks up the peel from the table, pinching it between her thumb and index finger. With the balls of her feet, she pops the lid to the compost bin upon and tosses it in.

"I just want you to take care of yourself next year." She sits down across from Doug.

"You'd think the offspring of a healthcare professional would have a better sense of physical well being," says Doug.

Barbara pinches the bridge of her aquiline nose before resting her elbows on the table and cradling her chin in her hands.

"_"

"_"

"We do everything we can," she says.

Doug scratches at his chest, breaking open a thin whitehead. A small blood spot grows on his solar plexus.

"It's not an issue of blame," he says.

"You are not your body," she replies.

"I know that," says Doug snatching up the flyer. "So let me learn theremin."

Barbara straightens her spine and laces her hands flat on the table. "I suppose it's not my decision to make."

18.1 SHANNON

Isa sat in the bathroom during shows, away from the amps and the monitors, the shredding vocal chords and the moshers. She sat with the toilet lid down, chin cradled in her palms. Her elbows pressed a pink waning gibbous into the flesh of each thigh. If the band playing the main stage was especially loud, she inserted into each ear a wadded up sheet of the thin fibrous toilet paper **Futurabold** stocked Rule 30 with. The concrete walls and wooden door provided a pleasant muffle to the sounds careening in from the main room. Vocals became mashed together, lyrics incomprehensible. If the guitarists and drummer were especially sloppy—and they often were—the whole band would morph into a thick sonic mud pile.

The solitude that the average bathroom brought was an added bonus. Thank-fully the large majority of punk venues sported a single unisex inlet rather than a multi-stall Lysol and linoleum deal. Rule 30 was no exception. It was Isa's fortress of solitude. There was nothing to hear but amniotic whoosh occasionally broken by the thump of a pit-dweller getting thrown against the door.

Currently a six-piecer from Bayonne was at the mic. One drummer, four guitars and a saxophone. Isa couldn't recall the name but the billing read something like "No Wave Re-revival". She removed a bit of tissue to excavate a plug of wax. In the mirror above the sink, her reflection did the same behind the scrawls of sharpie and mascara writing.

Isa read and reread the graffiti messages coating the bathroom walls. Most were crude band names, catchy political adages or half-sober semi-Socratic musings amongst a forest of ejaculating penises. At least they distracted her from the chronic hum of anxiety she'd harbored since losing her Eyes. Verbal methadone to the heroin of hypertext.

The mirrors, too, provided a modicum of relief. Like many other solipsists, Isa could find herself easily taken up by her own reflection. If she squinted hard enough, her ears could be made to look like little babies curled up in the fetal position. Her irises had turned greenish without the back-glow of her Lazies.

The re-revivalists crescendoed outside the bathroom and grinded to a halt. They left only the trickling of their delay pedals rehashing those last few chords in their wake.

Isa caught a short bathroom syllogism penned to the side of her frowning face:

The surprising thing about music these days is it's never fucking surprising.

This rang true enough to her. Sound, by its nature, is always discrete, analyzable. Even the hairiest of sound waves can be broken down into simpler elements, thanks to Fourier. Though genres change and instruments evolve, one can never hear something novel. That which seems new and complex is borne out of a false multiplicity. Music is always familiar, always comfortably within the bounds of understanding. Even on first listen, good music always sounds recognizable. In that sense, No Wave needed neither reviving or re-reviving. The band had given themselves a meaningless billing.

Her frown vanished into a neutral expression. Paradoxes always did her well. She did not feel happy; she never did. At least she didn't quiver with nausea as simulations of life without her Lazy Eyes looped in her mind.

The wooden door thumped twice. Isa unplugged her ears, the tissues waxy and green. All seemed quiet in Rule 30, save the knocking.

"Isa? C'mon. People are leaving."

Another report on the wood.

"Open up. I want to show you something."

It was a recognizable nasally tenor.

"Seriously, I'm coming in. Are you shitting or something? If yr shitting you better speak now and save us an embarrassing situation. I'm turning the knob."

But the knob did not turn. Isa had locked the door nearly an hour before. The knocks increased in both frequency and force.

"Dammit, Isa."

Without lifting herself from the toilet Isa leaned over, unlocked the door and opened it. There stood Takashi, his face flushed, tight black shirt tighter and blacker with sweat.

And within milliseconds, seeing the face of another without layers of digital filtering triggered a wash of panic within Isa.

"You missed a rogue fuckin' set."

"Do you have Eyes?"

"What?"

"Lazy Eyes? Do you wear them?"

Tak blinked twice then forced out a chuckle. "Me? No way, smart lenses are way too corporate," he scoffed. "What kind of punk do you think I am?"

"I lost mine."

Takashi glanced over each shoulder before entering the bathroom. Behind him a tall mustached man, saxophone slung around his shoulder, smoked a cigarette as he wheeled his amp out. Tak spun around and gave him a chin-to-chest "nice set" head nod. It was reciprocated and Takashi closed the door.

"Sucks. Any family who could buy you a new pair?"

Isa slumped over, her forehead touched her knees.

"Sorry, insensitive advice," said Tak.

"Can you steal a pair?"

Takashi clicked his tongue. "I dunno Isa. Musician's Warehouse is one thing, but smart lens firmware comes with GPS tracking baked in. I couldn't disable that, not until at least a few hours after pinching em. They're just too expensive to leave vulnerable."

"_-"

"It doesn't really matter though," Tak added. "I've got an idea that'll start making us all some money. You'll be able to buy your own pair in no time."

"_-"

"Aren't you gonna ask what it is?"

Isa sat back up and took a moment to finger a lock of hair. "What is it?"

A smile broke across Tak's face. "I'm glad you asked." Takashi pressed his palms together and made a gun with his fingers, the barrel resting on the cleft of his chin. "I've made a bit of an executive decision with New Ape Idea."

"I don't know what you refer to."

"It's our new band name. My idea."

"_-"

"Anyway, I figured, we have a new name, new gear, new practice space. We basically hit the refresh button on the whole project. Right?"

"_-"

"So, I'm thinking, now that we're evolving past our old forms. Y'know, learning from our mistakes or whatever, maybe we should change our responsibilities within the band. Reconfigure the instrumentation a bit."

"I'm staying on guitar," said Isa.

"No-no-no. Not where I'm heading with this." Tak backed into the sink and hit the cold-water lever with his elbow. As he turned the water off, he gave himself a brief self-inspection in the mirror. Isa had not stopped staring at her reflection since the hebody had begun speaking.

"Although, I'm not too bad at guitar. Just saying."

"--"

And a strange form of eye contact emerged: each one looking into the irises of the other's reflection: the closest the two may have ever come to real-deal 100%-organic F2Fing.

"I want you on vocals."

Isa could see her reflection double. Her head felt swampy, her guts like they were tumbling in a gyroscope. A chorus of *shit, shit, shit* resounded in her ears. "I don't sing," she managed to muster.

"Good," Tak said as he spun around. A shit-eating grin was plastered on his face. "I don't want you to sing. Singing's old, tired, dead. You can scream or speak or whatever kinda shit feels best. I'm sure it'll work."

"I don't think you get it. I don't sing, meaning, I don't vocalize. Period." Isa's voice broke as she talked. "I don't go near microphones. I play guitar, mostly with my back to the audience, if I even have an audience, and I don't scream or shout or speak. I am silent."

"I can teach you to get over stage fright. There are tools for it, like anything else."

Isa gripped the rim of the toilet bowl beneath her. "It's not stage fright. I am not afraid of other people. I just will not sing. My voice will not be heard."

"Well, will you at least *think* about it?"

"I did."

"For a prolonged period of time."

"Why? I always simmed you liked fronting. Won't Doug have a problem with this?"

"DLG? Ha! He'd be glad to see me stop singing. Any way I can avoid interaction with the crowd is, like, majorly positive to him."

"--"

"And, to your first question, I have realized that even a man as viciously talented as I will not excel at everything. There are those of us programmed to solve nonlinear equations and play bass guitar, and others meant to shred their larynxes night after night after night. I am, lamentably, the former."

"_"

"Think it over will ya?"

Isa's grip on the toilet bowl relaxed. Her knuckles darkened back to their original pink.

"And feel free to opt out of the aforementioned larynx-shredding. It's been done before. Then overdone, forgotten about, revived, and overdone again. Do whatever feels best for your lyrics."

"My lyrics?"

"Yuh-huh. I'm not writing lyrics any more. Another of my lesser talents." Tak twirled a blonde spike between his index and ring fingers.

Even Isa could tell that such an omission of humility coming from Tak was rare. "They always seemed...felt...fine," the shebody said.

"Thank you, Isa. Really." Tak's voice turned soft and viscous. "I wish I felt that way."

A silence, but not on Isa's volition. For once, her mind flooded with say-able words, but Isa's mouth could not form them.

"But that's just not how I see it."

"_"

"Y'know? Take our song, *My Dad is Not a Riot Grrrl*"

"Which one is that?"

Takashi snapped his fingers and whistled a few tuneless bars. They sounded entirely unfamiliar to Isa.

"_"

"So, like, whenever I sing the chorus, y'know:

My Papa never seemed he knew it
When he voted for Pres. Pruitt
For terms one, two and three,
And I'm like, 'Fuck Authority'

"I feel like the crowd never gets it. That last line especially. Like, I'm being ironic but I'm also not. I mean, sure, I hated the man but that's popular sentiment. Plus he hasn't been relevant since, what, thirty years ago?

"I'm trying to mock the fact that I'm writing a punk tune about such a banal political statement, but still acknowledging the sentiment behind it. If only there was a way to vocalize the quotation marks around '*Fuck Authority*'."

"_"

"So I think we should scrap it. Scrap anything I wrote. Our music's good, we can keep the instrumentation, but you're responsible for the verbage."

"I'm not singing."

A knock followed by a muted voice, "Isa? When you're done in there, **Fu-turabold** requests your company."

"I think Doug should sing. Not me."

"Doug? Seriously?" Takashi's voice turned staccato and loud again.

"Takashi?" from behind the door.

"DLG has the charisma of a hemorrhoid. Yr on vocals Isa."

"Takashi, I can hear you!"

"Actually, I say go with mumbling. That's my point-oh-two."

"Mumbling?"

"Tak? Isa? Can I come in?"

Takashi leaned over and locked the bathroom door. "I'm taking a shit in here," he called to the outside before readdressing Isa. "Yeah, sure, mumble. Crowds will find signal in noise. Like Cobain."

Several more raps percussed from outside. "Hello?"

"That's kinda the point though. Nobody could understand what he was singing right? And yet he's remembered as this genius vocalist. Just do that."

"Takashi, you are being neither cute nor adorable. Isa, will you please let me in?"

Doug rattled the knob a bit, but the door would not budge. "Sorry!" he said from behind the door.

"Exactly. Folks give such a major, sphincter-splitting shit about lyrics. They don't realize half the time they're making them up themselves."

Isa grit her teeth until she could feel the lactic acid burn in her jaws.

"As I said Isa, think it over. It's yr call, no pressure." Takashi turned the brass nut, unlocking the door. "And by that I mean, the choice has been made, lots of pressure."

"I'm not singing. Again. I'm not singing."

"And yet you'll sing. Or scream, or talk, or whatever. When yr up in front of the pit with a mic in yr face, you won't have much of a choice." Takashi opened the door to Doug. The hebody stood bent over, his hands on his thighs and his face beetish.

"Thank. You. Isa." Doug managed between pants.

"Isa didn't do shit for you," Tak said as he stepped out. "And seriously Doug, cut the histrionics."

"You're. One. To. Talk," retorted Doug. "I'm. Asthmatic. Dick. And anxiety. Increases it. Tenfold."

"Anxiety?"

Doug stood up and plugged his nostrils for a count of three before inhaling through them sharply. "Well. I rightly thought you two were having a pow-wow in there. What, given that Isa is usually lavatory-bound during these shows. And yet I *assumed* you two would let me in if I knocked. I winded myself banging on the door only to realize perhaps I was disturbing some hebody's defecating, or a shebody greasing her mohawk and I subconsciously started to feel embarrassed.

"I start sweating and my heart beats faster. And then, I become aware of said sweating and palpitations. I went from embarrassed, to mortified to having a minor-scale panic attack. So I try to calm myself down: deep breathing, count to ten, to no avail of course. So then I start panicking that I can't overcome my panic attack, so my small anxieties turn into a full-on, self-aware fit of neurosis. And I get dizzy and really start sweating. I become so nervous, you know, that someone else is watching me have a panic attack. So I have a tertiary panic attack. A panic attack that others are watching my panic attack about my panic attack, and judging me. I shake. I feel nauseous. My spine feels like an over-boiled carrot."

"Recursion is a bitch," said Takashi.

"That's when you opened the door. Lucky for me I wasn't interrupting some innocent shebody's micturation. It's just Takashi and Isa. You two just suck."

"Courtney Christ, Ganoush."

"An apology would be nice."

"Yeah, well, not my style," said Tak. "But I have good news. Isa's on vocals."

"I'm not."

Doug's chin skewed sideways into a goofy open-mouthed smile. "Really? That's amazing."

"I never said that."

"Yeah, figured I'm not the front man type. Need to focus on playing out of the pocket or whatever the fuck bassists say they do. Oh, and we're scrapping my lyrics too. Isa's gonna rewrite them for all our tunes."

"Takashi, I'm astounded. Truly. I never expected this of you."

"I wish you weren't so excited by this, DLG. It's a bit, I dunno, patronizing or something."

The corners of Doug's lips twitched.

"I can't sing. I will neither mumble nor scream. I will not look at the audience. I will not, I will not I will not!" Isa's voice, pinched and anxious, climbed close to a shout.

Tak and Doug stood in silence, their faces fish-like.

"Maybe I can change your mind," Takashi started. "I have something for you Isa."

Isa kept her gaze at her knees.

"Check this out," Tak said. He pulled a tablet the size of a thumb drive from one of his impossibly-tight pockets. He sized it up and swiped at the surface a few times. Above the bathroom mirror, a projection of the tablet's home screen showed

itself to the three. For all to see, Tak clicked open a docs folder where a blinking pink
.jpg waited.

"Ready for this?" he said and clicked it open. Before them was a complex
schematic, sketchily drawn by Takashi.

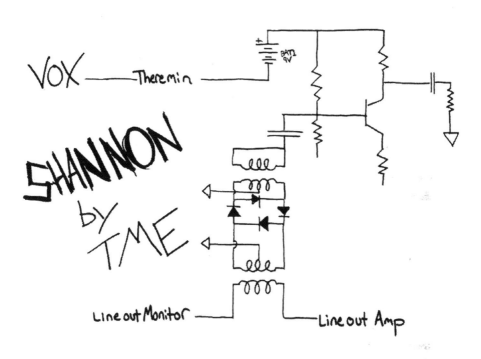

"What is this?" asked Doug.

"I hope you don't mind," Tak interjected, a vein protruding from his
forehead beneath his blonde spikes. "But I rigged some of our equipment together.
Created a revolution in sound design."

"*Our* equipment?"

"Well I stole almost all of it. So I guess it's mostly mine."

"It is so not yours," said Doug.

Takashi paused to thumb at his nose, either in diffidence or to swipe away a
booger. "Punk's not dead DLG," he said. "What you see here is my SHANNON.
The finest and most-cutting edge piece of vocal modulation hardware ever created."

Tak beamed at the crude schematic flickering in front of him.

"See, what we have here is an input, the signal from the microphone, fed into your old theremin, Doug."

"You can't use my theremin!" Doug shouted, his voice cracking pubescently.

"Too late." Tak shrugged. "It has already been subsumed by the SHAN-NON."

"I never said you could—!"

"Too. Late. Doug," Takashi repeated himself. "It's part of something greater now."

Doug swallowed.

"Where was I? The theremin feeds into an LBP-1 which you see here. That distorts the signal. Makes it richer. Following that we go through a ring modulator which, well, modulates it. All this is fed into the amp."

With a defeated tone Doug said, "Won't that sound like shit?"

Takashi smiled. "But punks love shit. Yr failing to see what this will do. We place the theremin in front of the pit. The heat and movement of the mosh will alter how much the signal is distorted or changed. The energy of the crowd modulates the vocals!

"You see, all communication relies on a good bit of ambient noise right? This puppy's namesake, Claude Shannon pointed that out first. Think about it, right now, I'm moving my lips and vocal chords, the vibrating air gets mixed up with the ambient noise of the band in the next room, yr bodily functions, whatever. But somehow yr able to parse out my signal from that noise. In fact, as our boy Claude pointed out, a good deal of that noise and redundancy is necessary for good communication!"

Doug scratched at his chin. "I don't follow he said."

"It's some tricky math," said Takashi, "But basically you've got to think about entropy—the amount of chaos in a system—as potential information. If a system is completely ordered, it has no entropy and no information to extract. If you want a message to have meaning, there has got to be motion. Communication works by patterning this entropy into redundancy. Redundant messages are easier to understand and difficult to fuck up. This is because communication has always fundamentally involved at least two parties: a speaker and a listener. My SHANNON essentially closes the loop that all of language has tried to do since we were early homos grunting on the savannah. It joins the roles of speaker and listener, or in our case musician and audience. Really, what I've invented is a new paradigm for punk rock!"

"So you destroyed my theremin for a half-baked experiment in information theory?"

"Well, the good news is, I'm not singing anymore. I thought you'd be relieved. Right Isa?"

Isa's face was in her palms.

"What did you do to her, Takashi?"

"Shit, nothing!"

"I don't want to sing."

"She said she'd think it over," said Tak.

"I *am* thinking it over."

"Well, don't think so hard. You'll give yrself an aneurism."

Isa was too entangled in her own thoughts to respond. Doug inhaled through his teeth.

"Why don't we give this a rest yeah? No vocals for now, we'll focus on instrumentals. It's not like we have a show coming up right?" he said.

"_"

"_"

"Anyway, **Futurabold**'s growing irate I'm sure," said Tak as he shut off the projection and minimized his tablet. "You know, she's been in her office waiting for us for the past half hour, I imagine."

From behind Doug, Tak espied the form of **Futurabold**'s Uncle Dee. He leaned against the doorframe to his niece's office, thick hairy arms folded across his chest. His shirt pocked with grease stains, his jeans tattered around his knees, he watched over them like a Golem over a small Yiddish village. Silent, formidable.

"Yeah, uh, let's do that," Tak said. He gave Uncle Dee a nod. It went unreturned.

Inside her office **Futurabold** sat at her desk. In the corner of her room sat her old PC tower and monitor, already home to a few different species of arthropods. In front of her was her new monitor: a clear golden rectangle propped up on a curved aluminum support, the screen three times the size and one two hundredths the thickness of her old one. Next to it was the tower, hand assembled by Takashi. The hardware sat inside an unused pizza box for the pizzeria across the street. Atop the screen was a tiny, almost invisibly small pinhole. Inside it lay a motion-tracker that allowed **Futurabold** to interface with the machine mouse-free. She could simply manipulate any item on the screen through simple hand gestures, or, if she was feeling particularly lazy, head nods. While convenient, these features required that users make little auxiliary hand gestures. An easy feat while alone, but difficult during meetings when she had to both use the computer and interface with whatever folks were populating the milk crates in front of her.

Futurabold said nothing when the three entered. She merely waved her hands toward the three overturned crates in front of her desk waiting for them. That, or she minimized a window on her display; it was difficult to tell.

"Uh, sorry that took so long," Doug said first. He took the middle crate. "We had to have a little band powwow beforehand."

"Uh huh," **Futurabold**, nonplussed.

"You know. Internal politics needed sorting out. You understand how these things go." Doug removed his glasses and buffed the lenses with the edge of his shirt.

Figure 3: SHANNON

"Right."

"Who were the guys just playing?" Tak asked. "Killer set. Tell 'em I said that."

"Pontius Pilates," **Futurabold** responded. "From where else but Brooklyn." Her voice was flat and disinterested.

"Shit, how'd you schlep them across state lines?"

"A few old colleagues from the Neo-!Kung ferried them across the Hudson. It's getting expensive though, bringing bands in from out of state. We might have to cut back to local acts."

A faint hack sounded in from outside. Most likely Uncle Dee. Otherwise the room was quiet. The silence roared on for several seconds at least. Doug and Takashi squirmed on their crates. Isa sat, somehow more silent than usual.

"So how're you enjoying the new setup?" Tak broke the quiet. "The pizza box definitely gives yr office a DIY appeal in my opinion. Plus the cardboard should provide excellent cooling for the hard drive."

Futurabold rolled her eyes up like, whatever. "My news RSS pulled out an interesting article this AM," she said. "I simmed that the three of you might find it worth seeing."

Futurabold waved her hands in front of the monitor for several seconds. "Oh Courtney Christ," she muttered.

"What is it?" said Doug, fidgeting with his glasses.

"My internet is ungodly slow," the shebody replied. "What did you install Takashi? Broadband?"

"Lemme see," replied Tak. He swung around her desk and peered at the screen. Slack-jawed, he scratched at the nape of his neck before wiggling his fingers around and mumbling to himself. "Everybody turn off yr electronics," he said, pulling his tablet out of his pocket and depressing a button on the side which dimmed its screen. "Phones too, Doug."

Doug unearthed a boxy Paleolithic flip-phone from his shorts. He pressed a button and turned it off.

"Well fuck me," said Takashi.

"What's going on?" said **Futurabold**, now with some urgency in her voice.

"Yr getting DDOS'd. Somebody is pinging your machine with an onslaught of information, but I can't determine the sources."

"What do you mean?"

Tak scratched at his chin, his pupils darting across the screen. "Well, govware—while generally secure— will handle information requests from verified sources if they are within a small radius. Like a federal agent's Eyes or something. Somebody's phone, or Eyes or something is radiating of fuck ton of information within this office."

"Wait hold on," said **Futurabold**. "Govware?"

"Yeah, well this whole transmission handling functionality is pretty tightly encoded into yr OS. I couldn't really untangle it when I was setting up yr computer," said Takashi. As he spoke he swung his fingers around as if conducting an orchestra through a highly polyrhythmic score.

"How did you get me a government computer?" **Futurabold** asked, eyes darting between her computer screen and Takashi.

"I pirated it."

"What?"

"Well, I should correct yr mistaken assumption. It's not a government computer, its government software. The hardware I put together myself. The software I pirated."

Doug's breath rate audibly accelerated. "Are you *trying* to get us arrested?" Doug said. " Takashi, how can you be so reckless?"

A sigh and a quick rolling of the eyes from Tak. "It's mostly risk-free, Doug. The number one rule of net pirating: the bigger your source ware, the easier it is to cop. And now I ask you, what source is more overwhelmingly huge than the government?"

"I don't follow," said **Futurabold**.

"See, the government has put a heavy investment into regulating the internet, an otherwise free flow of information. If you are a ruling body, cyberspace is scary as shit. It's distributed, lawless but democratic. That's why their software picks up whatever information is being transmitted by nearby dyads. It allows the NSA a distributed network to access everyone's digital communication in this country.

"The problem though, is that the government is run by old fogies. Graying dudes who went to Yale and Harvard when Apple was considered cutting edge. They had zero idea how the net, or most modern technology for that matter, worked when they were elected. And it's not like they put in much effort in keeping up with that wonderful exponential curve of growth and development.

"What you get, basically, is a set of lawmakers who, although their membership is ever-changing, are always lamentably behind-the-times."

"And this helps me how?" **Futurabold** asked.

"Well, old fogie politicians hire old fogie technocrats to enact their politics, right? If they write up a 3000 page cybersecurity bill say, monitoring all search engine keystrokes that contain a possible iteration of the Chinese characters for 'zoo porn' and 'Dennis Vreeman', they need to also find a team to create the software to implement said tracking. Problem is, though, while these Stanford elites were sipping espresso and leisurely programming on their subsidized tablets, some fourteen year old black hat from Nebraska with pubes growing on his chin read the news and already figured every possible hypothetical way to crack to their code *in advance*. Hard as the powers-that-be may try, they will never be able to keep pace with the basement-dwelling masses. You follow?"

All faces in the room—save Takashi's—were lacquered with varying degrees of confusion. Isa especially seemed stoned on her own thoughts.

"While I'm not the, uh, shall we say technophile that you are Takashi, I can't quite find the takeaway here," Doug said slowly, his upper lip twitching. "Political vindications aside, it seems to me that the lack of comparative efficiency between government officials and the hacker subculture don't have a lot of, well, relevance to the situation at hand."

Tak emitted a histrionic sigh. "You missed my point, Doug."

"I wasn't aware you had a point, Tak."

"Isn't it obvious? The government is massive and slow with an enormous bank account. But govware is still state of the art. Or what the state of the art looked like two years ago. All it takes is one guy to figure out how to crack it and in three days copies in forty different languages are available for pirating for all his friends. It's so closed it's practically open source."

"Isn't that illegal?" asked Doug.

Takashi shrugged. "I mean, I guess so. But it's not that heavily prosecuted. A good hacker doesn't get caught. A bad hacker gets caught and then hired by the government to help formulate the next report of wares. Half the time he'll still be black-hatting and leave some obvious holes for his darkly-capped buddies to snatch up from the underground.

"Besides, the Federal Government has all but collapsed anyway. That's why it's near impossible to get a permit to cross state borders. The government knows folks will pirate their software, so they just use that as an opportunity to monitor everyone's info. It's a win for them too, the fuckers."

"And that's where you got the—"

"—The OS for **Futurabold**'s computer." Takashi snapped his fingers. "Okay, I managed to open up a cache of your news reader," he said to **Futurabold**.

Futurabold shook her head. "Well, here's the article," she said, and turned the monitor around for all to see. "I managed to cache it when I first saw it."

The North Jersey Journal: Police Blotter
New Suspects Emerge in Guitar Heist

Paramus, NJ

In a new development in an ongoing case in which a Musician's Warehouse Superstore was burglarized last month, Police Chief Jared Moucet announced that investigators are on to a new lead. One of the guitars stolen, a rare vintage model known as a "Fender Jazzmaster" was tagged with a GPS tracking sticker. Moucet has tracked the posi-

tion of the guitar to Lodi, NJ, although no arrests have been made. Moucet gave no further
information on the case.

Doug gulped audibly. "So, shall I state the obvious?"

"We're fine," Tak said, "I threw out that sticker into the Passaic a month ago. Guess it washed up in Lodi."

"But should I be paranoid, Tak?"

"Paranoia is just a realistic assessment of one's place in this vastly networked world. It's an existential security blanket. Makes you feel like you matter to something else."

"That doesn't help."

"Paranoia is realism, Doug," said Takashi. He pulled at his skeletal bass-guitarist fingers, cracking them as he spoke. "At least in this case it is. Whether or not the police have traced it back to us, in all likelihood, we're fucked. Or at least we will be, eventually."

Doug twisted a greasy lock of hair on the back of his neck. "It's not giving any suspect names. Just Lodi. It's a huge city." He glanced at **Futurabold** whose arms were folded under her breasts. "You're not worried by this?"

"Worried? No. Confused? A little. I was just hoping the fuzz don't snag you before this weekend."

"This weekend?"

"You're headlining on Friday."

"Seriously?" said Takashi and Doug in unison, albeit with vastly different intonations.

"Yuh-huh. Frida and the Felchers canceled. Tour van broke down. So you're booked for a forty-five minute set. Better get ready."

A wild grin broke across Takashi's mug. "You got it, sister."

1.82 MOSH

Dee sat at his stool, thumbing and folding over $500 bills into a thick sandwich while he marked thick Sharpie X's on the backs of hands of underage youngsters. Rule 30 had no liquor license, though it was policy to mark the hands of all attendees, regardless of their age. His niece had established the rule. It gave Rule 30 a 1980's vibe that she insisted concert-goers would appreciate. Today's punks are nostalgic for the day before yesterday's scene.

Dee McRogers lived through that time, and he could remember it too: the age of Black Flag and Minor Threat. The era of hardcore basement bands and trendy anti-trend straight-edgers. Of course, Dee's memories of that time mostly consisted of him parked in front of the TV watching The Muppets while he chomped down on single-serving packets of vanilla pudding.

Twenty-somethings haven't changed all that much in the six decades or so Dee had been alive. The majority have always preferred to be dead than be uncool. And that means that whenever a hot new band emerged, one always aspired to be amongst the few who discovered it first. Hop on the bandwagon too late and you're labeled out of it, or at worst a poseur.

"500 bucks," said Dee to the young shebody at the ticket desk. Half of her head was shaved, the other hemisphere was a thick tangle of lime green dreadlocks. She forked over a crumpled Obama. Dee X'd her hand with a black sharpie and she joined the crowd inside Rule 30's main space.

At a venue like Rule 30, there was an art to finding the right audience size. When he ran the place, Dee was always pretty savvy toward it. It looked like his niece had inherited the same set of management instincts. A smart venue manager wants a big crowd, but if the space gets overfilled, the audience will grow discontent. Not because they're too warm or they feel uncomfortable smushed against all the other bodies in the room; punks dig that shit. Unless the act on stage was extremely compelling, no punk would risk being seen in a large crowd for it, lest they lose any underground clout they'd accrued. It's always been a rule of the sub-culture: if you find yourself going to big shows too regularly, you might as well cast off your combat boots and start listening to Top 40s bullshit.

"Frida and the Felchers still playing?" said one skinny kid with astounding vascularity. Dee'd seen him before.

"No," said Dee. He reached out a hand for cash.

And the kid just stared back eyebrows all screwy like, what? He had two shebodies behind him. The one with pink hair and a Chapped Assholes tank put her hand on his shoulder.

"Who's headlining?" she asked.

Dee looked into the atrium. A handful of punks pogoed up and down, either out of boredom or to keep warm. Others scanned the plexiglass walls as they flashed countless insignias in a loop. In the corner that fat kid, L'Marque or whatever, was screwing together a high-hat stand. The other two were probably backstage with Ruthie or something. They'd been hanging around here for months; what did Ruthie say they were called?

"New Ape Idea," said Dee, the words taking their time to pour out of his mouth.

The kid looked at the two shebodies behind him. They shrugged together.

"Fifteen hundred," said Dee and they paid.

Over the years, Dee realized he could calculate the hipness threshold of a venue like Rule 30. On a typical Friday night show, concert-goers seemed the most contented with an audience size of 100 people. Rule 30 though could legally hold about two and a half times the amount. 300 if they were willing to forgo a fining from the fire department.

So the hipness limit was 100 people. When the audience size was less than or

Figure 4: New Ape Idea

equal to that, Dee figured those kids would likely have a good time and all consider themselves a bit more punk for showing up. On the other hand, if the audience size exceeded that crowd threshold, one was better off staying at home. You'd come off as more punk for abstaining from such mainstream drivel, and all those unfortunate enough to show up would lose a degree of counter cultural cred. It was practically algorithmic.

```
If Audience < 100:
  show = punk
Else:
  show = not punk
```

Dee thumbed through a wad of bills a gaggle of kids had handed to him. He'd seen them before; they were Rule 30 regulars. Somehow they'd always managed to look about 16 years old in the years they'd been coming to shows here. Someone from the crowd called over to them. Dee X'd the backs of their hands wordlessly and they went on their way. Kids like that had probably shown up to enough small shows to accrue a fair amount of clout. They came to shows every weekend, probably figuring that the majority of them would be attended— but not over attended— and they could thus further grow their scene cred.

Over the years, Dee had come to think of it like grinding a character's stats in an old Playstation RPG from his childhood. If a show was indeed punk, all members of the audience maybe gained +1 hipness points. Likewise, one's clout iterated similarly if they missed out on an over-attended concert. Those that showed up to an over-large crowd or skipped out on a small, intimate show lost points in equal measure.

As far as Dee could tell, attending these shows really was a game. Grow your P-score and become a staple member of the scene. Lose too many and you were ostracized to poseurdom. Those who were confident in their abilities to choose when to go to a show or stay home probably had fairly high P-scores. Those who guessed wrong too many times had low P-scores, as well as little faith in their own ability to predict a good show.

All these kids were self-conscious. Dee knew that much hadn't changed over the years. Over years of watching bodies meander their way down the stairs and into his venue, Dee realized his formula was too simple. In addition to carrying a P-score, these kids must also carry a score representing how assured they were in their ability to nose out a good show. If their P-scores were above that threshold, they probably had a fair amount of confidence in themselves. Their past guesses were a good indicator of future shows. If their P-scores were below it, they would second-guess their instincts. Their social strategy was completely the opposite. If one's P-score grew from low to high, or fell from high to low, the individual's confidence rating would have to change entirely.

```
If P-score ≥ Correct Guesses:
        instincts = good
Else:
        instincts = shit
```

Hipness is a limited resource. The strategies one uses to attain it probably do not differ too much from those hunter-gatherers used when deciding when to chase down some tasty big game. A big crowd meant for an easier hunt, but less meat to go around. Sometimes it was better, Dee figured, to just sit out a hunt once in awhile. Especially if the hunt seemed too popular.

Over the years, Dee had run thousands of simulations of concert-goer strategy in the integrated development environment in his skull. P-scores, he figured, were not evenly distributed. Rather, folks tended after several shows or nights home to accrue scores that were either quite high or quite low. The key ingredient was feedback. Everyone kept a tally of their wins and losses in the back of their head when making a decision. This—it seemed to Dee—was the basis by which different crowds were formed. Why some bodies came to a few shows and stayed forever punks, while others found themselves happy enough to attend stadium shows of whatever artist was perched atop of the Billboard that week. He could sim the complex mathematics at the very backbone of genre formation. Graphed out it looked roughly like this:

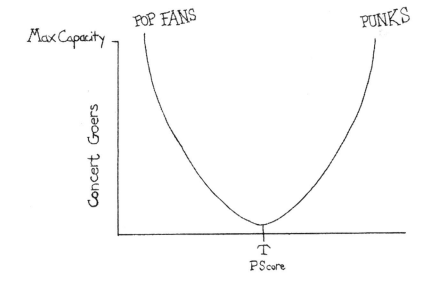

Shit, Dee was stoned.

A squawk of mic feedback silences the whirring calculations in Dee's skull. That blonde kid was fucking around with some knobs on this weird-ass pedal with glass tubes popping out of it. The feedback died down and he stood up and spoke into the mic. The shrieking returned. The chubby hebody ripped a few paradiddles on the drum set. Warming up with eccentric rhythmic patterns, alternating between traditional and matched grips. Dee didn't see Ruthie on stage or the pixie with the color-changing sleeve tats.

The blonde Korean-looking hebody marched off stage and returned with a blue Fender Jazzmaster. Dee hadn't seen a guitar like that in decades. The hebody plugged the guitar into a pedalboard and tuned it. He whammed out an E chord to an A, unplugged it, and leaned it against an amp stack before disappearing into the audience. The chubby kid set his sticks on the stand and followed suit. Weren't they members of the headlining band? Why did Ruthie have them set up for the opening act?

The first band had an old-fashioned drum machine wired to the PA. The gui-tarist started to hammer at a student's half-size guitar. The bassist played an upright, a mic dangling inside its F-hole. The chord swung about as he let loose a few open E's for tuning. He turned and squinted at the drum machine, activating it and giving a flat MIDI-fied 4/4 rock beat.

"Hello Hoboken! We are the Ass-Pube Snowmen," the bassist said, "And this song is in A minor."

And they started ramming at their strings. There was nothing original about this band. Plenty of groups lacked talent or musical ability, The Ass-Pube Snowmen just seemed to be mocking that old element of the punk aesthetic. There had been bands that brought down the house without trying. Then there were acts who tried so extremely hard to appear as if they weren't trying. The Ass-Pube Snowman, with their calculatedly sloppy music were obviously not trying to seem like they were trying to sound like they weren't. They were recursive and boring.

Ruthie had come out of her office, Dee noticed. She was standing along the wall, a notepad in her hand. Ever since she got back from living with the cavemen people, she liked to write about the kids, she told Dee, the younger of whom were spazzing out to this horseshit while the older, taller ones just stood there and yawned.

Dee had seen enough shit openers to know the architecture of how the audi-ence would react. In about fifteen minutes the elders would start to file out and puff on non-synth vape pens on the sidewalk and complain. By his calculations, Dee could slip out, enjoy a 10-minute spliff and re-enter in time to handle the wave of out-goers.

The Ass-Pube Snowmen announced that their next song was a Johnny Cash cover but neither the vocals nor the guitar lines were discernable. Somebody turned the bass mic way up. The plodding straight-eighths-on-the-root bass line didn't quite line up to tempo with the drum machine that'd been playing the same metronomic beat non-stop for the past three tunes.

Dee recalculated. He'd probably only have time for half a spliff before kids would start to leave.

From the sidewalk outside Rule 30 the band was barely audible. Dee sparked and inhaled. The synth stuff always smelled more sulfuric than plant-like, Dee had noticed. He used to get higher back when the stuff was illegal. The medical card felt good when he first got it, near two decades ago, but ever since the FDA bought out the whole hemp industry, Dee McRogers' felt like he'd been smoking the spindly leaves of pesticide-sprayed conifers rather than anything remotely cannabanoidal. The smoke left a metallic aftertaste and had an unpleasant, viscous mouthfeel. Not that these had been sufficient enough reason to quit smoking.

Mallorey always seemed to materialize out of nowhere. They were in the same black trench coat they always wore, collared shirt and tie beneath. The theebody was tall, sported a conservative crew cut and smiled a lot—all qualities more commonly exhibited by investment bankers than zine journalists.

"Mr. McRogers," Mallorey said with a nod. Kid still called Dee mister, which both cracked up Dee and infuriated him in equal measure.

Dee didn't say much and held out the spliff, two-thirds gone currently. Mallorey put up their palm like, no thanks, and Dee, stoned into synchronicity, did the same.

Night fell on Hoboken to the warm drumbeats leaking from Rule 30 and the soft purr of Waymos driving past. A couple bar hoppers yelped at each other as they stumbled into the pizza joint across the block. Mallorey, hands in pockets, seemed to take it all in too. Another quality atypical to his peer group the theebody seemed to have: An appreciation of ambience and quietude.

"**Futurabold** tells me she's debuting a band that's not to be missed."

"Tonight?" mumbled Dee.

Mallorey smiled. "Apparently their bassist had the idea that they should plug a Frida and the Felchers show on every music blog they could find. Y'know, bring in a crowd. Then change the headliner to the new folks when it's too late for anybody to leave."

Dee scratched at his head and tried to remember which one of them was tuning the bass before.

"Ballsy move no?" said Mallorey. "I mean, if those cats can't play we'll have a small scale riot inside. Never seen mass phishing like this pulled off."

"_-_"

"_-_"

"What about fish?" Dee mumbled.

"I'm gonna head inside. Put the ticket charge on my tab, will you Mr. McRogers?" Mallorey depressed the knot of their collar and the theebody's outfit changed to a sleeveless white muscle-tee, camouflage shorts and combat boots.

And the two entered Rule 30. Just as a threesome exited, cigs already in hand.

Down the stairs The Ass-Pube Snowmen were already getting booed off. The bassist held his large upright on his back like a pack mule. The other kid looked like he was tearing up as he turned off the drum machine.

Ruthie exited her office with the two hebodies from the headlining act. The tall skinny one leapt up on stage while the fat one took his time, wringing his hands and stretching his wrists. The former picked up his Rickenbacker bass and plugged it in. Real high-quality instrument, by the looks of it. The latter sat at his throne and picked up his sticks. At least they had an organic, embodied drummer, New Ape Idea. The bassist looked miffed and so did the drummer. With even longer strides than before, the bassist leapt off stage and through the crowd, navigating the growing pit with ease. He skirted toward the bathroom and, without knocking, opened the door and pulled out the short shebody with the changing sleeve tats. He led her by the wrist up to the stage.

After slinging that blue Jazzmaster around her shoulder she stepped up to the mic, eyes closed, biting her lower lip like, "Oh shit". The crowd was restless and murmuring to itself. Dee simmed that they were probably all piecing together the witty insults that they'd later hurl up at her unless she started to play something stat.

A couple beats and the bassist leaned forward and yelled, "Hello, we are New Ape Idea, and this is our first song!" and a few younger shebodies in the crowd hooted in mock-adoration.

For someone his size, the drummer could sure move. He was all over the set, Hawaii Five-O-ing up and down the toms and snare. The cymbals sounded crisper than Dee remembered. His face was calm and cool if not a bit nervous, and his shirt already seemed to be logged with sweat.

The bassist, however, was hopping up and down. His rhythm was uneven, his mids were turned up a bit too high and was that a flanger that he was running the signal through? Why a bassist would use any phasing on their sound was beyond Dee, but the audience didn't seem to mind terribly. A couple nodded their heads and shifted their body weight from knee to knee in time with the bass drum hits. Then again, there was always a few audience members willing to move to even the most atonal, arrhythmic garbage played at Rule 30.

The shebody with the guitar stared at her toes while the drummer and bassist exchanged worried looks, which was impressive given their level of simultaneous physical activity. The crowd started to jeer. Dee could see Mallorey and Ruthie leaning against the wall, Ruthie's hand cupped to her mouth speaking to him.

Dee took his seat at the stool in the venue's atrium. He watched the graffiti flash by; at this point he'd near memorized the order of tags as they changed. Monikers of bands, real and fake, elided into one another. The scribbled, looping L's and Anarchy A's blurring with over-recognition.

A trite "You suck!" enunciated itself from the crowd. The music had stopped, and the bassist's long arm was around the guitarist's shoulders, his thin muscles visibly tensed. He F2F'd with the shebody, his back to the sweaty mass at the drum kit who craned his neck like he was trying to join in too.

"No refunds," said Dee to a shirtless ectomorph, an X'd hand outstretched.

"Fuck off," the hebody retorted and left.

A small gaggle of regulars, unlit cloves already wedged between lips, turned to leave. Dee, tongue to palate, already began to enunciate another "No Refunds," when the bassist took the mic.

"Hold yr horses. We're gonna try that one again."

The drummer clicked off four on the rim of his snare. And the guitarist turned her back to the audience, lips to the mic like she was Miles fucking Davis. The guitar line was articulate yet fuzzy. The bass was just fuzzy. Cloves descended from lips and reentered pockets. Heads nodded, hips swayed side to side. These kids were *dancing*. At Rule 30 no less: a space where kinesthetic activity consisted of either ingesting nicotine while deriding the act on stage, or full-throttle body-slamming. The rare bird that was dancing only showed itself with the most ironic of plumages. The audience though looked like they were earnestly enjoying the music.

From their wall, even Mallorey and Ruthie tapped their toes, lips pouted and impressed. Dee was the only body at rest. From his stool he played the spectator. He found the guitar hooks infectiously catchy. If he was a younger hebody he too would be swinging his hips and shimmying his shoulders with all the rest. The arthritis and Lithium pills made that too difficult though. From within his steel-toed boots Dee could feel a big toe sliding about with the jagged bass line. He stood up as the guitarist played a line of rapidly descending pinch-harmonics.

The two hebodies on stage shared a nod and transferred their gaze to the shebody guitarist. She leaned forward into the mic, her back still to the crowd.

The shebody's voice sounded both liquid and cutting. The stuff of stretched and lacerating vocal chords. Both a howl and the cooing of mother to her child transubstantiated into one single aural force, rippling with harmonics.

You can't change [INDECIPHERABLE] *it's lost and abominable.*
Without your mother's [INDECIPHERABLE] *happening this way.*
Molding minds from your first steps.
And [INDECIPHERABLE] *your indifference.*

Don't you know it happens within and between?

Of course the crowd erupted at all this. Bodies leapt and tumbled over one another. Limbs flailed. Heads bobbed up and down. The audience's movement oscillated with the music, the whole of Rule 30 sat on the limen between chaos and synchrony. The synergies of the crowd's moshing made the pit look like a living super-organism, emergent from the bumping and grinding of its parts.

The Pit-Thing undulated and writhed. Its internal movements seemed to be the engine of the sound coming off stage. As if as the Pit-Thing grew and expanded, drawing more head-nodders into body-slammers, the music too scaled up. Not so much a discrete modulation—a change in key, a crescendo, a quickening of tempo—but an increase in viscosity. A thickening, an enriching of the vocals and guitar and bass and the pops and fizzes and hums and whirs that arise between them.

A hebody with a husky frame and a shaved head arabesqued above the mosh. He grabbed onto a heating pipe overhead and reflexively released his grip. A dozen others hoisted him up and crowd-surfed him across the Pit-Thing, after which he was deposited by its perimeter. With his arc and fall over the many-bodied body, Dee could hear the slightest swelling within the vocals. If the mosh pit was a super organism then New Ape Idea was its voice. The sound of its own growl igniting it all the more.

Fuck yes, they're eating my SHANNON up. And who said dropping out of University to play bass was a bad idea? Nobody, but that's not what I'll tell 'em in my memoirs. A good show is a complex system, fundamentally non-linear. And once you can specify the math behind a system, you can cheat it. That's the golden rule of cybernetics. If you want the crowd's adoration then engineer 'em into yr stomp boxes. These fuckers don't even realize how much I'm blowing their minds tonight. Should I smoke a cigarette right now, or would that look to cliché?

The visitats of those in the Pit-Thing whorled and pulsed together: Mandelbrot sets in an infinite state of genesis, Fibonacci spirals rotating endlessly, the whole Pit-Thing was a recursive sort of animal, exhibiting patterns within patterns within patterns. The shifting shape of a single tattoo mimicked the behavior of the entire Pit-Thing, Dee thought to himself. He felt warm. Not feverishly so. It was a kind of comfortable heat that blanketed him, uterine in a way.

Why draw so close to me? Do you not [INDECIPHERABLE]
"Not so," said the ghost to the machine.
[INDECIPHERABLE]
Can't you hear it scream?

Dee looked over to his niece by the wall. She was still with the Mallorey theebody, both moving to the music. Mallorey's face looked smushed and scattered, not unlike that of a Picasso painting. Ruthie sported a grin almost too big for her face. Dee's skull was humming, the music massaging a psychedelic sort of affect from his synapses.

1.	I do not wish to turn around.
1.1.	Should I turn around the crowd will show itself to me.
1.1.1.	Of course, this will make me nervous.
1.1.1.1.	By that I mean, I already entertain a state of anxiety. A viewing of the crowd will increase that.
1.1.2.	I have never been in a crowd before.
1.1.2.1.	By that I mean I have never been in a group of people during a musical performance.
1.1.2.2.	I prefer to listen in an isolated area.
1.1.2.2.1.	Like a bathroom for example.
1.1.2.2.2.	Mosh pits seem too dangerously unregulated.
1.1.2.2.2.1.	There are no rules in a mosh pit.
1.1.2.2.2.2..	It is like speaking a language without a grammar.
2.	Vocalizing is not too scary when I cannot see the audience.
2.1.	I can easily simulate that I am vocalizing to nobody but myself.
2.2.	And vocalizing to oneself is almost the same as remaining silent.

The Charybdis-like Pit-Thing swirled clockwise. Somehow. Dee couldn't calcu-late whether this was due to physics or psychology. Do all mosh pits eventually turn clockwise? Dee had never made note of such before. How could such a pattern emerge from the actions of a hundred or so individuals?

The music made Dee feel stoned. Even more stoned than he already was. Not in the couch-locked gravity-on-Jupiter weightiness of the usual stoned. Nor the somatosensory zigzagging high synthesized stuff usually gave him. This was something stimulating. Electric. Bizarre. He found his legs walking. Arthritic stiffness evaporat-ed from within his joints. He approached the Pit-Thing. He could smell its musk of perspiration and smoke.

&-//-1-&-2-E-&-A-3-E-A-4//1-A-E-A-3-4//-&-&-A-3-4//EAT-YOUR-GOD-

DAMN-SPINACH//EAT-YOUR-GODDAMN-SPINACH//-2-4//BOYSENBER-RY-4-&//

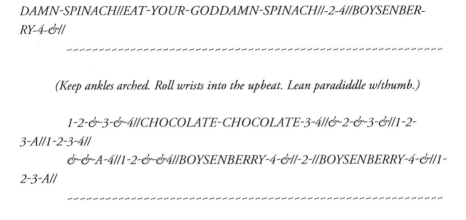

(Keep ankles arched. Roll wrists into the upbeat. Lean paradiddle w/thumb.)

1-2-&-3-&-4//CHOCOLATE-CHOCOLATE-3-4//&-2-&-3-&//1-2-3-A//1-2-3-4//

&-&-A-4//1-2-&-&4//BOYSENBERRY-4-&//-2-//BOYSENBERRY-4-&//1-2-3-A//

(Flexion in lower-back. Shift to ¾. Christ, Takashi don't do that with your hips)

Dee took an elbow to his jaw as he entered the Pit-Thing. The pain did not faze him. Although Dee himself did not mosh, the moshing grew all the more because of his presence. Just as the kinetics of a pinball increases with the addition of bumpers. The Pit-Thing bursted into a wall of shouts and cheers when the music ceased.

"Thank you and go fuck yourself! We've got 32 more for you!" said the bassist, snatching the mic from the shebody's mouth.

Part II

"The more specified a system is, the easier it is to cheat it."
—Heinz Von Foerster

2.10 Feedback

Takashi lay on the sheetless mattress unable to sleep. His skin was lacquered with a thin film of perspiration and dirt. Removing his clothes was difficult; Tak's sweat had likely damaged his shirt's resizing functionality. His eardrums had not stopped ringing for the past 72 hours, the high-pitched buzz of tinnitus was even more painful when he lay on his sides or attempted to cover his ears. DLG and Isa had been prescient enough to wear earplugs during the show.

After Friday's show, **Futurabold** had asked New Ape Idea to play last-minute sets on Saturday and Tuesday. The audience seemed to grow larger and more raucous with each show. Performing left Takashi exhausted. After taking down his equipment and stowing away his SHANNON in its hard plastic case, Takashi would crawl into this back room for a post-set schluff. Now though, his body hummed with adrenaline. While resting was possible, sleep itself would not come easily.

Takashi sat up and removed his Lazy Eyes from their case on the bedside table. He tilted his head back and placed the smart lenses on his irises. He blinked several times to lubricate away the dry pain. Tak laid back down, staring up at the ceiling. He activated his Eyes with two deliberate winks. Before him appeared the familiar torrent of windows within windows within browsers within screens. He closed down a series of pop-ups advertising weight-gain shakes and vegan quarter-pounders with cheese. A fitness app blinked in the corner of his peripheral gaze; Tak had not exercised in 276 consecutive days. Meanwhile, several social media accounts informed him that he had 1076 unread messages, 13 video calls to return, 4,517 articles he might find inter-esting and one photo of him on stage on Friday had been shared 13,893 times. He cleared the cache with an eye roll.

Though it took no more than a few seconds, Tak felt his head swell with frus-tration as he navigated through the onslaught of data structures and media updates, opening and closing window after window, before finding his Reader: a small API he had constructed in his free time. He pulled in the search terms "New Ape Idea" and let it run. There were 216 mentions in the last 4 days, largely personal blogs or social media accounts from the looks of it. The top trending article was from *Staph Infection*. Takashi blinked it open.

Editor's Pick—Go Bananas for New Ape Idea!
By Mickey Mallorey

Hebodies, Shebodies, Theebodies and Betweenbodies: Cast off your Lazy Eyes! Throw your tablets to the linoleum! They always made better doorstops than listening devices. I am here, donning my only formalwear that isn't totally trashed to eulogize with you—dear readers—over the death of the Digital Age.

For too long we have consumed our music—our Goat Boners .mp4s and pirated Judith Butthurt demos of yesterday—through the most unsavory of mediums. Those suits at the so-called "major labels" have doggedly tried to cut the immaterial cojones off the punkgeist. They have tried endlessly to exorcise the holy ghost of all that is rebellious, rude & DIY, clogging our sense-holes with their late capitalist pig-rock. Music consumption in the past 30 years has grown from a simply aural expe-rience to an entire epileptic fit of stimulation. To think that an "album" used to just contain 80 minutes of sound, not a prepackaged applet containing games, animations, and advertisements to bombard yourself with. Art is not made for your smart lenses!

Believe me dear readers, I was sick of it. We've all bared witness to today's godawful music scene. Pretentious poseurs polluting our ears with their noxious aural poison. It is no exaggeration to say that I was driven mad by it. But, just as I was pre-paring to go out with the music, my vodka and benzodiazepine cocktail sweating on my nightstand, I decided to pay one last to one of my favorite Hoboken haunts: Rule 30[1] .

The place was packed with the grungy rawkers that normally frequent it. Apparently, venue-manager **Futurabold** McRogers tells me she originally booked Frida and the Felchers to headline, but some territorial hunter-gatherers turned their van's tires to Swiss cheese. Needless to say, when New Ape Idea took the stage, the crowd was already simming ways to heckle them off and then blog of their awfulness.

Did you read the headline? Of course they didn't suck. And no, New Ape Idea is not one of those cerebral avant-thrash units that coat their caterwauling in some sort of post-postmodern pretense. Neither are they electronic beat-machines that only sound passable when your neurochemistry has been sufficiently saturated with non-synth and MDMA. New Ape Idea puts out good vibrations that are more organic than a vegan's diarrhea and fresher than the kale paste they ate for breakfast. In fact, New Ape Idea has such a medulla-meltingly original sound, it may be easier to describe the band by what they are *not*:

- Hyper-produced automated tween trash
- Highschool hxc tough-guys
- Gender-bending Queercore Burlesque-rock
- Jock rock, stoner sludge, or anything with the word "pop" in it
- Forgettable

This trio is *it!* Guitarist/voxist/Visitat enthusiast Isa Spines works the fretboard of her Jazzmaster like it's a hated ex in a gimp suit. To say she rips or shreds is to vastly underplay it. Spines is the rare guitar virtuoso who can milk her nickel-plated Ernie Balls for every harmonic they've got. Yeah, the shebody is that good.

---

[1] Dedicated *Staph Infection* readers may notice a trend in my reportage. Chiefly that I tend to give glowing reviews for just about every act to emerge from New Jersey's crustiest of coves. This is neither conspiracy nor fraud. Trust me, beloved readership, when I say that under the management of scene queen **Futurabold** McRogers, Rule 30 has been putting up the crunchiest, most brewtal riffage to date. I don't know what it is with the place, but if you haven't made pilgrimage to this new Mecca of Punk get on your knees and start scurrying! If you're from out of state, let's hope you have some connections to get you across state lines.

Spines' six-stringed heroics, though, are effectively counterpointed by New Ape Idea's solid rhythm section. Bassist Tak Miyagi-Edelstein plays like Sid Vicious with twice the taste, 2/3rds the talent and way, way, way more expensive gear. I've never seen a Rickenbacker withstand such abuse[2]. Drummer Doug Lamarck-Ganoush blasts beats with monk-like focus and Spartan athleticism. Watching New Ape Idea play[3] I get the feeling that this Lamarck-Ganoush guy was into some serious math-core as a young'un.

New Ape Idea's sound is like a spike of speed to the skull. It'll awaken your inner chimpanzee, and, let me tell you, it hasn't been let out in a while. In fact, he'll probably want to scream, hump, and pummel the nearest hominid into submission. And that's what the fuck happened to all the moshers in attendance. I have never seen a pit so wild in a few geological epochs. New Ape Idea is composed of the sort of virtuosic thrashers that can adapt to their crowd. It's as if the musicians on stage finely oscillate their tunes in sync with the pit in front of them. It's a feat rendered even more impressive when one realizes that Spines has kept her back to the audience the entire set. The shebody must have ESP.

Traditionally, the punk aesthetic has privileged attitude over sound, emotion over skill. While the New Ape trio produces music that is hardly baroque, the three are goddamn good at what they do. That's not to say that Spines can't wail. She can, and her lyrics are like something written by Shakespeare with a hangover. I tried to isolate a couplet for this print, but I couldn't pin the exact words. That's not to say I couldn't tell they were profound as fuck though. I couldn't tell what she was saying all the time, but I knew what Isa Spines was feeling when she took the mic. Although Spines was more than certainly available for an interview, she refused to comment on any of the post-set questions I volleyed at her backstage. Maybe it was the goofy look on my face.

New Ape Idea is both a force-to-be-reckoned-with and a trio not-to-be-missed. Ten out of ten. Five stars. Two thumbs up. You get what I'm saying. Yeah, I know this is an unusual review. No snarky irony. No accusations of poseurdom. Too much music journalism these days is dedicated to critics trying to reify their own political ideologies in terms of what they're listening to. Loads of isms: 5th wave feminism, corporate abolitionism, Neo-!Kung primitivism. Whatever. Nope. Not doing that here. No political manifestos this time. These fuckers sound so good they've left me humbled an inarticulate. I can't say that New Ape Idea is anything but 'good'. What's the matter? You gonna stop subscribing? I'll print out issues and personally deliver them to your parent's subterranean apartment if you do. Nobody's gonna be

---

[2] Speaking of equipment, New Ape Idea packs more gear than a Musician's Warehouse. For a trio capable of producing such raw, unbridled punk, they step on more stomp boxes than I knew even existed.

[3] And you *have* to watch New Ape Idea play. Seriously, it's the best live show I've seen in, like, years. And I go to a lot of shows.

able to deny this. Listen to New Ape Idea. It's not a recommendation, it's a command. Currently, they have no music available for download/torrenting so any interested parties will have to see them live. **Futurabold** McRogers informed me, given the trio's astounding debut, New Ape Idea will be headlining weekly shows every Friday night for the next three months at Rule 30 in Hoboken.

Takashi bolted upright. He blinked off his Lazies, took them out and deposited them back in his case. Had **Futurabold** read the article? A top review from *Staph Infection* was rare enough, surely a huge amount of popular interest was to follow this.

The possibility of a nap was now impossible. The mattress felt especially old and springy, the cloth itchy on Tak's skin, as if it was exhorting the hebody to get up on his feet and F2F with the rest of the band. A female voice beckoned to him to stay. In his peripheral vision played a popup add from a softcore cam site. With a wink Tak closed it, leaving silence in its wake. Tak's head swam. He needed a drink of water. Tak rolled over and stood up out of the bed, feeling a sharp pain in the back of his hamstrings. Reaching back he felt shards of something hard and wet pricking at his skin. He brushed them off his skin and examined them in his palm: the remnants of two Lazy Eyes, shattered under his weight.

2.2.0 BODY

It takes Doug several minutes of concerted effort to open his eyes. His head sloshes with dizziness, and his tongue feels as if it is made of steel wool. Above him hangs an IV bag filled with liquid the color of a well-hydrated body's urine. It feeds into a needle stuck into the crook of his left elbow. There is a faint soprano beeping in the background.

"Are you conscious?" says Isa.

Doug laboriously turns his head to the side to see her. She is seated at his bedside, her petite frame a bit too small for the chair. Next to her is Barbara Ganoush, passed out with her head tilted back against the wall. Her mouth is open, her sleeping expression displaying some internal cocktail of worry and fatigue.

"Yes," Doug rasps. "I am."

"You haven't been for the past eight days," says Isa. "Should I wake up your mother?"

"How long has she been asleep?"

"About twenty minutes."

"And how long was she awake before that?"

Isa leans forward in her seat and thumbs at her chin. Her visitat sleeves seem to be radiating violet like St. Elmo's fire. "I can't say for certain," she says. "I believe she's been here when she's not on her nursing rounds. So possibly a few days."

Doug blinks. Even his eyes feel crusty. "Don't wake her up then," the hebody says.

Isa nods and leans back in her seat.

Some irritation begins to germinate in Doug's lungs. He coughs, causing paroxysms of pain to erupt across his chest. He spasms in his hospital bed, gritting his teeth and groaning.

"Douglas," says Barbara, now awake. Immediately, tears begin to descend down her cheeks.

"Mom, what happened?"

"Sweetie, you're awake. Oh thank God, you're awake."

Doug turned his head and gazed up at the ceiling. A large screen hung above his bed, displaying a milieu of graphs and figures.

"How long was he up?"

"Only a minute or two," said Isa. "He asked to let you sleep."

"What is this?" said Doug, his eyes tracking the fractalic spiking of a heart monitor.

"Those are your vitals," says Isa. "You've been inoculated, but with far more modern technology than what I was given. It's standard procedure for IC admissions I suppose."

"Where are the doctors?" says Doug.

"They're on their way I imagine," says Isa. "I'm sure the microbots alerted them when they sensed you woke up."

Barbara pulls a tissue from a box atop a nightstand next to her. She dabs at her tear ducts before blowing her nose. An attempt at speech quickly breaks into more heavy sobs and her groping for several more tissues.

"You haven't had that much in the way of human care," says Isa as Barbara swallows her crying. "It's mostly been automated doctors, including the surgeries."

"Surgeries?" says Doug. "As in more than one?"

"You've had two according to your chart," says Isa looking up at the screen. "They've managed to remove three of the bullets."

"Out of how many?"

"Four," says Isa.

At this Barbara Ganoush begins to sob, her face in her hands.

A bell rings and a white coat enters the hospital room. The doctor is a tall hebody, with old-fashioned classes and a tablet held in his armpit.

"Good afternoon Douglas," the doctor says before making eye-contact and giving him a perfunctory smile. "How do you feel?"

"Well I'm conscious," says Doug. "So at least I have that going for me."

The doctor says nothing as he sizes up his tablet and fingers in some notes.

"It hurts when I cough, though."

"How much? On a scale of one to ten."

"Eight."

The doctor nods. "I'll have a nurse bring you some morphine. You have several wounds on your stomach. We removed the bullets but we can't stitch them up until we're sure you're not at risk for developing sepsis."

Doug fights the urge to cough once more. "How many are left inside me?"

"One," says the doctor, still focusing on his notes. "It entered through your chest and is sitting awfully close to your aorta. We don't have any automated surgeons that are sophisticated enough to remove matter from such a high-risk area. The good news is though that there is no hemorrhaging. We don't have to rush while trying to find a plan for you."

Barbara, who had been softly weeping lets out a moan. Isa, to her side, fidgets in her seat before placing a palm on Doug's mother's back.

"That's good news?"

"Well I'm sorry to say your insurance doesn't cover human surgeons. Not anybody good enough to do this yet. They have some better bots up at Mt. Sinai, but we're waiting on some paperwork to get processed before we can helicopter you there."

Doug exhales, his torso aching. "How long will that take?"

The doctor shrugs, his lips pursed.

"And what should I do until then?"

The doctor downsizes the tablet and puts it in his breast pocket. He snaps on a pair of latex gloves and approaches Doug's bedside. He pulls apart Doug's eyelids with his thumbs and shines a light in one pupil, then the next. "It's more a matter of what you should not do. Namely move, eat, or drink."

"We'll at least I'll lose some weight," says Doug.

At this, the doctor laughs before sticking two fingers into Doug's mouth and palpating his tongue. "Having a sense of humor is good," he says. "It speeds up the healing process."

"_"

"_"

"_"

"Well your nervous system is starting to reboot," the doctor adds. "This is a good sign. Your charts indicate you've had lots of visitors too. I'm sure they'll keep coming."

"Do you know who?"

The doctor shakes his head. "Not besides these two. And me. But if you'll excuse me, I have to continue my rounds. Press the orange button to your right if you need a nurse."

"I've got one right here," Doug says, gesturing to his mom.

The doctor wags a latexed finger as he stands in the doorway. "Careful now. Remember, no moving." And he disappears.

"Are his visits always this brief?" says Doug.

"This is the second time anyone's come," replied Barbara. She crumples a tissue in her hand and deposits it on the face of the nightstand next to her.

"He didn't even give me his name." Doug could hear the languidness in his own voice.

The slow beeping of Doug's heart monitor marks time for the next hour and a half. Barbara, eager to F2F with her son, asks him many questions: how he feels, if he's hungry, if he had any dreams while comatose. Doug of course feels like week-old shit and is starving but solid foods were strictly prohibited by the nameless doctor and the morphine dispenser seems to be there to elicit a palliative placebo effect rather than provide any actual opiates, and no he didn't have dreams per se but maybe he could occasionally hear the spectral traces of the voices of those talking to him just past the limen of his consciousness. His responses are irritated and terse. The F2F soon turns to Barbara monologuing at the hebody. Isa is mostly quiet, though she looks like she is listening as well.

"I need caffeine," Barbara says at last. "My rounds start in 20 minutes."

"Okay."

Barbara winces and grimaces and clutches her fists in synchrony with her son. The mimicry, likely unconscious on her part, does not go unnoticed by Doug. Mother-child empathy being among the strongest relations two bodies can appreciate. That twenty-five years prior they were not two, but one shared body. Knowing that one's pain is not private but shared can be an extremely potent analgesic, Doug finds. But the painkilling effects of solidarity bring with it a festering guilt that you were somehow subjecting another to your own suffering.

Barbara kisses her son on his forehead. Her face is beetish and swollen from crying. "I'll be back in 8 hours," she says.

"Goodbye Mom. I love you."

"And I love you," she says, searching the tissue box for another Kleenex before leaving.

"Courtney Christ," says Doug. He tries to lift his head, but his greasy hair is matted to the pillowcase. "I've never seen her so worn."

"She's been at your bedside constantly," says Isa. "At least whenever I've come."

"How often have you visited?" says Doug.

"Daily."

Doug exhales through his nostrils. The pain of breathing had begun to dull just pass his threshold of awareness. "Thank you for that."

Isa chews at a hangnail on her thumb. "I'm scared of being anywhere else.

Futurabold was arrested last week. Harboring terrorists."

"I sim you feel worse about that than I do."

"Perhaps," says Isa.

"I doubt you're liable for arrest."

"I just don't want Halisdol to find me."

Despite the discomfort, Doug turned his head to look at Isa. "Melodica knows where you are anyway."

It surprises Doug when Isa chuckles at this. "I suppose you're correct," she says. "Though hopefully not for much longer."

"Do you know how much of this my Mom knows? Re: me getting shot," Doug asks. He had kept her largely in the dark with regards to his recent musical endeavors. It wouldn't even be that surprising if she had never noticed Takashi's boxy blue van parked in the garage through the spring and summer months.

Isa returns to going at the hangnail before speaking. "I don't know. She hasn't asked me anything. Maybe Takashi said something to her, but that would be too insensitive, even for him."

"She probably doesn't want to know. The fact that her only child was shot multiple times with a Desert Eagle is probably horrifying enough. Unravelling the narrative behind could only bring about more upset." Doug runs his tongue across his lips, flaky and chapped with dehydration. "When was Tak here?"

"A couple times in the past few days."

"Did he stay long?"

"Fifteen, twenty minutes. He talked to you the whole time."

"Figures. I can't imagine the hebody feeling comfortable with quiet for too long."

"I simmed that your mother found it sweet."

A shuddering exhale. Doug clicks the morphine button three more times. "Who else did I miss?"

"Mickey Mallorey put up a get well page for you on *Staph Infection*. You had 30,000 posters last I checked."

"You know I'm off social media."

Isa's visitats display a pointillist matrix of shifting blues and greens. "Julia came too."

Doug tries to spit, but he cannot not summon the moisture. It is as if each of his various bodily tissues— dermis, smooth muscle, bones—are all composed of sandpaper of varying grades of friction. "I'm glad I was comatose for that. I never want to see her again."

Isa shrugs. "The shebody was, well, lachrymose to say the least. I don't think I heard her say anything beyond how sorry she felt."

"Was she talking to you or me?"

Isa leans back into her chair. "Both of us I suppose."

An automated nurse rolls into the hospital room. It navigates around Isa to Doug's bedside with the slow, unceasing deliberation only non-organic agents are capable of performing. Its display is a simple smiling face with wide cartoonish eyes. The nurse extends a small limb with a sponged tip and sterilizes an exposed patch of skin on Lamarck-Ganoush's shoulder before tattooing a flurry of injections into his skin. Its childish visage does not change as it exits the room, save for a few animated blinks.

"You'd think they'd program it to at least say something to me before doing that," says Doug.

"It may still have you registered as comatose."

He runs his hands across his belly, lightly fingering the staples holding his wounds shut from over his paper hospital gown. "Maybe it just realizes how overrated consciousness is." He breaks his F2F with Isa, looking up at the fluorescents overhead. "And don't give me the whole spiel on having a bad attitude. I've said that to myself enough."

"I've never been the type for spiels."

"Yeah, I suppose you haven't."

For a brief moment, a closed-mouth smile shows itself on Isa's face before quickly neutralizing.

"They'll probably sue us when I'm out of here," said Doug. "Melodica, I mean. If nothing else because we didn't honor their recording contract."

"They've been an invisible hand guiding my life thus far," said Isa. "At least litigation is relatively visible. For me, that would be a change for the better." Another smile, this one toothy and longer lasting. Doug met it with a puzzled curl of the eyebrows.

"I apologize," said Isa. "I'm not good at making jokes."

"It was a solid effort," said Doug.

"_"

"_"

"_"

"That was a joke too," said Doug. "I guess I can't say I'm any better." He winced. "Whatever morphine drip they have me on is fucking with my words."

"I'm tempted to say fucking with words is the essence of being human," said Isa. "But that sounds a bit reductive."

The stinging in his shoulders help to distract Doug from the burning of shrapnel in his chest. "I can't believe my mom has had to endure this. I am crushed with guilt."

"None of this was your fault."

Doug chuckles, then winces. "You're starting to sound like a therapist now."

"I should know," says Isa. "I've been to enough of them."

"_"

"_"

"You know what's interesting?"

"Tell me," says Isa.

"What I said before. How I was 'crushed' with guilt."

Isa blinks.

"Well," Doug says, "I've spent so much time religiously holding on to the belief that there was some aspect of myself independent of, well, this." Doug slowly runs a hand down his torso. "I'm now starting to find though that all of the words that are used are tied to my body. Even if there was some piece of an immaterial soul connect-ed to my pineal gland, I don't even know how I would be able to talk about it."

"Elaborate."

"One can't speak without using metaphor. And all metaphors come from hav-ing a body. Think about it. Getting crushed is something that happens to your body. I'm trying to express some abstract emotional state, but I can't get past my own fleshy shell."

"I sim this upsets you."

"How could it not? To think that I am nothing more than a set of irritable bowels and a julienned cardiovascular system, all wrapped in pus-pocketed skin. It's all pretty fucked."

"Pretty fucked," Isa repeats. "One word is aesthetic, the other a bodily func-tion."

"My point exactly," says Doug, his speech turning slow and belaboured. "The limits of my language, the limits of my world, it's all in my overactive sweat glands and man-tits."

"You don't get to the limits of language," said Isa. "New ways of expressing oneself are always frothing up. Don't take that for granted."

"_"

"_"

"I think I've found it," Doug rasps.

"What?"

"The outer borders of all human expression. The pith of meaning-making. The Ur-truth."

"May I ask?"

"Banana," says Doug. "As sung by you." He forces a smile.

Isa swallows. "I don't think I can sing anymore," she says.

"Who says you could in the first place?"

Isa's visitats on her arms turn an explosion of fractals, a chaotic pattern neither Doug nor her had ever seen before. Her lips pursed, Isa begins to hum an im-provised tune. It is soft and in a minor key. The stuff of real lullabies sung by mothers to their young as they wriggle little limbs about in a slow but spastic proto-dance, training up neural circuits that would later allow them to crawl then walk then make their own song.

Isa's tune decrescendos to silence after a few bars. Doug is asleep; hers being the last human voice he would ever consciously hear.

V.3.0

SETS

Julia's boss looked underfed. Even when she stood several feet away from him, she could still smell his rank ketotic breath. Fortunately, Julia's workstation was on the other side of the office from Mr. Halisdol's. F2Fs with him were rare. He'd generally message her over her Lazy Eyes: the only required piece of dress at the Meadowlands Melodica complex.

The two of them were the only bodies in the office. At one point, the space would have teemed with engineers, though their own work had rendered the current need for them obsolete. The spacious room was otherwise populated by several potted shrubs in the corners and a stack of servers running along the southwestern wall. The servers would purr gently, harmonizing with the air filtration system. The office was otherwise silent, save the occasional reports of Julia's keystrokes on her old-fashioned plastic keyboard. She had specially requested the keyboard; no way would she type on those immaterial displays. She needed the give of cool plastic under her fingertips.

"Do you like children?" Mr. Halisdol asked, not looking at her. Instead, he directed his gaze out through the room's high expansive windows. This had to have been the third or fourth time he'd asked Julia this question since she started at Melodica.

Julia pushed herself back from her desk and turned to him. His irises glowed as he futzed around on his Lazies. He had a large projection of several strange attractor mappings that he manipulated with his fingers.

"I have no experience with them," Sets replied. "Check my CV."

Mr. Halisdol brought his index fingers to his chin and pursed his lips. He was silent for a long while before he blinked off his Lazy Eyes and turned to her. "So you don't like them?"

Julia sighed and returned back to her monitor. "No not really."

"Would working with children with developmental disabilities upset you?"

"That's not really my area of expertise."

"What about underprivileged youths?"

"--"

"Orphans. Children born into extreme poverty. Wards of the state."

"What age?" asked Julia.

"Toddlers at the oldest. Infants mostly."

Julia began to resume her coding. Perhaps that would get her supervisor to break off the F2F.

"So?" Mr. Halisdol pushed further after a couple beats.

Julia Sets exhaled. "I just don't know if I'm really qualified. I'm not really the caretaker type."

"You wouldn't be doing much caretaking. Just helping to implement software for parsing and analyzing data."

Julia pulled at her fingers, cracking her knuckles. "Well, if these kids were dealt bad hands, I suppose it's not their faults. I'm not really bothered by the idea of trying to help them."

Mr. Halisdol returned a smile. Sets could see both of his gum lines. "A degree of clinical distance is necessary for the work we'll be undertaking. It's not exactly for bleeding-heart types."

Secaucus smelled like dead birds. Even the building's air filtration system couldn't mask the stench completely.

"That's not to say a great number of individuals won't be helped by what we're trying to do," Mr. Halisdol continued. He sat back down at his desk.

Julia scanned her monitor: a thin screen split into four quadrants. Each was half a meter across. The top of the shell she was working in was a dragon's back of tabs across two different panels. "Whatever you say Mr. Halisdol," she said.

Since that morning, Julia's code wouldn't compile. It was an hour after lunch now. There was probably an errant semicolon camped out somewhere in the dozens of functions she had in front of her. During the year she'd spent at Melodica, Sets had been working specifically on the back-end implementation of various data filters for one of the company's many research projects. Data science wasn't her specialty at UZ, though it wasn't uncommon for alumni to enter the field after graduation. The details of any of the projects she was currently involved in were kept pretty hush-hush to lowly technicians such as herself. Melodica had a very closed-book corporate culture. She knew the company developed educational and developmental eupsychics technologies, though the exact products were a mystery to her. They certainly weren't making anything that showed up in classrooms or toy stores. Melodica seemed to have a large cash flow, but the inputs and outputs were indeterminate. At least based on her interactions with Mr. Halisdol, Julia could infer she was either currently developing studies involving children in need, or she would start shortly.

Mr. Halisdol was probably the only individual Sets encountered on a regular basis at Melodica. Throughout the enormous campus, she might occasionally see other employees walking to the restrooms or vending machines. Almost always they were too absorbed by their smart lenses to notice Julia, let alone F2F. Apparently, most of the other developers worked in the campus' sub-basement laboratory. Though Sets had card access, she'd never entered. There was no reason to. Sets enjoyed her workplace's lack of sociality in a manner common to data engineers. Even the cafeteria was sparsely populated at lunchtimes. Either Sets' colleagues took their meals at odd hours or they produced energy via autotrophy. Either way, Sets ate most of her meals in her own company.

Others might have found the corporate culture at Melodica stifling. To Julia, it was just mildly curious. Like why couldn't she call her supervisor "Evan," his first name? On her first day he had extended a sweaty palm and said, "Call me Mr. Halisdol." Julia had complied ever since. It wasn't alienating to her so much as perplexing. No matter though, it was not like she'd be dying to talk to him either way.

Maybe it was a sneaky company trick to encourage productivity, Julia simmed. As if by limiting her social prospects to only the most uncomfortable of individuals, Melodica had forced Sets' hand into immersing herself fully in her programming. There were no appealing interpersonal distractions.

For a man who constantly wore a straw hat, Mr. Halisdol didn't seem to comprehend the cardinal rule of good headwear etiquette: never wear one's hat indoors. The hebody kept his cheesy cap on constantly. It wasn't until four months into the job that Julia Sets learned he was balding. She then estimated that Mr. Halisdol must've been creeping up to his mid-forties age-wise, but a quick internet search told her he was instead just under thirty. Only a half-decade older than her, and Sets still had to call him Mr.

At least Julia could wear sweatpants and a t-shirt to work. Her boss often wore a tweed blazer, but he'd never vocalized any issue with her casual dress. And with the large windows shining artificial sunlight into the office year-round, Julia enjoyed getting some UV rays on the back of her neck and shoulders. It was more vitamin D than she ever got while in University.

Mr. Halisdol left for one of his frequent bathroom breaks. The hebody must have diabetes, he took piss-breaks so often. When the doors closed behind him, Julia was alone in the office. She was never eager to leave, even when she herself had to urinate. The air was warm and smelled perpetually of a springtime thoroughly different from the putrid aroma of the Meadowlands outside. She had a state of the art computer, and her chair could be set to massage her lower back, hamstrings and glutes whenever she wanted.

No massage chair could soothe her eyes though, aching with screen fatigue. Julia's code looked impeccable. She had stepped through all her programming, refactoring the thickets of monospaced type dozens of times. Nothing seemed to need patching, and yet no sensible output was produced whenever she ran it. She swiped out of her development environment and opened her email. Clearing her spam folder had the same cognitive effects for Julia as nicotine has on others: it was a quick procrastinatory measure that occasionally massaged her brain into insight.

Her spam folder was the usual litany of drek: Nigerian princes in need of fiscal consult and Lazy Eye applets that offered to scan for malware while rooting their own little worms. She snapped each email one by one into the trash bin. In the half century since its emergence on the world wide web, the conning tactics of spam hadn't changed all that much. It was laughable really. Perhaps it would take more than a few generations to weed out all the chumps from the gene pool.

Though one flagged message somehow was miscategorized by the server's spam filter. It was a message from an old college friend, Doug Lamarck-Ganoush. Julia marked it Not-Spam and opened it.

From: LamarckG@zappos.alumni.edu
Subject: No soap radio
Date: 6/25/42 11:44:32 PM EST
To: Julia.sets@melodica.meadowlands.com

Hey JS,

It's been a while. How's the real world? I'm sure you're working more efficiently now that I'm not numbing your eardrums with my theremin practice. I'm still playing drums with Takashi and Isa Spines, if you remember them. We're called New Ape Idea, and we play weekly shows in Hoboken. If you need a break from the corporate grind you should stop by. I know you're a recluse, so I've attached a recording of our last show. Apologies for the low quality and outdated file format. It was the best my phone could do.

Kind regards,
DLG

Julia twiddled her index and middle fingers, downloading and unzipping the attachment. She took a peek at the metadata and confirmed it was indeed recorded by Doug's old Nokia somewhere in Hoboken.

The shebody would be the last to deny that Lamarck-Ganoush was a competent musician. Back in University the two spent a lot of time in one another's company, usually in an unoccupied dorm room they had nicknamed "The Dojo." There, Sets would plug away at one of the many assignments from the several CS courses she was taking. Simultaneously, she'd switch back and forth between schoolwork and whatever MMO the school had her playing—she got in on an E-Sports scholarship after all. Student athletes had to learn to leverage distractions. They kept her wits sharp and her attention-span short, just as she liked it.

Lamarck-Ganoush meanwhile, would practice his theremin. He had a small Youtube channel where he would post grainy videos of himself playing some tune every week. He had mastered most of the classics, exhorting everything from Skrillex to Rimsky-Korsakoff from those two glass tubes. Though his channel only had a couple dozen subscribers, Doug practiced relentlessly. Together, the two of them honed their skill in mutual silence. Julia Sets never had simmed that DLG would wind up playing punk, though she never doubted talent like him would always find a way to keep making music.

The door slid open and Mr. Halisdol re-entered the office, mumbling to himself. He sat down in his chair and cleared his throat before blinking on his Lazies.

Julia dragged the audio file to her desktop and plugged earbuds in her ears. It was a welcome distraction from her work, and maybe Mr. Halisdol wouldn't try and speak with her while she listened. She clicked play and leaned back in her chair.

Her ears were awash with the din of a large crowd chatting and hollering at one another. There was a squeal of guitar feedback. She could hear Doug warming up on his floor toms while a bass and a guitar tuned their strings.

Eventually a chant snowballed out of the crowd. "Fucking play! Fucking play! Fucking play!" Their collective voice did not sound frustrated so much as eager. It was as if the band on stage was taking its time, almost flirtatiously, in order to build a riling anticipation in the crowd. After a half minute of cheering, Julia could hear a voice amplified by a microphone address the crowd.

"Well, Courtney Christ, I guess we don't have a choice now," it said. It was a recognizable tenor; could it have been that kid who roomed with Doug their freshman year? Julia remembered a lanky, frustratingly extroverted hebody with a strong, pinched-sinus Hudson County accent.

The crowd cheered. "My name is Takashi Miyagi-Edelstein, and we are New Ape Idea!"

Yep, that was the hebody alright.

Four snare clicks and New Ape Idea erupted into sound. The recording clicked, evidently the phone was jostled from its recording position by the bodies around it. The band was tight, its punk sloppiness evidently well-rehearsed. The guitar was driving, spewing a whorl of power chords and distorted hooks in an expertly controlled frenzy. It was complemented well by Doug's athletic drumwork. Despite his pudginess, that hebody had honed an incredible sense of hand-eye coordination from his theremin years. Maybe he couldn't climb a flight of stairs without losing his breath, but put that hebody behind a drum kit and suddenly he's an Olympian.

Though it was a male voice that introduced the band, Julia could hear a distinctly female yowl singing over the instrumentation. Perhaps "yowl" wasn't the right word: the shebody's vocalizing seemed to vacillate between a guttural scream dripping with pathos and a gentle maternal cooing. Though the lyrics pouring into the microphone were indeterminate, Julia had no doubt that she was hearing something poetic, maybe even profound. That much was obvious. Though the identity of the she-body singing was unknown to Sets, she felt a personal intimate connection with her crystallizing. Like the glassy threshold of her own ego was slowly growing porous. The recording was rough and over-compressed but Julia's synapses still snapped and tingled with excitement. She simply had to see this act live.

After a too-short two minutes the song ended and the audience burst into applause. Julia felt tempted to re-listen to that one tune, but she still had another 36 minutes of the recording ahead. She could feel her heart rate accelerating. She clicked pause and removed her ear buds, taking a deep breath to calm her body down.

"What was that?" Mr. Halisdol said. Julia spun her chair around to face him. He was looking directly at her, his back to his workstation. His Lazy Eyes were off too.   "What was what?"

"That music," Mr. Halisdol seemed to be stifling a smile.

"You could hear it?" Julia said.

"Of course," her supervisor replied.

Julia looked back at her computer. Her ear buds were unplugged from the audiojack. She must have had the recording blasting from the twin speakers at her desk.

"I'm so sorry," she began. "I didn't realize my ear buds were unplugged."

"No need to apologize. Just tell me, what is that band called?"

"_"

"_"

"New Ape Idea."

Mr. Halisdol blinked on his Lazy Eyes and turned back to his desk. He had switched to private browsing mode, there were no projections being emitted from his eyes, just a soft greenish glow to his irises. Sets remained facing him. Her boss seemed to be kneading his knuckles into one of his palms as he browsed the internet.

"So Isabel Spines is a member, no?" Mr. Halisdol said after a few beats. "Are you acquainted with her?"

"Who?" replied Julia.

"She's apparently the frontwoman."

"__"

"__"

"No. I don't know her," said Julia.

"But how'd you find a recording? Was that a bootleg? I'm reading that they haven't released anything, nor do they plan on it."

Julia pulled at the collar of her t-shirt. "Listen, I'm sorry if I was distracting you. I should really get back to my—"

"It's okay," Mr. Halisdol gave her another two-gummed smile. "I'm just curious."

"One of my good friends is the drummer," said Julia. "We went to school together."

"So that would be Doug Lamarck-Ganoush?"

"Yeah," said Sets. "Exactly."

Mr. Halisdol nodded to himself. "You know they are in trouble with the law right? Under police investigation for breaking and entering."

Julia swallowed. "I didn't know that. Doug never told me."

"Their records are more accessible than one might think," replied Halisdol. "Your friend, he may not have realized the full extent of it. They won't have to worry anymore. You can tell him that."

"__"

Mr. Halisdol nodded at her. "Our chief technologist is on very good terms with a large amount of the state's criminal justice system. We'll have them cleared of all investigatory charges."

Julia inhaled through her nose. "That's very kind of you," she managed to say. "But why are you doing this?"

"You know, I'm not a big fan of punk rock usually," said Mr. Halisdol. "Often I can't stand it, but I was enticed by what I heard."

"They've been getting a lot of attention for such a new band."

"Evidently," Mr. Halisdol cracked his knuckles. "Could you play the rest of the recording? I really enjoyed what I heard. You can tell them that too."

"Okay," said Julia.

"You will tell them that, right?" Mr. Halisdol stood and walked toward the window. He folded his hands behind him priest-like and looked at the marshes below.

"__"

"__"

"Okay, I'll tell them," said Julia before clicking play.

2.4.0 Selection

"You weren't referred by anybody?" says the hebody.

"No," replies Julia Sets.

"We have a big dropout problem with newly inducted bandsmen," says the other, a shebody. "They'll talk and talk about how much they want this lifestyle, only to flee back to modernity once they realize they'll go a few weeks without a hot shower."

"I understand," says Julia. "I'm here to commit."

"Commitment means a little more than doing the paleo diet from you apartment in Nanuet. Everyone's a hunter-gatherer faddist. Especially shebodies like you."

Julia tries to discreetly massage her right hamstring, where pins and needles are beginning to emerge. "What does that mean?"

"Sorry to profile," the bandsman continues, picking some schmutz out of his beard, "but these fair-weather primitivists are almost always white folk. They think this is their college year abroad or some shit and think this life's ideal for them because they read *Ishmael* as sophomores or something."

Julia looks toward the other. She seems to flare her nostrils in slight offense, but is otherwise silent.

"I already graduated university," says Julia. "If that helps."

"It really doesn't," says the bearded Neo-!Kung.

"Not at all," the other finishes. Her speech is coated with a mild Carolinian drawl.

The three of them sit on a dirt floor, sheltered by several birchwood joists supporting a large translucent tarp. The two Neo-!Kung bandsmen seem relaxed in a full squat, their glutes just grazing the earthen floor. Julia, not in possession of such flexibility, sits cross-legged on the ground. Her knees ache, and the whole tent smells vaguely gastrointestinal to her.

"Again," says the male Neo-!Kung, a broad-shouldered shirtless hebody whose long hair is matted to itself with grease, "Why are you interested in joining?"

Julia had found the encampment after spending several hours scouring a satellite mapping of Rockland County. The site was difficult to spot from above: the Neo-!Kung huts were camouflaged well with the surrounding conifers, and they were located far away from any major roads. She used a supervised learning algorithm to trace her as she scrolled around the map, only to let it run wild overnight. The next dawn she was presented with several possible camp site locations in the form of an array of histograms of oriented gradients. The site she was presently situated in was the first guess she had driven to.

"In all honesty," says Julia Sets, smoothing the wrinkles in her gray sweatpants against her thighs, "I'm in some trouble with the law."

Both the Neo-!Kung do not attempt to stifle their laughter.

"On the lam?" says the bearded one. He sports an anarchy A stick-and-poke on his wrist, though it seems faded with age, perhaps a remnant from adolescence. "Just what we need. Another suburban wastoid avoiding community service for dealing non-synth."

"It's nothing like that."

"You know, joining a federally-recognized terrorist cell may not be your best course of action if you wanna stay on the right side of the law," says the other.

"Terrorist cell?"

"Oh yeah," the beard adds. "As of two weeks ago. Maybe earlier. We don't really engage with the modern media."

"Such bullshit. Goddamn government trying to take away our guns is what it is."

Behind the two Neo-!Kung is a hand-carved wooden gun rack. On it sits a half-dozen military-grade assault weapons. Julia had purposefully avoided learning the exact type of gun that had killed Doug, not that it would even be there in front of her. They are cleaner than any other piece of equipment or food she has seen since entering the campsite.

"We here in the Neo-!Kung are like porcupines. We just go about, living our lives the way it was meant to be lived. We don't try and harm nobody, but when folks fuck with us, they get pricked."

"They get pricked real bad."

"You're nonconformists. Counter-culturalists," says Julia. "I get it. I used to have a lot of friends who were punks."

"Were they your clientele?"

Julia picks at the sole of one of her shoes. "I guess so."

"Some punks. Calling your ass in for dealing."

"That's not what I'm looking at time for," says Julia.

"Then what was it?" says the shirtless Neo-!Kung. He leans forward until his knuckles are on the ground.

"It was a bit more white collar," Julia replies.

"Goddamn," his partner says. "You're sure not gonna fit in here."

"Shut the fuck up May," says the other. "I'm intrigued."

Julia takes a long draw of air through her nose before speaking. "Corporate espionage."

"Shit."

"Where you're going," says May, "I don't blame you for wanting to hide out in the woods. You received your subpoena yet?"

"I'm not worried about prison," says Julia. "Or that is to say, alongside whatever illegal activities I may have done, I also screwed over a lot of friends."

"Corporate drones," says the other bandsman. "Fuck em. So you embezzled some funds? Dropped them down a tax-bracket? Most of those fuckers don't even have the emotional capacity for friendship, let alone sustaining F2F."

"They weren't my coworkers," says Julia. Already she can feel her throat begin to burn with stifled guilt.

May clicks her tongue. "You're so young too."

"All these finance types usually are."

"I wasn't in finance," says Julia. "I'm a data scientist. Research analytics."

"Ooh we gotta mung-hole over here," says the other. "I'm gathering you're really gonna have some trouble adjusting to the hunter-gatherer lifestyle. Sure is different from the world of numbers and stats."

"Like you'd know anything about that Raymond."

"Raymond?" says Julia, looking up. "That doesn't sound very hunter-gatherer-like to me."

"You reckon we change our names or something when we get here," May returns.

"That's what I've heard."

A smirk spreads across Raymond's face. "Some of us do. Again usually white girls who later drop out."

"That makes sense," says Julia. "Based on the one ex-member I knew."

"And that was?" May asks.

"Well I don't know what her name was here, but she now lives in Hoboken. She goes by **Futurabold** McRogers."

"Oof," says May. "You are really not doing a good job convincing us that the Neo-!Kung is right for you."

"Not at all."

"You didn't like her," says Julia, shifting her weight from one ass-cheek to the other.

"Couldn't stand her," says Raymond. "The shebody spent all her time playing anthropologist. Just like taking notes on us while we were hunting food or maintaining the campsite or whatever. Always standing there writing notes on her little pad."

"Lazy as hell. She was just watching us for some little intellectual endeavor of hers or some shit," says May. "Made only the feeblist attempts at pulling her own. When she wasn't exhausted to bits going on how appropriative our name was."

"Well" says Julia, knowing she had betrayed herself as soon as that syllable escaped her lips, "It's not like there are any actual !Kung people here." She swallows. "Per se."

"It's 2043, not 2017," spits May. "We can call ourselves what we like."

"Excuse us for not getting the chance to study anthropology at Zappos or Beats University or wherever," Raymond adds.

"_"

"_"

"I honestly never got to know her that well," says Julia. "We only F2F'd maybe once or twice."

"May and I couldn't stand her," says Raymond. "But she stayed on relatively good terms with a few other bandsmen. Plus now she employs a couple of our members. The extra cash flow is a nice thing to have."

"You use money?"

Raymond leans back on his haunches and cracks his knuckles. "I mean we don't, but several other members do."

"We need supplies, ammunition."

"Capitalism is a necessary ecological factor to contend with."

"I see," says Julia, nodding. "So some of you have to interact with the modern world."

"Sure," says Raymond. "We have an entire unit of Envoys, in charge of all modern interactions."

"Is that **Futurabold**'s job?"

"Was," says May. "Until she defected."

Julia exhales slowly. "You think I'll be another one like her, I sim. You'll think I'll weigh down the band before quitting, right?"

"Undoubtedly," says Raymond, smoothing his dark curly beard. "If it was my say, I would bar you from joining."

May nods, twirling at an auburn lock of hair.

"Well whose say is it?" says Julia.

The two Neo-!Kung share a look before turning back to Julia Sets.

"Well, it's yours," says May. "We can't stop you."

"So I want in—"

"—Then you're in."

"We believe us humans have an inalienable set of rights to live the lives Mother Nature designed us to," says May. "This is what life, liberty, and the pursuit of happiness is all about. It's against our credo to prevent any interested parties from joining."

"So there's no application, no test I have to pass?"

"Nope," says Raymond.

"Physical fitness requirements? Anything?"

"If you're interested," May begins.

"I am."

"Then welcome to the Neo-!Kung."

A machine-gun rapport cuts across the air. Julia yelps as she ducks and covers her head with her hands.

"Courtney Christ," she says, then looks up. "Are we under attack?"

"Nah," says May, rising to her feet. She approaches the gun rack, picks off a sawed-off Smith and Wesson and cocks it. "I'll be right back," she says, and exits the tarp.

"Damn," says Raymond, still squatting. "Must've been a sizable kill." He side-eyes Julia, who says nothing. "You sure you really want to commit to this?"

"Good hunt!" hollers May, before Julia can muster a response. She lifts the entrance flap to the tarp and peeks inside. "Three wild turkeys," she says. "You picked a good day to join, uh—"

"Julia."

"Right, Julia."

Raymond stands to his feet and stretches his arms. Although likely an older hebody, his body is tight and sinewy from a forager's lifestyle. He unracks an Uzi and gestures with his head for Julia to approach. Getting up from the ground is much more difficult for her. Her legs ache and her back is tight and hunched from years of slinging code seated at a desk. Julia Sets approaches Raymond and reaches for a gun.

Raymond slaps her hand. "You've got any experience with these kinda arms?" Julia shakes her head no.

A histrionic sigh. "You'll learn eventually. But not now." He cocks the Uzi and ushers Julia outside the lean-to.

The Neo-!Kung campsite is a strange attractor of foragers in motion and ad-hoc huts and tents like the one Julia had just exited. All the buildings are open-air. Some older installations take the form of thatched huts, carefully engineered to withstand summer superstorm and brutal winter alike. Several modest lean-tos and tents dot the forest clearing in equal numbers. Many of the younger bodies are at work, thatching foliage, carrying buckets of water or berries from shelter to shelter, though even more are at rest. Topless mothers sit on oak stumps and gossip as they breastfeed their young around a fireless pit. Their guns sit unloaded on the ground. Their older children shout and ambulate around them, locked in some fluid game with dynamic rules. Inside one of the bigger buildings, a heavily visitatted hebody strums an out of tune acoustic guitar. A pair of broken eyeglasses sit crookedly across the bridge of his nose. As he sings, a bevy of ex-hipsters join in, tapping their bodies or the floor in percussive synchrony. They bellow a cover of *The Battle Hymn of the Republic*, though as far as Julia can hear, with altered lyrics.

> *"My eyes have seen the glory of our species' oldest truth.*
> *I suffered in modernity before the Neo-!Kung.*
> *Foraging and gathering's what we were built to do,*
> *The hunter marches on."*

"Over there," says May. She points to two burly hebodies emerging from the pines. They drag the still-twitching corpses of three birds behind them. The turkey's heads appeared to be blown completely off; staccato jets of blood spurted from their necks, creating a dotted maroon trail behind them.

Raymond and May take off toward the hunters. What is a light jog for them is a near sprint for Julia. She catches up to the other bandsmen, her face flushed and her breath heavy and phlegmy. The thongs of her flip-flops had drawn blood from the webbings between her big and index toes.

"You should go barefoot," May says. Julia can see that all the other Neo-!Kung are without shoes. Their feet are thick and hard with round knobby callouses.

Both Raymond and May hand their weapons to the returning hunters. They turn on both their safeties. The Uzi is holstered, while the other drops the turkey and takes the shotgun in both hands, making sure to keep the barrel out of line with any of the other bodies. Raymond takes one of the fowl and tucks it under his arm, the pressure of which causes a large ejaculation of blood behind him. May follows suit.

Julia gets down to the ground on her knees and puts her arms under the dead turkey. It gives one last life-like shake, causing Julia to yelp and withdraw. The four bandsmen laugh loudly. Julia repositions herself and manages to lift the fowl, though not without a large amount of blood staining her sweatshirt and pants.

She shudders. "I don't know if I can do the hunting thing."

Raymond chuckles. "Nobody ever was considering you for that." He shares a look with the other two hebodies. They look older and are a bit huskier than Raymond, and their smiles evince a lack of routine dental hygiene.

"New recruit?" says one. "You'll be foraging for berries and legumes."

"She's got a bit of fat on her," says the other. "Might make a suitable breeder."

A wave of nausea breaks across Julia. Though not without a libido, the shebody had little sexual experience beyond internet porn and the occasional paycam of some anonymous hebody. Simming intercourse with any of the specimens around her elicited feelings ranging from apprehension to disgust. And she only could cognize the idea of carrying and birthing their offspring in the most abstract of ways. Anything more detailed might cause her to drop the turkey.

"What about working as an envoy?" says Julia. "I can mediate between us and them."

May drops her bird in a large woven straw container. Raymond and Julia follow suit.

"That will not happen for a long time," May replies. "We only let our oldest, most longstanding members do that kind of work now. The kind of bandsmen who will be least likely to be seduced by the outside world's evils. "

"But that couldn't have always been the case," says Julia. Her hands are slimy with turkey entrails. She picks little bits of feather out of her clothes.

"You're right, it wasn't," says May. "But we've had enough ex-bandsmen like your friend in Hoboken leave us that we had to make a band-wide rule. And we generally hate making band-wide rules."

"What'd I say bout these white girls?" says Raymond. He nods to two potbellied middle-aged shebodies. Their breasts are uncovered and they wear tattered visors on their foreheads. The women squat down by the turkeys and begin defeathering them, their stubby fingers moving with a sort of unconscious mastery brought about by hours upon hours of practice.

"I just," says Julia. "I don't know if I can, well, be a breeder." Even saying the word left the sting of bile on her tongue and throat.

"We wouldn't force you to do that," says May.

"Even hunting. I mean, I can learn. But I don't think I have the physical fortitude to do that all day."

"Believe us," says Raymond, "Nobody was thinking that here." And the other hebodies laugh, again.

A bellowing mechanical sound cuts across this sky. Julia compresses her palms to her ears by instinct.

"What was that?" she asks.

"Probably nothing," says Raymond. "A surveillance chopper, maybe." Raymond nods to the other hebodies and takes his Uzi. They brandish their shotguns and follow him into the pines.

Julia looks toward May. She seems unfazed, squatting down and assisting the women with the defeathering.

"None of this work is 'all day'," says May, curling fingers smeared with blood into quotes around her speech. "Any one of us puts in only maybe 2 or 3 hours of labor into the band a day. The bulk of our time is spent doing, well, this." She gestures out to the rest of the encampment: a panoply of gossip, music, and recreation.

"I worked 65 hours a week at my last job," says Julia. "And data science is supposed to be cushy." She takes a seat with the rest of the shebodies but does not touch the turkey carcasses.

"Humans are not meant to live like that," says May. "Life is to meant to be enjoyed. Savored. That's what we do here. It's an adjustment initially, but in time you'll learn to be quite happy here."

"Then why so many defectors?"

The three shebodies pause from preparing the bids and look up at Julia.

"It's a minority of bandsmen that leave," says May. "But the outside world is brimming with addictive technologies. It's impossible to live a life of meaning and balance out there. Not when you're constantly trying to manage a schizophrenic set of social media personalities and stressing about the strength of the Wi-Fi routers embedded under your skin."

"Those are mostly for show. You know, a fashion accessory. I don't think people actually get too worked up about the signal strength of their subdermals," says Julia.

Another bellowing mechanical chopping. This time the sound is much more obviously that of a low-flying helicopter.

"I hear now you can embed your computer into your contact lenses," says one of the older shebodies, yanking off the last white down of the turkey's breast.

"Those have been around for years," says Julia.

"It's poison," says May. "But this," she continues, holding her bird up-side-down by the legs, "This is intimacy."

Julia gives a tacit nod.

"What are you waiting for?" says May. "Get intimate!"

Suppressing her hesitation, Julia begins to pluck one of the birds, one feather at a time. The other shebodies unsheathe knives from their waistbands and begin to eviscerate the bodies, dumping the entrails into the original straw container.

"What's your name?" says the elder to Sets, forgoing eye-contact.

"Julia."

"_"

"Here," says May, "Why don't you take the innards to the cooking tent. It's the hut about 500 meters south."

"Okay," says Julia, lifting the wicker basket up with both hands. Already a small cloud of black flies have begun to buzz around her. "Is there, like, a composting area I should dump them in?"

"Give them to one of the cooks," says May. "We're eating that, not tossing it."

The organs, a pinkish bloody mass of indiscernible tissues, jiggles with each step Julia takes. She can hear more helicopter sounds, and in the distance a sort of rhythmic chanting coming from an array of baritone hebodies. The words are indecipherable.

"Hey!" yells Raymond, sprinting toward her from the forest. "Get a fucking gun!"

"What?" says Julia as he passes by her.

"Drop whatever you're doing and arm yourself."

"I've never shot a gun before," Julia says, but Raymond was already out of earshot. She drops the organ basket to the ground and begins to double back to the fire pit. The encampment snaps into a sound vacuum. There is no music, no playful hoots and shouts, only Julia's heavy breath and plodding footsteps. In her peripheral vision she can see young children carried by their mothers into the larger buildings. Those beyond a certain threshold of fine motor-development carry pistols and light crossbows and hide themselves behind boulders and felled logs.

"Damn Feds," Julia can see May mouth as she cocks her shotgun.

"What is going on?" Julia pants as she approaches her.

May turns toward her. "Our rights are being robbed from us is what's happening. You need to arm yourself."

"I don't know how," says Julia. The corners of her eyes begin to sting with panicked tears.

"Time to learn," says May. "If we're a terrorist organization those Feds can kill us on sight. The semi-automatics are the easiest to use."

"My car is a quarter-mile away," says Julia.

"And?" says May.

"If we can get to it we can drive away. Pretend we're hikers or something."

"I'd let you do that an hour ago, but you joined the band. This is tribalism. Only if—," May says before catching a stray round in her left eye socket. She sways and falls to her side onto the screaming Julia.

The screaming of a rocket propelled grenade Dopplering overhead. The projectile hits the blades of a drone copter the size of a lap dog, which spirals into the eaves of a pine tree.

Sets' mouth tastes salty with nerve tissue and blood. Though May is waifishly thin in comparison to her own mass, Julia is brought down to the ground by the shebody's limp weight. Julia heaves the seizing body off of her and rolls onto her stomach before crawling her way into the fire pit. There at least she would have some cover from the endless reports of gunfire tattooing through the air all around her. She reaches out and blindly gropes for May's shotgun. Her fingertips graze cool metal and Julia is quick to pull the gun into the pit and hold it tight against her breast.

The sky is a cloudless, sunless blue. Two black helicopters fly by before descending to the ground. Julia rotates herself slowly, trying to get a better view of federal agents in their all-black Kevlar pouring from the bellies of the choppers while still playing dead. Though not a sliver of unprotected skin can be seen, a few of the Feds crumple bloodlessly from the expert marksmanship of a bandsman peeking out from behind an evergreen. The whirling helicopter blades now obfuscate the noise of any gunfire or death songs from federal agent and bandsman alike. Though, curiously, the loudest sound of all is Julia's own cardiovascular workings. The oceanic whoosh of her deep, urgent breaths and the hummingbird palpitations of her heart against her aching, anxious ribcage.

U pon reawakening from his post-set schluff, Takashi reentered
Futurabold's office. He'd gotten into the habit of taking naps after shows. First
he'd chat with the audience for a little while; swap stories, give tips to up-and-comers,
generally shoot the shit. What band is successful without self-promotion, he figured.
When the copious F2Fing grew too exhausting, he'd retreat into the back room for a
cig and a rest. Now, his joints aching, his tongue mossy with stale smoke, he navigates
through the near-empty concert-space with the unconscious precision of a sleepwalker.
He mumbles meaningless phonemes to himself, his oratory circuits unaccustomed to
staying silent for more than a few minutes.

    Futurabold's Uncle Dee sat on a wooden stool outside the doorway. The
neck brace he wore bunched the fat of his jowls up around his cheekbones, giving him
the appearance of a sedated bulldog. His eyes shifted toward Takashi, but he said nothing as the hebody passed him by.

    Inside, Doug and Isa were locked into their own post-show rituals. Doug was
sitting on an overturned milk crate reading a loggy paperback by some dead neurol-

ogist named Feldenkreis. Doug claimed the text helped him drum better; it allowed him to totally reframe his mind/muscle connection or something. While he read, he sat up straight, his spine perfectly erect.

Isa was slouched against the wall. After shows she'd immediately retreat to **Futurabold**'s office. Members of the audience would mob her otherwise. With each passing performance, the crowds that filled Rule 30 grew bigger and bigger. **Futurabold** couldn't even stand on the sidelines and watch, the venue would get so packed. The audience now always chanted Isa's name too. Before New Ape Idea took the stage and when they exited. And Isa never was one to bid affection from anyone, let alone the audience. She still performed with her back to them and her eyes shut tight. That shebody was so cool her temperature couldn't break into the double digits, Kelvin. Alone in the office, Isa tended to spend large amounts of time tuning her guitar. This attention to tuning was useful before shows, but redundant once they were off stage. She leaned over, her blue Jazzmaster slung across her torso, and plucked the strings as she twisted the instrument's chrome tuners contemplatively.

Meanwhile, **Futurabold** sat at her desk staring at her computer screen. She pressed her index and middle fingers to her lips as if to mime smoking a cigarette. Though she made eye contact with Tak, she passed over his entrance in silence.

Takashi planted himself in the middle of the room. He began whistling a few bars from an old Dennis Vreeman Sodomizes Gandhi in Purgatory tune, hoping to capture some attention from the others. It was ineffective. The hebody cracked each of his knuckles, then his neck, then his knuckles again.

"Gonna take a nap," Tak said and about-faced.

"Can you headline another show on Wednesday?" **Futurabold** said.

Doug glanced at him from his paperback. Tak turned back toward the shebody. "Why?" Tak asked.

"Remember the hebody who you kicked in the chest two shows ago?" said **Futurabold**.

"Not particularly." Tak preferred to jump around the stage, playing grabass with the pit. He'd pluck at his bass and play grab ass with the moshers at the lip of the stage. Sometimes things would turn playfully violent, but hey it wasn't a good punk show unless somebody's nose was bleeding by the encore, right?

"He's the frontman of a band called Greenberg's Sphincter. I had them booked for Wednesday. He just messaged me. Apparently after taking your steel-toed boot to his solar plexus, he has hairline fractures in three of his ribs. He says he's in too much pain to perform, so I have to rebook."

"Courtney Christ, is he okay?" said Doug, casting a consternating look at Takashi. "Do you think he's the litigious type?"

"He's fine," replied **Futurabold**. "The hebody is excited enough that he came into physical contact with a member of the great New Ape Idea. Apparently, he sold his t-shirt with Takashi's footprint to a kid in the crowd for 2K."

"Only that much?" Tak had an ebullient grin smeared across his face.

Both **Futurabold** and Doug rolled their eyes. Isa's gaze was still focused on her Jazzmaster.

"I suppose we could cover a Wednesday," Takashi said. He nodded at Doug, who returned the gesture.

Futurabold waved her finger in the air in front of her monitor, likely marking off a calendar. "I'm considering making it permanent. Could you do every Wednesday for the next two months?"

Takashi smirked. "How big of a cut from ticket sales are we gonna get?" he answered.

"You want a cut now?" said **Futurabold**.

Takashi pulled a red milk crate across the floor. It emitted a thin friction groan as he did so. "Your ticket sales must be at an all-time high—"

"—Bands have always sold out shows at Rule 30."

"Yeah, but you paid most of 'em right? We're local. No gas costs. Nothing. If you want us to play, yr gonna have to pay."

"You're not our manager," interrupted Doug.

"Shut up DLG," said Tak. "Yr just as broke as I am." He sat.

Futurabold scaled down her screen and pushed it to the side before leaning over her desk toward Takashi. "I thought letting you play here was a favor. You needed asylum. I said I'd give it to you for a few months, and I've followed through. Besides, it's not very DIY to ask for payment."

"Well I built you a computer and brought in absurd ticket-sales on the regular," Takashi folded his arms across his chest.

"With stolen software—"

"Pirated!" said Takashi quickly. "And upgraded by hand. Don't pretend it isn't, like, the greatest, sleekest, most useable OS you've ever encountered."

Futurabold engaged a strange matrix of facial muscles, forming a weird smile-smirk, at least as far as Takashi could scan. He couldn't sim whether any of his arguments were effective or not.

"You want extra cash, start selling some merch," **Futurabold** said. She neutralized her facial expression and looked at Takashi in silence.

Doug laid the Feldenkrais paperback across his lap, careful not to bend the spine. "Takashi," he said, "**Futurabold** has done us a favor, letting us play here. We don't need extra conflict." He raised a didactic finger up, swallowed what he was about to say next, and lowered it.

"A favor?" Tak snapped. "Puh-leeze The Neo-!Kung profiteer is working us over while fattening her wallet. We owe her nothing."

"I'm putting myself at legal risk harboring you," **Futurabold** said.

"You think any of the other punk bands you put up here don't have a crimi-nal record?"

Futurabold sat back in her chair. "Probably not. This isn't like it was fifty years ago. Punk is just a word; a label suburban poseurs affix to themselves. Most self-avowed punks don't have much on their records other than 'honor student'."

"Not us! We're the real thing!" said Tak, happy to be speaking in earnest. "And we fill up Rule 30 night after night because of that. Because we're not just po-seurs!"

"Speak for yourself," said Lamarck-Ganoush.

"Rule 30 fills up because there is nowhere else to go," said **Futurabold**. "Those 'real' punk bands live in their van and, well, tour. From what I gather."

"We could go on tour—"

"And what? Transport millions of dollars of stolen goods across state-lines? You know the police will inspect your vans at the borders. Unless you try and cross through Neo-!Kung territory. And you'll need either lots of money or an inside connection to do that." She smirked. Was she blackmailing them? It seemed uncharacteristic of **Futurabold** to threaten to sick the paleo-people with their guns on New Ape Idea if they defected from her venue.

What was **Futurabold** trying to say? Did she think Tak was a poseur? Takashi tried to sim **Futurabold** simming him back. The recursion of mind-read-ing made him dizzy. He realized he was grimacing and twisted it into a smirk.

Paranoia was Takashi's primary mental state. A constant fear that his thoughts in all their surreal perversity were somehow leaking out from his head and into the atmosphere for all to see. That every other person was cued in to some impossibly accurate real-time transcript of his thoughts but was too mortified or polite to ever tell him.

"I'd just like to be able to receive some compensation for my work here." Takashi muttered. "Exchange some of my services for capital. It's basic economics."

"Three unemployed UZ grads hungry for money," **Futurabold** smiled coyly, fingering the top ridge of her monitor. "You could get a job. Work as a code monkey, I'm sure there are thousands of gullible contractors deluded enough to hire you."

"And you would be out of a band."

"If you want to earn anything substantial," said **Futurabold** frankly, "Why not record an album?"

"And have it pirated?"

"So now, Mr. Miyagi-Edelstein, you are anti-piracy?"

Recording was, in itself, a problem for New Ape Idea. If situated in a record-ing booth with flat snowshoe condenser mics and a sound-board with an impossible number of switches, the three would be doomed to sound ordinary. Like the semi-amateurs they were.

Takashi recognized this from their first show. A recording booth would deprive them of a necessary context for their sound. What transformed Doug, Isa, and him from three musical bumpkins toeing up against poseurdom, to the primal punks of New Ape Idea was Rule 30. Or, more importantly, the élan of a few hundred visitatted punks thrashing out their collective discontents for Takashi's SHANNON to blend with Isa's voice.

Tak took a moment to crack his knuckles in satisfaction, simming it all. Though far from the musical talent that Isa or even Doug was, Takashi felt he had successfully earned his place in the band. Sure DLG and Spines had ability, but the SHANNON added a new dimension of nuance to their sound. It allowed them to sing the siren song of the pit's own moshing back to itself. The SHANNON was the necessary feedback component that turned a chaotic phase-space into a dynamical system. Without the necessary left hand side of the equation: mosh pit + SHANNON, there could be no equivalence to the right: New Ape Idea. During practice the band sounded flat, weak, banal.

"It makes sense you joined the Neo-!Kung," said Takashi to **Futurabold**, smiling with calculated insouciance. "You are a natural-born capitalist."

"Excuse me?"

"I bring you millions, maybe billions of dollars of new equipment plus revenue," Tak attempted as best he could to affect a cocktail of Japanese humility with Jewish guilt, head bowed slightly, voice nasalized, "And you only seek to alienate me from my creative labor, like—"

"—Shove it up your ass," said **Futurabold** sharply. She resized her monitor and pulled it in front of her face. Perhaps Marxist rhetoric was not the best approach to win over an ex-anarcho-capitalist, Takashi thought. Good thing **Futurabold** stopped him then, he was just about to quote Adorno.

Doug leapt up to his feet, folding the book under a dampened armpit as he did so. The hebody seemed to be moving faster in recent weeks, Takashi had noticed, maybe lost a few lbs around the chin too. Isa looked up as well with an expression of consternation mixed with surprise. Her hands remained on the Jazzmaster.

Doug took several slow breaths, in through the nose out through the mouth while he spoke. His voice was level. "Please Takashi, let's not bite the hand that feeds."

"You call this feeding?" Takashi could feel a vein showing itself on his forehead.

Doug cleared his throat, as if summoning the logical faculties necessary to counter Takashi's remonstrance. Meanwhile, **Futurabold**'s nostrils flared. Takashi had never seen the shebody—normally cool and nonchalant—so royally pissed.

"I'm with Tak," said Isa, setting the blue axe by her side.

The other three shared a quick glance, with looks of surprise plastered across their faces. Takashi himself frothed with a sort of warm pride, like that of a parent whose mute child uttered her first words.

But with its old tweedle-dee ringtone, Doug's caveman Nokia flip-phone had to ruin Tak's scheppin nachas. Courtney Christ, the phone must've been from 2010. Didn't Doug at least get a training smartphone back when he was in kindergarten?

"Excuse me," said Doug in a hush as he pulled the brick of Finnish plastic out of his cargo shorts. He depressed a button on the phone's side, silencing it.

"If I'm going to continue to vocalize for an audience, I'd like to at least get payment for it," said Isa, an unusual fierceness in her expression. "I've been playing with the idea of quitting. Or, rather, at least stepping down from vocals."

"Why?" said Takashi, breaking the ensuing silence.

"I hate singing," she said.

"So, what's new?" said Takashi. "You always hated singing."

"You fail to simulate. I *loathe* it. I feel nauseous. The crevices of my brain fill with pus."

"Well Isa," Doug started, "You're really talented at it. Perhaps you don't realize your own potential. Bad posture can do that."

"I should correct myself," said Isa. An expanding Mandelbrot set worked its way across her forearm. "It is not the singing I loathe, rather, it is the singing in front of others."

"Stage anxiety," said **Futurabold**.

"How do you even see the crowd?" said Tak. "You keep yr back to 'em the whole time."

"I am still aware of their presence."

Again, the trebly digital ringtone of Doug's phone cut in. Takashi could hear it hum and vibrate in Doug's pocket.

"How does that still work?" Tak, massaging his temples.

Doug coughed a bit. "I, uh, well, I take good care of my belongings. It was my Dad's. From when I was a toddler."

"If you need money, you should sell that. I'm sure the Smithsonian would put it on display," said **Futurabold**. "It must be an antique."

"Worthless," said Takashi. "Maybe save for the little powdered gold inside some of the transistors. We have landfills full of these. Besides—"

"—It has sentimental value," Doug added.

"Well, turn it off!" said Tak. "Or put it on vibrate. Or something."

"I can't shut it off," said Doug. "I'm afraid I'll blow the system when I turn it on again. It's a very fragile device."

"It's a fucking Nokia," said Tak.

It rang again, causing Takashi to tug at one of his blonde spikes. Doug flipped the screen up, the phone giving an audible plastic clack as it did so.

"Excuse me," he said. His shorts made a swishing sound as he exited **Futurabold**'s office and closed the door behind him.

Tak eyeballed the closed door. "Well," he said. "If we were to take a vote, of all currently present on the issue of New Ape Idea's future payment, I would suspect you would be outnumbered, Ruthie."

"Don't call me Ruthie," **Futurabold** said. "You didn't know me then."

"Uh huh. All in favor of future compensation in the form of a percentage of the box office revenue to New Ape Idea, please raise your hand." Takashi grinned at **Futurabold** monkey-like as he raised his.

"Look behind you," she said. He turned to see Isa palms were at her sides.

"What? Spines, I thought you said—"

"I said I'd prefer compensation if I am to keep singing. However, ideally, I would prefer not to sing at all."

"Well, that screws us both," Tak said to **Futurabold**.

"How so?" **Futurabold** replied.

"If Isa won't sing, we have no band. You have no profit. We're at a stalemate."

From outside Takashi could hear the muffled sound of Doug pacing, talking on his phone.

"Why can't you just put a video on your Lazies or something?" Tak craned his head around to Isa, his body followed suit. "It's the 21st century rule for social anxiety: Stare at a screen with your digital happy place until the presence of all others seems to evaporate."

"I would," said Isa, "but I've been playing blind."

"Excuse me?"

"I lost my Lazy Eyes. Two months ago. I haven't found them since."

"Couldn't you buy another pair?" **Futurabold**, kneading the knuckle of her index finger.

"Nah. Too expensive."

"Aha!" Takashi extended a digit up in the air. His nail overgrown and purpled from vigorous bass playing. "A classic triple bind. Each of us is imposing a condition making the wishes of the other impossible to actualize." Takashi brought his finger to his lips and began to gnaw at his nail in contemplation. He unearthed a bit of the dirt caked beneath the keratin with his teeth.

The door creaked as Doug opened it, panting as he entered the room. Beads of sweat dribbled down his neck, zig-zagging around his stubble like metal balls in an old plinko game.

"We're having a vote," said Takashi without missing a beat. "Do you think we should be getting a slice of ticket income?"

"Did **Futurabold** consent to this?" Doug asked.

"You think democracy requires complete consent?" was all **Futurabold** replied.

"I voted for no conflict." Doug said.

"No longer an option, DLG."

"Well," Doug pulled a handkerchief out of one of his bulbous pockets and dabbed at his neck and brow. "I suppose I vote for payment. But we may have other options."

"See!" said Takashi. "Fifteen percent. Five for each of us."

"Other options?" Isa picked up her guitar and slung the strap over her shoulder. She chucked out a muted chord.

"I received a phone call from an old friend from university—"

Takashi emitted a loud guffaw. "A phone call? Seriously?"

"My phone was ringing."

"I can't tell if that's hip or obnoxious," said Takashi. "She couldn't, like, email you?"

"She apparently tried, but got no response."

"Who was this?" said **Futurabold**, leaning over her desk.

"Julia Sets. A good friend of mine."

"Your girlfriend from sophomore year?"

"Not exactly girlfriend, wasn't that sort of shebody."

"But she was always with you when you practiced theremin."

"This is true," said Doug. "Apparently, she's working for a satellite R&D department for some microtech company. She heard a bootleg I sent her of our first show and, for reasons indeterminate, her company is looking to book recording artists, and she'd like to have us come in."

"You recorded us?"

"With my phone," said Doug. "I keep recordings of all my musical endeavors. It was a habit I developed back when I had my theremin."

"Why didn't you tell me?" said Takashi. "Us."

"I didn't sell it or anything like that," replied Doug. "Just a few low-fi recordings for Babs and a few friends. They came out surprisingly well given the limited capacities."

Takashi pivoted the ball of his foot into the shag carpet below, rotating it back and forth as he thought. "You realize, whatever deal they may offer us, Lamarck-Ganoush, we will likely not be able to sound anything like we do live. Different SHANNON parameters and all."

"I assumed that," said Doug. He looked toward Isa; she seemed unusually interested in the conversation. "Though, I'm not exactly sure they want to do anything traditional with us. At least not in a standard record deal. You know, make a whole applet with audio and visual effects for mass consumption. They're a microtech company, after all."

"So what do they want with us?"

"Again, indeterminate."

"A phone call," said Isa. "It makes me shudder."

"What do you mean?" said Takashi.

Isa shrugged and shook her head. "Speaking into a microphone and having another's voice spoken directly into your ear. It's so, well, intimate." She sat back down on the crate and twiddled at one of the potentiometers by the Jazzmaster's bridge. "How does one stand it? Why not send a message. Something written, typed out, epistolary."

"Sets did try to contact us apparently," said Doug. "For weeks. The call was a last resort."

"I saw nothing," said Takashi. "And I'm pretty vigilant about this kinda stuff."

"She apparently also sent a message to **Futurabold** via Rule 30's website."

"Strange," said **Futurabold**, "I didn't see anything either."

"Hold on," said Takashi, "Lemme see." He walked around her desk, trailing the pads of his fingers along its wooden top as he did so.

With an audible exhale **Futurabold** stood, relinquishing the black desk chair to Takashi who took it without looking at her.

In a series of movements, so fluid and skilled they required little conscious thought, Tak picked up the monitor from the desk top, affixed it to its stand and expanded it into a Golden rectangle. Like the conductor of a symphonic orchestra he waved his hands in the air, sliding through screens and windows. **Futurabold** watched silently. He hoped she was taking mental notes.

"The only results I'm getting for the search terms 'Julia' or 'Sets' are irrelevant. 'Sets' is giving me way too many set-length requests from booking bands, but I don't find much scanning over them," he said. "What was the name of the company she works for?"

"Something like 'Melodica'," said Doug.

"Spelling?"

"Unsure."

"Say it again," Tak ordered.

"Melodica."

"Like the keyboard?"

"Yes," Doug replied.

"Say it again. Slower and more loudly."

"ME-LO-DI-CA."

"Thank you," said Takashi all singsong. "I'm running a search using your voice input and a text-to-speech patch." He thumbed at his nose. "Still nothing."

"How bizarre," said **Futurabold**.

"Agreed," Doug wiped at the lens of his glasses with the bottom hem of his shirt.

"Ah! Hold on, I've got it," Takashi popped a little bit out of his seat as he spoke. He twirled his index and middle fingers in a spiraling pattern like an amateur hypnotist, lips closed but obviously grinning behind them. "Yes, she's been emailing us, several times now for the past 22 days."

"So why didn't we get it?" Doug asked.

"For whatever reason, all the messages were filtered out as spam."

"How could that be?" said Doug. "The Gmail accounts from school?"

"Rule 30 isn't on the UZ server," said **Futurabold**.

"Correct," Tak added, eyes still glued to the giant translucent screen. "I built the spam filtering system myself."

"So was it a bug?" Doug, like c'mon.

"As I said, I built the system myself. There are no bugs."

"So what was—"

Tak swatted his hand in front of him, as if batting away Doug's nagging. He initiated two media players and an internet browser in doing so. "I'm looking, I'm looking. Oy." Takashi called upon the laser keyboard and typed soundlessly while the other three waited. "Bizarre," he said. "Sets tried to reach us through her company email address right? But it was filtered out because it was a governmental ISP."

"State?" said **Futurabold**.

"Nah, Federal," said Takashi, bewildered.

"Why are messages from governmental ISP filtered out?" said Doug.

"Mostly cuz they piss me off."

"Maybe **Futurabold** would want those messages—"

"I was under the impression that **Futurabold** is a punk."

"I just study them," she said.

Takashi rolled his eyes.

"Even so," said Doug. "We're in a legal snafu, shouldn't we be keeping a close eye on anything we get from the government, not shuffling them away?"

"What, are the feds gonna subpoena us via email?" said Takashi.

"Not my point," said Lamarck-Ganoush.

"You never have one, boyo."

"Are we back to that again?"

"What does she ask?" said Isa.

Doug approached the desk and read over Takashi's shoulder he said.

"Wants us to record something for R&D," said Takashi. "The fuck?"

"She's offering us a tour of the facilities," said Doug. "Maybe this will make more sense in that context."

Tak squinted to read. "In Moonachie? Ugh! How are we s'posed to get there?

Motorboat?"

Doug swallowed, moved away from the monitor and retook his seat on the milk crate. "I guess we're driving," he said.

2.6.0
Asylum

The automated emergency room doctors had wrapped Halisdol's hands with thin clear bandages to protect them from infection while the spray-on dermis grafts itself to his palm and fingers. The whole healing process was said to take no more than a few hours, though it has been almost two days and the burn blisters aren't fully healed. Tasks involving fine digital movement such as typing or writing are painful, and Halisdol's hands constantly itch even when they are not being used.

Halisdol's office is cluttered but empty of any other human company. He sits back in his chair, attempting to blink on his desktop console via his Lazy Eyes. They are unresponsive. His fingers are too wrapped and stubby to change the lenses. Even manipulating an eyedropper to wash them in saline solution might be too difficult. The other workstation at the far end of the room is unoccupied. Sets had stopped showing up to the Meadowlands office almost a week prior. She wasn't there to at least help him boot his computer or lubricate his smart lenses. Her absence would likely be deemed as another one of Halisdol's recent failures by the higher-ups as soon as he could reach them.

Halisdol winks twice and finally his monitor shutters to life. An awkward one-eyed squint to open up the shell, and he vocally changes the input vector to gestural. Halisdol waves his stiff bandaged hands in front of the screen, opening up the Melodica conference line and then joining the call circle waiting for him. According to the display, the others had been waiting nearly twenty minutes for Halisdol to log on.

Tardiness, yet another strike against him.

Mercado's mustachioed lack of smile appears first, in the top-right corner of the screen. The other three quadrants are black, though Halisdol reads that a vocal signal is being transmitted from their respective offices.

"Good afternoon Evander, I hope you're well," he says.

Halisdol straightens up in his seat. "I'm just fine," he replies.

"Yes, well. You do not look it."

"When we're done here feel free to take the rest of the week off," says one of the interlocutors. "More if you need it." It is a shebody's voice, a gruff alto. Halisdol has never heard it before. Her quadrant blinks to life. Her face is immediately recognizable, it is that of Emily Calbert, Melodica's Chief Operating Officer.

Halisdol's eyes saccade between the two C-suiters. "I suppose I should be flattered that you're not just having some HR schmoe do the honors."

"Present," says the bottom-right box. "Hey, my name is Randolph Barnes, head of Human Resources for the north eastern branch of Melodica." His speech is lilted, almost chipper. "Sorry you can't see me. I'm having some trouble with my camera."

There is a sound of shuffling before Barnes' face blinks into existence. He is the only person not currently wearing a tie. "There we are," he says.

"I apologize for being late," Halisdol begins. "I had some difficulties accessing my computer, you know, without hands. Though I guess it doesn't really matter at this point."

Calbert smooths one of her suit's lapels. Her hair is cropped short in a dated business cut. "We're still waiting on another individual," she says. "An Asylum First representative."

"Has anyone reminded you lately Evander," says Mercado, his gaze directed somewhere to the side of his camera, "That it is rude to cover your head when speaking with superiors."

"I don't think—" Barnes begins, when Halisdol pinches the brim of his hat, his hands aching with the movement, and removing his hat, revealing a swath of male-pattern baldness.

"Asylum First?" says Halisdol.

"A subsidiary of the FirstLife PAC," says Calbert. "One of our largest partners."

"May I kindly suggest that you refrain from relaying classified information to Evander," says Mercado. "It was, after all, from his office that various high-profile information was leaked to, what were their name?"

"New Ape Idea," says Barnes, evidently reading the name off of his screen.

"It was my assistant who did that," says Halisdol. "The one you hired for me."

"Well, you let them on the premises."

"Of my own office! And they saw nothing. Hell, I don't even know the half of what we do here. I supervised them the whole time."

"Evander," says Calbert, evenly. "Can we please calm down?"

"And, to be fair, they also received server access from your nephew," says Halisdol. "Who you insisted produce their music."

"Mr. Halisdol..."

"What does it matter?" Halisdol spits, his body swimming from a cocktail of exhaustion, malaise, and frustration. "Are good manners going to give me a bigger severance pay?"

"There is no severance pay," says Barnes.

Halisdol sits back and closes his eyes. "Well, I could just shit." He attempts to massage the bridge of his nose, but his fingers protest in pain. "I could litigate you know. I'm almost positive I was promised severance pay when I transferred to god-damn New Jersey."

"There's no severance pay because you're not getting laid off," says Barnes. Halisdol can hear the raps of keystrokes as Barnes types at his workstation.

"Oh, so I'm fired?" says Halisdol. He looks at himself in the conference call screen. In retrospect, it is an almost laughable irony that he felt his baldness was the biggest feature to conceal. He is a mess. Not only are his hands visibly mummified, but his left eye is still swollen and purple. The stitches on his upper lip give him the appearance of having a cleft palate that was never covered up, and his suit is rumpled and in desperate need of dry cleaning.

"Quite the opposite," says Calbert. She displays and quickly neutralizes a smirk. "I don't want to say much more before the Asylum First representative connects. I don't like to reveal too much of my hand until betting takes place."

"Excuse me?" says Halisdol.

"One moment," says Barnes, and the bottom quadrant, heretofore black, displays a pale, well-groomed hebody sporting an obviously-practiced smile.

Calbert clears her throat and addresses her camera. "Gentlemen, allow me to introduce Vincent Dewert from Asylum First."

Dewert nods. "Pleasure to meet you." The hebody somehow speaks without ever closing his mouth, as if he is a badly constructed animation with a speaker hidden behind his perfectly straight teeth.

"Likewise," says Calbert. "We also have Maximilian Mercado, one of our Product Leads at Melodica as well as Randolph Barnes from HR." Both hebodies nod and smile as they are introduced. "And lastly we have Evan Halisdol from New Jersey. He is the eupsychics research technologist we briefed you on."

"Very happy to meet you Mr. Halisdol," says Dewert.

"Yeah, well, same here." Halisdol can see that the hebody wears a small platinum American flag lapel on his suit jacket.

"And I'm so sorry to hear about your injuries. I speak for the entire FirstLife family when I wish you a speedy recovery."

"Thank you, though I hate to say it hasn't exactly been 'speedy' thus far." Halisdol by instinct tries to carve finger quotes around his speaking but winces at the pain of digital movement.

Even the hebody's laugh sounds pre-recorded. "Yes, well, have some patience. You should be receiving a care package from us in the coming days."

Halisdol looks to Calbert then to Barnes. Both are grinning in obeisance to the lobbyist. Mercado however has his lips pursed; Halisdol sims annoyance.

"Mr. Halisdol is one of our finest researchers," says Calbert.

"Yes, an excellent employee from the start," Barnes adds on.

Halisdol sits upright in his chair, shifting his eyes back and forth among his interlocutors. Years in front of shell script and data munging software had atrophied his F2F muscles. He couldn't quite sim what everyone else was thinking. Board meetings especially being an entirely new genus of human interactions, the scripts of which Halisdol was only familiar with in the most cursory of ways. Were these simply corporate niceties belying more sinister mental states amongst the others? A way to gently coax Halisdol into their graces before exiling him back to a basement cubicle in some lowly position for him to count the weeks until his position is automated away. Or had some bureaucratic snafu occurred, a misplaced decimal somewhere or an uncommented-out print statement somewhere deep in an obscure piece of company software that somehow prevented any word of Halisdol's colossal fuckup with the Spines subject and her crew from reaching New York?

"I've only heard good things," says Dewert.

And Halisdol gives a smile with too much gum; the kind that most non-*sapiens* would read as an expression of bare-teeth malice.

"Evan—can I call you Evan?" says Dewert. "How do you like New Jersey?"

"This is a big fuck up," blurts Halisdol. "I didn't even come halfway through finishing my project."

Dewert shakes his head and chuckles, his shoulders bouncing theatrically.

"And yeah. Evan is fine."

"Mouth of a sailor, this one's got," says Dewert. "Well Evan, I have to ask, how much of our beautiful country have you seen?"

"America?" replied Halisdol. If his eyes weren't so swollen they would be nearly bugging out of his skull. "I mean, I was born in New York. Up by Poughkeepsie."

"We know that," says Barnes.

"I guess I haven't been able to see much beyond the tri-state area then."

"Yes, you Yankees always seem so reluctant to step outside of your comfort zone."

At that, Calbert and Barnes share a look, mediated through their screens.

"Well, bureaucratically it's very difficult," says Halisdol. "Not to mention the fact that hunter-gatherers might decide that your scalp might make a nice handkerchief or whatever."

"You've worked with those savage bohemians before," says Dewert. "Surely you can't hold so crude a stereotype."

"Look at me," says Halisdol. "Surely I can."

Dewert slowly looks up then down, likely appraising Halisdol's previously tenderized face. "There's a lot of evil in this country. A lot of it. God has blessed our whole human family with freedom and a consciousness more deeply complex than any other system in our universe. And what do some of our cousins do with them?"

Halisdol's eye flicks to the other quadrants of his screens. He can sim a look of pained tongue-biting at Dewert's religiosity shared amongst all the Melodica employees.

"This is, in essence, what has drawn FirstLife to your work with euspychics. Y'all seem to make the prospect of courting in these wayward sheep so simple."

"It's much more complex than you think," says Halisdol. "TANSTAALF."

"What now?"

"Please ignore him," says Mercado. He clears his throat. "Evander has a proclivity toward inundating others with jargon. He is a much better researcher than he is a conversationalist."

What was that? A compliment, however backhanded, from Mercado?

"Needless to say," says Dewert. "If you decide to come work with us, you'll have that deep-seated satisfaction of knowing you are working to benefit all Americans across our nation, not just those locked up here in New England."

"I wouldn't really call Moonachie 'New England'," says Halisdol. He looks to Calbert, then to Barnes. "So I guess this is about me getting fired."

Dewert smiles then leans back. "Did you even debrief this poor man?"

"As far as I know, I wasn't," says Halisdol.

"Mr. Halisdol," says Randolph Barnes, "Given in part to your extraordinary work leading research in our New Jersey eupsychics branch, Asylum First has shown an interest in buying out our entire branch."

"Seriously? Is this even standard business practice?"

"Not at all," says Calbert. "But considering how much of our work was leaked by your lab assistant, we've decided this is the best course of action. We're so close to an important breakthrough, and we'd rather see it get done by other capable hands than not get done at all."

"Consider this one of those ball and cup games," says Dewert. "We're hoping to discreetly pass the ball off from under one cup to another and keep none of the general public the wiser."

"Okay," says Halisdol. "So why talk to me, if my entire department is getting transferred?"

"It's not quite that simple," says Dewert. "We're buying all Melodica's previous research but not necessarily their staff. We want you to manage that aspect of business. Once you finish convalescing of course."

"Not to mention that we simply don't know how trustworthy other employees are, as much as I hate to say it," says Barnes. "We can't risk handing over another Sets."

"Where is she now?"

"Indeterminate," says Barnes.

"So, uh" he says, "I'm being offered a promotion now?" says Halisdol.

"Don't sound so incredulous Evander," says Mercado. "Even I must admit you've done good work, these leaks aside."

Halisdol wants to chew on his nails or crack his knuckles but resists. His whole set of somatic subsystems feel like they are clunking along without doing much in terms of helping him process what he hears or read the emotions encoded in the four faces displayed in front of him. It's as if a set of functions in his reptile brain in charge of keeping his heart beating and lungs breathing has encountered some unforeseen runtime error, junking up his higher, more computationally-heavy cranial modules.

"We're looking at extending your research to institutions all along the eastern seaboard," says Dewert. The hebody has the kind of face of a politician from last century, confidently WASPy, his chin with an almost caricatured cleft, and with a build that suggests he spent time in the armed forces even though he was born into wealth. This in comparison to Halisdol who—injuries notwithstanding—tended to recog-nize himself as looking like an archetypal code monkey. That all the testosterone in his blood stream never helped facilitate a muscular build or sculpted jawline, instead giving him premature baldness and an anxious bladder.

"That's fine," says Halisdol. "Well, it's more than fine. It's great. Terrific really. I just can't exactly grok how extendable anything I've done is. We barely managed to produce a song with New Ape Idea and—"

"—We learned a tremendous amount from that," says Calbert. "Mainly how unimportant those morons are to successfully developing a completely dynamical eupsychics system."

"With all that emphasis on Spines though—"

"—Irrelevant," says Calbert. "Really."

"Well, even so," says Halisdol, "I was barely able to reduce any of the exten-sive ontogenetic data we've collected into anything significant, let alone musical."

Calbert looks at the face of her desk, she seems to be smiling to herself. "I think you misunderstand," the shebody says. "Mr. Halisdol, we weren't trying to have you analyze any data yet, we were still in the mapping phase. You know, creating different vectors out of tons of data, key pairs. Seeing what pieces could fit together before identifying whether that fit was useful or important. In that sense, you've done a great job."

"We have plenty of recordings of those simians now," says Mercado, "Not to mention exchanges between you and the subject captured on your smart lenses. And she is just one of a cohort of several dozen scattered across the state."

Halisdol's office begins to feel very warm. He is several stories up, and the climate control seems to have shut itself off. He allows himself a quick glance out the window. The sun is setting though the swamps below are still amply illuminated from stray metropolitan lights, caught in the polluted ionosphere. Very few people must be left in the building. Nobody at Melodica works OT voluntarily, what kind of human would be so masochistic?

"The main idea here is that we're exiting phase one of development," says Calbert, "and it looks like Asylum First will be contracting individuals to take up phase two."

"And we'd like to get the jump on you Evan," adds Dewert with a wink, "Before you decide otherwise."

Halisdol swallows. "So if I decide to stay with Melodica, what will I do?"

"Nothing," says Mercado.

"What he means," says Barnes, "Is that once you're done with your convalescence, we can't guarantee your employment with us. It's nothing personal, as Ms. Calbert said, we're laying off our entire eupsychics research branch."

"So I don't have a choice," says Halisdol. "I never do."

"The good news is, if you decide to come with us we'll be finishing up some operations in Jersey City and Camden for about 18 weeks before we head down south. We've already established some basic operations in Baltimore, DC, and Atlanta."

"I've always wanted to see scenic Baltimore," says Halisdol.

Dewert chuckles without smiling. "I must warn you that the First Life family doesn't take sarcasm very well. Irony isn't so appreciated when you're trying to save millions of lives."

Halisdol sniffs. "I see."

"After about 9 months we'll be settling in DC, which I'm sure you can learn to enjoy. Not to mention I've already enquired Mr. Barnes about your salary Evan, and right off the bat we're willing to double it."

"Two times shit is still a multiple of shit."

Calbert screws up her eyes and checks a nonexistent wristwatch. "Are we almost done here?"

"Alright," says Halisdol. "Can I at least have a week to think this over?"

"I wish I could give you that time Evander. I really do," says Dewert.

The air filtration system seems to have shut itself off for the night. The tower must think it is empty, save a few automated custodians and interns asleep at their desks. The faint uretic odor of a draft from Secaucus begins to seep inside the building. Halisdol can just barely smell it. It's slightly piquant, like ammonia and left-over curry. That, at least is one thing Halisdol wouldn't miss about New Jersey.

2.7.0 Attractor

"I'll fucking build you a new phone," Tak said. "If this record deal proves to be the least bit lucrative."

"I need to focus Tak," said Doug. He turned the steering wheel with both hands as he looped around a cloverleaf off of the freeway. Highway driving like this provoked a small-scale existential fear that made interlocuting with Takashi difficult, if not frustrating.

"And you can recycle all your loggy paperbacks too. Read'm electronically." Takashi picked at some schmutz lodged between his bottom teeth. "Better for the ecosystem."

"If we sign the record deal," said Doug, his dermis growing slick with sweat as he watched an eighteen-wheeler swerve around him.

"Yeah," said Tak. "Exactly."

"Which we know nothing about."

Tak clicked his tongue against his palate. "Isn't that why we're schlepping down here?"

"I just never thought you'd be so enthusiastic about the prospect of selling out," said Doug.

"You're one to talk," Tak snapped. He picked his feet up from off the dash and sat up. "With your shitty flip-phone and loggy paperbacks. It's all hipster retro faddism."

"Major untruth Miyagi-Edelstein."

"At least I'm not the one who's failing to reckon with today's post-post-modern technological landscape, boyo."

"I have no idea what that even means," replied Doug.

"Please," Isa intercut. "Please be quiet."

This muted Takashi.

Swamp grass was about the only flora left that could grow in wild abundance in New Jersey. Most of the Garden State had been deforested to make room for highways and turnpikes on which Waymos would zip by. Even the Pine Barrens down south looked more barren than pine. Doug had heard trees once grew there, though superstorm after superstorm tore up the shoreline every summer, which coated everywhere from Longbranch to Mahwah in countless grains of sand and rendered the soil infertile.

But somehow the swamp grass—species indeterminate—blades more brown than green, rose from the muddy crust of the Meadowlands. Though Moonachie smelled like death it was in fact teeming with a certain abundance of life. The grass grew over two meters tall, making it difficult for any of the passengers in Doug's sedan to see the Melodica tower until they were in its parking lot.

After a quick but deliberate angle-parking job, the three exited the sedan. Doug locked it, turning the key into a metal lock on the driver's door, which elicited a scoff from Takashi.

The Melodica tower was the tallest skyscraper in the Meadowlands area, next to the gargantuan Bank of America NY Giants Memorial Stadium and Recreation Complex. It had the appearance of a giant tree rather than a man-made structure. It was the largest ecobuilding Doug had seen firsthand, though Takashi quickly remarked they were "no-big-deal Green Capitalist scams" that were "like, everywhere" in the NYC area. The front door was locked.

"Julia said there was a face scanner by the door," said Doug. He found a black camera lens to the right of the entrance.

"Gotcha," Tak stepped forward and mugged into the camera. A red line began to blink indicating that permission for entry was not granted.

"It's your hair," said Doug. "Didn't you style it specifically to thwart this kind of technology?"

Takashi stepped back, smiling. "Indeed I did," he said, flicking a devil lock hanging in front of his face like the elm of a willow. "You have any other ways to get in?"

Doug sighed and removed his Nokia from his pocket. He kept Sets on speed dial. "She'll buzz us in," said Doug, flipping the black device shut and pocketing it. "Her lab is on the twentieth floor."

And with that, the glass doors parted, and the three entered the building. Takashi's teeth chattered as they walked through the lobby. The air smelled minty and over-processed. Isa pinched her collar, and her shirt grew long sleeves that obscured her tattoos. Doug, the type to wear shorts and tennis shoes independent of air temperature, humidity or precipitation, was unfazed.

The five elevator doors were made of steel, the only visible metal on the entire floor. From the lobby extended two long hallways, each with ten or fifteen bamboo doors. Occasionally, a hebody or shebody in a darkish suit would slide one of the doors open and power-walk to another, eyes downcast and a visage displaying solemnity or boredom. They spoke few words to one another, only brief nods devoid of any F2F contact. Doug cleared his throat and summoned an upward bound elevator, which dinged with its arrival almost instantaneously. For a company called Melodica, the atrium was whisper-quiet, almost clinically so.

"Shit, this set-up is, like, corporate to the tenth power," said Takashi.

"—"

"—"

Takashi sniffed as the elevator beeped with each successive floor it ascended past. "No comment?"

"It's rude to talk in an elevator," said Doug.

"Yeah, but it's just us in here, boyo."

"Don't call me boyo."

"—"

"—"

"I'm just saying," he said, "I don't quite get what he wants with us."

"Julia is female," said Doug. His voice was followed by a gaseous stomach rumble.

"Not her, this he," Takashi windmilled his arms about, gesturing across the elevator.

"Why is Melodica male?" Doug asked.

"Corporate personhood law dictates that all incorporated businesses and ventures are to be designated as either male or unisex," said Isa.

"Yeah, a bunch of those fourth-wave feminists tried to start referring to all corporations in the female," said Tak. "Which caught on, to the point where SCOTUS got all tied up trying to gender traditional corporate law. It was big on the news blogs for, like, five hours back in the late twenties. To think before then most Americans woulda thought of sex and gender as separate things. But here we are now, calling ourselves shebodies, hebodies, theebodies, betweenbodies. Because that's what we got that Melodica, or Zappos, or Alphabet doesn't: bodies."

"I have heard that at one point it was fashionable to give one's preferred pronouns at the onset of F2F," said Isa.

"I'd say mine were, 'You there!' and 'Seize them!'" Tak snorted at his own joke.

"_"

"_"

"So why wouldn't, uh, he want us?"

"Because we're punk as fuck," said Takashi, volume rising, "and Melodica is so white collar it's blinding."

"You can be white collar and punk."

"You, Doug," said Tak, "Need to look up the definition of your terms. Logical fallacy, of the—"

But before Takashi could finish yammering, the elevator doors parted, revealing a long hallway that stretched out before them. Windows took up the majority of the walls' surface area, and Doug felt as if the sunlight streaming through them was brighter, cleaner, more intensely saturated than the smog-encumbered waveforms outside. Takashi, adjacent to Doug, hinged at the waist and adroitly unlaced his combat boots. Doug could pick up a brief pungence as Takashi slipped his feet outside the boots, but the building's too-clean aroma quickly masked it.

"The floor is so cool," said Tak, standing still. "Like, in Kelvin."

Although Doug wanted to verify the claim, he was not willing to risk removing his footwear. He simmed a highly-probable scenario of an unpleasant scent articulating itself, much worse than Tak's. He instead squatted down and touched the floor with his fingertips.

"It's chilled," Doug said. He noticed that he was not sweating. At the far end of the hallway he spotted a lone bamboo door. This must have been where Julia Sets was waiting. Isa departed toward it while the two hebodies remained behind.

Tak stood, boots in his hand, wriggling his toes. His feet, small for his height, were a bit gnarly with overgrown toenails and blisters. He did not wear socks under his combat boots, and it looked like he never had for a few years.

"Something about a clean bamboo floor just makes me wanna remove my footwear," Tak said, nesting his boots in the crook of his elbow.

Isa approached the door and stopped a meter away. Tak and Doug took a minute to catch up. There was no discernible way to open the door: no knobs or handles. Doug waved his hand in front of the door, but the beige rectangle remained closed. He unpocketed his flip-phone, ready to redial Julia Sets, when Takashi approached the door, and stood, on a slight square recess in the floor.

The door slid open, revealing a wide room, that somehow seemed both cluttered and spacious. One wall was a giant window, overseeing a vista of unused

train-tracks, overused highways and a sea of the brown-green marshiness below. The
Bank of America NY Giants Memorial Stadium and Recreation Complex was just a
cerulean ellipse in the distance. The opposite wall contained a row of server stacks,
and the corners sported small arrangements of banzai shrubbery, arranged like the first
image on a Google search for Feng Shui. The air filtration system sounded as if it were
whispering a conspiracy to itself. There were two desks in the room, bamboo as well.
They were cluttered with fat stacks of paper, huge gaping display monitors, and PC
towers tall enough to look like they were from the mid-naughts. One desk, the closer
one to the door, was unoccupied. Julia sat at the other, hunched over, some Gothic
Mumblesludge droning on speaker. Her Eyes projected a high-lumen interactions window and shell filled with colorful lines of code. Sense-holes plugged, she was unaware
to the arrival of Takashi, Doug, and Isa.

"Julia?" said Doug, though she still remained unaware. They stepped forward
into the lab anyway, Doug leading this time. The door shut behind them, eliciting a
turn from Sets.

"Ganoooooush!" she said, beaming. The various projections and sounds
ema-nating from her area disappeared. She pushed herself away from her desk, stood
from her chair, and walked toward them.

"Good to see you Julia," Doug said, and they entered a meaty embrace. Unafraid of body odor (though not entirely devoid of it), this was the first hug Doug had
initiated in years so far as he remembers.

"I haven't seen Perl in years," said Tak, sauntering over to them.

"And you still haven't," Sets said. "This is a language I've written myself.
It scales a bit better for the immense amount of information I need to handle. I'm
blinding myself with data entry." Sets let out a chuckle.

"Really?" said Takashi. He scratched at the back of his head and smothered
an impressed smirk. "Looked like Perl to me."

"Ah, good eye, Miyagi," she said. "Honestly, they're pretty similar. I was a bit
lazy when developing the lexer. I've still got some old habits hammered into me from
when I was getting my bachelors." Julia turned toward Doug. Her smile widened.
"But I'm sure no one else really wants to listen to me blather on about coding syntax."

"It's Miyagi-Edelstein," Takashi corrected her.

"They only gave you one degree?" Doug asked.

"No, three," said Julia. "That was a plural S. Bachelors." She turned her gaze
toward Isa. "I don't believe we've been introduced. I'm Julia Sets." She extended a hand
that went unreceived.

"This is Isa. Isa Spines," said Tak.

"Isa Spines," Julia repeated slow and conscientious-like. "I've heard great
things."

"From who?" said Tak.

"From Isa," she said. "The recordings Doug sent me. This shebody can wail."

"Well fuck DLG," said Takashi sharply. "I never gave you permission to do that."

"Do you write your own lyrics?" Julia turned to Isa. She picked at one of the several earrings hanging from her right lobe.

"I didn't sell them or put them on the web," said Doug.

"How do we know they haven't leaked?" Takashi, eyebrows squinted together.

"We would know. They'd be all over the net," Doug replied. "Has Mallorey told you about their write-ups in *Staph Infection*? Anything tagged "New Ape Idea" has more hits and individual visitors, by a factor of ten compared to any other articles."

"They don't require much thought," said Isa, recoiling a bit.

"Besides," said Doug to Takashi, "The recordings were crap quality. Sounded like they were mixed in a tin can."

"The recordings you sent me?" Julia turned from Isa, who refused to grant her eye contact. "They were obviously not professional quality, but they weren't bad for demos. I've heard worse from Ganoush."

"Really?" said Doug. "I just recorded them on my phone's built-in condensor mic."

"The quality was clear though. Almost too clear. I could understand the lyrics, hear the different instrumental lines. Everything."

"Courtney Christ!" said Takashi, pinching the bridge of his nose. "Yr flirting with disaster Lamarck-Ganoush."

"Disaster how?" said Doug. "Free publicity. Isn't that what you want?"

"I want money too, DLG."

"More people'll come to Rule 30—"

"We're selling shows out already."

"What about free information? Your whole white hat pirate spiel." Doug pawed at the back of his head, undoing and rewrapping his bun in frustration. "Or are you only okay with taking what's not yours."

"Not what I meant," he said. "Information transmission error. Noise has been confused for signal." Tak flared his nostrils. "I'd just like to be in the know about these things."

"I believe I'm the only one who heard them," Julia said. Like Doug, she preferred clothing of the loose, baggy and earth-toned variety. Not the skin-type black denims and crusty band tees that could change at the push of a collar button the rest of the punks preferred. She tugged at a loose thread on her hoodie, likely a thrift store buy. "And Mr. Halisdol too. And maybe whatever NSA agents had access to our email."

"Who?" said Tak.

"My boss." Julia scanned around the room. "Likely in the restroom. He'll be here soon, likely asking for the evaluation of two to the nth power."

"Uh-huh." Takashi nodded his mouth slightly agape, which, for whatever reason, made Doug smile a bit. Isa, too, seemed to be paying attention to the F2F, likely for lack of a better digital distraction. She, of course, did not smile.

"That's his workstation," Julia gestured toward the bamboo block across the room. It was covered with an array of manila folders, all overfilled with papers.

The lavatory door slid open, revealing a lanky hebody, unshaven and gaunt. His hairline receded to a spot under the cover of his tacky straw Panama hat.

"Ah," he said, scratching at his whiskers. "These are the musicians."

"New Ape Idea," said Julia. "Mr. Halisdol, this is Takashi Miyagi-Edelstein, Douglas Lamarck-Ganoush and—"

"Isa Spines," Mr. Halisdol said, approaching them. He offered a hand toward Isa. "Heard great things." His attempt at a smile only evinced how rarely genuine that facial expression was for him.

"How?" Tak asked. He folded his arms across his thin ectomorphic chest.

"Julia showed me," Halisdol replied. "Or I overhead. Listening to music in order to increase work productivity is allowed here at Melodica."

"Up the punx," said Takashi, his voice dripping with sarcasm.

"Right, well. I liked what I heard. Or, I should say, my Lazy Eyes did."

"They have an audio input?" Isa asked, now drawn in.

Halisdol tugged at the sleeve of his blazer revealing a small skin color square, slightly darker than the peach complexion of his wrist. "Externalities feed," he said. "Can measure sound, humidity, temperature, air pressure, and wind current, Geiger counter. Really everything except the visual spectrum which your standard pair of eyes will cover."

"Do you have one?" Doug asked Julia.

"All Melodica personnel do," said Mr. Halisdol. "We're a share holding partner with Lazy Eye's parent company: North Hampton Solutions."

"A conglomerate?" said Isa.

"Never mind," Halisdol volleyed. He took a step back. "Should you decide to do business with us here at Melodica, I can see to it that you can have Externalities Feeds for all your Lazy Eyes."

"Thank you," said Doug. "Though I don't wear them."

"Me neither," Tak added quickly.

"Isa does though," said Doug.

"Did." Isa sighed.

"Right," said Mr. Halisdol. "That makes sense. The artistic types usually forgo modern digital conveniences. I'm happy to have lenses fashioned for any of you, should you choose to work with Melodica. Pro bono, of course."

At this, Isa snapped her gaze up toward Mr. Halisdol.

"So why are we here?" said Takashi.

"Do you work well with children Tak Miyagi?" Mr. Halisdol asked.

"—Edelstein."

"Of course," he said. "Not too long ago, Melodica launched a venture into, erm, child welfare futures. We're looking to start a line of music products for children in need."

"Like, what kind of music?"

"Lullabies, specifically."

Doug and Takashi glanced sideways at one another. "I think there's some mistake. We're a punk rock band," said Takashi. "Like hardcore shit. Total post-shoegaze Darwinian thrash."

"I am no genre expert, though I suppose those adjectives could be applied to what I heard." Mr. Halisdol tugged at the knot of his necktie and forced out a laugh. "Though I did realize one thing: You three have talent."

"Lots of bands have talent." Tak, again.

"Not a lot of punk outfits," said Julia.

"Major untruth Sets, yr not accustomed to stylistic—"

Doug raised a pacifying hand. "Can we let Mr. I'm sorry sir, what was your name?"

"Halisdol."

"Mr. Halisdol finish his pitch?"

"Yr right, I'm being very rude," said Takashi. "Please excuse my unprofessionalism." He pinched at the collar of his t-shirt. At once, his charcoal *Leftover Smegma* tee loosened and became a white pinstriped dress-shirt with a blue bowtie. "Please continue," he said.

"Right," Mr. Halisdol said, nodding. "We're currently scouting musicians with ability, which, from my understanding you have. As well as a degree of cultural sway."

"Cultural sway?" Lamarck-Ganoush, like what?

"You have quite a presence on the blogosphere," Mr. Halisdol replied. "The number of mentions about New Ape Idea on social networking and music journalism sites is significant. Additionally the rate at which new mentions occur are on par with several top 40 bands."

"Were you aware of this?" Doug to Takashi.

"We don't have any music up, at least, I don't think so," Tak said.

"Which makes it all the more impressive," Mr. Halisdol said with exaggerated prosody. "And yet your popularity increases. All due to circulating legend regarding your stellar live show, stage mannerisms, lyrics, et cetera."

"And we're cheaper than any top 40 act with a similar blogosphere presence,"

Takashi said.

Mr. Halisdol shifted his headwear. Doug hadn't realized before how small the man was. An inch or two shorter than Doug, at least a head below Takashi. Maybe several inches taller than Isa. "It is important, our marketing department tells me," he said. "To recruit musicians that have achieved a certain degree of popularity."

"Even for lullabies?" said Takashi, like the hebody was trying to lose Melodica's business.

"Young hip parents want their children to listen to young hip tunes. Not to mention the, well, structural simplicity of the punk genre makes for easily digestible music. Young, developing perceptual circuits in the process of bootstrapping into maturity. Fragile aural canals and whatnot. I am not an expert in these matters."

"I thought these," Takashi cast a glance at Julia. She had remained silent since Mr. Halisdol's entrance. "*Lullabies*, were for children in need."

"They are," said Mr. Halisdol.

"With hip culture-saavy parents?"

For a pregnant moment Mr. Halisdol looked as if he was chewing on the meat of his inner cheek. "Yes, well, this is what our marketing department tells me. I'm not one to question their praxis, as paradoxical as it may seem at times." He shifted his weight from one foot to the other as he spoke. Back and forth and back and forth. "It's all oriented in cognitive science really. Not my specialty."

Doug spoke first. "And your specialty, Mr. Halisdol, is?"

"Eupsychics theory," said Julia, finally speaking. "At least in this lab."

Mr. Halisdol nodded. "Ms. Sets is correct. My focus has been on human applications. Specifically those regarding the ontogeny and development of human perceptual and cognitive schemata."

Takashi's spine straightened followed by a half-smile to Doug and Isa. "I see, chaotic systems," he said. "Applied complexity theory."

"Indeed," said Mr. Halisdol. "What began as a popular subgenre of physics in the 1980's has since grown to an all-encompassing mathematical descriptive model for a huge matrix of studies. My work is primarily concerned with mapping it onto human neuromotor systems. I guess it does fall under the psychology/cognitive science umbrella. Though it is mostly just number crunching."

Takashi toed the floor, pivoting the ball of his foot like a nervous flirt. "Makes sense. I've had similar thoughts myself," he said. "With regards to treating the human individual as a dynamical system."

"Oh, it's hardly a new practice," replied Mr. Halisdol. He and Tak were F2F-ing pretty intensely, Doug noted. "For all its early history, the study of psychology has basically been the uprooting of old, tired, useless theory and supplanting it with new fresh equally-incorrect paradigms. Freud and his analysts distilled basic appetites to perversion and Mommy-issues. It all culminated in a style of therapy targeting wealthy

narcissists who were willing to spend ample time on their backs lamenting their own
unwieldy egos. From whence came the Behaviorists. Operant conditioning and stimu-
lus-response tests. And they all pretended that there was nothing going inside the head
at all. They of course were overthrown by the cognitivists who pretended the mind
was a meat-based Turing machine and consciousness was all symbols and syntax. The
Evolutionary Psychology craze of the tens and twenties was not—"

"—I thought you said you weren't an expert," said Lamark-Ganoush. Mr.
Halisdol had been monologuing straight at Takashi the whole time, speaking at an
accelerando clip.

Mr. Halisdol cleared his throat and tugged at his collar. "This is history. The
backdrop to my research. Not to say that I'm a psychologist. I just research what I'm
told to. Though we do employ some very intelligent psych consultants that dictate the
direction of our R&D. I have little reason to doubt their collective intelligence."

Takashi was quick to interject. "What's the problem with evo psych? Are you
one of those Evangelical Christian guys?"

"Oh, evolution is a fact," said Mr. Halisdol, turning again toward Takashi.
"Though what are the driving forces behind it? Darwinian natural selection? Gould's
punctuated equilibrium? And while the genome may change through a Darwinian
scheme, cultural evolution, well, doesn't." Mr. Halisdol glanced at Doug. "Memes are
either used or abandoned."

"Not that I didn't buy into the whole thing when it was faddish," continued
Halisdol. "I did the paleo diet back in the tens. If I was a younger and braver man
I may have joined the Neo-!Kung a few years ago. Though the whole field of study
can get too speculative. What, trying to delineate the evolutionary history of all our
humanity. I do numbers. Dynamical systems, Eupsychics. It's more, erm, grounded."

"Absolutely," said Takashi. "Makes sense to me."

Doug could feel something bilous gurgling in his intestines. "I don't get it,"
he said.

"My research?" said Mr. Halisdol. And then with a nod toward Julia he corrected himself. "Our research?"

"This is the strangest record deal I've ever heard of."

"We live in the age of strangeness DLG," said Takashi. And to think only
moments ago he was the most vocally opposed to coming to the Meadowlands.

"I would like to see your laboratory," said Isa, her gaze still downward cast.

"I've been doing a lot of the talking here, I understand that." Mr. Halisdol
attempted another smile. "Perhaps Ms. Sets would like to show you some of the
work she's been undertaking at her console."

"It's mostly raw data that I'm sorting through. Or rather I'm trying to automate the whole data-sorting process," said Julia. "But I'm mostly working with highly
abstract points of information. I don't really know what they represent." She emitted

a weak chuckle. "Honestly, this is the first I'm hearing about a lot of my research as well." Julia looked to her boss. His lips were pursed and his nostrils flared a bit.

"Lemme see your code," said Takashi. "I'm sure I could figure the gist out."

"No problem," Sets said. She turned and walked with Takashi and Doug toward her desk. Mr. Halisdol had his hands in his pants pocket and kept wetting his lips.

"Did you ever meet this girl back in school?" said Doug. "One Ruthie McRogers?"

"Doesn't ring a bell."

"You should meet her," said Doug. "Or rather, she should meet you. I sim she'd appreciate your technical expertise."

"I'd prefer to see the main laboratory," Isa said. She hadn't moved with the rest of them. "If that is possible."

"Yes, well," said Mr. Halisdol. "I don't even think Julia has had a tour yet. We tend to keep the exactitudes of our research relatively hush-hush. Corporate espionage being a consistent threat and whatnot."

"_"

Head tilted back and mouth agape, Takashi stared at the litany of code projected in front of him. "I wouldn't mind seeing the lab," he said. "See what you've got under the hood."

"If it's not too much to ask," Lamarck-Ganoush added. "Perhaps you could give us a little more detail on this whole lullaby project?"

"Yes, well," Mr. Halisdol pressed his palms together. "We could perhaps have something arranged with the Eupsychics Division, if it will inspire a degree of confidence in any future music contracting."

The main laboratory was in the subbasement of the Melodica tower. Aside from the five of them—Halisdol, Sets, Tak, Isa, and Doug —no one else boarded the elevator during their trip down. The downward acceleration of the elevator made Doug feel as if his bladder was swelling. A sensation unabated by the fact that the other four of the elevator's passengers all remained completely silent for the duration of the ride. Even Tak did not speak. He kept his head bowed and lips sealed, as per timeless elevator-riding etiquette. Quietude from Isa was expected, Julia too perhaps. Mr. Halisdol didn't speak per se, though Doug noted that he seemed to move his lips, as if chewing words he wished to say to the rest on the way down.

While above ground, the building seemed almost empty, the rooms well lit and elegantly furnished, the basement was overcrowded and concrete. White lab-coats bustled back and forth, swinging fingers around in front of them as they manipulated items on their Lazy Eye displays. The whirring of a giant industrial fan covered the rest of the ambient noise; Mr. Halisdol sounded slightly strained when he announced "Here we are" to the other four.

"You study children down here?" Takashi yelled.

"Not quite," replied Mr. Halisdol. "This is our Systems Application division. Very little of our research corresponds to actually working with human subjects here. Our goal is to outline the architecture of the data we find. Attractors, repellents, phase-space delineation et cetera."

Doug leaned in toward Julia and attempted to make an aside. "Does this make any sense to you?" he asked, though the laboratory's din masked his vocalizing. Mr. Halisdol walked backwards as he talked, every so often looking behind him to avoid backing into another employee or a server stack.

"So yr intending to construct the human subject as an autonomous system," said Takashi, his voice lilted with content in his ability to spit out jargon. "Computationally complex in that it is not easily decomposed into smaller sub-systems."

"Ah-ha, well you are talking the capital-B capital-I Big Ideas." said Mr. Halisdol as they approached a large steel door. He pressed his thumb against a fingerprint scanner for several seconds, before the doors slowly swung open. With a wave he ushered them into an over-white, over-bright room, the only sound the amniotic hush of old fluorescent lighting. A water cooler gurgled on the orthogonal wall.

"Break-room," he said, though there were neither chairs, nor tables in it. He pulled a thumbnail sized square from his jacket pocket from which he removed and inserted two clear lenses. He blinked them on.

"I thought we'd have a tour," said Takashi.

"Well, I can't show you around too much," said Mr. Halisdol. "Security policy, as I've said. But I assure you, our research is cutting-edge." His voice sunk into a baritone as he spoke. "As vice-president of Research and Development, I can assure you we at the Meadowlands branch of Melodica, we are *seekers of truth*."

Doug took a quick look at Julia. She stood in the doorway with her back to the rest, craning her neck to take in as much of the lab as possible. Mr. Halisdol approached her and placed a remonstrating hand on her shoulder before blinking the door shut with his Lazy Eyes.

"In Eupsychics we concern ourselves with understanding healthy human ontogeny. That is, growth and development of an individual subject through time." Mr. Halisdol pulled a white kerchief from his breast pocket and dabbed at some sweat dripping down his neck.

"Using that, what was it—"

"Dynamical Systems Theory, yes. It's a subset of Complexity Theory that was from the end of last century through the late teens. Its applications ranged from traffic jam avoidance algorithms in Waymos to mapping out Dengue epidemiology in South-east Asia. It wasn't until the last two decades or so that researchers began to apply it as a means of understanding human psychology."

Takashi nodded along with Halisdol's speaking. Isa too seemed to be listening, though she kept her gaze directed at the rectangle of floor in front of her toes.

"Allow me to show you," Mr. Halisdol continued. He removed his straw hat and used it to fan away some airborne dust particles. He then blinked on a projection of an empty two-dimensional Cartesian coordinate plane on one of the break room's sparsely-decorated walls. His pupils were no longer visible through the bright glow of his Lazies. "Essentially, what we are doing in the Department of Eupsychics is attempting to map out possible developmental attractor states within infancy and early childhood.

"Attractor states?" said Doug. He side-eyed Takashi, who now sported a simian grin, both rows of teeth visible. Apparently this all made sense to the hebody, as obvious as basic geometry or single-variable calculus. Or at least, Tak was trying very hard to give that impression.

"Development in all organisms, infancy through senescence, is not monotonic. A baby does not grow taller and fatter its entire life, dying as a giant. Rather there are certain states that the system approaches. These are known in the field as 'basins of attraction'. Imagine a ball rolling down a hill and into a canyon. If the canyon is deep enough, no matter the ball's momentum, it will be unable to roll out of the canyon and eventually settle at its lowest point. Likewise, there are certain physiological and cognitive pits that direct the momentum of growth."

"So," said Doug. "You're trying to figure the, like, developmental ruts children run into as they grow?"

Mr. Halisdol did not break is gaze at the wall, lest he skew the projection. "Not quite," he said. "Allow me to put it this way. Children are born across the globe into innumerable social and familial contexts. Languages, cultural child-rearing patterns and family structures vary enormously, yet largely the same kind of human is produced: one that can walk bipedally, manage at least one language fluently and understand the social conventions of its habitat. Computationally, that is like having a function that, despite having vastly different parameters, produces a relatively constant result after iterating several million times.

"This may not sound so impressive," Mr. Halisdol continued, "Unless one takes into account the vast number of degrees of freedom within a human system. Trillions of potential neural connections, multiplied by the hundreds of muscular motor systems in the body; there are nearly infinite combinations between the two, ways the brain and body may interact. For a child to take its first steps, it must learn to prune away all the possible neuromotor circuits that prevent it from moving its legs properly. This is a removal of degrees of freedom within a system in order to assure a consistent performance. A proper step, we can say, is a behavioral attractor basin."

"So what's the graph for?" asked Doug. The blank projection still remained in front of them all. Mr. Halisdol spoke facing it, his retinas glowing.

"I surmised a, erm, graphical representation of this theory may prove useful for the laymen among us."

"We don't need it," said Takashi.

"I would prefer a picture of what you say," said Isa.

"Of course," said Mr. Halisdol. "Suppose we have two simple equations mapped on the plane. Say, a simple quadratic such as $y = x^2 + 5x$ and a simple line $y=x$. Now let us put in a third function that is governed by a couple rules. Say, it will approach the parabola in a vertical fashion until they touch. Then, it will approach the diagonal horizontally until they touch. After the first epoch it will look like this."

Mr. Halisdol squinted and a thin line began ascending toward the curve. As predicted, once it grazed the curve it veered right until it hit the straight line.

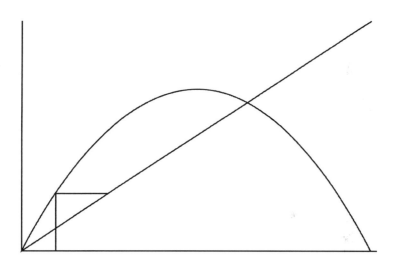

"Now, human ontogeny is essentially a giant feedback process. The end result of one iteration becomes the starting parameters for the next iteration. Much like childbirth—the end of development in utero— becomes the starting conditions for infancy.

"If we have our function reiterate itself over and over, soon it will become enclosed within a specific area of the coordinate plane."

Sure enough, as Mr. Halisdol spoke, the function kept repeating itself: moving toward the parabola then the diagonal in turn. Eventually it became enclosed within a square in the upper-right corner of the screen. Its movements were too small and quick to be perceptible.

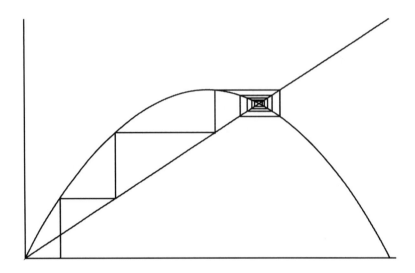

"This is what is called a 'point attractor'," said Mr. Halisdol.

"Yeah, we know," Tak interrupted. "The function approaches a single point and more or less stays there. Elementary stuff."

Mr. Halisdol blinked off the display. The meat of his eyes returned to an organic non-glowing white with black pupil. "While I am impressed with your knowledge of dynamical systems, I was under the impression your, well, colleagues, were not of the same erudition."

"I fail to see how your picture corresponds with a human being," said Isa Spines, ever the tough sell.

Mr. Halisdol chuckled humorlessly. "Yes, well, that was an oversimplification to be sure. My point being, we try to look for milestones in human development as attractor states in an ongoing system. And, even as simple algebra can show you, attractor states are begotten by the rules and parameters of the phase space in which it is set coupled with feedback between its past activity and the present."

"So if it's all about rules and parameters," said Doug as he circled a finger around his bun, "Why not focus on that stuff, rather than these points of attraction on whatever. I'm not an expert, but couldn't you learn a lot about a child by, like, examining its genome and various organ tissues and stuff? Wouldn't those provide the 'rules' you're after?"

"Complex systems are not easily broken down, DLG," said Tak. He stared at the now-blank wall, as if waiting for another projection to light across it. "If you change the parameters within a phase-space, even slightly, results can become unpredictable in a huge way." Takashi paused to pick something green from between two teeth. "Imagine if we replaced the diagonal with a sinusoid, or a logarithmic ascent. The same point attractor might not even exist."

"Mr. Miyagi-Edelstein is correct," said Mr. Halisdol. "Though I wouldn't have put it so aggressively.

"Imagine a waterfall. I could change the mass and direction of every drop of water within it, and yet the waterfall will still appear the same. The fact is, when dealing with these systems, we know it is somehow dependent upon its initial conditions, but we can't explain exactly what's going to happen explicitly in terms of those factors. It throws a wrench into the whole idea of causality really. Things get even more complex when you take the notion of feedback and apply it to such systems. Maybe not waterfalls, but to anything involving human cognition or communication."

Perhaps it was his Lazy Eyes that propelled Mr. Halisdol to ramble on. Lazy Eye wearers were never the most conscientious type; they tended to get lost in their own world. Lamarck-Ganoush could sim Mr. Halisdol forgetting he had an audience just then, and hence talking too much. There were enough Takashis in this world, flapping their tongues about subjects too prolix and esoteric to be of interest to the folk. Lamarck-Ganoush found it all obnoxious. As if the user's private show of images, hypertexts, and videos siphoned the essential cognitive faculties necessary for successful F2Fing. And if the user wasn't an over-talker, in Doug's experience, he became like Isa. Paralyzed by anxiety and skepticism. Pretty much impenetrable. Talkative or tacit, a shower or a sayer, they were all solipsists the lot of 'em.

"Bioinformatics was thought to hold the key to unlocking the human several decades ago. To think that decoding a single *Homo sapiens* genome was a process that once took months, let alone hours. Microtechnology, too, was thought by some to solve all problems, become the proverbial holy grail of the sciences. That prospect was stillborn, in my opinion." Mr. Halisdol turned toward Isa, looking her up and down. She seemed oblivious, or at least parsing some internal recursion of contrapositives and obscure conditions deep inside her. "Believe me," he said. "We tried."

"I'm a bit confused," Doug again. "You want us to record an album of lullabies to assist in your child development research, or are these to be marketed toward new families?"

"I'm perplexed too," said Julia, her voice edging on an anxious valence. "I had no idea this facility even existed, let alone the research we were doing."

"Well, research confidentiality is a paramount concern in all east-coast branches of Melodica," said Mr. Halisdol. "Besides, you never asked. And to you Mr.," he squinted, "Lamarck-Ganoush, the lullabies are intended to be a marketable educational device. We intend on incorporating a wide range of musical genres; however, New Ape Idea is the first band we've managed to ask."

Figure 5: Evan Halisdol

"And we'll get paid?" said Takashi.

"Of course. You'll receive a contract with the details, should you agree to record. We're offering 15 million up front as well as a 3% royalty on all sales."

Doug opened his mouth, about to ask for a brief consultation with his bandmates. Of course, Takashi had already grasped Mr. Halisdol's hand before any words were emitted.

"I'm hesitant to accept," said Isa. Doug could see Takashi's hand go limp in Mr. Halisdol's.

"Me too," Doug followed. He swallowed. "Could the three of us have a moment to talk this over?"

Mr. Halisdol smoothed his lapels then cleared his throat. "Was my explanation not satisfactory?"

"C'mon DLG," said Takashi. "I know yr confused, but I get the gist of it. I can explain it in the ride back."

"I think it would be best if we just could talk about this before signing on to a record deal."

"I see," said Mr. Halisdol. "That is understandable." He nodded toward Julia. "Miss Sets and I will be waiting outside. Take your time." He then blinked open the door and exited. Julia followed.

"_-_"

"_-_"

Takashi emitted a dry cough, as if to exhort an F2F from his bandmates. It was not effective.

"_-_"

"_-_"

"_-_"

"Well aren't you awfully eager to sell out," Doug spat out at last, his voice a bit more biting than he intended.

"We all know we need the money," Tak retorted. "And I wouldn't shit talk Melodica too much, they're probably listening in on us right now."

Doug looked over each shoulder. Although there were no visible cameras or mics, he knew Tak was correct.

"So they can't give us details about their project. It seems random yeah, but that's modern corporate security. I wouldn't give two fucks. We know it's for some research. How bad can it be DLG? Our art is being used to advance the sum total of human knowledge."

Doug nodded pensively. "What say you Isa?"

"_-_"

"I don't know," said Doug. "This big company that sprung up in the middle of the Meadowlands that nobody's ever heard of. Why are they the ones doing this research? Why not like, some university or something?"

"Courtney Christ DLG," said Takashi. "What year do you think it is?"

The hebody sighed. "Yeah, but what is the research department called? Eu-psychics? I've never even heard of it."

"Well psychics probably refers to psychology and Eu is Greek for good. What's to be so afraid of?"

"And its 15 million dollars."

"15 million dollars," Takashi repeated.

"That's a metric shit ton of money."

"It is. It is."

"Well what about our performances? Will we have to sign away the right to that? I'd hate to give up Rule 30."

"So we insist on that. We have some negotiating power too I'm sure," said Takashi. "I don't see why they'd want to take that away from us anyway. Those shows just increase our marketability."

"I'm still apprehensive," said Doug. "But—"

"But what's the worst that could happen?" Takashi sported a crooked smile.

"A lot of things, Miyagi-Edelstein. A lot of things."

"Are the children raised with any sort of religion?" says Congressman Duffy, surveying the playroom.

"No," responds Dewert. "We can't. A technicality of voucher reform."

The two dozen children in front of him mill about quietly. They do not shout or run, and when they speak, the children address one another in low polite voices. To Duffy's side, a trio of mixed-gendered kids—age four as displayed on their breasts—play a drawing game on one of the orphanage's tablets. One draws an array of geometric shapes, while the other two color and animate it. Based on their facial expressions it is difficult for Congressman Duffy to sim whether they are competing or working together. Across the room, a sextet of five year olds perform a calisthenics routine together. They alternate between push ups on their knees, running in place and performing jumping-jacks. They do not count aloud but manage to keep in sync with one another. Above them the wall displays an animation of the orphanage's name. Several cartoon animals beam at Duffy and wave at him. Their collective gaze follows him and Dewert as they stroll across the room.

Dewert places a hand on the wiry crown of a 4 year old, gender indeterminate. The child does not seem to be occupying itself with any games or activities. It
simply sits on the play mat meditatively with its legs crossed.

"This one is Sam," says Dewert.

"Pleasure to meet you," says Sam, standing up and taking three of Congressman Duffy's fingers in its little hand. Duffy can see the child's hazel irises are glowing
with active smart lenses.

"Sam," says Dewert slowly with a toothy saccharine smile, "Do you know who
this man is?"

"Congressman Patrick Duffy," says Sam. "Republican, New Jersey."

Duffy straightens his spine instinctually on hearing his name. "That's extremely
impressive," he says. "Do you know what a Congressman is?"

"No," says Sam with neither meekness nor temerity. "I read it off of my Eyes."

"Very good," says Dewert, giving Sam a pat. "Isn't that impressive?" he says to
Duffy. "Sam has apparently been literate for the past 14 months."

"A living miracle," says Duffy getting down on one knee. He is now eye-level
with the child. "With an intellect like yours maybe one day you'll even grow up to be
a Congressman like me," he says.

"Maybe," says Sam. "Although Nanny tells me I could make a good politician."

"That's exactly what a congressman is," says Duffy.

"Oh," replies Sam. "Okay."

"Do you want a picture with him?" says Dewert. "It'd make great publicity."

"That's okay," says Duffy. "I let my interns handle my social media presence."

"How rare," says Dewert.

Duffy stands back up. He sees another three year old, plucking out notes on
a small keyboard. Though his motor skills are appropriately poor, a coherent melody
jaunts forth; however, Duffy does not recognize it.

"What is he playing?" he asks.

"Probably one of his lullabies. We use a lot of music for our instructionals."

"I see."

Below the men's feet the playmat displays a busy city street. Animated cars loop
around the parochial streets, yielding to crossing pedestrians dressed in antiquated
work garb: blue-suited policemen, nurses in white hats and blouses, Duffy could even
espy a mail carrier with too-short shorts.

"And what are they like when visitors are not around?" says Duffy.

"Their behavior is impeccable," Dewert responds. "As always."

"Do you spank them?"

"Rods are spared, but the children are hardly spoilt," says Dewert. "To say we've
boiled down parenting to a science is an understatement."

"I'm inclined to agree." Duffy scans the room. He has toured military bases that were more disorderly. "But one thing Mr. Dewert."

"Yes?" Dewert clasps his hands clerically behind his back and gives the congressman a postured, close-lipped smile.

"It's all too uncanny. Foster children shouldn't be this polite. I can't imagine that most honest folk wouldn't get a little disturbed F2Fing with one of them."

"They won't," says Dewert. "Not when the children are so young. Your constituents only need to hear the statistics to have full faith in this project. Tell them the test scores, the violent behavior incidence rates, and in a few years the university matriculation rates."

"We won't have those numbers for another fifteen years," says Duffy. "Well, I should hope you don't plan on staying in Congress for the rest of your career."

Duffy adjusts the knot of his necktie. "I appreciate a partner with a vision."

"20/60 vision to be exact. And you'll be approaching the century anniversary of *Roe V. Wade* too."

"You have this all figured out, don't you?"

"I'm only repeating what I know you've thought," says Dewert.

A bell chiming plays crisply over speakers. All the children calmly put away whatever toys or educational devices they had been playing with and begin to ebb around the two hebodies, forming a queue by the room's entrance. They stand in pairs, holding hands with partners. A few swing their partners' arms playfully to and fro while they chat quietly with one another. Dewert leads the congressman to take a few steps backwards into the room's center. Duffy can see that the playmat animations have been replaced by a static hardwood floor pattern.

"Hello Miss Allison," a chorus of little voices says in unison.

One of the chaperones enters the room: a middle-aged shebody with her dyed-dark hair tied up in a tight bun. She holds a tablet in the crook of her arm that she briefly consults before addressing the line of children waiting for her.

"Hello my little chipmunks," she says, her voice sweet and maternal. She wears a matronly blouse with a name tag clipped onto the breast. "What time is it?"

"3 O'clock," they say.

"So what will we study now?"

"Math."

"Very good," she says. Only now does she acknowledge the two men standing in the center of the playroom with a slight nod. "Who needs their Eyes?" she says back to the kids and a series of hands shoot up.

Miss Allison depresses a button by the doorframe, revealing a compartment containing a series of vials. She removes four of them and squats down. The four Eyeless orphans break from the line and approach her, one at a time. Gingerly, she peels their eyelids apart with two fingers while dropping in a few drops of saline solution from a pipettes, first in the left eye, then the right. She then removes a pair of smart lenses from one of the vials and places them over their irises before wiping away the salty runoff tearing down their cheeks with the back of her hand. The children are stoically quiet during the whole procedure.

Miss Allison stands and replaces the vials back into their compartment which she then closes. The children meanwhile take a seat at the triclinium of tables along the three playroom walls. They blink on their Lazy Eyes, insert small colorful buds into their ears and begin fingering the air in front of them, navigating through bubbles of content visible only to them.

"Congressman Duffy," says the chaperone, "Allison Hernandez. It's a pleasure." "Nice to meet you." Duffy extends a hand, which she takes. Her palm is sur-prisingly callused.

"Hello Vincent," she says, nodding to Dewert.

"Amazing work you're doing here Miss. Hernandez," says Congressman Duffy.

"Thank you," she says. "I take it this is your first visit to It Takes a Village."

"Correct," he says. "But I'm already impressed. You can rest assured this will not be my last visit." He punctuates this with the rehearsed laugh of one who aspired to join the senate.

All the orphans seem silent and docile during their class. One six year old's face erupts in a quick grimace. He clenches a tiny fist in frustration before his expression neutralizes and he resumes his course.

"What's he studying?" asks Duffy.

"Who, Milo?" says Allison Hernandez, before blinking on a Lazy Eye display of her own and activating a few sliders. The child's display turns from private to public browsing. Milo does not seem to notice or care that the adults can all see what he is up to.

Before him are four cartoon monsters, they carry oversized paintbrushes drip-ping with different colors. They stand to the side of a large blank map of the European Union, the various countries are unlabeled. Milo selects orders from a drop-down menu to the left of the map, and a monster lumbers over to a given country and hur-riedly paints with his enormous brush.

"Milo's trying to paint each country a different color, in such a way that no two countries of the same color touch," says Hernandez. "He doesn't know it, but he's learning basic algorithmic thinking."

"Right," says Duffy, "I'm sure he is."

The chaperone blinks back on her display and slides Milo's into private before blinking hers off.

"Is he on an advanced track?"

"No sir. We don't track the children. They all can learn at the same rate, an ex-tremely accelerated one at that. All the three-to-six-year-olds are doing the exact same activity now."

"Three to six year olds," Duffy says, only half aware that he is speaking aloud.

"That's the age group I work with, yes."

"What about the older children?"

"The six-to-tens are on a field trip," Dewert cuts in, leaning forward as he speaks. "Once they hit the double digits though we either move them to foster care or to our halfway house up the parkway."

"And what about the toddlers?"

"They're in the nursery," says Dewert.

"May I seem them?"

"Of course," says Dewert. He nods to Allison, who side-steps away from the entrance to the playroom.

"Down the hall and to the left," she says.

The whole nursery is softly lit with a deep azure tint, giving the room an amniotic under-water quality. There are none of the cartoonish drawings or animated educational posters the hallways or playrooms are equipped with. Instead the walls display aggregates of the bodily informatics of the toddlers laying in the grid of cribs at the room's center. All of the cribs are tented with translucent mesh. Large cables dangle from the ceiling. Each has a large glass sphere that hangs about ten centime-ters above each crib. A damp fuzzy wash of sound echoes throughout the nursery. It sounds almost human to Duffy, though he cannot parse out any individual words or sentence fragments.

"What are we listening too?" says Duffy.

"We aren't listening to anything," says Dewert. "The children; however, are listening to their lullabies."

"So this is their nap time?" says Duffy, lowering the volume of his voice.

Dewert clicks his tongue. "Apologies. I suppose that title is misleading. These children interact with the recordings nearly all hours of the day. Because each melody is individually tailored to each crib, the lullabies slip in and out of phase with each other. What you're hearing now is the mush that comes from all these asynchronous recordings playing at once."

Duffy nods. He and Dewert begin to stroll along the perimeter of the nursery, both men's legs swinging metronomically. "Is there any chance I could have a listen to what they're hearing?"

"I apologize, but no," says Dewert, stopping. "That would require opening the tent. "We try and limit the amount of F2F interactions the children get at this age, it can throw their target developmental trajectories severely off course."

Duffy places his hands along the metal railing circumscribing the nursery. It is cool to the touch and feels recently cleaned. "I'm no psychologist," the congressman says, "but I fail to see why that would be the case."

"As you know these are very high-risk youth," says Dewert. "Often born into poverty, broken homes. Most would be aborted if their parents had the funds. At a certain age—younger than you may be inclined to think—these children begin to internalize this parental void. Their minds become the perfect ecosystem to nurture mood disorders, substance addictions, and criminality."

"You are preaching to the choir here Vincent."

"Yes well, research at our sister institutions has opened the doors for discovering new methods of effectively rearing these highly special individuals."

Duffy raises a hand to Dewert, silencing him. "Vincent, do you know who I work for?"

"I'm sorry," says Dewert. "I don't follow."

"The federal government of the United States," says Duffy. "And in my tenure I have smelt a lot of bullshit. I can tell what some folks have eaten for lunch three days prior my nose is so good."

"With all due respect congressman," says Dewert. "I wasn't bullshitting you."

"I wasn't saying you were," says Duffy, eyeing him. "And honestly, I don't harbor a huge amount of resentment toward bullshitting. I'd call it a necessary evil, but frankly I don't see it as so evil these days. What I'm saying though is this: I can tell you were about to start bullshitting me, and I'd like to ask you to stop doing it before you've even started."

"_"

"You don't have to put any gloss on it," says Duffy, his tone softening. "Just tell me what you do here. I have people who will be able to spin this way more effectively than you ever can."

"Well I'm no scientist," says Dewert. "Lobbying requires an entirely different type of smarts. But what from what I understand, the human organism is a vastly complex system. This is almost cliché, but the extents of this complexity are only becoming fathomable thanks to our use of computational technologies exponentially more powerful than our own brains."

"You're still making my nostrils tingle Vincent."

"Right, well. When a child grows up, we like to think of its development occurring across a few different spectrums. A child develops motor skills that let it crawl, then walk. Linguistic abilities that let it babble then form words and in time sentences. Interpersonal intelligence that lets it recognize faces and names. I could go on and on. But what we're seeing now is that these separate faculties aren't so separate after all. They overlap."

Dewert leans over the railing and gestures out toward the matrix of cribs in front of him. "As these babies listen to this music, they exercise their limbs. It's like a little dance. They wiggle their fingers and kick their legs. This trains up the neural circuits that allow them to later walk and run or what have you. But it also helps them grow on a deeper psychological level. Moving their bodies, it's like they realize, 'Hey, this is where I end and the rest of the universe begins'. This of course is only reinforced by hearing the voice of their mother. Or whoever their caretaker is, I guess I gotta be politically correct here."

"No need for political correctness with me," says Duffy.

"Good," says Dewert. "They hear their mother singing and realize that they are not the only conscious entity in the universe. That other humans exist alongside them. Basically, by listening and dancing in their own infant way, the seeds of having a human identity are sown within them."

"And this is fact," says Duffy. "Not just speculation?"

"Corroborated by years of research," says Dewert. "What's fascinating to me though, is that this singing and dancing between mother and child, it's like there aren't even two people involved. It's a joint act. The mother sings, her child moves, the mother's singing changes in reaction to her child's movement. It's a feedback process right? Like two become one. It's the way we get a sense of self, and through ourselves we sim the thoughts of others. Public language begets private thought. This whole lullaby song-and-dance thing apparently runs very deep in our evolutionary history, but it's still highly fine-tunable from what I understand." Dewert cocks an eyebrow. "Unless you're one of those folks I shouldn't bring this sort of Darwin stuff up around."

Duffy shakes his head. "This is New Jersey, not Mississippi."

Dewert lets out a convulsive, laughless "Hah."

"But I still try not to talk about this sort of matter around my constituents. I'm sure you understand."

"Of course," says Dewert.

"But one question," says Duffy. "At age three you say they're let out of here. Why? Isn't that transition, I don't know, abrupt."

"We slowly introduce them to other supervisors beginning at age two. By the time they exit toddlerhood they start having playtime with one another. At that point they've simply outgrown the music work we do here," says Dewert.

"It's not a shock to them?"

"Not at all," says Dewert. "We have people who studied this all very carefully so we here can essentially manipulate this innate mother-child relationship to put these wards on the best developmental tracks possible. You see, in effect we raise them from very early on to believe that they are completely alone in the universe. That their own experience is the only valid consciousness in existence. If they blink, poof, there goes the world."

"It sounds like we're raising them to be sociopaths," says Duffy.

"Not at all," says Dewert, shaking his head metronomically. "Once the children meet other caretakers and wards, they can't quite differentiate them as separate. They deeply see everyone they meet as an extension of their mind. At this point, utter solipsism, narcissism, what have you and total empathy and brotherly love become one and the same. Any chance of future criminality or antisocial behavior plummets. It's cognitively impossible for them not to be good Christians."

"Or so you say."

"Or so I *promise*," says Dewert.

Duffy checks his wristwatch: a once high-fashion antique from last century. He forgets to note the time while staring at the analog hands ticking before returning his hand to his side and readdressing Vincent Dewert.

"I've spoken with several of your colleagues across the House," Dewert continues. "If the six of you form an investigative sub-committee and push this through Congress we can have orphanages such as this nation-wide. We've already established branches in states across the eastern seaboard. We just need some momentum to move west."

"Sounds very good for you."

"Very good for us," says Dewert. "We'll have a cheap and effective Federal institution for dealing with abandoned or problem youth, and you'll have spearheaded its national development. Liberals will love it because it's a safety net that actually works; one that may sway the people toward re-Federalization. The Right, too, will also now have one of the best arguments for overturning *Roe v. Wade* in nearly a century."

"You know," says Duffy, "I tend not to appreciate when folks try and do all my thinking for me."

"Like you haven't imagined any of this before?" says Dewert. "It'll be another 'Morning in America'. You'll be able to rally around the family through those without one. This could turn our country purple."

Like a series of coupled oscillators running in tandem, the dozens of warbling lullabies emanating from each of the cribs began to slowly snap into synchrony. What at first was a soft wash of static waveforms coalesces into a polyphonic chorus, the voices obviously synthesized but still uncannily human. Within each of the dark tents, those babies must've begun flexing and distending their little limbs in rough symmetry. Whether this is a highly unlikely occurrence of pure stochasticity, or the result of melodies bleeding from one crib to the next is unknown and for the moment unknowable. Congressman Duffy is not a man of science, yet he can intuit that speaking could disturb the delicate equilibrium before him. And so, he just breathes softly through his nostrils, drinking in the whole nursery in silence.

"I've heard of stranger things," said **Futurabold**. "I mean, I wouldn't have guessed your first album would be children's music but—"

"Lullabies," Takashi interjected. He lay supine on an uncovered mattress that **Futurabold** had installed in her office at his insistence. After a show two weeks prior, a gaggle of post-crusters found Tak amidst his post-set nap. According to Takashi, the interaction-effect of their non-stop adulations and foul body odor made the prospect of a twenty-minute schluff impossible. He thus asked if he could transfer the mattress to **Futurabold**'s office, which tended to get much less intrusion after shows. Likely because Dee tended to stand outside the entrance and serve as bouncer.

"Even moreso," **Futurabold** said. "I can't exactly sim any babies finding your music soothing. But I guess there's a market for it. They're probably trying to pull in some young gen-Z parenting demographic or something."

"That's what I thought," said Doug. "However it's entirely, like, a charity project. Apparently this music—our music—is supposed to be distributed amongst orphanages and detention facilities or whatnot. You know, wards of the state."

Futurabold nodded as she twirled at her mohawk's anterior end with an index finger. "Bizarre. Then I guess we can assume they're not in it for the profit. Maybe they're trying to condition a new generation of hipsters."

"I'm thinking more or less the same," said Doug, his Feldenkrais paperback splayed open across his lap. "I wanted to investigate further, of course Takashi signed a contract almost immediately."

"It's good money!" said Takashi as he sat up, his hair matted against the back of skull. "With what Melodica pays us we could buy out Rule 30. And that's not even including the royalties."

Doug turned to **Futurabold** and put forth a supplicating palm. "I can assure you, we have no intent of doing such."

"We could've bought our whole set-up." Takashi fell back onto the mattress: an ancient spring-style likely older than he was. "No need for me to have jacked it."

"You should keep that in mind next time," said Doug, looking over his shoulder at Tak.

"So babies without parents?" said **Futurabold**.

Doug turned back toward the shebody. "Apparently," he said.

Futurabold looked up toward the ceiling and nodded. "Actually, on second thought, that does make sense," she said. "To a degree."

Tak sat up. Combing his fingers through his hair, he unmussed his bed head. His blonde spikes bristled out anemone-like. "Now this I gotta hear."

"From what I understand, your album is to be marketed toward orphans, or children from broken homes. I'm sure these researchers at—"

"Melodica," Doug said.

"Melodica are looking to try and compensate for that missing act of care."

"Bleeding-heart bullshit," said Takashi.

"You're the vegan here, Tak," said Doug.

"Yeah but, like, so a few toddlers don't get to hear a nursery rhyme before they go to bed. Is that really the biggest problem society is facing today?"

"You're thinking of reneging on the contract?" **Futurabold**, expanding the desktop screen and swiping across its broad face.

"As I said, the money's good. Beyond that, I give a very minor-league shit."

"Huh," said **Futurabold**, shifting her weight forward in her chair. "You know lullabies are culturally ubiquitous? Everyone from hunter-gatherers to 5th Wave Feminists sing to their young"

"Is that so?" said Doug. He had returned to his loggy paperback. "You learn this in your Evo. Ludology degree?"

"Nope," said **Futurabold**. "Internet."

"Are they, like, counter culturally ubiquitous too?" said Takashi rolling onto his stomach, his back to the other two. "Like will ravegoth parents sing their brood Kamikaze Khrist riffs at bedtime?"

"It is highly unlikely that whoever would call themselves 'ravegoths' could successfully reproduce," said Doug.

"And the word 'lullaby' is misleading," added **Futurabold**. "Parents, especially mothers, will sing to their infants at all times—not just when trying to put the kid to sleep." She swiped her hand in front of her, scrolling through some wiki invisible to Doug and Takashi. "Apparently caretaker-child song can occur while feeding, playing, whenever."

"So we're not trying'ta put kids to sleep," said Tak. "Maybe our tracks will be for feeding."

"Or recess," said Doug.

"Infants don't have recess, boyo."

"They have a huge amount of developmental benefits too," said **Futurabold** squinting at the screen. "Lullabies, I mean."

"I guess it depends on the songs they want us to sing," Takashi, face half-buried in a thin pillow. "Like, if we're doing *Hush Little Baby* the applications will be self-evident."

"Melodica wants us to do originals," said Doug.

Tak turned 180 degrees onto his back. His forearm covered his eyes as he spoke. "Wait, seriously? They're asking for a lawsuit. I'm pretty sure our lyrics are in violation of, like, three thousand federal speech codes."

The paperback made a thin thumping sound as Doug closed it. "Courtney Christ, did you even read the contract?"

"I assumed you would, DLG."

Lamarck-Ganoush felt his body ossify with frustration. "I did, but what if I didn't? What if I skipped over something?"

"Well fuck," **Futurabold** muttered. "There is an overwhelming amount of research I'm getting, even with just a cursory-level search."

"You're too thorough for that. I simmed that you simmed that I wouldn't read it, and therefore would go over the whole spiel in painstaking detail. And it seems I simmed correctly."

"—Most of the publications are behind a paywall. Is there any way we can get around this?"

"Why do you feel that's an okay thing to do, Tak? My eyes are shit. How do you know I didn't skip all the fine print?"

"I simmed you wouldn't. It's called theory of mind, Ganoush. The reading of one's mental states by projecting them onto your own. A basic component of human psychology."

"Which is also a side-effect of singing to infants," said **Futurabold**, enveloped by her wiki wonderland. "At least according to the study abstracts I can access for free. Bootstrapping of theory of mind. But that seems more speculative."

"Well, shit," said Takashi. "I guess we'll have to clean up our lyrics."

"Like which ones?" said Lamarck-Ganoush.

Tak propped himself up on his elbows and cocked his head at Doug. "Do you not know the words to our own songs?" he asked.

"I don't pay much attention. I'm mostly trying to keep time," said Doug. "What are the really bad ones?"

"Y'know," said Tak, his rate of speech slowing. "I'm not so sure myself."

"Some anthropologists speculate that lullabies are a vestige of an earlier form of human communication. There are even more links to articles by evolutionary psychologists. The abstracts read that early hominids communicated musically, and that has since evolved into a syntactical verbal language."

"I think Isa's been changing some of them since she started singing," said Takashi.

"We should ask her," said Doug.

"There's so much to read here on lullabies," said **Futurabold**, "I found an old academic journal on something called *Communicative Musicality*. Apparently toward the end of last century, a few psychologists were looking at these early mother-child lullaby interactions as the key to the formation of the child's sense of self."

"Well, where is Isa?" Tak again, louder this time.

"Likely the bathroom," said **Futurabold**, lifting her gaze from the monitor, snapping back into loggy reality.

"Why?" said Takashi. "We just played a set. I thought her rule was pre-set: bathroom, post-set: office."

"She's not an automaton, Tak," said Lamarck-Ganoush.

"Might as well be," said Takashi. One eye closed, he played with his eyelashes as he spoke. Pinching them with his index and middle fingers as if they were wired to some neural pleasure center.

"Shut up Takashi," said both **Futurabold** and Lamarck-Ganoush in concert.

"And you do have a set coming up," said **Futurabold**. "FYI."

"No shit?" said Takashi.

"Double-feature Fridays," said **Futurabold**. "On the condition that you get 15% of ticket revenues. Remember?"

But Takashi, sitting up, could only look at her in groggy confusion.

"You're up in another two point five hours."

"You never told us!" said Takashi.

"She absolutely did, Tak," Doug replied. "This is the second week in a row we're doing this."

"Yr shitting me. I don't remember last week."

A sigh from Doug. "You were crossed on a case of low-carb corn beer and non-synth," he said.

Takashi smiled. "Now I remember. I hope I didn't sound too fucked up. Or if I did, I hope I was fucked up in the right kinda way. Y'know?"

"You're the bassist," said **Futurabold**. "Nobody gives a shit what you sound like."

Takashi emitted a curse that seemed to combine both Yiddish and Japanese phonemes. "Well, I thought today was Wednesday," he said.

But **Futurabold** and Doug had already returned to their respective texts. Doug, back erect, digesting his hip paperback; **Futurabold**, chewing on the meat of her lower lips as she pawed through cyberspace.

The mattress groaned as Tak rose to his feet and leapt off it. "I should probably get her," he said, and shuffled out. Doug could hear a muffled interchange with Dee after the door slammed.

And for the next several minutes, the two continued to read, involved in their arrangements of letters. It only took a few minutes, three or five, no more than ten, the overhead ceiling fan providing a uterine whoosh of white noise, for them to grow deeply unaware of one another's presences.

*   *   *

1.	I prefer to keep my eyes closed as I play guitar and sing.
1.1.	Although I am unsure as to whether "sing" is the proper label for what I do.
1.1.1.	Yell? Intone? Vocalize?
1.2.	Of course, aspects of set-up, which necessarily precede playing guitar, require that I keep my eyes open.
1.2.1.	These include tuning, plugging in my guitar to my pedalboard and my pedal board to the amplifier, sound checking the vocal mic, presetting my distortion, flanger, auto-wah, chorus, fuzz, overdrive, reverb, digital delay, compressor and volume pedals to their proper settings. In order to properly calibrate the SHAN-NON, Takashi will have me vocalize into the microphone as he manipulates a series of potentiometers on the machine's chassis.
1.2.2.	Currently, I have turned my back to those who are filling the room.
1.2.2.1.	I do this because I do not prefer to look at them.
1.2.2.1.1.	"Them" of course referring to the others.
1.2.2.2.	Ideally, I would prefer simply to cloud my vision with applets from my Lazy Eyes. This having the effect of obscuring the others' faces.
1.2.2.2.1.	I cannot do this currently because my Lazy Eyes have gone missing.
1.3.	Occasionally, playing guitar requires that I open my eyes. This is because I am unable to coordinate the proper movements of

	my wrists and fingers without visual input.
1.3.1.	Of course, opening my eyes for this purpose fulfills a similar role as my closing them in the first place.
1.3.1.1.	Ibid 1.2.2.1
2.	Four drum stick clicks are usually the cue to begin our set.
2.1.	By this I mean that, as a rule, four clicks introduce the ensuing music.
2.1.1.	Although, I can imagine three clicks beginning our set.
2.1.2.	By that manner, five or six clicks as well.
2.1.2.1.	In this way, the music to be played is not dependent on the number of drumstick clicks preceding it.
2.1.2.2.	However, I cannot recall if I have ever played after hearing three or five clicks.
2.1.2.2.1.	What is it that stops me from playing after click three and waiting until click four?
2.1.2.3.	Most songs which I play are in a 4/4 time signature.
2.1.2.3.1.	I could infer that these four clicks are a convenience, symbolizing the four beats per measure.
2.1.2.3.2.	However, Doug begins each song with four clicks, regardless of time signature.
2.1.2.3.2.1.	This practice, though, was adopted at the insistence of Takashi.
2.1.2.3.2.1.1.	Takashi claimed starting songs as such was "tradition" that others would recognize.
2.1.2.3.2.1.1.1.	By "tradition" I assume he refers to a practice undertaken by bands of a similar ilk as ours.
2.1.2.3.2.1.1.2.	In this sense, one can see the truth in calling Takashi a Poseur.
2.1.2.3.2.1.1.2.1.	A "Poseur" is one who carefully calculates their outer expression to appear in a certain manner, regardless of whether it is consistent with their internal experience.
2.1.2.3.2.1.1.2.2.	Takashi is concerned with his appearance, not with his inner life.
2.1.2.3.2.1.1.2.3.	He once admitted to fearing that his brain might spring a proverbial leak, and all his innermost thoughts would be broadcasted for everyone to hear. The world would thus shame him for his poseurdom.
2.1.2.3.2.1.1.2.4.	Whereas I fear that I am no more than a bracket on the world. That

	everything which seems outside me is actually contained within me.
2.1.2.4.	How I am able to synchronize the tempo of my playing guitar with Doug and Takashi is curious.
2.1.2.4.1.	Especially in cases when four clicks precedes a song with an alternative number of beats per measure.
2.2.	The onset of my playing correlates with a cheering from the others pooling around the stage.
2.2.1.	As with the drum clicks, this cheering precedes my shutting my eyes even tighter.
2.2.1.1.	Ibid 2
2.2.1.2.	Although this ritual was not in place when I still had my Lazy Eyes.
2.2.1.2.1.	Ibid 1.2.2.2
2.2.1.2.2.	The last time I was in contact with my Lazy Eyes was in the cot room of Rule 30 approx. 86 days ago.
2.2.1.2.2.1.	I thus believed they were lost within the sheets of Ruthie's bed.
2.2.1.2.2.1.1.	After much searching, the objects could not be found.
2.2.1.2.2.1.2.	Takashi even insisted on moving the mattress into Ruthie's office to abet my search. The Lazy Eyes are still in an unknown location.
2.2.1.2.2.1.2.1.	Unless of course Takashi found them but has hidden his acquisition from me.
2.2.1.2.2.1.2.1.1.	I do not like to think about this possibility.
3.	Admittedly, I do not know the names of any of our songs.
3.1.	By which I mean, I am unable to identify any of the songs by their titles. I instead recognize them based on the quality of their sound, their melodies and rhythms as well as the proper digital maneuverings I must undertake to play them properly.
3.1.1.	Perhaps one could differentiate most songs by their lyrics.
3.1.1.1.	This process, however, is not possible for any songs that I "sing".
3.1.1.1.1.	Ibid 1.1
3.1.1.1.2.	I justify this argument because all songs I sing have the same lyrics.
3.1.1.1.2.1.	"Banana, Banana, Banana, Banana, Banana"
3.1.1.1.3.	Any lyrical difference between one song I sing to any other is de facto arbitrary.
3.2.	Although several others have claimed to have preferred songs within our repertoire.

3.2.1.	It would thus follow logically that preferred songs are selected based upon metrics separate from lyrics.
3.2.1.1.	Although, Takashi, Doug, and Ruthie have all drawn my attention to texts praising my innovative lyrics.
3.2.1.1.1.	Three distinct propositions may follow this:
3.2.1.1.1.1.	That there is a discrepancy between the lyrics I think I "sing" and the lyrics I actually sing.
3.2.1.1.1.1.1.	Then what is the relationship between what is thought and what is said? If I attempt to vocalize the word "banana", and yet the word "orange" comes out unbeknownst to me, what have I really said?
3.2.1.1.1.2.	That there is a discrepancy between the lyrics I sing and the lyrics the others perceive.
3.2.1.1.1.2.1.	This mishearing could be traced out by examining the logical structures underlying the following: the montage of neural firings representing what I am to sing, the sound waves emitted from my throat, the stimulation of hair cells within the eardrums of the others, and their corresponding neural representations. One could thus pinpoint the exact failure in this correspondence.
3.2.1.1.1.3.	Unless the reasons why the others hear different lyrics is not easily broken down into the discrete subsystems I listed before.
3.2.1.1.1.3.1.	While perhaps possible, I do not wish to entertain such, as it requires meditating on the outer and inner experiences of others.
3.3.	The vocal melodies of different songs I sing are negligible too.
3.3.1.	Just as the corresponding lyrics are undifferentiable.
3.3.2.	By this I mean it is almost impossibly difficult to differentiate songs based on vocal melodies.
3.3.2.1.	That is not to say that every song has the exact same vocal melody. Rather, the vocal melodies of varying songs are indistinguishable.
3.3.2.1.1.	This property of all my melodies is likely due to distortion and modulation from Takashi's SHANNON.
3.3.2.1.1.1.	By measuring the heat and kinetic energy generated by the others, the SHANNON alters the signal travelling between the microphone and the amplifier.
3.3.2.1.1.1.1.	Thus, even when performing the same song twice, the vocal melodies will be different.

3.3.2.1.2.	Though the vocal melodies are not indistinguishable in the same sense as my lyrics. The lyrics are indistinguishable because they are all alike. The melodies, however, are all unalike.
3.3.2.1.2.1.	And yet how peculiar the word "indistinguishable" may be rightly applied to both opposite cases.
3.3.2.1.3.	Though if the vocal melody of a song is influenced in part by the movement of the others, to what extent am I even singing?
3.3.2.1.3.1.	This is another reason why I prefer not to use the word "sing".
3.3.2.1.3.2.	Though if I am not the performer, why do I feel such stage anxiety?
3.3.2.1.3.2.1.	Logic would dictate that such anxiety is meaningless.
3.3.2.1.3.2.1.1.	Although who or what determines what are the criterion for a proposition being logical?
3.3.2.1.3.2.1.1.1.	Takashi and Doug are performers, as are the others, as am I. They all perform with their eyes open. If logic dictates what I ought to do, I ought to open my eyes as well.
4.	I have vastly underestimated the number of others in the audience.
4.1.	Before, I had assumed there would be no more than one or two dozen.
4.2.	Rule 30 is packed. There are likely several hundred bodies filling the space.
4.2.1.	And yet they move, despite their congestion.
4.2.1.1.	They move in the following ways:
4.2.1.1.1.	Some will windmill about, arms outstretched, pummeling those nearby.
4.2.1.1.2.	Their knees locked, several pogo up and down, their hands balled into fists.
4.2.1.1.3.	Couples throw themselves at one another, as if to tackle or otherwise subdue each other. I do not believe, they intend to hurt each other, as their smiles evince an amicability.
4.2.1.1.3.1.	This behavior is often referred to as "moshing". The setting it occurs in is concurrently the "mosh pit".
4.2.1.1.4.	One hebody glides across the mosh pit, held up by the supporting arms of the others below. His smile too evinces a content inner experience.
4.2.1.1.4.1.	And from surfing across the crowd he manages to grab a metal

heating pipe overhead and brachiates from it. He swings his legs to and fro before dropping down back into the pit. Upon landing he pounds upon his chest.

4.2.1.1.4.2.   Although the palms of his hands look severely burned, he does not act as if he is in pain.

4.2.1.1.4.2.1.   It occurs to me that his actions, atavistic as they are, may be a reference to the name of my band.

4.2.1.1.4.2.1.1.   "New Ape Idea".

4.2.2.   Within the center of the mosh pit a circle forms.

4.2.2.1.   It consists of several others moving about in the same direction, creating a human whirlpool.

4.2.2.1.1.   Those who attempt to travel in a direction opposite to that of the current are pummeled by the masses moving against them.

4.2.2.1.1.1.   Likewise for all those who attempt to stand unmoving within the perimeter of the whirlpool.

4.2.2.1.2.   The whirlpool seems to emerge from the chaos of the mosh pit.

4.2.2.1.2.1.   That is to say, there are no prescriptive factors that dictated the formation of the whirlpool.

4.2.2.1.2.1.1.   Other than the laws of physics and human anatomy of course.

4.2.2.1.2.1.2.   What I mean to say is the emergence of the whirlpool was likely not premeditated. It is a large pattern that arises from the activity of its sub-components.

4.2.2.2.   Does the whirlpool within the mosh pit have a meaning?

4.2.2.2.1.   It certainly does not have a grammar.

4.2.2.2.1.1.   What I mean is, although there are rules dictating what cannot happen in the mosh pit (one could not fly about the room for example or turn into a pineapple), there are no rules for how the pit ought to function.

4.2.2.2.1.1.1.   Ibid. 4.2.2.1.2

4.2.2.2.2.   Though I can imagine several uses for the mosh pit.

4.2.2.2.2.1.   Physical exercise.

4.2.2.2.2.2.   Emotional catharsis.

4.2.2.2.2.3.   Social intercourse.

4.2.2.2.2.3.1.   These uses inform its meaning.

4.2.2.2.2.3.2.   The mosh pit does not have one single meaning.

4.2.2.2.2.3.2.1.	Meaning varies among those within the pit.
4.2.2.2.2.3.2.2.	Therefore the mosh pit is more meaningful than the strange jargon Takashi employs.
4.2.2.3.	As the whirlpool grows, consuming more and more of the pit, it subsequently modulates the vocal melody to a greater degree.
4.2.2.3.1.	Hearing the sound of my voice grow more and more distorted, those that make up the mosh pit begin to thrash about more vigorously. The human whirlpool at its center increases in velocity.
4.2.2.3.1.1.	This feedback loop seems as if it will continue indefinitely.
4.2.2.3.2.	I refrain from vocalizing.
4.2.2.3.2.1.	I fear that should I continue, the dynamism of the mosh pit will engulf me completely. I too will be swallowed up by the whirlpool.
4.2.2.3.2.2.	And yet, the mosh pit continues to grow more chaotic and complex.
4.2.2.3.2.2.1.	Its movement must be enough to activate the SHANNON and create the auditory illusion of my vocalizing.
4.2.2.3.2.2.1.1.	To what extent, then, am I still singing? I do not vocalize, and yet lyrics are heard.
4.2.2.3.2.2.1.2.	In this manner, I realize, the music I produce is in some ways independent of me.
5.	Takashi is mouthing "Holy Shit! Holy Shit! Holy Shit!"
5.1.	He may be vocalizing, although I am unable to hear his voice over the din of our playing.
5.2.	A large, open-mouthed smile accompanies his vocalizing.
5.2.1.	Both upper and lower teeth are visible.
5.2.2.	Likely, the smile evinces a positive internal state.
5.2.2.1.	I suppose this is why one smiles: to symbolize an internal state as such.
5.2.2.1.1.	But can't one also smile deliberately, despite not experiencing a state of happiness?
5.2.2.1.1.1.	In such a case, one says to herself, "although I feel depressed I will still choose to smile so as to symbolize otherwise."
5.2.2.1.1.1.1.	I cannot imagine a case in which one manages to choose the expression before the interior experience.

5.2.2.1.1.1.2.	Expression cannot precede emotion.
5.2.2.1.2.	One may also smile spontaneously, as if the interior emotion is leaking out.
5.2.2.1.2.1.	In such a case, the smiling is intentional, though not necessarily deliberate.
5.2.2.1.2.2.	The smiling occurs in concert with the emotion: either simultaneous or with a slight delay after the experience.
5.2.2.1.2.2.1.	In both cases the marking does not precede emotion.
5.2.2.2.	Both a deliberate fake smile, and a genuine spontaneous smile are symbolically equivalent.
5.2.2.2.1.1.	To what extent then is it fruitful to attempt to parse a genuine from an affected smile?
5.2.2.2.1.1.1.	Or to ask whether any emotional display is spontaneous or feigned for that manner?
5.2.2.2.1.1.2.	Decoding the internal states of others is an impossibly difficult endeavor.
5.2.3.	I realize that I do not smile very often.
5.2.3.1.	This lack of smiling in itself may mark an array of certain internal states.
5.2.3.1.1.	The large majority of which are painful, depressive or anxious. Some are neutral.
5.2.3.2.	Perhaps this is why I find smiling so perplexing: I have little experience doing so.
5.2.3.2.1.	Although, I would prefer not to dwell on why I have such trouble remembering the last time I smiled.
5.2.3.2.1.1.	Or how smiling even feels for that matter.
5.2.3.2.1.2.	I suppose I could smile now and note how it feels.
5.3	Takashi is concurrently playing the bass guitar as he speaks.
5.3.1.	Although his technical proficiency at the bass guitar may be too poor for him to actually be considered a bassist.
5.3.1.1.	Though this lack of skill is in itself a popular mores of the punk community.
5.3.1.1.1.	In this sense Takashi may not be considered a poseur, as his lack of skill is genuine.
5.3.1.1.1.1.	If, however, he purposefully prevented himself from becoming

skillful at the bass, would he then be a poseur?

5.3.1.1.1.1.1. Such questions lead me to capitulate on the value of estimating the corresponding inner and outer states of another.

5.3.1.2. I'm inclined to think of Takashi as too poor a musician to be labeled as a "bassist".

5.3.1.2.1.1. Of course the criteria for what is poor musicianship color the meaning of the word "bassist".

5.3.1.2.1.1.1. There are no criteria outside of myself by which to affect the decision to call Takashi a "bassist" or not.

5.3.1.2.1.1.1.1. And yet I find myself using the word "decision" when expressing myself. As if meaning lies in agreeing with another.

6. I now wonder about the amount of truth that lies in solipsism.

6.1. That is, to what extent do my mind and my world overlap?

6.2 Of course, solipsism feels true.

6.2.1. In that I experience only my own experiences.

6.2.1.1. That is, obviously, a tautology and therefore without meaning.

6.2.1.1.1. Much in the way that saying "a banana is a banana" articulates very little.

6.2.2. But how a proposition "feels" shouldn't affect its truth-value.

6.2.2.1. I therefore may not accept solipsism on such grounds.

6.2.2.1.1. Although perhaps I have done so for most of my existence.

6.3 It occurs to me that these private monologues that I have are not possible under the conditions of solipsism.

6.3.1. This proposition in itself feels oxymoronic.

6.3.1.1. Ibid 6.2.2

6.3.2. How can I have a language, if I only communicate with myself?

6.3.2.1. What I mean by this is, why attach words to propositions I already know.

6.3.2.1.1. It seems language is, in itself, an argument against solipsism. There would be no need for me to employ it unless I wished to communicate with another mind.

6.3.2.1.1.1. And in some cases, this other mind is myself.

6.3.2.2. Language is the trails of footprints in the snow that lets one know she is not alone in the cold winter.

6.4. One cannot be a solipsist in the mosh pit.

6.4.1.	After all, how can one be involved in the constant motion, the jostling, the bodies slamming together and yet find themselves truly lonesome?
6.4.2.	The mosh pit, as stated earlier, has its own grammar.
6.4.2.1.	Ibid 4.2.2.2.1.1
6.4.2.2.	The existence of the mosh pit, like that of language, flies in the face of the solipsist's hypothesis.
6.4.2.2.1.	How ironic that for so many weeks these punks before me were so excited by the paradoxical vocalizing of a solipsist.
6.4.2.2.1.1.	Paradoxical in that the solipsist did not realize her own vocalizations negated the one hypothesis she held true above all else.
6.5.	It seems though that there are several factors that would lead one to embrace solipsism.
6.5.1.	Active Lazy Eye use.
6.5.2.	Losing one's parents at an early age to an act of terrorism.
6.5.3	Allowing oneself to be seduced by logic to the point of failing to grasp the world beyond what is analyzed.
6.5.4.	Countless hours in solitude spent practicing guitar.
6.5.5.	Immersing oneself in digital realities.
6.5.6.	Having thousands of robots several micrometers in length course through one's bloodstream, recording, and computationalizing every aspect of their body.
6.5.6.1.	Although this will not necessarily lead one to solipsism in itself, it will certainly enforce the idea that one's identity is mathematically—and therefore logically—describable in its entirety.
6.5.7.	A lack of F2F interaction.
6.5.7.1.	The solipsist's condition will be exacerbated if her only avenue of F2F is sexual intercourse.
6.5.8.	Constant interior monologuing.
6.5.8.1.	And herein lies the challenge: how should I break out of my own head, as it were?
7.	After taking a guitar solo that lasts several choruses, I bring my lips to the microphone and begin to vocalize again. The pit responds

as one might expect: an explosion of bodies twisting, leaping
and slamming about in sync. There is a certain joy, I suppose, in
eliciting such action from an audience. I imagine this is what draws
Takashi and Douglas to performing. I increase the volume of my
voice, though perhaps not consciously. The music and dance elicit a
deep-seated, primal vibration within me. A sensation that emerges
in part from some matrix of subsystems of immense complexity.
I can barely comprehend the winter tree neural constellations
crackling in concert between me and those around me. My cere-
bellum keeps me upright and my fingers moving. Mirror circuits
snapping within and between Takashi, Doug and I; how else could
we achieve rhythmicity with one another? I feel the awakening of a
limbic system that has been dormant since puberty. And that is just
the neuromotor level of analysis. Change the size of the frame and I
could sim the machinations present at the physiologic, perceptual,
cognitive, linguistic, phenomenological, and ontogenetic levels, to
name a few. I could change the size, direction and movement of
every single person in the pit. Sing different notes. Strum different
chords. And yet, what is in front of me, the mosh pit, will still
somehow appear the same: a massive whorl of bodies. The same
scene emerges from radically different preconditions. And yet I can
sim scenarios that, despite having consistent preconditions, exhibit
different results. I may flip a coin in the same manner repeatedly,
but the face it lands on is not describable in such a way. This is
the first time I have opened my eyes and looked upon the mosh
pit. My Lazy Eyes are lost. I am naked. And what strange word to
use: "I". Any pronoun for that manner. As if any one individual is
easily parsed from her surrounding contexts. This unearths another
great unfounded belief: that in attempting to describe a state of the
world, you are somehow making that state clearer or more understandable. It would seem the very methods of communication, language itself, is what causes such myopia. Whereas even ten minutes
ago such a syllogism would cause me acute distress, I find this lib-
erating. I sing. I do not vocalize. I do not yell. I sing. And perhaps
Takashi and Doug notice because their playing changes in character

too. Not in volume, pitch, timber, wave shape. A quality that if I were to attempt to describe it I would surely fail to communicate it accurately. The activity of the mosh pit has changed too; however, I did not notice this at first. I am too caught up in the rapture of my own music. Too enchanted by the scene to actually pay attention, to maintain awareness that the pit has changed from a peaceable mosh to an all-out brawl. Fists are hurled. Noses bloodied. Bodies fall to the ground wrapped around other bodies in baroque wrestling holds. Ruthie's Uncle Dee is at his feet and enters the pit. I watch as he is swallowed up in it. The hebody pulls two bodies apart though they still swing fists at one another before he is taken to the ground by a dozen black-clad punkers like ravens descending on a carcass. The walls flash brilliantly the names of bands I've never known and Dee lies face down unmoving and Takashi and Doug cease to play but I cannot stop myself from singing.

Figure 6: Isa Spines

2.10.0 Consultation

The waiting room Isa sits in is almost completely bare save for a few potted shrubs and a faux-wooden coffee table in front of her. Upon it sits a tablet with a small library of self-help and popular interest media feeds. It's attached to the wall behind her with a thin rubbery cord. Next to the tablet lies a sculpture of old plastic slinkies jumbled and intertwined beyond use. Though there are several seats for patients, Isa has sat for forty-five minutes alone. A small white-noise generator buzzes on in the corner, though Isa can still hear the neurologist talking quite loudly in his office. She does not bother to try and eavesdrop though. There is a potted plant to her right, though when Isa touches its leaves she feels that it is made of wax.

When the neurologist opens the door to usher her in, Isa sees that there was no patient in his office. He opens the office door remotely, not getting up from his chair.

"Welcome Isabel," he says in a rehearsed, sing-song manner. He gestures for her to have a seat across from him.

The neurologist's office has a similar sculpture sitting on the doctor's desk, and Isa now wonders if they were purchased in series as ready-made artworks, or whether they were instead the result of several fumbling patients with maladaptive and overac-tive motor systems attempting to play with the old plastic toys.

"Well. You are due for surgery in two weeks," says the neurologist. He is a zaftig bearded hebody with almost no hair on the crown of his head but the rest of his body is woolly enough to pass for an early member of the homo genus.

"Three," says Isa. She sits in the same kind of chair as the doctor: a thick large recliner made of leather that both feels and smells very authentic.

"Mhm," the hebody nods as he fingers in some notes onto his medical tablet. "And you'll need to see me at least three more times before I can legally approve you for microfactory removal."

Above his head hangs a Byzantine collage of his various diplomas, degrees and certificates. It is through examining them that Isa learns the neurologist's name is Xander Mercer.

"I understand," says Isa.

"And that's a best case scenario," he says. "It's a very intensive procedure. A complete blood transfusion, not to mention that you'll suffer some cognitive impairments for a few weeks afterwards."

"Yes. I know."

"You ever had dialysis?"

"_"

"_"

"Do you mean to say you're one of the few who doesn't have access to my medical history?" said Isa.

"The removal procedure is similar to dialysis," said Dr. Mercer. "Or a blood transfusion."

"_"

"_"

"Additionally, I'll likely want you to have a dozen counseling sessions when you're out. Just to make sure you're adjusting healthfully."

Isa scratches the crook of her elbow. She wears a long-sleeved business shirt. She had put it on that morning with the express intent of obscuring her visitats, simming that should the neurologist catch a glimpse of them he might require her to attend additional consultations and thus further delay the clearing of these damn micros out from her bloodstream.

"So," Dr. Mercer says, resting his tablet on his rotund belly. He presses a button under his armrest. His chair emits a mechanical buzzing sound as it slowly eases him back until he is almost at a full recline. "Tell me about yourself."

"Myself?" says Isa. She remains upright. What is she to say? Of course the shebody intends to give off an impression of mental hygiene. How do people normally respond to such an inquiry? And wouldn't Dr. Mercer, somewhere in attaining his myriad degrees, have learned to see through a bluffing patient? Or does he sim her simming him? In that case should she give a weak lie, a feeble "I'm fine," followed by theatrical tears so that he may feel like he successfully healed her and can send her off to scrub up? Or would even that be easy for Dr. Mercer to spot?

Fuck, Isa thinks to herself. Theory of mind is a real shrewd shebody.

Dr. Mercer peers at his tablet again. "You have an impressive profile. Lost your parents at an early age. Recently witnessed the murder, well, manslaughter, of a close friend and creative partner. Significant other in the state penitentiary." He whistles. "How's that feel? A bit maudlin, no?"

"Maudlin," says Isa. "Yes." She replays what Dr. Mercer says to her. "State penitentiary?" she says.

Dr. Mercer nods, producing a couple extra chins as he does so. "Yes, says so here. Awaiting trial. Accessory to manslaughter. When was the last time you spoke to her?"

"I don't know," says Isa. "A month maybe?"

"And you two were sexually involved," says Dr. Mercer. Isa cannot tell if it is a statement or a question.

"--"

"--"

"Yes," says Isa. "One could say that."

"--"

"--"

"Do you have any information pertaining a man named Evan Halisdol?" Isa asks. She rubs her big toes against each other through her canvas shoes.

Dr. Mercer fingers in a few more notes on his tablet. Isa can barely see the full of his face beyond the soft rolling mass of his stomach every time he inhales.

"I had a girlfriend once who was no good," he says after nearly a minute has passed.

"--"

"--"

"Did you?" says Isa, sitting perfectly upright. For the previous length of the conversation, the shebody had tried to initiate eye contact with the neurologist: a basic element of healthy F2Fing aptitude and a sign that she surely was well enough for microbot removal. The doctor however, seemed to prefer keeping his gaze leveled at his notes.

"Broke my heart," he says. "I'm married now though."

"I see," says Isa.

"Would you say you relate well with others?" Dr. Mercer asks.

"That's a very loaded question."

More notetaking. It took Isa almost an hour to shuttle up to Montclair for the appointment from Takashi's parents' house in the Oranges. Tak had offered to drive, but even Isa could read that the hebody still had some hesitation regarding riding his old van up the parkway. Takashi himself has turned slightly agoraphobic in the past months. His hair returned to its original semitic brown curls as he stopped tending to it. He'd mostly stay in his childhood bedroom as far as Isa could tell, taking apart and rebuilding fuzz pedals with a screwdriver and an old soldering iron. He had stopped speaking too, though not out of a lack of having anything to say. In times of grief language does not seem to line up so neatly against the world as one would want it to. This Isa knows too well.

The neurologist opens his mouth as if to say something, but instead closes it, cracks his knuckles and continues fingering his tablet screen.

This was a kind of silence that Isa did not entirely enjoy. Where would she go after the procedure, considering she gets approval? Could she still count on Takashi to let her convalesce on the living-room futon where she now sleeps at night? And anything further along than that seemed too blurred over in her mind to be truly imminent.

"And it says here you're a musician."

"Yes."

"A guitarist."

"Yes."

Dr. Mercer chuckles and places his tablet on the surface of his desk behind him. "I play a little guitar myself. Music can be highly therapeutic. I'm glad you play," he says before wiggling himself up, reaching around behind his chair and pulling an expensive-looking acoustic guitar from behind his desk. "I myself have written quite a few tunes," he says, returning to a supine position.

"Yes. Music can be very cathartic," Isa manages to say, but she sims that Dr. Mercer is not that interested.

He plucks a few harmonics out, tuning the instrument. Isa can hear that it is tuned to an open chord. "Here's one I wrote when coping with the death of a good friend," he says. "Suicide. Maybe you'll appreciate it." He unclips a capo from the guitar's head and places it high up on the 7th fret. He strums a few chords, each played by barring his index finger straight across all 6 strings.

And Isa sits quietly as the neurologist strums an E major chord and an A major chord back to an E major chord. He stares at the ceiling and wiggles his body a little bit to the 4/4 rhythm and sings vaguely about loss. From the awkward planting of his thumb on the back of the guitar's rosewood neck, to his clumsy percussive fingerpicking far too close to the bridge, Isa can think of a thousand pointers to offer Dr. Mercer. Even Tak had better technique. But instead she summons a thoughtful close-lipped smile of one who finds all this therapeutic.

2.11.1 Drive

Isa sat in the leather back seat of Takashi's van looking out over the foggy Hudson. Takashi at her flank, Julia Sets and Doug in the row behind them, and two nameless Neo-!Kung in the driverless driver's seat and shotgun. Both lean, muscular hebodies, likely in their mid-twenties, they sat statue silent, their guns on their laps at the ready. They wore blue cotton shirts, leant to them by Doug. The kind that couldn't scale to fit at the press of the collar, the clothing sat loosely over the men's bodies, obscuring unchanging ink tattoos of various tribal insignias.

The exact mechanisms by which the Neo-!Kung rationalized riding in the Waymo were a mystery to Isa. What with the hunter-gatherer band's abject refusal of almost all modern technology. By that logic, almost all forms of ammunitions should be prohibited, and yet nearly every other Neo-!Kung member the shebody had met carried at least a semi-automatic slung across their backs.

"Old habits die hard" was what **Futurabold** had said with a shrug when Isa first inquired about the weapons paradox. And then later "any successful hunt-er-gatherers need to be attuned to ecological pressures and constraints." At the time, **Futurabold** herself was too busy editing a style sheet for Rule 30's Lazy Eye applet to really F2F.

Perhaps whatever North Jersey fauna they hunted—deer, squirrels, the occa-

sional wild turkey—were too difficult to poach without such arms. Or maybe the
rifles were acquired due to a need for self-defense. It wasn't hard to sim the discontent
the Neo-!Kung might receive from outsiders, especially disgruntled residents along the
NJ/NY border. The state had little affection for them either. Assaulting or murdering
a Neo-!Kung bandsman was hardly prosecuted. Isa could remember reading about
bits of legislature floating around Congress trying to demarcate the band as a terrorist
organization back when she had her Lazies.

Futurabold had hired four of these Neo-!Kung to serve as security for
Rule 30. She told New Ape Idea they would work as long as her Uncle Dee was in the
hospital; however, even once he had returned, his jaw wired shut and his right arm
fixed in a sling, the Neo-!Kung had stayed. The four of them, two hebodies and two
shebodies, stood vigil during shows. One in each corner of Rule 30's atrium. So as
not to scare the concert going audience, they left their rifles in **Futurabold**'s office.
Instead they discreetly carried Desert Eagles in hidden holsters. Not once did they
mosh or nod their heads or tap their toes. The bandsmen seemed somehow immune
to the atavistic power of New Ape Idea's sound that seemed to enchant anyone else
that listened. Maybe they wore earplugs. Another form of technology, albeit a simpler
one, that they paradoxically accepted.

The technology use of the Neo-!Kung was but the mildest of a long list of
cerebrum-crushing unknowns Isa had mulled over recently. Some proved too scary to
dwell on for too long: her palms would moisten and, after an hour or so, a vasovagal
headache might appear as if the blood in her brain turned viscous and syrupy. The
problem was sweet and mild in comparison to heavier items. Items such as "Why am I
on the flash drive Takashi stole?" or "Why does **Futurabold**, after months of sexual
relations, now seem to avoid even casual F2F?" made Isa feel as if her frontal lobes
were beginning to hemorrhage.

Takashi claimed the drive was just, like, laying there when he picked it off
the mixing board. This was during New Ape Idea's second studio session with Melodica. He claimed Mr. Halisdol must've left it behind, which is likely an untruth given
that the hebody had not accompanied New Ape Idea to the studio with them for the
past month. Mr. Halisdol only showed up to the first one wearing the same tweed
jacket and Panama hat as when Isa first met him. Some hebodies just liked to set their
clothes to the same outfit every day. He seemed jittery and nervous like before as well,
though perhaps such was his emotional base state.

The sound engineer—a bearded hebody the shape of an upside-down pear—
had been in attendance for each of their weekly sessions. Unlike Mr. Halisdol, he
seemed to possess an almost Taoist aura of contentment and smelled faintly of non-
synth. The sound engineer, who asked that he be called Toad, was genial to all except
Takashi, who Isa simmed Toad took a quick disliking to. During their first session,
after New Ape Idea gunned out a quick demo of one tune, Takashi drew vocal offense

to the auto-tuning of his bass track. The vibrations emanating from Isa's amplifier stack were still reverberating around the booth when Toad, with a smirk, turned a complex array of knobs on his baroque soundboard and played the demo back to the band. Their rendition of "Banana", flat and nowhere near as energetic as any of their live performances, sounded completely different, as if played on several glockenspiels rather than electric guitars and drums. Isa's vocal line was somehow morphed into a wordless series of metallic chimes.

"This is what it'll sound like in post," Toad had said. "All lullabied up."

For reasons Isa could not immediately garner, Toad's mixing incensed Takashi. He nearly threw his Rickenbacker to the ground, angry veins protruding from his forehead and blurted a string of morphemes referencing "artistic integrity" and "creative licensing". From his throne, Lamarck-Ganoush picked at his top-knot of hair and reminded Tak that he had signed away their rights to such months ago. If his intent was to calm Takashi, thought Isa, his efforts were ineffectual.

The recording sessions occurred every Thursday and lasted an entire workday. About 9 hours, including a lunch break, catered by Melodica. Isa didn't mind the cold cuts and cheeses provided for them every noon. Takashi refused to touch the stuff, citing to Toad a litany of anarcho-veganist philosophy during their first session.

"Asshole" was a kind euphemism for how Takashi acted throughout the sessions. Last lunch break, Doug, between bites of Petri-dish prosciutto, said he thought Takashi was suffering the "Sisyphean agony of self-actualized poseurdom," That a record deal—often the sign of having "made it" as a musician—failed to grant Tak any feelings of accomplishment or satisfaction. That even since UZ, the hebody allocated more effort toward *appearing* a talented creative musician rather than spending time cultivating any skill. That should New Ape Idea continue to ride along this eigenvec-tor of small successes—the glowing write-ups in *Staph Infection*, which began to spill over into mainstream blog aggregators, the chronically oversold tri-weekly concerts, contract w/Melodica notwithstanding—each and every vector of accomplishment would continue to be rendered unsatisfactory for Takashi. The hebody was a narcissist but not delusional, said Doug. Tak was more than aware of his lack of talent or ability. He was always concerned with appearance upkeep, you know, external measures of success. Each of these past studio sessions likely made Miyagi-Edelstein feel as if he was drawing an inch closer to being found out for the poseur that he feared/knew he was. His mood swings a sort of manifest interaction effect between a phobia of being outed as a poser, and a calculated affect drawn from legends of mercurial punks in the recording studios of yore. If he didn't claim to be whatever he meant by vegan-post-straight-edge, he'd probably string himself out on organic non-synth H just to seem like Richard Hell.

The overarching irony was that Takashi, for all his efforts to avoid being found out as a poseur, was easily judged as such by the few that bothered to get to know him.

The closer the roads got to New York, the less they seemed to be maintained. The passengers bounced as the van the rumbled down route 9, the pavement acned with potholes. The Neo-!Kung sitting shotgun pressed his nose to the window, smushing it cartoonishly. A flattened hand shielded sunlight from his eyes as he kept watch in silence.

Isa pinched the drive between her index finger and thumb. The thing was no bigger than a discontinued penny. It was coated in a slick black plastic, no marks or corporate insignias showed themselves.

"Why did you take this?" said Isa to Takashi.

"I've got a nose for juicy data," Takashi replied.

"Is 'juicy' really the word for it?" said Doug, fingering air-quotes around the morpheme in question.

"Alright. 'Suspicious'. Or maybe so much as 'horrifying'."

"You're reading into it too much," said Julia Sets, looking out the vehicle's windows.

"Well you were curious enough to come," said Tak.

"No. I'm not. I just owed Doug a favor."

"A favor worth risking your job over?"

Sets swallowed. "No. It's not that."

"_"

"_"

"I'm just willing to go to great lengths to prove to you that you're just paranoid," Julia finished.

"I'm inclined to agree," said Doug "Maybe it's meaningless corporate noise from Melodica, and the three of us are now at risk of losing our record deal because you pinched it."

"I don't know if we're gonna wanna keep working with these suits once we find out more about what's on the drive," said Tak. He turned toward Isa with an open palm. Isa handed him the drive and Takashi plugged it into a USB on the underside of his armrest. A large screen appeared, taking up the majority of the Waymo's front windshield. Takashi waved his hand around to open the contents of the drive. The screen went dark as Tak opened the Waymo's OS terminal and began to decrypt the drive. Thousands of lines of white code, the print too small to be read easily, began to flood the windshield.

"What you see here are thousands of pieces of information being appended hashed to a remote dictionary every millisecond," Takashi said. "This database has been running for nearly fifteen years. The data hasn't even been cleaned or wrangled on the server side by the smell of it."

"Why did you steal this, Tak?"

"I'm not the thief here, Lamarck-Ganoush, if you can believe it." Like a cephalopod swimming through turbulent water, Takashi waved his arms about in front of the screen, opening and closing windows as he did so. "Check out the name of the file," he said.

Isa squinted instinctively so as to zoom in on the letterings. Cyborg behaviors uninstall hard. In the lower right-hand corner read **Spines.Isabel.sh**.

"Courtney Christ," Doug said. "What the fuck is this?"

"Well I've been combing through it," said Takashi. "The tables that I could read seemed to correspond to different somatic functions I guess. Heart rate, blood pressure, basal metabolic rate, you get the idea."

The van, sensing a clear road ahead, sped up to 150 mph.

"This belonged to Toad?" Isa said.

"Not necessarily," Takashi shaking his head. "The only evidence suggesting so was that I found it in Toad's studio. That's it. Against a large pool of data suggesting he has little knowledge of the contents of the drive. In fact, I'm willing to risk the hypothesis that Toad has nothing to do with it at all."

"Why?" Doug asked.

"Well, decrypting the drive's contents was initially stupidly easy," Tak said. "A real piece of cake as they say. Whoever encrypted it used a SHA2 with their state's area code as a key. Elementary stuff, first semester cryptology. Akin to prepubescent-boys-in-a-treehouse-with-a-plastic-decoder-ring level encryption. Of course, most gov code monkeys don't know any better." Takashi had paused to tilt his head left and then right, cracking his neck both times. "I used 212 as my second guess. Manhattan, NYC. It's not a huge inference to assume the database originates from there."

"So it's not Mr. Halisdol's either," Doug said. "By that logic."

"Improbable, yes. I generally agree, DLG, but I'm unwilling to rule out the possibility. Didn't Sets say he came from New York?"

"But he's a corporate suit," Doug had added. "Not involved with the state. Plus to cross between Manhattan and Jersey would require a connection with either the Neo-!Kung or the feds. Both maybe."

As they entered Fort Lee the driver disbanded the self-driving modules of the Waymo and switched to manual drive. Immediately the van slowed down, the driver reducing the speed to about a sixth of what it was before. A spore of nausea began to germinate in Isa's intestines as the deceleration threw her along with the 5 others in the van forward. Tak, who had not worn a seatbelt for the drive, was thrown from his seat. He emitted a string of curses in three languages before lifting himself back up unharmed.

Through the van's windows, dayglow restaurant signs shined down from outside buildings, the neon bright enough to pierce both the afternoon daylight and the windows' tinting. No other vehicles—Waymo or otherwise—were on the road. These shifts from self-driving to manual were not possible on crowded streets. Even with their ultra-fast response times, 20x times faster than the average human's parasympathetic reflexes, any nearby Waymos could have wrecked themselves against the slowing van.

How odd that these anti-tech paleoliths made the deftest drivers, thought Isa.

Takashi shook his head from side to side. "The fuck is that for?"

The Neo-!Kung riding shotgun, an unshaven hebody appearing to be in his thirties turned his body around in his seat and eyed Takashi. His face seemed to be more chin than anything else. He did not speak, unsurprisingly, only nodded at Takashi while he fingered the safety of his gun.

But the rationale behind the van's shift to manual drive soon showed itself. Turning the steering wheel hand over hand over hand, the driver took the van off of the Fort Lee backstreets and down onto the sandy shoals of the Hudson River. After pulling over, he gave a thumbs-up gesture, signaling to all the passengers to exit the vehicle.

"Get down!" said Doug as he belly-flopped to the rocky sand. He gripped Isa by the wrist and yanked her with him as the pullulating metallic clicks of the drawing of armaments cut across the air. Lying prone on the ground, sandwiched between the masses of Sets and Lamarck-Ganoush, Isa peaked out and could see two more gunmen emerging from the riverbanks. They too wore the body paint and loose-fit-ting, unwashed clothes of the Neo-!Kung. The driver raised a hand and the other three mimicked before lowering their guns in synchrony.

Following Julia, Doug and Takashi, Isa rose to her feet. Three of the Neo-!Kung retreated down the river bank. Only the driver remained with the four, silently unloading his rifle.

"Will I get shot if I move?" said Takashi.

"_"

"_"

"_"

"I need the drive," he followed, before creeping toward the Waymo, opening the door and plucking the flash drive from his seat.

The last time Isa had seen the Hudson River, the water was much bluer. It had been dyed as a massively-funded tourism ploy in the early twenties; Mayor Swift's logic being that the old river, more gray-green than blue or clear, disgusted potential visitors and gave New York City a dirty, polluted aura. When she had been eleven or twelve, the orphanage took her, along with the nameless others, to the river banks as a field trip. The river still had the same cerulean hue—so vivid it was almost a parody of what water was supposed to look like, like water on an atlas map—and it smelled of hand sanitizer. This though, said the chaperone, was a marked improvement over its past state.

Memories dating this far back were difficult for Isa to grasp, as were most of her years as a ward of the state. Her stored sense data felt corrupted, remembered faces had the quality of print photographs smeared with petroleum jelly. An immediate clarity began around puberty when she was moved from the asylums, given a public school smartphone and social networking account, and sent via DIFUS through the New Jersey foster family system. Discovery of the cello at age 13 clearing the fog further. By the time she had matriculated to University, her memories, like the Hudson appeared to her as almost artificially clear. Perhaps that could be attributed to the Lazy Eyes she began wearing freshman year, once all her social, academic and romantic interactions could be logged, edited, and stored externally to her meatware.

The Hudson no longer smelled antiseptic, Isa noted. Instead it had a fishy quality, not unlike canned tuna. Ironic, given that the river was completely incapable of sustaining any form of marine ecosystem.

These other Neo-!Kung were much louder than the two drivers **Futurabold** hired. They had mild Appalachian accents, though the content of their speech was indecipherable from the distance. Along with the two drivers, they returned up the bank and gestured for the five by the van to follow.

An additional Neo-!Kung was standing in a small ferryboat. The boat had two wooden seats and a modest motor at the bow side. He laughed at some unheard joke as he tugged the motor to life. Though the boat seemed to be able to carry at most one or two individuals; however, all four were to board. The second of the river Neo-!Kung offered a hand to Julia and then Isa as they were lead onto the motorboat. Takashi and Doug were not proffered such chivalry. Isa immediately fell to a sit, lacking sea legs even when the boat was at a dock.

Overhead she could see the George Washington Bridge with maybe a dozen cars making use of it. The canary yellow border checkpoints on each end contrasted greatly with the old steel girders of the bridge. Isa couldn't sim whether the patrollers 150 meters above her could see the little motorboat zigzagging across the water, white-capped tail wave at the bow. Or if they did, whether they cared. Isa considered breaking the silence of her shipmates with this question but could not. Maybe because her conversation-starting muscles had atrophied to thin gristle with years of minimal use. Or the gasoline hum of the motor coupled with the sloshing of the waves made conversing below a yell impossible. So she sat in silence. Like she was used to.

About ten meters out from the Manhattan bank, one of the Appalachian Neo-!Kung killed the engine before leaping out of the boat and wading toward the shore. His partner followed, both gripping the stern tip and pulling the metal thing toward the sandy shoal ahead. The beach wasn't wide, the majority of it cut off by a concrete wall below the parkway. Besides the Waymos zooming past on the highway above, the group was alone. About a quarter-mile down, Isa could see a man snoozing in a plastic lawn chair, a cast fishing reel anchored in the sand. No other sapiens were present on the beach.

"Alright," said one of the Neo!-Kung, the first of the hunter-gatherers to address any of the others for the duration of the trip. "Walk about a half-mile north along the beach and you'll find a slope that will take you to the city proper. Whereabouts you headin'?"

"Chelsea," said Julia Sets. She had the blank fish-face of one reading off of her Lazies while pretending to F2F. "27th and 6th."

"Whew, Chelsea," said the Neo-!Kung. He squatted down and scraped mud off of his feet and calves as he spoke. "You'll have to call a cab to get there."

"**Futurabold** didn't arrange a ride for us?" said Tak.

"I heard nothin'," said the Neo-!Kung. "We man the ship." He nodded at his partner who proceeded to re-enter the motorboat, one leg at a time. "That's all were paid to do fer y'ins."

Tak turned toward Doug, but the glance went unreturned. Hands in his pockets, Doug milled about the beach, eyeing the concrete barricade covered in unchanging graffiti from decades past. With a shudder, the motorboat came to life. The Neo-!Kung inserted two fingers into his mouth and whistled to his partner. A quick hand wave was returned.

"Maybe call a cab," said the bandsman before he turned toward the boat.

"Call a cab?" Tak's speech had a nasally, viscous quality to it. "Like, on a cell phone?"

The Neo-!Kung, satisfied that his legs were thoroughly de-caked of Hudson ooze, stepped into the boat. "I'm not the one to ask," he said before grasping his other by the shoulder and motoring off.

"I already placed an order," said Julia. She blinked twice, implicating her Eyes. "They're meeting us near here, on the Upper West Side." Her voice sounded hollowed out.

"I'm not paying for a fucking cab," Takashi said. He waved his hand flippantly as he spoke. "One K a piece just to travel two miles. Can't afford that shit."

"You've been making twenty grand a week from shows," said Doug. "Where'd that go?" He caught himself mimicking Takashi's hand movements, winced and removed a kerchief from a cargo pocket and dabbed at some perspiration dewing up around his neck.

"None of yr goddamn business, Lamarck-Ganoush."

"I'll cover it," said Julia.

"Is Melodica comping this?" asked Doug.

"No." Julia shook her head. "I'll cover it. I insist."

With a pre-recorded "THANK YOU" upon the closing of its doors, the Citicab zipped off. It seemed Julia paid through her Lazies as no paper, plastic or digital capital was visibly handled.

Like the Meadowlands complex, this Manhattan Melodica tower was living, though in New York, about half of the skyscrapers Isa could see had the bamboo-and-foliage thatching for walls and roofs checkered with solar cells. The concrete, steel and glass of the older buildings seemed desperately antiquated in comparison. The building had a semicircular car roundabout, though the three dozen or so parking spaces were all unoccupied. Takashi approached the plexiglass sliding doors, though they did not open in automated obeisance when he stood in front of them.

"Here I've got it," said Sets. She flipped an adjacent plastic latch and stared into the retinal scanner. The doors swooshed open.

"Employees only?" said Doug.

Sets shook her head. "Not even," she said. "I had to design a patch to make my Eyes have an identical registration code to Evan Halisdol's."

"I don't remember this in New Jersey."

"The going-ons in Manhattan are a bit more, well, high sec," said Sets. She pinched her collar turning her tank top into a pink blouse. "From what I understand."

"Are we gonna be able to even walk around in here?" said Takashi, craning his neck into the lobby.

"If it's anything like New Jersey, the building's so-called 'smart' security system is anything but that," said Julia. "Just act like an intern."

Sets approached Tak and looped her index finger into the vertex of his vintage-style v-neck. He screwed up his eyes as an eggshell button-down emerged, larger than the previous tee by at least two sizes. His sleeves extended to his wrists and then retracted, giving the impression of full sleeves rolled up to the elbow. A maroon tartan tie slithered out tongue-like and pacified when it had reached full length.

"Do employees really dress like this?" he whined.

"No," said Sets. "But you will."

She nodded toward Isa, then Doug. Isa's tank turned to turtleneck, obscuring her undulating tattoos. Doug unzipped a hoodie and removed it, revealing an undersized hand-tied bow tie knotted through the collar of a sweat-stained business shirt. Doug tied the hoodie around his waist.

"How, though?" Isa caught herself mumbling.

"What now?" said Takashi. The building's doors began to close. He extended a hand between them, reversing their direction.

"Acting like an intern," said Isa, this time at a more conversational decibel level. "Are there recommended techniques for doing so?"

Tak and Doug shared a look, and Doug spoke. "Just pretend you work here. I don't know, watch how you hold yourself. Walk like it's all familiar, but not too familiar."

"I just feel apprehensive," said Isa. "Without delving too far into it, I am the reason we've come here."

"And a gnawing curiosity about that database," said Takashi. The doors began to spasm jaw-like, closing then opening then closing again but never completely chomping down on his elbow, still extended into the portal. "Though that isn't exactly extricable from you, Spines. Guess yr right."

"And paranoia," said Doug. "I'll admit that I feel it too."

"I empathize. Though if I am indeed a person of note to Melodica, perhaps they are expecting my presence here."

"We can't refute that, no," said Lamarck-Ganoush. "Though for all we know, Melodica could have analogous flash drives for all of us, Takashi just happened to pilfer only yours. Right Julia?"

Julia made a sound. Isa could not decipher whether it was a hum of affirmation or a happenstance non-verbal utterance, devoid of any meaning.

"Speculation," said Isa. "But Melodica may recognize us, whether or not we can pass as interns."

Sets sighed audibly. She grabbed both Isa and Doug by the wrist and led them into the tower lobby. "Just keep quiet," she said. "Like usual. I can guarantee most folks working here are intimately acquainted with monotony. Pretend you're an automaton, executing lines of code."

"I can do that," said Isa, following her.

"I've noticed," said Sets. The plexiglass closed and locked itself behind them. "As have many others."

The lobby was expansive and empty. To the left of the entrance was a bamboo receptionist's desk, the majority of its top a large viewport running an idle animation of the company's logo: *Melodica* written in a golden serif font. Behind it, animated strings vibrated soundlessly. And below the title a catchphrase shimmered gently: *Live in Harmony.* At the far end of the room were six elevator shafts, five of which waited unused at the ground floor according to a rectangular screen above them. The room was illuminated with a fresh clean light, like sunlight on a cloudless spring afternoon; however, Isa did not see any lamps, fluorescent tubes or similar light sources.

Takashi whistled. "Where is everybody?"

"It's almost 8 pm," said Sets. "The complex has been closed for two hours."

"But we got in."

Sets brushed a thin skein of hair out of her eyes. "Evan Halisdol was a research tech before moving to the Meadowlands," she said. "It's Melodica policy to keep facilities available for R&D folks 24/7. I was banking on New York being slow to pop Evan Halisdol off of some approval list."

"There's no, erm, *security*? You know, in-the-flesh guards." said Doug. He twirled the tip of his business tie between his porcine index finger and thumb.

"A few may be patrolling here and there," said Sets. "Though I've never come across them in Jersey."

"It must be automated," said Isa.

The twirling of Doug's tie began to accelerate.

A beat. "Though most security at Melodica is automated," Sets added. "Like you saw at the door. Nothing worth sweating, I'd say."

Doug moseyed around the lobby inspecting the space, his mouth slightly agape. The fabric of his pants covering his inner thighs swished as he walked. A long meditative inhale through his nostrils. "Impressive building," he said. "I don't think I took the time to appreciate the architecture in New Jersey." He paused beneath a large framed print of a French impressionist painting hanging above a pair of love seats and a worktable. Isa recognized the print as a Mary Cassatt, the image stored in a memory of another field trip from the orphanage, this one to the Metropolitan Museum of Art. The softly colored mother caressing her baby was the giveaway, though Isa couldn't remember the painting's title. Perhaps she never learned it in the first place. A shame, with her Lazy Eyes she'd be able to drawn out the work's title, painter, date and several important related works of criticism with just two squints and a nod.

"So where are we going?" Doug said. "We've infiltrated Melodica, now what?"

Takashi held up the flash drive between his index and thumb. "Let's mine a bit, boyo," he said and approached the receptionist's desk. He disappeared beneath it before emitting a "Eureka!" and returning upright. His blonde spikes seemed to hum electric as he excitedly ran his hands across the tablet screen.

"What are you doing, Takashi?" A grace note of worry preceding every word he spoke.

"In a nutshell, DLG, I'm pinging the disk here to find a means of installing the software on the drive. From there, I can run these little rootkits I've built, nothing too invasive or noticeable. But they're gonna dig out all references to Isa, You, Me, or New Ape Idea and compile them to a list which I'll import back onto the drive. From there we should find what we need to find."

Sets, unseen by Takashi's manic tableting, approached the desk and peered over the screen. "He's just searching Isa's name in various directories," she said.

Takashi looked at her something poisonous.

"If you're going to lie," said Sets, "At least know the parameters of your audience. You can maybe fool Doug and Isa with badly rendered computer jargon, but not me."

"Well, my efforts are paying off," said Takashi between closed teeth. "Both my name and Doug's return a little over 50 results, the large majority seem to be just contractual/legal shit." Takashi shrugged. "But Isa, or actually the search term was

'Isabel Spines' returns thousands of links. All to other host refs in Melodica's server system."

Isa felt her intestines calcify. "Are these largely pertaining to New Ape Idea? Lullabies?"

"Indeterminate," replied Takashi. "But probability suggests otherwise, meta searches indicate most of these results do not even mention Doug, the band or yrs truly."

"_"

"Any idea what Chaperoni is?" Takashi looked up from the screen. "Maybe an acronym for something?"

"_"

"_"

"_"

"It's an early nanorobotics network prototype," said Julia, cracking the shared silence. A sidelong glance to Isa, then to Tak. "I know Halisdol worked for a guy who helped build it. A simple enough decentralized network, mostly tested on non-human primates, built for somatic monitoring, cheap preventative healthcare as I recall."

"Checks out," Takashi again, "Save the 'non-human primates' bit. Seems prototypic subjects were quite sapient."

Julia squinched up the corners of her eyes, likely manipulating her Lazies. "I don't feel good about being here. **Futurabold** said our ride will be waiting for us, right?"

Doug approached the elevator shafts. All appeared to be stagnant. "As long as the building's clear—"

"Microbots, not nanobots," said Tak, shaking his head. "Ancient stuff. This ringing any bells Spines? Any familiar lines?"

"More pictures than words."

Takashi removed his gaze from the console, though his fingertips kept up their interfacing. "Yeah? What of?"

"A doctor. I was younger then. Early pubescence. He couldn't walk. His legs were manipulated by an old automatic exoskeleton, highly outmoded by today's standards."

Takashi bobbed his head in an excited nod. "Fascinating but fruitless. No names? Locations? Yr full name and paraplegic yield an entirely new list of results, probably confusion regarding the term 'Spines'."

"I can't recall."

"Can't really discern what a lullaby company has to do with failed microrobotics, but whatever," said Takashi. "Connection's there, and hell, this is a receptionist's desk."

"Does this have the same layout as the Meadowlands complex?" said Doug, hands folded clerically behind his back.

"Does it look it?" Julia returned.

"The lobby is certainly different, obviously," said Doug. "What I mean is, how similar are they? Offices above ground, labs in the basement?"

"I'd assume so, I believe that's protocol."

Doug nodded. "Peculiar. The elevator landing displays don't indicate any basement floors."

"No, they're here," said Takashi. "But it looks like they only have two basement floors, not some Willy Wonka sub-ground complex like in Jersey. I guess going deeper would interfere with the subway system or something."

"People still use that?" said Doug.

"Wrong hebody to ask, Lamarck-Ganoush." Tak broke from interfacing to crack his knuckles. "Though the drive's pin number has a laboratory key. I'd assume we make use of those elevators."

"I wouldn't," Sets cut in.

Three sets of eyes affixed themselves to her.

Julia picked off a crescent of fingernail hanging off the pink of her middle finger with her teeth before speaking. "The white-collar employees may have turned in for the day, but I'm sure there are at least two dozen technicians in the lab. As you saw before, they have 24-hour access."

"We can pass as techs," said Takashi. A wry close-lipped smile as he set his shirt from business-casual to include a white lab coat overtop.

"You look like you walked out of a 20th century sci-fi film," said Lamarck-Ganoush.

"This is how the techs dressed in New Jersey," said Takashi. "Least the ones I saw. How's the accuracy, Sets?"

"It's accurate enough," Sets, shaking her head. "Lamentably."

Tak's smirk evolved to a toothier genus. No cue, verbal or gestural, was necessary for Isa to follow suit with her outfit.

"Well, I'm stuck," said Doug gesturing toward his tie. "This is all I brought."

"I'm staying here," said Julia. "I'm not risking it."

"I'll keep you company," said Doug.

"Romantic," said Takashi. He dipped beneath the desk to remove the flash drive. Upon re-emerging, with a broad two-fingered stroke he reset the tablet to its welcome screen. After planting his hands on a non-digital desktop surface, he vaulted over the desk and stuck the landing. "Let's go, Spines," he said summoning one of the at-the-ready elevators.

Julia Sets had highballed the laboratory population. The lab—a sea of cubicles and overhead fluorescent tubes—also seemed to double as a server room. The whole room felt under-lit, as typical for basements. A stack of deep blue mainframes in the center had the strange property of seeming to absorb light. They remained almost invisibly dark save the blinking of LEDs across their chasses. Across the labyrinth of white half-walls were a series of doors. Above one Isa could read "Storage", another "Nursery". Perhaps 20 meters away, in the outer orbit of the lab's server nucleus, a few wild-haired hebodies conversed inaudibly. Both had a set of Lazy Eyes on full projection mode. They paid Tak and Isa no mind.

Takashi surveyed the chiaroscuro laboratory, wetting his lips with a few lupine licks. He held the flash drive to his breast like a medieval pilgrim clutching a lock of hair from a deceased saint.

"What's our next step?" Isa, barely above a whisper.

"We're well outside the atmosphere of speculation," Tak returned.

"About me?"

"Oh yeah." said Tak. He approached one of the white cubical walls and peeked over it. "Yr name is all over this place. We know that. I'm interested in on honing in on the exact correlation between you and Melodica."

"Perhaps I don't want that."

Tak craned his head around. "You don't *want* that?" His voice at a biting whisper. "Listen, I don't doubt the truths we may uncover will be, to a degree, *inconvenient*. For you at least. But Courtney Christ if that doesn't make it, like, imperative that we figure out what's up."

"Think about it. You: Isabel Spines orphaned at a young age and thrown around the NJ foster system until college. Despite having the interpersonal skills of a fungus colony, you manage to front a band, which folks like Mickey Mallorey says has single-handedly revived punk counterculture. Before that can even happen though, yr approached for a children's music record deal by some inter-state conglomerate, which apparently has years of weirdly intimate data on you. There are just too many loose ends floating about. I mean, like, how could you not be insatiably curious?"

Isa inhaled through her nose and shut her eyes. "I'm curious," Isa said, re-opening her eyes. "But not enough to risk physical harm."

"Grow a backbone Spines," said Tak. "Where's the risk? I don't see it." Palm up, he panned his hand across the cavernous, beeping laboratory. The two overtime scientists had retreated into the room marked "Nursery".

"But what if these things: the flash drive, me, New Ape Idea," said Spines. "What if that is all indeed random synchronizations? Unrelated happenings, etiologically disparate. What if we are simply paranoid?"

"Connecting the dots in front of you isn't paranoid, Isa," said Tak. He swung around a cubicle and activated a fluorescent desk lamp. "It's narrative. Everybody craves a good story. Glucose for the mind."

The cubicles, like the receptionist's desk, contained a large flat touch screen computer embedded into the desk. Takashi deftly found a USB jack and plugged in the drive. Isa stood around the other side of the eggshell wall and observed.

"Here we go," said Takashi. His index and ring fingers traced the tablet in gridded strokes. A snort. "You'd think they'd at least password protect these consoles."

"They didn't?"

Tak flicked his pupils upward at Isa for a second before returning to the tablet. "I mean they did, but I managed to finagle my way into sudo access on my three-hundred thousand seven-hundred fortieth guess." His face briefly turned zombie-pale by the pallor of the bright white screen, before shunting back into a deep blue shadow, no less corpse-like.

The far-off mezzo-soprano of an infant crying. Tak and Isa could see the door to the Nursery open, though no bodies came in or out.

"Beautiful," Takashi said a bit louder than Isa would've preferred. "Yr every-where, Spines." Tak wore a palsied smile as his arms marionetted around the glowing rectangle. His fingers scrolled, swiped and typed with practiced fluency. Though most of his face was darkened by shadow, the screen cast a messianic halo over his over-dyed piles of hair.

"This makes sense," said Takashi. "Melodica apparently has managed to buy out almost all companies involved with commercial microrobotics in the tens and twenties. Which is of course why such stuff isn't available on the marketplace. We'd probably have automated cybernetic immune systems by now otherwise."

"_"

"You don't remember anything about the procedure, right?" said Takashi head still bowed.

"I remember the procedure, yes," said Isa.

"And you were never curious 'bout it? Never did any research? I mean, this is the first time I'm hearing about it."

"It was just one of many childhood traumas."

"Courtney Christ," said Takashi. "No need to get all, like, Freudian or some-thing. All I can tell you, and let me articulate this for you nice and clearly, is that Me-lodica has more or less had access to your body for the past fifteen years. And I don't mean your health charts, I don't mean your IQ scores. I mean your body. Any aspect of your physiology that can be computed, that can be signified with a number and stored, that is on this flash drive. Blood content, liver functioning, hormone levels. They even have records of activity across various neural circuits. At risk of sounding reductive, they've been reading your mind."

"_"

"_"

"If Melodica could read my mind," said Isa, "Couldn't we assume they know I am here with you right now?"

Tak cocked his chin. "Plausible," he said. "But I don't know if they're doing so actively. They may just be recording all this information for later review."

Isa approached the cubicle and leaned over the wall, the plastic giving slightly under her weight. With great rapidity, Tak was swiping rectangular .pdfs into a blue square marked drive. "These are the only text documents," said Tak. "The rest are data clusters that I don't have the knowhow to defrag immediately. But look at this," Takashi tapped twice on one document and with a scissoring motion of his fingertips, expanded it to screen size. **Towards a New Paradigm of Theory of Mind and Social Delinquency** it read. Below the headline was an abstract and several charts of data, which Isa did not have the time to read.

"Hard numbers will take time to crunch through," said Tak. "But words on print, that shit's platinum. I could probably map a set of reducers onto all of these .pdfs and extract the info relevant to us over the boat ride home. Or at least, maybe Julia could."

"Why do you think these studies have anything to do with me?"

Something softened in Takashi's face, though the bright digital glow shining on it had not. A montage of eye, cheek and lip muscles relaxed giving Tak a wise but resigned affect. "Yr name's all over them Isa. I'm just skimming through, but you've been a subject in what looks like hundreds of studies. Some are longitudinal, they may be happening right now."

"But they can't print my name," said Isa, backing away from the cubicle, her speech rising in both pitch and tempo. "I thought that was illegal."

Takashi had either refrained from manipulating the tablet, or he had auto-mated the file-copying process while he spoke. Regardless, his hands above him, in the zone typically relegated for gestural communication. "For all institutional or public research, yes, it is illegal to print subjects' names. I'd assume that carries to the corpo-rate sector as well. My hypothesis is Melodica either has no intent of publishing these results or they've made a deal with some bureaucrats in Albany and Trenton."

Isa closed her eyes and inhaled. It was hard to believe that tens of thousands of microscopic self-driving robots swam through her capillaries. She simmed a night-mare of mechanical spiders creeping up her innards.

A childish laugh, then a scream, then a laugh emanated from the Nursery.

Tak had resumed his maestro tableting. He stuck out his tongue in concen-tration, his forehead showing veins Isa had never seen before. "Almost done," he said. He took a second to wipe his brow with the back of his wrist. "Give me 120 seconds and I'll have copied off every file with your name on it," he said and winked. "In the meantime, I want you to summon an elevator and hold it open. Message Sets to call us a cab. We're gonna wanna scoot from this building as fast as possible."

"I can't message anyone," said Spine, who began toward the elevator shaft. "I lost my Eyes."

"Then we'll have to do it F2F and run. DLG's gonna love that," he said.

Isa called the elevator and it opened obediently. She stood in the portal so as to prop it open.

"Takashi," Isa said. "Why is it that I have never seen you wearing Lazy Eyes?"

"They make me nauseous, to be honest," said Miyagi-Edelstein. "You can see I'll engage in most contemporary wearware. But retinal interfaces give me the crawls." Tak popped the flash drive from the tablet, and with a diagonal swipe powered the desk down. He pocketed the black thing as he approached Isa.

"And, to be candid, which I'm not sure is a phrase I've ever said before," Takashi entered the elevator. The doors dinged closed before him and Isa. "Going without Lazies does have a set of social affordances."

"I've realized you can make more of a statement about yrself by refraining from a select few items of the modern era's technofascism. It's strange, but pragmatic. I see hundreds of these budding cyberpunks, more through various digital interfaces. They're all decked out with neon Lazy Eyes, chest-piece visitats and subdermal Wi-Fi hotspots, thinking they're so hip and unique. Of course I like to be considered a member of that in-group."

"But that's the prevailing culture. And to be a good punk, I've got to rebel against that. So I abstain myself from wearing Lazies in public."

"In public?"

"_"

"_"

'Okay, I do have a pair. I just don't put them on around you or Doug. I've got an image to preserve."

The elevator dinged with each floor they descended.

Isa exhaled. "I believe this is the most honest you've ever been with me, Takashi."

"Probably," Tak agreed. "But coming clean to you is like coming clean to an undecorated wall."

"Doug doesn't wear Lazy Eyes."

"Lamarck-Ganoush is a hipster," said Takashi, "Don't think he isn't."

The elevator emitted an automated "Thank You" before opening, revealing Julia Sets eyes tightly closed, pinching the upper bridge of her nose. Lamarck-Ganoush had his hands folded across his chest. His thick-framed glasses, slick with facial sweat, drooped down along his face, the bulbous tip of his nose preventing them from falling off completely. He shook his head, Isa simmed disappointment.

"I'm sorry, I'm sorry, I'm sorry," said Sets. She shook her head as she spoke.

"What'd I miss?" said Tak.

"Julia ordered a cab," said Doug. "And **Futurabold** assured us transportation back once we get to the river." He turned his gaze toward Sets, "It's up to you if you'd like to accompany us."

"I'm sorry, I'm sorry, I'm so, so sorry."

"We really oughta leave," said Doug. "As soon as possible."

Tears began to bud and drip down Julia's round cheeks.

"Let me in the know," said Takashi, his volume increasing, "I really hate not being in the know."

Doug sighed then swallowed audibly. Pools of perspiration around his nipples, underarms and neck grew and began to coalesce. "To put it pithily," Lamarck-Ganoush said. "Shit's fucked."

"Shit's always been fucked, DLG, where's the novelty?"

A triplet of Waymo honks undercut Takashi. Outside the tower a yellow service car waited for them.

"I'll explain in closed quarters," said Doug. The doors opening obediently for him with little of the hassle entrance provided. Takashi and Isa exited. Doug turned toward Julia, who gave a lachrymose "No thanks," followed by a litany of "I'm so sorry, I should've said something."

Doug took the driverless driver's seat. He hooked his arm around the headrest and rotated his body to face Isa and Takashi, who sat in the row behind him. "While you were snooping in the basement," he said. "Julia informed me that Melodica has been conducting research on children and infants that, at times, toes the line between morally gray and just plain cruel."

"Could've guessed that from our tour of the New Jersey lab," said Takashi.

"Surely, but what surprised me was her admission that Isa has been a research subject of theirs for nearly twenty years."

"Lines up with what we found downstairs," said Tak.

"What kind of research?" said Isa.

The cab began to accelerate to its top velocity: 200 mph. Each Manhattan pothole and speed bump sent the two lighter-weight passengers bouncing off of their seats.

"Orphans, foster children, children diagnosed with mental illnesses," said Doug, sturdy in place, "are statistically more likely to grow up to commit crime, evade taxes, and become generally bad citizens. Melodica, is one of a series of government-subsidized businesses aimed at making these at-risk youths less, well, risky."

"Sets told you this?"

"As soon as you and Isa left for downstairs she broke down. Tears and everything. I assume she was too weighted down with guilt."

"And so we're making lullabies why?" said Takashi. "Put kids to sleep so they won't hold up liquor stores?"

"Not quite," said Doug. "Remember what Mr. Halisdol told us about Eupsychics. Melodica's research is centered on reducing human development to a mathematical system. A healthy, productive citizen could be, in his language, a specific attractor state in a phase space."

"But lullabies?"

"I'm getting there," said Doug, like relax. "Apparently lullabies are an evolved predecessor to learning language. Mothers sing to their young in every culture around the world. Psychologists at Melodica suggest that it thus plays an important role in the dynamic system of development. Think about it: every infant is born a solipsist. It doesn't see any difference between their thoughts and the world at large. When its mother sings to it, that's the first indication that a person outside of themselves exists. Lullabies lay down the base state for communication between others to develop."

"And language is the building blocks of the human psyche," said Isa, tracing the outline of a royal purple Koch snowflake germinating on her wrist.

"Exactly," said Doug slapping his headrest. "According to Julia, Melodica thinks that by engineering the perfect lullaby they can set the developmental course for these at-risk wards of the state. Make them, well, pacified."

"Courtney Christ," said Takashi. "And Julia knew too."

"Well, I don't think she realized Isa was a subject herself," said Doug.

"But why us?" said Isa.

"Maybe by having one of their subjects producing the music," said Tak, running a hand through his mane, "Melodica hopes to produce some weird feedback loop. Hacked orphans making music for hacked orphans. But that's just speculation."

"Can we pull over?" said Isa quietly.

"But Courtney Christ," said Tak. "Mind control? Social programming? I thought the punk lifestyle would keep me away from this fascist bullshit."

"Please. We need to pull over."

"I don't know how we're supposed to get out of it too," said Doug. "We signed a contract. Or rather, *you* signed it Takashi."

"Like you wouldn't have Ganoush."

"Pull over!" said Isa, her voice stifled but shrill.

Doug depressed a button on the car's dashboard and, with breathtaking control, the cab pulled onto the West Side Highway's capillary-thin shoulder lane, slowed to a complete stop and unlocked all doors and windows. Wordlessly, Isa opened her door and crept out of the vehicle. She leaned against a guardrail and doubled over, her vomit falling hundreds of feet to the dyed-blue Hudson below.

2.11.2 MOSH III

Evan Halisdol should have never trusted those punks. They probably signed the contract with full intent of skipping out after seven recording sessions. All out of some juvenile anti-corporate, anti-sellout, anti-conformist anti-anti-anti credo. Kids don't realize that there's such a thing as conforming to nonconformity.

They completely cut out all contact too. No response to messaging of any kind: Eye messenger, email, SMS. Even antiquarian phone calls to Lamarck-Ganoush's cell wouldn't go through. Evan Halisdol went so far as to email their hangout, Rule-Some-thing, with the owner named after a typeface. Nothing in return. The shoulder they gave him was so cold, it could shatter if dropped on the ground.

Julia wasn't being too helpful either. Whenever Halisdol brought up New Ape Idea she shook her head and said it wasn't her job. Her work output was fine, nothing spectacular though (and she was hired on the premise of a constantly spectacular output. Halisdol flirted with the idea of firing her. Just to stick it to the punks so bent on sticking it to him. But he needed her; no way he could sift through all that data corporate sent to his office by himself.

If he fucked up this lullaby project, shit, Halisdol didn't even want to think of that. Slinking back to Mercado, head hanging low, his spine curved in defeat. He'd likely resume his position as a lowly tech. Trade off his premium dental plan for a stoic four-cornered workspace with eggshell colored walls and manic-depressive fluorescent lighting. And that's a best-case simulation. Together, each of Halisdol's simulations of the coming times—should he fail to sort this New Apeshit out—formed a certain eigensystem. Though their topography differed, they all pointed in a common direction: he would be humiliated, reprimanded by his superiors, the chambers of his heart would shudder in angst with each palpitation. Not to mention he'd likely take a significant pay cut. Failure to produce the album would mean a whole downgrade in workplace ecology too. Though his coworkers were by no means friendly in New Jersey, at least he could F2F with them about the banalities of the wife and kids (Halisdol would usually bullshit, he had neither). Back in Manhattan though, folks weren't so amicable. Hell, coworkers could be so cool to each other, they didn't even deserve the sense of warmth the label "folks" implies. Zombified by the private digital universes their Lazy Eyes afforded them, they'd not even give so much as a nod to a passerby.

But how nice it was to ride in a Waymo and be able to vent and rant and rave as he pleased. There was a comfort in it. The steel chassis and glass provided a little bubble in which one could throw a tantrum of little consequence. Those poor drivers of yesteryear: having to devote a significant chunk of cognitive capacity toward steer-ing, applying significant pressure to pedals, all in concert with other cars and drivers. Plus the small-but-pervasive threat of accident. It soothed Evan Halisdol to note that, despite his absolutely fucked predicament, he could pitch a huge private fit about it in a manner not possible a mere 25 years ago. Through his windows he could see a hypnotic trail of sediment layers scrolling past—the interiors of mountains bifurcated to make room for highway lane upon lane. On his other side there was the highway divider snaking along, other vehicles, the recursive, and enchanting vista of the deforested Garden State.

When really royally peeved, Evan Halisdol felt more like a body than like a person. A collection of physiological states: vasovagal headache, perspiring skin, unfavorable systole/diastole ratios, gritted molars. He tried to counter this like he tried to counter most embodied anxieties: simple number manipulation. It took less than a minute though for Evan Halisdol to realize the simple by-ones counting he'd been conducting in his head coincided perfectly with the reading of the exit numbers zooming past as he traversed to Hoboken.

Evan Halisdol kneaded at the brim of his Panama hat, twisting it and ma-ligning its creases. "Shitty motherfuckers got my fucking shit fucked!" he said, letting it go and seeing its crookedness. He twisted a dial on the car's console. The dashboard clicked into a mirror surface. Evan Halisdol watched himself place his hat on its head. It wobbled a bit, the inner ellipse form-fitted to the contour of his head was stretched more circular in his frustration. Those fucking punks even made him ruin his lucky hat. Halisdol switched off the mirror back to the standard window HUD.

The Waymo glided off Route 3 and turned southbound toward the two-lane streets of Weehawken with a sort of balletic fluidity. Halisdol supposed few human drivers could pilot a car with such liquid grace. Maybe that's the heart of the problem: You can't fucking trust humans for anything. From driving a car to recording a series of twelve four minute lullabies. Why trust them in the first place? If the human agent really was a dynamic system—the fundamental axiom underlying all of Evan Halisdol's research— then there was an inherent degree of unpredictability to them. He was a fool for assuming that the album recording progress would be a steady state affair: Every week he got reports that the three would show up, pitch in a solid eight hours, and leave. He should have known any progress would be non-linear: four weeks of excellent work followed by a month of stagnancy. The only reason the sound engineer hadn't quit, Froggy or whatever he asked to be called, was the pro bono lunch spreads provided by Melodica. Well, thought Halisdol, TANSTAALF. There Ain't No Such Thing As A Linear Function. Not when it comes to the chaotic messiness of *Homo sapiens.* How though was he to explain this to Mercado, a man repulsed by even the mention of 'strange attractors', let alone convince him not to sever Halisdol's employment entirely?

The cab door opened below the sign of Wolfram's automata: Rule 30 in faux pink spray paint. Evan Halisdol stepped to the curb and slammed the door shut five syllables into its automated departing thanks.

Every Friday night at 10pm is what Rule 30's site lists. A few gaggles of adolescents strewn about. Only a small minority seemed to be wearing Lazy Eyes. It was shocking, given that most 12-28-year-olds rode the wave of increasing cyborgization. They seemed to F2F organically in a way Halisdol hadn't seen save for members of the Neo-!Kung. Halisdol himself was not so good at juggling the real, material world concomitantly with the digital. Especially if the Lazy Eyes were in private browsing mode. Maybe that's what the punks did these days, rebel against the minor threat of digital interfacing.

Inside Rule 30, a large tuber of a man in a Black Flag tank sat on a folding chair behind a wooden table. He wore a medieval contraption around his and head and neck, his jaws too looked wired shut. He made eye contact with Evan Halisdol and outstretched a meaty hand, palm upwards. Halisdol did not take it.

"Hello?" said Halisdol. "Is anybody in there?"

The man kept eye contact with Halisdol for several seconds before a dreadlocked hebody checked Halisdol in the shoulder.

"Don't fucking mock him, piece of shit," The dreadlocks brought the tip of his index to Halisdol's clavicle. "Either pay the cover or don't, but you don't need to assert your voice over those that can't speak!"

Evan Halisdol swallowed audibly before synthesizing a verbal reply. "I'm here to see New Ape Idea," he said.

"Well, you're with like-minded folk," replied the hebody, his edge softening. "But you gotta pay cover first. Look," he tapped Halisdol on the shoulder and pointed, "You're already holding up the line."

"No," said Halisdol. His Panama hat wobbled as he shook his head with vigor. "I need to speak with them. I am their record executive and this is urgent."

"Oh man, we gotta label pig!" the hebody hollered. He grabbed Halisdol by the lapels and pushed him backwards into the queue. His comrades by the entrance aided in shoving Halisdol through the building's open door, hurling a flurry of insults at him on the way out.

Out on the humid sidewalk, Evan Halisdol contemplated activating his Lazy Eyes and placing an order for a cab back to the Meadowlands. An interchangeable swath of youths loitered around as before, each micro-clique having a sort of family resemblance to one another. A specific theebody appeared unique to Halisdol. A tall, Scandinavian phenotype, leaning against the brick facade of Rule 30 jotting into a real analog Moleskine. They wore a white business shirt with a black tie, an almost Mormon ensemble. Evan approached the individual with a plastered on smile.

"Hi," he said.

"Greetings," said the theebody. They returned a much more genuine smile before bringing their attention back to their jottings.

"Are you here for New Ape Idea?"

The theebody looked up. "Yeah of course. I'd assume you are too." They wet their lips. "You're a fresh face. Is this your first show?"

"I know them. The members. I know them all very well."

The theebody nodded. Halisdol could sim that all his words were being perceived as hyperbole. "But yes," Halisdol continued. "I suppose it is correct to say this is my first show."

"My name is Mickey Mallorey." They clicked on their pen and flipped to a blank page in their notebook. "Editor-in-chief of *Staph Infection*. Mind if I pick your brains for a few?"

Evan Halisdol gnarled up his face in frustration. A fuzzy wash began to emanate from within the venue. "Do you know their manager? I've been trying to contact her for weeks."

"**Futurabold** McRogers," said Mallorey. "Of course I know her, her office is inside."

"I know that," said Halisdol. "But the bouncer at the front won't let me in."

"Aw, Dee's a sweetheart," said Mallorey. "He very rarely gives anyone trouble. Didja try making an appointment with **Futurabold**?"

"Listen," said Halisdol. He smoothed his tie to his chest. "I need her pretty urgently, it's about a record deal I have with New Ape Idea."

Mallorey stepped back, their face looked like the ventral side of a manta ray.

"A label guy. Fuck! Why didn't **Futurabold** tell me they were signed?" They wrapped their fingers around Halisdol's bare wrists. "C'mon I'll get you to her. Fuck, I hope this news hasn't broken yet."

Mallorey pinched their shirt and tie getup into a fake-leather studded jacket worn over a fabric sportsbra. Their chest had an adolescent grazing of fuzz. They pulled Evan Halisdol into Rule 30, snaking past the ticket line.

"Yo! That's the fucking cheapskate from before!" hooted a queued punk.

"He's with a label," Mallorey volleyed back.

"Oh we know," replied another, before flaring his nostrils and oinking at the two.

The whole interior was bordering on sensory overload for Halisdol. He and Mallorey pressed themselves against the walls, which were not graffiti-covered cement as Halisdol assumed they were, some kind of plexiglass displaying weird illegible hi-def animations. The room smelled of non-synth, clove tobacco and body odor from the mass of hebodies, shebodies and betweenbodies packed together. Some nodded, others had their hands folded across their chests in boredom, and many pogoed up and down, colliding into one another. On stage four individuals stood wearing clown makeup. A bass guitarist plucked loud, droning walls of fuzz with no coherent rhythm to it. A bebop saxophonist and drummer added to the noise. A fourth member did not appear to play an instrument, rather he stood behind an old-fashioned laptop computer and intermittently pressed keys and waved his hands in the air in excitement.

"Is this shit what kids really listen to?" Halisdol yelled to Mallorey over the din.

"They're called Erectus Dysfunction. A lotta bands have been picking up on the whole early-homo motif after New Ape Idea. Obviously, no worthy imitators yet that I've seen." Mickey Mallorey had the uncanny ability to have their voice heard over the loudest of music, while never appearing to yell, scream or otherwise distress their vocal chords. "I gave 'em a decent write-up after their debut show. They make solid openers for New Ape Idea." He gestured toward a door, a stern-faced Neo-!Kung stood at parade-rest in front of it. "That's **Futurabold**'s office," Mallorey said.

Evan Halisdol nodded thanks and sidled toward the door. He caught the Neo-!Kung's eyes and the guard shook his head before Halisdol's vocal chords could even vibrate.

"I need to speak to Ms. McRogers," Halisdol cupped his hands to his mouth as he yelled.

Another head shake no.

"Maybe you know her as **Futurabold**?"

An applause from the audience as the laptop member of Erectus Dysfunction took the mic. "Thanks y'all," the musician said. "You know what's coming up." And the four descended from the stage, further crowding the audience.

"It's a matter of legality," said Halisdol.

The Neo-!Kung stepped forward as the door opened behind him. The three band members marched out and onto the stage. Despite much yelling and hand waving, Evan Halisdol was unable to capture any attention from them. He must have blended in with the crowd's deafening cheers of adulation as New Ape Idea took the stage and plugged in.

"Thanks for coming," said Isa into the microphone. Her voice was mild and shaking a bit. She turned a few chrome knobs on her blue Jazzmaster and stomped a few pedals to life before turning to acknowledge her two other band mates. They both nodded, Doug clicked off four, and they launched into music.

Evan Halisdol had heard the bootlegs, but those tinny recordings sounded like the live band the way scrolling through a wildlife blog feels like being mauled by a grizzly. They were loud, pounding, and chaotic, sure, but Halisdol had heard plenty of loud, pounding and chaotic bands before. What was novel to him, what liquefied his bones and calcified his arteries was New Ape Idea's amniotic wash of fuzz, coupled with lyrics that sounded like a Petri-dish child of Flaubert and GG Allin. They made Evan Halisdol want to smash something. Or embrace the nearest shebody and weep into her breasts. Or find anything living and make love to every available orifice it afforded. Or quit his job at Melodica and join the Neo-!Kung. Or all of the above. He felt a strange attraction to the other moshers, throwing themselves about in front of the stage. Like Halisdol's mind was just one node in a vast neural network made up by everyone in the room. Even the Neo-!Kung bouncer seemed to enjoy the music, tapping his foot and nodding his head in synchrony with the snare hits, though Halisdol could see he was wearing ear plugs.

And Isa Spines seemed to smile as she sang and shook her hips from side to side. Most of her peers he'd heard, those wards inoculated with the Chaperoni prototype had fallen into a deep clinical depression. Some had committed suicide. The majority of them were still wards, though in asylums rather than orphanages. But Spines was free and exhibiting authentic joy at that. And somewhere inside Halisdol knew he should be feeling frustration with her. Frustration with her skipping recording sessions, frustration for her elation at playing hooky, but all he could feel was entrancement by the music. Real world details became blurry and difficult to parse against the atavistic single-minded impetus to dance.

Looking left then right, Halisdol removed a pair of foam earplugs he had stowed away in his breast pocket and inserted them into his waxy canals. Rule 30 was silent but dynamic, and Evan Halisdol felt his head return at once. If he couldn't get to McRogers, perhaps he could get the band's attention.

Evan Halisdol, pressed between mosh pit and monitors, inched his way toward the center of the stage, waving his hands overhead and yelling at them. The drummer, barricaded by his massive set was invisible to Evan. Spines seemed lost in the rapture of her own vocalizing. Only the bassist, Takashi, caught Halisdol's glance. Immediately, his expression turned from one of contentment to an Oh Fuck! countenance.

"I need to speak to you urgently!" Halisdol yelled. He could feel his own words humming in his skull from the earplugs.

Takashi locked eyes with Halisdol for several beats, continuing to pluck at his bass strings as he did so. He squinted a bit, then looked away, smirking as he did so.

Halisdol was smushed against the stage by the hundred or so moshers behind him, crushing him against the stage. He felt his face redden, both out of anger and the crushing of his internal organs. One hebody behind him, decided Halisdol's shoulders afforded a good stool to see the band better and leapt onto to Halisdol's back. From his peripheral vision, Halisdol could see Takashi laugh to himself as he toppled over, only to be helped back to his feet by a few Good Samaritan hands.

"You little prick! We signed a contract! I could sue!" Halisdol screamed, he could feel his carotid artery pulsing out beneath his dermis. But he went unheard, either through deliberate ignorance on the part of Takashi, or simply because Halisdol's voice was but a drop in a torrential rainfall of bombastic punk rock.

The stage was only a few feet off the ground, coming up to Halisdol's shoulders. It was largely lined with monitors, too tall for Halisdol to climb over. About a yard to his left though, Evan Halisdol espied an opening. A clearing made for a black box, wires sticking out along with two glass tubes. If he could move them out of the way, Halisdol could have a foothold to get on stage. Good luck to Miyagi-Edelstein if he tries to ignore him then.

Halisdol planted his palms on the black painted stage and pressed. A lack of muscle mass belied a sinewy strength, as Halisdol heaved his slim frame off the ground. Perhaps mistaking him for an eager crowd-surfer, two young moshers behind him grabbed Evan Halisdol by his glutes and heaved him overhead. Halisdol watched Takashi visually track him as he rose above the masses of Rule 30; he could read the insouciance in the bassist's almond-shaped eyes.

"Letmedownletmedownletmedown!" hollered Halisdol, having never found himself supported by the collective arms and hands of teenagers and, moreso, finding the experience eliciting an acute sensation of vertigo scintillating between his ears. Rule 30 began to spin, the scrawling on the walls blending with the piping overhead. Halisdol felt like a balloon, specifically an over-inflated rubber one. The membrane between his body and the world seemed to become diffuse, Halisdol and his surroundings blending via osmosis. Whether this was sparked by the hypnotic music, or a fear of heights was indeterminate. Desperate for stability, feeling as if his body would explode or melt or both should he not immediately grasp onto something solid, Halisdol wrapped his fingers around a rusted pipe overhead. Chinning himself up, off of the joisting arms of the mosh pit, Halisdol kicked his legs back and forth. His leather shoes smashed into the faces and backs of necks of several individuals below.

Though scalding to the touch, the piping afforded Evan Halisdol some relief. He could feel the snapping of his neurons quell. His dangling feet were at about head height of the average mosher. Halisdol ran a quick simulation of swinging himself to the stage and deemed the act plausible. Praying his calculus was accurate, Evan Halisdol threw his ass back while brachiating from the pipes. Though some momentum was lost as his feet and shins collided with moshers below, Halisdol was able to throw his legs forwards and swing himself monkey-like, releasing his overhand grip and flying forward.

His gymnastics were a net success: Halisdol found himself lying prone on the stage, the gizmo with the glass piping smashed beneath him. Ignorant of his lacerated torso (and reddening shirt, Halisdol rose to his feet. The music, he noted, had changed in quality. Isa Spines was too busy locking eye contact with Lamarck-Ganoush to see Halisdol. Though the band played on, the instrumentation sounded stripped apart, disconnected. Amateurish even.

"My SHANNON!" he heard Takashi scream. "YOU RUINED MY FUCK-ING SHANNON!" Halisdol lifted his head to see the bassist, eyes wide, nostrils flared, a wicked trickster grin pasted onto his face like now was his big fucking chance to be Sid Vicious.

Unslinging his bass guitar from his shoulders and gripping it by the neck, Takashi quickly smashed away any of Halisdol's pointy rodent facial features. The body of the Rickenbacker proved to be an excellent cudgel for gross amateur facial reconstruction.

Twin streams of blood gushed from Halisdol's nose, his nostrils rendered to look more like flat serpentine slits on his face than orifices on any mammalian proboscis. The blow to his face turned Halisdol 180 degrees around. Though Isa Spines and the drummer had stopped playing, the mosh pit did not seem to cease its activity.

Perhaps, Halisdol thought, moshing and full-out rioting were parallel attractor states. The presence of music in the system's phase-space being the differentiating factor.

A second Rickenbacker smash to the base of his skull knocked all thoughts of applied Dynamical Systems Theory out of Halisdol's meatware. As he crumpled to the floor, Halisdol saw two Neo-!Kung sprinting from their posts toward the stage. With the third blow to his face, Halisdol lost track of the hunter-gatherers as they mixed into the crowd.

"Stop it! Stop it!" shrieked Isa Spines, her face pale. Halisdol could read his own face in Isa's reaction: he wore a mask slickened with a paella of blood, mucous and tears. Whereas Miyagi-Edelstein was performing the role of old-school brute, Spines fell to her knees, stymied with empathy.

Figure 7: Takashi vs. Halisdol

From his drummer's throne Lamarck-Ganoush rose, dropping his sticks. "Takashi stop! Please!" he added to the chorus of shouts.

Ignoring Doug, Takashi raised his guitar over his head, about to bring it down in a wood chopping stroke. As the bass descended, Evan Halisdol, on his knees, brought hands to his face in protection. Through some miracle of parasympathetic reflexes, Halisdol found himself having caught the body of the Rickenbacker and ripped it from Miyagi-Edelstein's grip.

"You little motherfucker," Halisdol held the bass like a sledgehammer and intended to reverse the assaulter-assaulted relationship he'd been sharing with Takashi. His swing was interrupted by Doug Lamarck-Ganoush, who threw his mass over the drum kit toward the two. Arms outstretched, he caught both Halisdol and Miyagi-Edelstein in the crook of each of his arms and the three tumbled off the stage.

The bass guitar knocked out of his grip, Evan Halisdol found himself sandwiched atop of Takashi Miyagi-Edelstein and beneath a supine Doug. He wriggled his upper-body free as Doug rolled off the two, and attempted to strike at Takashi's face. His slaps pained both parties, as the top layer of dermis had been burned off of Halisdol's hands by the venue's steam pipe.

A flurry of kicks and stomps cascaded from the moshers-turned-rioters surrounding them. Takashi's face too had turned to bloody soup, though his grin sat upon it unchanging. Despite punch after punch delivered by Halisdol, Takashi refused to relinquish his smile. It was the reports of four gunshots that finally wiped away his Cheshire cat grin. Impressions of Doug's collapsed and bullet-holed body, the smell of smoke and the parting of the crowd around the shaking Neo-!Kung were like after-thoughts to Halisdol: the last to notice that all of Rule 30 had been rendered silent aside from the wet slapping sounds of punch after punch after punch delivered to Takashi's head.

About The Author

Dan Sohval is a writer, teacher, and stand up comic from New Jersey. Dan studied English and Cognitive Science at Vassar College and received a Fulbright Fellowship to S. Korea. He currently lives in New York City. This is his first novel.

About The Artist

Isaac Fisher is a cartoonist from Pittsburgh, Pennsylvania. He met the author during his time as a Fulbright Fellow in S. Korea. Isaac writes and draws *Cock and Block Comix* and *Heil Silver* for the Burlesque Showcase. He currently lives in Atlanta.

The Burlesque Showcase is Incubator Comics Company's imprint for adult themed content. At the Burlesque Showcase, we celebrate authors and artists who are unafraid to address taboo subjects in their work. Read our featured content at www.theburlesqueshowcase.net. We are open for submissions.

Incubator Comics was founded in 2017 by Pittsburgh based author Alex K.A. and Atlanta based cartoonist Isaac Fisher. Incubator Comics is a grassroots media production company dedicated to hatching the careers of emerging storytellers and artists. We currently produce comics, fiction novels, and mobile games for a variety of audiences. Our products have been used as teaching aids in high school biology curricula and middle school How-To-Make-Comics workshops. Learn more at www.incubatorcomics.com. We are also open for submissions.

Made in the USA
San Bernardino, CA
17 October 2018